AS A LAST RESORT

"Fresh, funny and crisply written, *As a Last Resort* is a rom-com for lovers of second chances and meant-to-be lovers. Don't miss this one."

—Annabel Monaghan, *USA Today* bestselling author of *It's a Love Story*

"What happens when the place you've sworn off forever becomes the one place you just might belong? Witty, heartfelt, with sparkling chemistry and laugh-out-loud moments, this charming debut reminds us that sometimes love—and healing—find us where we least want to look. Wollett's debut rom-com is a breath of fresh Florida coastal air. Not to be missed!"

—Sarah Penner, *New York Times* bestselling author of *The Lost Apothecary*

AS A LAST RESORT

KRISTIN WOLLETT

FOREVER

New York Boston

This book is a work of fiction. Names, characters, places, and incidents are the product of the author's imagination or are used fictitiously. Any resemblance to actual events, locales, or persons, living or dead, is coincidental.

Copyright © 2025 by Kristin Wollett

Cover design and illustration by Elizabeth M. Oliver
Cover copyright © 2025 by Hachette Book Group, Inc.

Hachette Book Group supports the right to free expression and the value of copyright. The purpose of copyright is to encourage writers and artists to produce the creative works that enrich our culture.

The scanning, uploading, and distribution of this book without permission is a theft of the author's intellectual property. If you would like permission to use material from the book (other than for review purposes), please contact permissions@hbgusa.com. Thank you for your support of the author's rights.

Forever
Hachette Book Group
1290 Avenue of the Americas, New York, NY 10104
read-forever.com
@readforeverpub

First Edition: September 2025

Forever is an imprint of Grand Central Publishing. The Forever name and logo are registered trademarks of Hachette Book Group, Inc.

"Lost In Your Eyes" Words and Music by Deborah Gibson, Copyright © 1987, 1989 by Music Sales Corporation (ASCAP). International Copyright Secured. All Rights Reserved. Reprinted by Permission. Reprinted by Permission of Hal Leonard LLC.

The publisher is not responsible for websites (or their content) that are not owned by the publisher.

The Hachette Speakers Bureau provides a wide range of authors for speaking events. To find out more, go to hachettespeakersbureau.com or email HachetteSpeakers@hbgusa.com.

Forever books may be purchased in bulk for business, educational, or promotional use. For information, please contact your local bookseller or the Hachette Book Group Special Markets Department at special.markets@hbgusa.com.

Print book interior design by Taylor Navis

Library of Congress Cataloging-in-Publication Data
Names: Wollett, Kristin author
Title: As a last resort / Kristin Wollett.
Description: First edition. | New York, NY : Forever, 2025. |
Identifiers: LCCN 2025014587 | ISBN 9781538773239 trade paperback |
    ISBN 9781538773246 ebook
Subjects: LCGFT: Romance fiction | Novels
Classification: LCC PS3623.O5927 A8 2025 | DDC 813/.6—dc23/eng/20250404
LC record available at https://lccn.loc.gov/2025014587

ISBNs: 978-1-5387-7323-9 (Trade paperback); 978-1-5387-7324-6 (ebook)

Printed in the United States of America

CCR

10 9 8 7 6 5 4 3 2 1

For Justin.
Every good thing about Austin came from you.
♥

As A Last Resort

1
SAMANTHA

At any given time, there are twenty different imaginary conversations taking place in my head.

For example, reminding my mother (nicely) vodka does not count toward your recommended daily liquid intake of ninety ounces.

Or, reminding my coworker Robby (nicely) I'd prefer if he didn't take credit for all the work I actually did. Again.

Or even, encouraging my sort-of boyfriend, Jack, (nicely) he should chew with his mouth closed because then he wouldn't sound like such a cow when he eats.

I was in the middle of having one of these imaginary conversations, reminding the waitress (nicely) I ordered my salad with dressing on the side, as I shoved sopping wet lettuce into my mouth, when I noticed Jack staring at me from across the white linen tablecloth like I was supposed to say something.

"Did you hear me?" he asked.

"Of course, I did." I hadn't.

"So, you agree on our problem. It's not me, it's you."

Right. It's me.

Wait.

What's me?

Servers zoomed by our table with fried spring rolls and chiming wineglasses. He gulped down the rest of his wine and snapped to get a waitress's attention.

My phone dinged for the fifth time in three minutes.

"Sorry, just hold on a sec." I grabbed it out of my back pocket and read the text from my coworker. "You've got to be kidding me."

"What now?"

"It's Robby. He's changing the offer price on the contract for Rock Island. Again."

"I don't mean with your work, Samantha."

My feet fished around for the heels I'd secretly discarded somewhere under the table and I reached for my purse.

"You're leaving?" he asked with a mouthful of food. A piece of rice shot out and stared me down from the tablecloth.

"It'll just take a minute. I can't access the contract on my phone and the office is only two blocks away." Our acquisition team worked on the final draft of the development contract for hours—*hours*—and of course, the minute I leave for a microsecond of personal time, Robby sends an SOS that lands squarely on my plate.

A waitress appeared at our table. "How are your appetizers?"

"They'd be much better if we had wine to go with them." Jack motioned to the empty glasses.

Her smile fell just a bit and I cringed.

"Of course. Just a moment." She hurried off as I stood up.

"You can't be serious," he scoffed.

"Robby's technically my boss on this project. I can't just ignore him."

"But you've barely touched your food."

"I'll be quick. I promise."

As I pushed the key into my apartment lock two hours later, it hit me that I was supposed to head back to the restaurant.

After a slew of unanswered calls and texts, I backtracked to Pho Quyen on the off chance Jack was still there.

"He left this for you," the hostess with bright blue eyeliner said as I walked in the door. She handed over the bill. A table of off-duty servers in the back eyed the host stand and grew eerily quiet, filling their salt and pepper shakers with a bit more aggression than necessary.

Jack had ordered another bottle of wine before peacing out for the night. I paid, vaguely remembering the end of our conversation. Had he broken up with me? I couldn't completely remember the details. My brain was fried after working sixteen-hour days for two weeks straight.

I called Jack again on the walk back to my apartment. No answer.

I texted again. No response.

Now, admittedly, work was a little hectic, but nothing we hadn't weathered before. There were more take-out nights and sleeping-at-the-office-again nights than usual, but we generally worked.

He worked a lot. I worked a lot. We just worked a lot. Separately.

It had been this way for almost six months and the convenience of it was marginally better than the stigma of being alone. I thought we were chugging along just fine. Not like, *best-relationship-ever* working out, but *better-than-dating-the-creepy-taxidermy-guy-off-Tinder* working out, for sure.

Until he'd said it wasn't.

At least, that's what I think he said. It was all still a bit hazy.

☼

My alarm went off at 5:30 a.m. I checked my phone—no texts or calls. After a quick run and an even quicker shower, I pulled my hair back in a low bun and put on one of my seven rotating tailored suits.

I loved New York City. There were always a few ladies meeting on the street corner for coffee, leaning their heads together, gossiping about who their neighbor had come home with the night before. Always someone running down the street, determined not to be late. The loud flower guy on my corner, known by locals as Italian Marco, always called me sunshine as I walked by, even though I'm pretty sure the next warm body who passed got a similar greeting.

I walked the four blocks to work in my favorite nude Weitzmans as I checked my email. Somehow the chaos outside on the streets was the perfect accompaniment to the chaos inside my head, and made me feel just a little more in sync with the world.

The double glass doors of 44 Union Square opened to the familiar friendly eyes of Bo, the overnight security guard. He tracked me and tipped his head.

"Samantha Leigh. I hope I live to see the day you walk in after I've already clocked out for the night."

"The early bird catches the worm, Bo," I said, falling into our cheesy greeting for the early mornings.

"Yeah, but the second mouse gets the cheese!" he called after me as the elevator doors shut, hoisting me up to the top floor where Goodrich Equity Partners, LLC, operated from.

The doors opened to a darkened reception area. I stepped out and took a deep breath. This was my favorite moment of the day. The smell of paper and corporate carpeting accosted my nose, the space filling with the buzz of printers gearing up for a day of abuse.

Thirty minutes later the hallways teemed with chatter, clicking heels, and steaming stainless steel tumblers of coffee. First on the agenda was a debrief of yesterday's deal memo we'd sent down to Florida for the new resort development contract. The land in this small town of Rock Island we bid on was nestled on the north end—a ten-mile stretch of undeveloped beachfront with a $20 million price tag. It was a perfect spot for a new resort.

It also happened to be where I grew up, though *hometown* wouldn't be the first word to come to mind. It was a fun fact I tried to avoid telling people, just in case they were the type to google police records and stumbled across my mother's mug shot for disorderly conduct. Or public intoxication. Or my favorite, where she's giving the camera a thumbs-up for indecent exposure. Luckily, Robby was managing it since I was already assigned to another project, and new developments from the ground up weren't my thing anyway. They were Robby's forte, thank God.

"Good work so far, everyone," Glenn said as he walked into the conference room, Robby trailing closely behind our boss on an invisible leash. "Rock Island verbally accepted the offer this morning. Legal's got it in their hands and along with some minor requests we need to sift through, I think we'll be able to call it officially closed by the end of the week."

You could hear the collective breath everyone was holding release at the same time. Surviving weeks of late nights, countless rounds of edits, and Glenn's never-ending commentary on the "lost art of professionalism" had finally paid off. Everyone was exhausted and mildly traumatized, but we could smell the victory.

As president of Goodrich Equity Partners, LLC, the leading venture capital firm in the Northeast specialized in resort development deals, Glenn Goodrich is old-school in more ways than one. He likes all offers printed, bound in leather, and hand delivered to the recipient. He says if we can't spare a few hundred dollars on a presentation for a $20 million contract, we're not charging enough. First impressions are a big deal.

He's also old-school in the sense that men do the heavy lifting and women are there to look pretty and fetch coffee. Not that he'd verbalize that out loud, of course. That would be an HR no-no.

"Don't relax yet," he said as the air puckered again. He grabbed Robby on the shoulder and squeezed. "Thanks to Robby for running point on this. This is an example of someone gunning to make director in the next couple years."

Yeah, gunning to see how far up Glenn's—

Robby looked at me. And *winked*. The hair on the back of my neck crawled to attention.

Now, on the surface, Robby was the poster boy of a vintage Ralph Lauren print ad shot on a Martha's Vineyard back lawn at sunset. You know the ones I'm talking about—Dad's in pale pink, Mom's wearing a skirt that a small village could fit under, the towheaded kids are wearing white. Yes, he was objectively attractive. But he followed Glenn around like a lost puppy, and when he laughed, he snorted like a pug with a mild case of asthma. The reality that Robby and everyone else in the room, including Glenn, knew I pulled together 95 percent of the work on this offer yet received 0 percent of the credit, solidified his douchebag status for me. And this wasn't the first time I'd been glossed over after pulling more than my fair share.

"Happy hour at O'Keefe's after work," Glenn called out as people started to file from the room. "We'll celebrate Robby's thirty-day due diligence vacation in Florida." A little cheer erupted from the room, mostly celebrating the fact Robby would be gone for thirty days and we wouldn't have to put up with him.

I gathered my folio and stood. My assistant, Ivy, snatched it from me and said under her breath, "He's such a jerk."

"Which one?" I asked. She smirked.

I walked past Glenn and Robby still cuddled up together on my way out.

"Samantha," Glenn called out to me. "Stick with this kid here. You could learn a thing or two from him."

"Of course, sir. I wouldn't miss an opportunity to learn from the best." I gritted my teeth so hard I'm surprised they didn't crack.

Robby flashed his pearly whites in my direction. I tried to wink at him, but he looked at me like I had a baby dragon protruding from my neck. For some reason, my wink didn't land as seamlessly as his did.

Winking's a lot easier in theory.

"See you at O'Keefe's, Leigh?" he called on my way out.

"Absolutely."

I shut my office door thirty seconds later with Ivy hot on my feet. "Absolutely not."

"I don't need to tell you that you're going. Puggle will be there."

One of Ivy's oddly impressive talents was her plethora of canine nicknames for Robby. I couldn't recall the last time she used his real first name behind a closed door. And yes, I was aware he would be there.

I also knew Glenn was going to be looking for me to check off the team player box. But Jack finally texted me back during the meeting and I felt like trying to see him to clear the air was the right thing to do.

She sat on the tiny couch in my office. *Learn from the best.* That was good, by the way."

"Bile was literally crawling up my throat by the end of that sentence."

"Could've fooled me."

"I really can't tonight though. I walked out on Jack last night at dinner and didn't even say goodbye. He's only responded to one of my texts since."

"Check in with Jack *after* O'Keefe's. Just one drink. You can show Glenn you can be just as personable and charming as his little Pugsworth."

I sighed. "Jack broke up with me." I turned my phone around so she could read the text that came in during the meeting.

> **JACK:** Yes. I broke up with you.
> And the fact you're texting me this
> should confirm why.

"Yikes."

"He's upset that he was trying to break up with me and I wasn't listening. I was distracted by Robby's text, asking me to change the offer price last night."

"So you left dinner…"

"To fix Robby's enlightened stroke of genius, which was being bound at the printers," I answered. "But when I got to the printers they had already finished and we needed to reprint the entire proposal."

"All one hundred pages of it?"

"Apparently, it was just easier to print the entire file because the offer price was listed on quite a few of the pages. But then after it was bound, Robby asked if I'd just drop it off at the courier's since they were still open so they'd get it first thing this morning. It was right by my apartment anyway, so…"

"Of course, you did."

"And then I forgot to go back."

"You forgot to go back."

"Yes." I knew it sounded horrible.

"To the restaurant where your boyfriend of six months was waiting for you."

"Correct."

She sat back and kicked up her feet on my Knoll tulip coffee table. The bright red bottoms of her heels screamed at me.

"I mean, here's the thing though. Do you really like him? I mean like, *rest-of-your-life* like him?"

Besides having the uncanny ability to come up with the most creative pug-themed nicknames I've ever heard for Robby, Ivy was also never afraid to ask the hard questions.

I met her two years ago while interviewing candidates for an assistant. As a Brown graduate near the top of her class, she was overqualified and sharper than any other candidate I considered. When I asked her why she was applying for a job well below her experience level, she made me sign a nondisclosure. Apparently, she had once written steamy romance novels under a pen name, and she was seeking a job as far removed from that as possible.

I was the only female lead on the acquisition data team when she applied. Actually, one of the few women at Goodrich Equity Partners, LLC, period. So by default, I was her best option.

"It's not like I'm madly in love with him right this very second or anything. But doesn't that kind of thing ebb and flow anyway?" I asked.

"The honeymoon period should ideally last more than a few months."

"We have so much in common though. We both like to work. We both run. We both eat a lot of takeout. We can talk to each other about anything."

"Except when you're not listening."

I sighed. "It's convenient."

She narrowed her perfectly lined brown almond-shaped eyes at me. "Every woman's dream."

"What? Convenient things can be good for you," I argued, "like toilet paper."

"That's not convenient. It's necessary."

"Have you ever been in a situation without toilet paper? Pretty sure you'd figure it out."

"Jack is not your toilet paper."

"I feel like we're losing the metaphor here." I cradled my head in my hands.

"Look, all I'm saying is you need to show up at O'Keefe's."

"And I agree with you. But I don't want to."

"But you want *it*. Yes?" She raised her brow.

Ah. *It.*

The thing we do not speak of out loud. The *promotion*.

The other teams focused on new developments and were composed of male hotshots with deep pockets from the Ivy League schools. And here was me, a small state school graduate from a tiny Florida beach town no one's ever heard of. I led the data acquisition team for mixed-use space projects that needed a bit of reengineering. Got a city center or dated downtown that needs revitalization? I'm your gal. While my family wasn't six degrees away from the Kennedys, at the time I was hired there wasn't anyone else who did what I did at GEP. Glenn needed me. And that's how I landed a spot on his sacred data team in the first place.

The promotion Ivy referred to was the next step to being a director at GEP. It was a trial run taking on all the responsibilities and duties of a director without the official title. If you've checked off all the necessary boxes by the end of the year, you've made director. Which means you're not filling days with research and spreadsheets anymore. You're the one finding and negotiating the deals and creating the big-picture ideas that could change the landscape of entire cities.

And that's exactly what I wanted to be doing.

There was only one coveted spot. And here's the catch—for once, it wasn't Glenn's sole decision. GEP had gone public, and now there was a whole board he answered to. Sure, he'd make his strong recommendation and give his supporting evidence skewed in favor of who he wanted, but all director roles were now voted on by the board. After being nominated a few months ago, it was a game changer for me. And the company. Glenn wouldn't dare promote a woman to director, but apparently, his board had joined the twenty-first century and the nomination was pushed through.

And numbers don't lie. Because of my track record, I was leading a team on one of the biggest revitalizations of the century for Oakstone Springs, North Carolina. I was in charge of expanding the quaint little city everyone knew and loved, to a booming metropolis with nationally recognized music festivals, art galleries, and upscale co-op markets filled with local vendors.

The honest to God truth was I loved my job. I really did, but being passed over multiple times as lead for other projects was getting a little played out. This time it was statistically in my reach to get this promotion, but I couldn't lay back and just wait for it to happen.

"One drink to show I'm charming and lovable and social," I said, giving up. "Then I'm getting the hell out of there."

2
AUSTIN

"Dude, c'mon. It's been three years." Bits of lobster roll rocketed from Patrick's mouth onto the checkered plastic tablecloth.

"*Dude*, you're never going to land a girl eating like that." I sipped my beer trying to find a way out of having this conversation again. "And, it's not that. I'm just not that into her."

"How can you be *not that into her?* Look at her, Austin. She's smokin'. She's as hot as a Fourth of July firework." Always the cliché warrior. He flashed his pearly whites, which popped against the dark melanin of his skin. "And you're only giving me fifteen minutes of your precious time before you abandon me for your real family, *Capt'n*. How else am I supposed to finish something this big?"

As we churned into the heat of Florida summer, people were swarming in like ants all over the island, and it was my ferry company, Scuttle's Ferry, that brought them here in droves. After the rush of tourists who came in for the weekend, Patrick and I would down a quick drink exchanging war stories right before my weekly family dinner commitment, a tradition etched into my existence as far back as I can remember.

Patrick and I always went to Charley's Lobster Shack, the first restaurant you saw once you crossed the water by boat, which was one of the only ways to get to Rock Island. There weren't any roads or bridges that connected it to the mainland, so my ferry or a private transfer, if your pockets ran deep, were how you got to the island.

The shack's red picnic tables and white awning stood out from the shoreline like something plucked from New England and dropped onto a random island in Florida.

Charley, the owner, hobbled over and swatted Patrick on the back. "Patrick, Capt'n Austin—what's fizzlin', boys?"

"Besides Austin's love life, not much, Charley. Not much." Patrick took another obscene bite of his lobster roll.

"Aww, chin up. There's plenty of fish in the sea." Charley chucked my chin with his knuckle like I was still some schoolboy. That's one of the fun things about living in such a small town. Everyone remembers when you wore diapers.

"Speaking of, who's the newbie?" Patrick asked, nodding his head toward the subject of our earlier conversation who was serving the next table over.

"Ah, my niece Sherry, in for summer break from Jersey. She takin' good care of ya?"

"She's doing a great job. Austin and I were just saying if you don't work her too hard, how it'd be nice to take her out on the ferry and show her a sunset run."

I threw darts at Patrick with my eyes.

"I'm sure she'd love that, Capt'n." Charley squeezed my shoulder just a little too tight. "Business is pickin' up. Feels good to see them boats putzin' around, doesn't it?"

The shoreline outside Charley's was littered with rental crafts buzzing around the water. The dock was full, all the tables taken by laughing tourists two beers in. Charley's was a staple to regulars but packed to capacity and thriving during tourist season. The energy lifted the hairs on my arm.

"Sure does." Patrick patted the name tag hanging on his shirt and smiled. "And tips skyrocketed, thanks to your genius idea."

We both wore teal shirts for Scuttle's Ferry, but Patrick's sported a new addition—a name tag that declared him as USAIN BOLT in all caps. I'd been wondering who gave Patrick the harebrained idea to use a fake name on my ferryboat.

"Oldest trick in the book. You think my real name's Charley?" He winked at Patrick and hobbled off, favoring his right leg. "Enjoy your food, boys."

"What? It works." Patrick stopped chewing to give me his million-dollar smile again and went back to demolishing his lobster roll. He'd made me a RYAN GOSLING name tag, but I refused to wear it. No one would believe that guy knew how to run a boat.

"You know, he probably fakes the wooden leg too. I'm telling you the concept is genius. And"—he slid into his well-honed Usain Bolt persona—"I get to practice my Jamaican accent."

"For all those Jamaican acting auditions you're getting."

"Can't be too prepared. Never know when a Hollywood director will come on board and give me my big break."

Patrick changed career paths as often as underwear. Something I couldn't relate to. Since I was five, I knew exactly what I wanted to do. After my dad took me out on his boat and I caught my first fish, my dream has always been to own a fishing charter. There was something about the quiet stillness of the water that steadied me. And nothing compared to the feeling of that first catch—the patiently waiting, the building tension and anticipation, wondering if you'd return to shore with an empty hook or prove yourself a true angler.

But when your dad's a high school football legend who's coached five teams to state championships, there are expectations. Big ones. You're not just asked to follow in his footsteps—you're drafted into the family tradition. He's football royalty, the former head coach of Rock Island High School, the man who turned a team of nobodies into heroes, who united an entire town over blades of grass. Hard work, sweat, and determination on the field—that was his creed.

But football was his dream, not mine. And I saw the gap between what I was and what he needed me to be every time he looked at me.

Even when tourism exploded on the island a few years back, and the need for boats to ferry people became a clear path to success, it wasn't about business for me. It was about creating something of my own, something as far away from the dirt of the stadium field as possible. I seized the opportunity and built the only open-water ferry running six days a week.

So turns out, neither of us got what we wanted. I didn't become his champion on the field, and he couldn't see the man I became on the water.

But on the bright side, business was booming. And I was slammed. I was in the market for another boat, a larger one that would accommodate double the people and cut down on the number of trips across. We had a pretty decent following on social media, thanks to a recent video of Patrick dancing on the top deck with an eighty-year-old guest that went viral on TikTok. She said it was the best day of her life and half the internet thought it was actually Usain Bolt.

The Bolt himself even commented on it and shared it.

So, I was busy. Too busy to be dating.

"So, what's the verdict?" A silky voice pulled our attention to the end of the table, where a very persistent SHERRY—according to her name tag—stood with her hip cocked to the side.

"I can't tonight." I tried to sound as neutral as possible. "Got family plans with an early morning tomorrow."

"He'd *love* to, Sherry." Patrick piped in, glaring at me. "But he'll take a rain check. My boy needs to get out and I can't think of a girl more beautiful than you who'd be more fun on a beautiful night like tonight."

"Sure, rain check it is." She eyed me and laid the cash-only bill at the corner making a quick pivot to saunter off to another table.

"I mean, do you see that walking away?" His eyes were about to pop out of his head.

"Why don't *you* take her on a date then?"

"She's not interested in me. She's interested in some weirdo who hasn't dated anyone in three years because he's still sulking."

"I am *not* still sulking. And I've dated, just no one worth dating more than once."

"That doesn't count," he argued. "There are plenty of girls much better for you than Vanessa was if you'd just give them a chance."

That name still stung. Not like it used to, though.

I stretched my neck to loosen the sudden tightness. "I'm busy running a business, in case you haven't noticed."

"She's just here for the summer, man. Ain't no harm in getting to know her and having a good time."

"I don't want a good time. You know that's not my thing."

"But you *need* a good time." He leveled his eyes on me. "*Hey—*"

"Uh-uh, no time for a heart-to-heart, brother. The family's waiting." I threw a couple bills onto the receipt. "I need to save some energy for tonight's interrogation where my lack of dating prospects will be center stage. Again."

"Just consider it, yeah? My friend deserves to be happy again." His dark eyes did that lost-puppy-dog thing they do when he starts to get all serious on me.

"I am happy."

"The grump line on your forehead says otherwise, boo."

Here's the thing—I'm not an overly emotional guy. But if you were to ask me whose betrayal irrevocably rocked my world, I wouldn't have to think hard.

My fiancée left me for my best friend.

I feel like I should get a bit of an extended pass for dealing with the shitstorm of that particular situation.

The whole thing had blindsided me. Tom was the childhood friend who took refuge at my place for days when his dad was a little too rough with him. The best friend who was socially awkward for the first sixteen years of his life then all of a sudden over the summer entering junior year discovered contacts, got a tan, gained twenty pounds of muscle, and learned how to throw a football in a perfect spiral for seventy yards like he'd been doing it since he was born.

He was the best friend who'd introduced me to Vanessa, the woman who'd become my *fiancée*.

And the best friend who later stole her out from under me.

≈

"Here. Chop these." Mom handed me a wicker basket full of onions, brussels sprouts, and carrots.

"I know what you're doing and I'm not in the mood to talk."

Ever since I was little, she'd corner me in our kitchen and give me a cooking task to get my hands working, then she'd slowly start to grill me on life questions and before I knew it, I was spilling my guts out to her.

"What I'm doing is getting vegetables ready to throw on the grill before your father runs out of patience and burns the steaks."

Dad never wanted to put the vegetables on first. Always thought they took up too much room and his steaks couldn't *breathe* properly.

She handed me the knife.

"Fine, but no serious life questions. Deal?"

"Only *not* serious life questions allowed. Deal."

"Hi, Mom!" Lexi strolled in with her fiancé, Rex, trailing behind her. My little sister entered a room the same way Mom did—a lively little ball buzzing with energy locked in a five-foot frame. You couldn't help but be drawn in by her aura. They even looked alike, both with sandy blond hair reminiscent of Farrah Fawcett's heyday, naturally windblown and all bouncy like it had huffed a helium balloon.

And Rex was the perfect Ken doll to her Barbie. He moved here to coach the Mariners, the Rock Island High School football team. When Lexi introduced him to the family, it was like Dad had won the lottery. Rex slid effortlessly into the role I'd failed to fill—the Marcs family legacy carried on, but by someone else.

And when Rex took them to the state championship his first season—didn't matter that they lost. By the look on Dad's face, you would've thought they won. It quieted the doubters, sure, but more than that, it eased Dad's focus on me, at least for a little while, something I could never quite do on my own.

But I couldn't ask for a better guy for Lexi. He's a man of few words, but when it comes to her, he lights up. They met at Harpoon's Oyster Bar when she was saving up for photography school. He asked her out, and she shot him down on the spot. She had a rule about never dating guys who hit on bartenders. But it was love at first sight for him. He wouldn't take no for an answer, showing up every night just to order a Coke until she gave in. Then, three dates in, and she was smitten. He proposed after just a few months. Now, with the wedding a month away, all eyes are on me—the last one standing.

Which is ironic, since I was the first to get engaged.

"Hi, sweetheart," Mom said warmly. "Would you mind chopping up the lettuce? Rex, go distract Bill out there. He's fixing to start taking apart my chairs and throwing the wood on the grill if we don't put something on it soon. God forbid it sit there hot for a minute with nothing on it."

"Yes, ma'am." He winked at my sister on the way through the sliding glass door.

What's up with people winking all the time?

"Did your dress come in?" Mom asked Lexi.

"Yep! I have to go in for the fitting this week. And I confirmed the hotel is completely blocked out. Patrick said he'd man the ferry Friday night with his cousin until all the guests are over." Lexi faced me. "He promised me he wouldn't run it into any icebergs."

"Just a heads-up, he's wearing a formal tux."

"To the rehearsal dinner?"

I nodded.

"Of course he is," she said with a chuckle.

I wiped my eyes with the back of my wrist.

"Oh no! Are you getting emotional about your baby sister getting married off?" she joked.

"Oh, stop, it's the onions. And it's about time you got off Dad's payroll," I replied.

"Right. The onions." She smiled. "It's seriously not a big deal. I could always ask Mallory to go with you if you need emotional support." Mallory, a friend of my sister's from high school, had a major crush on me that bordered on stalker level territory. My hands still sweat whenever I meet a Mallory.

"Are we going to eat tonight or tomorrow?" Dad walked through the slider and wrapped his arm around Mom's waist. She playfully slammed the basket of vegetables into his stomach and told him to scoot along.

He did a double take when he caught sight of my eyes. "What's wrong with you?"

"It's the onions," Mom, Lexi, and I all chimed simultaneously.

Mom steered him back out the slider to put on the vegetables.

"Mallory would be a fun date." Mom's attempt to steer the conversation back to my dating status was predictable. It wasn't a matter of *if* she would bring it up at every family dinner night, it was *when*.

"Do you remember when she showed up on our doorstep with flowers?" I asked.

"I'm not opposed to a little role swap." She definitely was.

"She picked them from the front lawn. Bees were literally swarming around her head, and one stung her on her neck."

Mom's face puckered. "Oh goodness. I don't remember that."

"She used it as an excuse for me to take care of her."

"She wouldn't do that," Lexi replied.

"Okay, what about the time she slit her own tires, so I'd give her a ride home?"

"She didn't." Mom's mouth hung open.

Lexi pointed the knife at me. "There's no proof of that."

I narrowed my eyes on her. "But you admit it's a possibility."

"I mean..." Lexi trailed off giggling.

"And she definitely sent me that anonymous valentine senior year, the one that had the hand-drawn picture of a potato on it that said *If you were a potato you'd be a sweet one...*"

"That was actually a really beautiful watercolor of a potato though." One of Lexi's admirable qualities—always finding the silver lining. Even in a stalker situation.

"Crayon," I corrected. "It was crayon, Lexi."

"Well, everyone certainly has to have a talent." Mom pursed her lips together to desperately hold in a grin. "Let's perhaps pass on Mallory as a date option for now. Don't you worry, I have other options."

"*Single* doesn't sound so bad now, does it, Mom?"

"Okay, that's it, you two out back," she ordered. "I've got the rest. Shoo, shoo."

Lexi and I moved past the patio onto the grassy yard that overlooked the water. It used to be my great-grandmother's house, one of the first on the island, passed down generation after generation. It was right on a point of the island, jetted out onto a small strip of land. Little crabs ran around the pebbles at sunset. Small waves flopped against the rock barrier to the property. If you sat in the Adirondack chairs my great-grandfather had built with his bare hands and looked straight ahead to the water, it stretched out as far as you could see in almost every direction. It gave the illusion you were sitting at the edge of the world.

"Mom's not going to let it go." Lexi settled into one of the chairs' worn-in grooves.

"And I'll give her the same answer I always do. I don't need a date."

We looked behind us to Dad at the grill, his signature KISS THE COOK apron hanging around his neck, tongs in hand, and Mom running out another dish of salt-and-oil–tossed veggies she forgot about. He'd bark and complain about there not being enough room and she'd grab his rear as she dropped off yet another thing for him to maneuver onto the hot grate.

They had been high school sweethearts, my dad the quarterback of the football team—yes, the same high school team he coached to states and Rex recently took over—and my mom captain of the math team *and* the cheerleading squad. They were the perfect picture of what young love could morph into once you grew old if your fiancée didn't leave you for your best friend—boy, girl, a golden retriever, and a house with a view of the water. The only reason we didn't have a white picket fence was Mom said it would block the view of her hydrangeas from the street.

"Dinner's ready!" Mom called out.

"Brace yourself for the inquisition," Lexi warned with a grin. "I'll get you some liquid ammo." She headed inside first to grab a beer for me.

Even though our family dinners were technically relaxed, it was more like the laid-back outdoor setting of a Serena & Lily catalog. The table overflowed with food, Edison lights hung from the trees, and white linen napkins were intentionally crumpled on the table.

"Are we expecting company?" I asked.

"You know how your mother is," Dad replied.

"Where did the lobster tails come from?" Lexi asked as she dropped my beer off and plopped down in her seat with her own glass of white wine.

"Carl brought in fresh catch and I couldn't resist. Look at these!" Mom held a tail up and smiled like she was the poster child for Rock Island Lobster Hunting Tours. Without looking down I knew that each of us would have our own little white ramekin dish with melted salted butter. She was always prepared for everything, especially when it came to taking care of others.

"Speaking of," she continued, "I was thinking since we're doing the rehearsal dinner in the backyard, we could do a little cold seafood bar. I know you wanted to keep it simple, but maybe an ice bar with a few different options, like lobster, oysters, shrimp, and crab claws?"

"With a huge ice sculpture in the middle in the shape of two swans intertwined or something?" Lexi deadpanned.

"Yes! That's exactly what I was thinking!" Mom beamed.

"Mom. No. I said simple."

"But it would be so easy, and people would love it."

"Let your mother have her fun." Dad was always the first to defend Mom, right or not.

"Especially since you're the only one I'm going to be doing this for in the near future," Mom finished with a very pointed look in my direction.

Lexi eyed me.

Yes, I know what's coming.

"I'll call Carl and set it up. Tell him to add a few extra to the head count just in case."

She just wanted to get to the fact I didn't have a date, *again*, but in the most roundabout, respectful way possible.

"We don't need extra seats, Mom. My long-lost soulmate is not going to walk onto my boat tomorrow."

"You never know. I met your mother in line at the water fountain."

"We know, Dad," Lexi and I said together.

"We just want you to be happy, that's all. I'll set an extra table setting."

"She'll set an extra table setting," Dad echoed.

"It's your sister's wedding. You shouldn't be alone." Mom was relentless.

"It is my sister's wedding, which means my dating status is completely irrelevant to the conversation."

"I wouldn't say it's completely irrelevant." Lexi smiled into her wineglass. "But people do go to weddings single more often now. Better chance of meeting someone."

"Oh! What about Rex's cousin? The one who's the lawyer?" Mom asked.

"Married with two kids," Rex said.

"Oh, I must be thinking of someone else. What about your other cousin from California?"

"She's a lesbian," Lexi said.

"So, is that a definite no?" Mom asked.

"Mom, please."

"What? You have to ask these days."

"He and Patrick will adopt a baby girl one day if grandkids are what you're worried about." Lexi ducked just in time to miss the brussels sprout I aimed at her forehead. "What? I'm just kidding! I'm sure it'll be a little boy."

While I appreciated my mother's tenacity, our nights inevitably turned into discussions of why I needed a date. How else could I ruin the devil's plan to keep me a lonely single hermit who lived with only one plate and one fork in the kitchen the rest of my life?

I layered on my I'm-done-with-this-conversation tone. "We all can't be lucky enough to find ourselves at the end of a fairy tale with our soulmate like you two lovebirds did."

"Especially when the person we think is our soulmate turns out to be a cheating slut."

"Alexandra!" Mom cried.

"What? I'm just saying."

I had moved past the point of hating Vanessa a long time ago, but selfishly, it felt good to have someone dislike her more than I did.

"That's enough out of you, young lady." Dad's smile betrayed his stern voice.

Mom grabbed her wineglass and leaned back. I braced for the blow. "Speaking of, have you talked to her lately?"

Lexi dropped her fork. "Mom, seriously, what the f—"

"Language, Alexandra. I heard she and Tom were on the rocks. Maybe she's having second thoughts."

"Having second thoughts, three years later?" Lexi was getting pissed.

"Still were the best-looking homecoming king and queen I've seen in all my years." Dad was using his fork to talk to me again.

I took a calculated second to not throw my pint across the table. "That picture was taken years ago right after the game. Which, for the record, she was probably screwing Tom shortly after. So, let's not rewrite history just because our skin tones complement each other."

Mom patted my hand and lowered her voice. "People make mistakes."

Dad perked up. "Speaking of, Rex, have you told Austin about your offensive coordinator leaving? Spot's open. Got your name all over it."

My chair screeched against the travertine of the patio.

"I've got to prep for the morning. Got a full run tomorrow, Dad. You know, for the business I own. The job I already have." I downed the rest of my beer and turned to leave.

"Honey, don't get upset with him," Mom called out as I headed toward the patio slider. "He's just thinking about what's best for you long term."

"I like my job. And I'll say this once more then I'm done with this conversation for good. I'm not going to bring a random date just to have a warm body sitting awkwardly next to me at my sister's wedding."

As I slid the door closed, Mom's whisper floated in behind me. "I'll find him someone. We can't have a lopsided picture."

3
SAMANTHA

A warm limb snaked across my waist from behind.

"Glad you made it." The heat of Robby's breath tickled the back of my ear. *Ugh.* It really wasn't fair that he had such a velvety bedroom voice.

I shot him a tight smile and eased away from his arm, practically crawling into Ivy's lap next to me.

The sounds of the late happy hour filled the Irish pub. It felt good to be out and about after weeks of nonstop work, even though the lingering guilt of not heading straight to Jack's weighed on me.

"I didn't know they served pink drinks here." Robby slid his finger along the edge of my glass, stealing some of the colored sugar that lined the rim.

I flicked his finger off. "And you're drinking gasoline. How appropriate."

"There's my dream team," Glenn's voice boomed from behind us. He scooted in next to Ivy as he clinked Robby's own matching glass of poison, the contents of which probably cost my entire week's salary. "Ah, a man who knows his scotch. Good boy."

Ivy coughed into her drink and her eyes widened at me at the dog reference.

Yes, I heard.

"Is your drink pink?" Glenn asked.

Robby snorted.

"I'd say it's more of a *blush*."

"Excited to head to Florida for the month?" Glenn turned his attention to Robby.

"Absolutely, sir. Bags are already packed and parked by the door. Can't wait."

"Good. Enjoy your last weekend in the city for a while." Glenn clinked his glass against Robby's again and turned to spread his sparkling personality to the others.

Ivy locked eyes with me. "I've heard it's beautiful down there. How is it that you always get assigned the tropical destinations, again? We must be selling our souls to the wrong devil, Samantha."

"*Tropical* is code word for *sweltering heat*," Robby said.

I rolled my eyes. "Yeah, it's awful. Sunshine and palm trees for days."

Ivy lowered her voice. "I heard people don't wear shoes."

"Or shower," I added. "And it's not like you'll have time to actually see the sunshine, even if Florida does have the most gorgeous sunsets you'll ever see."

"Aren't you from down there?" Robby asked. I paused, quickly racking my brain for how he'd know a fact I never talked about.

Ivy stood and turned toward the bar. "I'm going to grab another round."

Robby turned his sparkly eyes on me and I could tell he was about to dive headfirst into the whole hometown situation.

"Are you really not excited about your trip?" I preempted him.

"I'm excited about a twenty-million-dollar deal. I'm not excited about being hot. Or the mosquitoes."

"They're not that bad," I said smiling, "as long as you don't go outside."

"I have a meeting first thing Monday with the seller. I can't believe this guy's been sitting on this jewel for thirty years. It's completely undeveloped with over ten miles of oceanfront property."

"I know. I pulled together the pitch, remember?" I wasn't expecting a response.

"It's going to be amazing once we're done with it. I couldn't imagine living there now though. That's really where you grew up?"

He was looking at me like I was in a glass case. There was a hard line between work and home for me, even though by choice, the latter barely existed at this point in my life. Once you started to let people see a more personal side, there were always questions. Lots of questions I didn't want to have to answer.

"Yep." Short and sweet usually moved the conversation along.

"What's it like? You know, so I can properly prepare myself for any alligator run-ins or shoeless people I may encounter."

The least I could do was help him prepare for the climate that was about to smack him in the face. "Honestly, it's hot, especially now in the summer. The days are really long. It'll be light by six a.m. and stay that way until almost nine p.m."

"Do people get all turned around like in Alaska when the sun never sets?" he asked.

"I don't think officially, but there are some super weird people who live in Florida, so you might want to carry pepper spray just in case."

"I think there are super weird people that live everywhere. They just hide in other places and in Florida it's too hot to care."

That's something we could agree on.

"Do you still have family there?" he asked.

I hesitated.

"Let me guess. The answer is yes and that's the reason you haven't been home in a while." For someone who kept his eyes mainly on golf and Glenn's rear end, he was coming across as quite intuitive.

"First of all, not sure I would actually use the word *home* to describe that place for me. And second, how do you know I haven't been back in a while?"

"I may not be the most observant person, but I have noticed you haven't taken a single vacation in years."

I paused. "It's a long story." And not one I necessarily wanted to dive into, thank you very much.

"It always is," he answered. After a few seconds of silence, he spoke. "Drugs."

My eyes flicked up to him.

"That's why I don't go back home," he continued. "When I was in high school, my dad fell off a ladder, shattered his leg, and has been a mess ever since."

That was a curveball I hadn't expected. "I'm sorry," was the only thing I could conjure up. I shook my head. "God, I hate when people say that to me. Never mind. That sucks. That's what I really mean to say."

"I couldn't agree with you more." He took another sip. "So, what's your deal, Leigh?"

I'm not sure if it was the couple of drinks, or the fact that for the first time, Robby seemed remotely human, but I answered him.

"Alcohol. Or pills. Or anything else she could get her hands on, honestly." I inspected the melting sugar on the rim of my glass. "My mom."

"Ah, that sucks too."

"Yes, it totally does." I hated when people looked at me with pity in their eyes once they found out my mom was an addict. But he didn't. He laughed. But not in a mocking way, in a knowing way. In a—*that sucks*—way.

"I walked in on my dad passed out butt-ass naked on the couch one time," he offered. "Couldn't wake him for the life of me. When

I called 911, my former kindergarten teacher, who was a part-time paramedic, was the one who answered the call."

I couldn't help but laugh. "The joys of living in a small town. I once got a call from my high school science teacher at midnight. He was fully bought into the idea that corporate America was controlling humans through the aluminum in their antiperspirant, so he refused to wear any."

Robby scrunched his nose as I continued.

"Turns out he'd been sleeping with my mom for a few weeks. She was on a date with him and mixed too many substances. She passed out at the bar and I had to come get her. Needless to say, the rest of the year was super awesome."

"I hated school." He started tearing up the bar napkin into tiny little squares. "All my teachers knew about my dad so everyone walked on eggshells around me. I was awkward compared to my older brother anyway. He was the star player on our high school baseball team. Took them to states. Was a big deal at the time. I was more the nerd with my head stuck in a spreadsheet."

I couldn't imagine Robby being awkward in high school. He was annoyingly confident. Self-assurance wasn't something he lacked.

"You're thinking it's hard to believe I wasn't always this good-looking, huh?" He winked. "Would you ever go back?"

"Like, for good? Voluntarily? Oh, God no." I shuddered at the thought. "It'd be like willingly walking into purgatory. More than half my high school still lives there. It's bad enough when I have to visit, running into the entire male staff of my high school who have most definitely seen my mother naked. Not to mention the gaggle of mean girls, the Blondtourage, who made my life a living hell. They're just older now, with little, grumpy spawns on their hips, patrolling the town with their perfectly coordinated strollers, ready to cut anyone without a matching pickleball paddle."

"I also had my fair share of classmates who weren't held enough as babies. My underwear got sent up the flagpole once."

"It did not."

"It did."

"I cheered for the football team and one time during a pep rally, the Blondtourage sent little mice in windup cars across the track to where I was sitting. Like, twenty of them."

His eyebrows pulled. "Where did they find mice windup cars?"

"You know, I have no idea." Of all the time I spent thinking about that pep rally, I never thought of where they actually came from.

"That must have taken some dedication to find. That was back before Amazon. They couldn't have been cheap."

"That never even crossed my mind."

"I finally found my groove when I took calculus as a junior." His face lit up as he said it. "Everything all of a sudden made sense once I could bury my head in numbers."

I remembered that exact feeling. Math always seemed easy. A place where I could focus my energy on figuring out complex problems that, at the end of the day, had a solution, instead of home drama that seemingly never ended.

At the beginning of senior year, I thought we'd turned a corner. Months had passed without a late-night pickup call from a stranger, or police showing up at my door, Mom in tow. We watched movies together. She cooked. She smiled. She seemed happier. Bright eyed. Full of energy. I came home one day and she was napping on the couch. But two hours went by and she hadn't stirred. I tried to wake her up and I couldn't. Apparently mixing amphetamines with alcohol awards you respiratory depression and overexertion simultaneously, which is a fancy way of saying her body couldn't regain consciousness on its own, according to the paramedic who also said, *Thank God you called us when you did.*

What if I had waited twenty minutes longer? What if I had gone and taken a shower instead of seeing the shine on her forehead when I walked by that made me stop and check on her? Would she have stopped breathing while I was shampooing my hair?

I hated myself for letting her lie there for hours. And decided I never wanted that responsibility again.

The next day, I went to the guidance counselor and doubled up on algebra and calc. I even signed up for night classes just to be able to catch up to the math honors track for college and make myself a shoo-in for a school far, far away.

I looked up. Robby's eyes were dissecting my face. I shook the memories and tried to change the subject.

"So, why Goodrich?"

He lowered his voice. "Happens to me too, in case you're wondering. It's hard to shake some of the stuff you see."

"Yeah."

He took a second, nodded, and moved on. "Had a small finance position with a housebuilder for a few years, which was great, but once I met Glenn and saw the scale of projects he was working on, I knew this was what I wanted to be doing. What about you?"

I told him about the neighborhood revitalization project I was working on when Glenn found me. Aimed at increasing community engagement for youth, our team threw a city block party to unveil a new skate park. It was the last piece in the overhaul of the area and it got a lot of attention. Glenn approached me after the event and offered me a job.

"And your goal is to sit in a corner office with your last name on the banner as a director?" he asked.

"Absolutely." The look on his face told me he didn't see the same future version of myself I saw at the firm. "What? You know I'm good at my job. And I'm good at finding and negotiating deals too. Glenn just hasn't seen that part of me yet."

Even though I wasn't part of Glenn's good ol' boys club, I knew I was the better choice for that job. Unfortunately, Robby was also nominated, and he was president of the Glenn Goodrich Fan Club.

"Well, when I get the promotion, I'll be happy to bring you in on finding the spots. Would be nice to have an attractive travel partner in tow searching undiscovered parcels of land in the boonies together."

"That sounds completely *not* aboveboard."

"Hey, I'd be a great boss. I know my employees' strengths."

"More like you use them to your advantage."

"I take credit for *steering* my team's work. There's a difference."

"That's completely untrue," I argued. "I've done the majority of the work on the Rock Island contract and you know it."

"Are your undies in a wrinkle about not being the teacher's pet?" He barely tilted his head, and I swear his eyes twinkled.

"First of all, my *undies* are none of your concern," I shot back. "Nor will they ever be."

"Debatable."

"*Second*," I continued, "a great boss doesn't try and pass their employee's work off as their own. That's where you and I differ. I actually give my team credit for what they accomplish."

He rolled his eyes. "It's semantics. You say tomato…" He downed the rest of his drink. "Why don't you let me buy you a real drink?"

"I happen to like my *blush* concoction," I replied.

He leaned across the table. "I love it when you say the word *concoction*."

I pitched forward and lowered my voice. "You know, I was just wondering where the real Robby was hiding. You almost had me fooled that you were of the human species."

Ivy came back just in time with a drink in each hand and landed them in front of us.

"Where's yours?" I asked.

"I've got family flying into town tomorrow. Stay late, have fun. Make questionable choices in my name." She kissed both my cheeks, winked, and flew toward the exit. Why did it seem like everyone else in the world could wink so easily?

"So, are all the rumors about Florida true?" he asked.

"Depends on which rumors." I gauged how many gulps it would take to down my newly poured drink and make for the exit.

"Google says oral sex is illegal in Florida."

"And on that note," I threw back the contents of the entire cotton candy martini in one sip and stood as it burned a trail down my throat, "have a safe flight, Robby."

I beelined it for the door.

4

AUSTIN

The ferry looked like it had been through a hurricane, trampled into submission by suitcases and sun hats. I couldn't remember it ever being this busy.

A whistle from behind me cut through as we idled in from the last run of the day. Patrick's eyeline focused at the end of the dock in front of us. "Now that's a young lady with a mission."

"You've got to be kidding me." A casual Sherry from Jersey leaned up against a wooden piling, an inch of white denim cutoff shorts covering her mile-long legs with a red tied-up half shirt, looped through the middle. She smiled with the innocence of a viper and waved.

"I think she lost half her clothes in a battle with the dock to get to you." Patrick leaned back against the rail, clearly enjoying the view.

You couldn't say the girl didn't have confidence.

He grabbed the intercom. "Good evening, beautiful people. This is the Bolt himself, welcoming you to Rock Island. Please stay seated as we dock and we'll have you folks off and on your way to paradise in no time."

After the last guest had exited, Sherry strolled over and propped herself up against the piling that flanked the boat. "How was family dinner last night?"

"Uneventful." I turned to start the mountain of trash pickup on the boat deck.

"You're back early. I'm not going to take no for an answer now. One drink."

Sherry wasn't my type. And I didn't feel like being charming.

"We were going out anyway, join us!" Patrick called from the top deck.

She leaned onto the boat and grabbed the railing. "One drink can't hurt. Right?"

When a flea sneezes on Rock Island, the gossip train barrels ahead full steam. So I knew the moment I walked into Harpoon's with Sherry, that the subject of town gossip the next morning would be my Friday night whereabouts.

And Harpoon's was never lacking for busybodies. They had cheap beer, good fried food, and a great view of the water. Patrick walked in first like he did everywhere else, waving and schmoozing like he owned the joint.

Sherry clung to my side as we walked in, a potent mixture of strawberries and that same hairspray my sister used that I hated because it burned my nose. I headed straight to the bar for drinks as she peeled off to the bathroom.

Becky, the bartender whom I'd gone to kindergarten with, raised her pierced eyebrow at me. She was like another little sister to me, and never missed a chance to get into my business.

She landed a frosty beer onto the bar in front of me. "Well, that's a new flavor of ice cream for you."

"That's one way to put it." I took the first glorious sip, which had little ice shavings floating on the head.

"She's something to look at alright, even though she's not your type."

"She's more *your* type."

"Too bad she's not into that if she's here with you. I'd take her off your hands in a heartbeat if she'd let me." Becky plopped another drink in front of me that had a red and white paper umbrella nestled into whipped cream and smelled of coconut. I raised my eyebrows. "Trust me, she'll love it."

"Put these on Patrick's tab. I have him to thank for this one."

"Don't you mean Usain?" The corner of her mouth pulled up. "I'm surprised he hasn't gotten sued for that yet."

Only Patrick would be able to steal a famous person's likeness and have said famous person on board with it. He ran through the bar like a tornado, capturing smiles and laughs like he was harboring them as currency for later.

I jumped as I felt a pinch on my butt.

Becky suppressed a laugh and darted the other direction down the bar as Sherry came up behind my barstool and wrapped her arms around my waist.

"Aw, babe, it matches my outfit!" Sherry whined as she reached around me to grab her drink. Great. We'd already reached *babe* status. "And how did you know I love Malibu?"

I looked at Becky who was choking back a laugh halfway down the bar.

"Lucky guess?"

"You're a gem." She grabbed my beer with her other hand, squishing her boobs against my shoulder. "Let's go play pool."

"Have fun," Becky mouthed with a smirk as Sherry strutted in the opposite direction, hairspray strawberries in her wake.

Apparently, *pool* was code for *let me show you and the rest of the bar my cleavage.*

Her chest practically spilled onto the felt. I looked around and she had every single eye in the place on her. I started to sweat. I was never one to relish attention.

She sunk three balls in a row and sauntered up to me like a Cheshire cat.

"Your turn."

I cleared my throat and tried to line up my first shot, but her thigh was against the table in front of me.

"Umm, you're sort of in my way a little. For the shot."

"Oh, my bad, I didn't mean to distract you." She walked her fingers up my pool cue.

There was flirting, then there was what Sherry called flirting. Apparently they did things differently in Jersey. This was part of the reason I didn't date. You never knew who was fun crazy or legitimately crazy. The line could be pretty thin.

Cheers erupted by the front door. Sherry's eyes darted toward the noise, giving me just enough time to slip out from under her arm.

Lexi's blond head popped up behind the bar, already laughing with Becky. And there was Rex, surrounded by the usual crowd like he'd parted the Red Sea. Rock Island's golden boy. People loved him. Hell, I couldn't blame them. But we hadn't had a game in six months, and people were still lining up to congratulate him on a good season. It was the kind of glory my dad had always pictured for me—the future he'd mapped out from the moment I could throw a football.

A future I never wanted.

My phone dinged twice just as Patrick walked over to check in on us.

"Hey, you got me for a sec?" I handed over my cue without waiting for an answer and stepped away to check it. One text was a subtle jab from my dad seeing if I'd caught the basketball game on TV that day, and the other was from my mom asking who I was at Harpoon's with. Great.

I needed an out. I was crawling out of my skin to get out of the bar even before Lexi and Rex showed up and it turned into a pep rally. It wasn't like I hadn't been on dates before, it just wasn't a priority for me. I wasn't a one-night-stand kind of guy, and I didn't see myself wasting time when I had so little of it to spare in the first place.

"Hey, Dad needs me at the house. Gotta go, man. Sorry to cut the night short." It was a lie, but I was desperate. "I'll see you around, Sherry."

I tried to ignore the wave of disappointment that crashed over her face as I turned around. I knew Patrick would flirt with her and make her feel like a million bucks. He'd lift her spirits and tell her I'd had a rough day. Which I hadn't. And that she'd get another chance. Which she wouldn't. Or he'd tell her I had just gotten out of a bad relationship and wasn't ready to jump back in. Yet.

I walked out the front door and took a deep breath. The chatter inside the bar died out as the door behind me closed. I ran my hand down my face and looked up. She was attractive if Barbie was your thing. And nice. And clearly into me. But she just wasn't who I wanted.

～

I opened the front door to my beach bungalow and threw my keys onto the little plate on the table. *It's a key dish*, Mom had said the week after Vanessa moved out. My keys were the one thing I just couldn't keep track of. It's funny how the basic things become the most difficult. I never saw the purpose of an entire plate made solely for the purpose of holding keys when the table underneath it did the exact same thing. It took me a few weeks to get into the habit of actually using it and now, that's just where my key ring belongs.

Mom came over to help me rearrange furniture and spruce up the place. She figured moving the love seat from the left side of the room to the right was at least one step toward mending my shattered heart.

I collapsed onto the couch—the couch Vanessa had picked out but that now lived on the other side of the room.

Tom would've gotten a kick out of the Sherry story. He'd reenact it, licking whipped cream off his finger, prancing around the living room with his shirt tied up like an idiot, and we'd laugh until we cried. He'd pass out on the couch and we'd roll into the next day easily, like brothers who were separated at birth.

I could hear Vanessa's laugh in my head when I'd tell her the part where my pool cue turned into a finger ramp. She'd throw her head back and laugh with her mouth open, with that twinkle in her eyes that sparked something in me.

I shut my eyes tight and counted to ten. I'd be up in a few hours with a full day of work ahead of me and once I got going, I wouldn't have the time or energy left to think about this stuff.

But these quiet moments were the hardest.

The moments when I still felt like calling Tom, even though we haven't spoken in years. Then, I'd think about calling Vanessa. Then it hits me—again—that they're both gone, like a kick to the chest I never saw coming.

I used to hate the quiet. It was a reminder of how empty everything felt. I'd have the radio on, or the TV going in the background just to fill the space. But after a while, I learned to sit in it, even if they showed up in my head when I least expected it. It doesn't happen as often now, but when it does, I still feel the hollowness in my gut.

That's the thing about staying in the same place. They moved on. They got to go somewhere new—together. But I'm stuck here, in all the places where their ghosts still look at me from across the room.

5
SAMANTHA

With the Rock Island contract in the near-distant past, I decided to trade in my predictable Sunday of run, shower, and work at a nearby coffee shop to browse the weekend morning market near my apartment.

Ivy said I needed to live a little. Breaking my routine was the least I could do.

Baby steps.

And Jack was still ignoring me. No response to any of my apology texts after *the text* on Friday. I debated going to his apartment but didn't want to look desperate. Maybe he just needed time to cool off. I did, in fact, forget his complete existence for a few hours. My feelings would probably be hurt too.

"Hello, sunshine!" Italian Marco called out as I walked by his flower stand.

I gave him my best smile. "Today feels like a flower day, Marco."

He clasped his heart and looked toward the sky. "I have nothing as beautiful as you for sale, but I will try."

I wondered if he grew out his mustache and dyed it black as part of his whole *thing*, a direct contrast to the vibrant rainbow of colors splashed across his stand.

As I wandered through the ranunculus and garden roses, "Tainted Love" blasted from my phone.

I pushed ACCEPT.

"Hi, Mom." My insides braced for what was to come. I never knew what version of my mother I'd be getting, especially at 9:00 a.m.—the *I-just-woke-up-twelve-hours-sober* version or the *I'm-still-awake-from-an-all-night-bender* version.

"Hey, sweet pea! How's your Saturday?"

"It's Sunday, Mom."

"Do you remember Melissa Makecroft from elementary school?"

Aaaaand here we go. "No, doesn't ring a bell."

"Well, I ran into her mother at the grocery store yesterday and she just got divorced. Apparently, her husband ran off with his secretary after she had a miscarriage. Isn't that awful?"

"Wow. Yeah, that is awful." I was half listening. My weekly calls from my mother always included thorough updates about childhood acquaintances I didn't care about.

"You used to run around with her when you were little. She's the one who froze your underwear at your fourth-grade birthday party. Do you remember that? She was always a mean little thing."

"Nope. Don't remember her." I picked up a bouquet of large white and light pink garden roses in full bloom. I loved the way the petals curled in on each other.

"Well, you remember Johnny, her brother. He's still sleeping around with half the girls in town, spreading syphilis like it's butter on a knife. That poor mother. She had a fifty-fifty shot at one of them turning out."

"Sooooo," I drew out, trying to change the subject without setting her off. "Have any fun plans for today?"

"Are you coming home for the Fourth?"

She was hitting all the fun subjects at once.

The famous Fourth of July block party on the island was when people from high school who never left poured into downtown, their kids running barefoot down the middle of the street holding a lit sparkler in one hand and a hot dog dripping ketchup on their Old Navy flag tank top in the other.

The last block party I came home for, I ran into Boston Smith, the star quarterback of our football team and my junior and senior year crush. He was the hottest guy in school, one of the nicest, and not surprisingly, not one of the smartest. There's that saying, *Not the brightest crayon in the box*. I don't even think his crayon made it into the box to be considered. We were partners for two years in chemistry, and I basically took every test for him. He turned and waved when he saw me, and gave me an enthusiastic "Hi, Sasha!" I was mortified.

A tall blonde turned around with a baby on her hip. Of course, it would be the one and only fearless leader of the Blondtourage, Crystal *apparently-now*-Smith because the mean girls always snag the hot guy in the end. She gave me a condescending smile. "Oh, her name's not Sasha, babe. What is it again? Gosh, it's been so long."

And that wasn't even the worst of the visit.

I got a call in the middle of the night from a rando saying he was with my mom, but she couldn't remember where she lived. I told him I'd meet him to come get her, and when I pulled up, my old gym teacher was waiting for me. That's when I found out my mother had a thing for dating my old instructors. He still looked exactly the same, wearing neon-yellow gym shorts with a slit up the side and a dry-fit sleeveless shirt. It scooped just a little too low in the armpits so that if he leaned forward at all, you had a clear shot of his side nipple and dusting of hair around his areola. He was an extra straight out of a Richard Simmons workout video.

I took a deep breath. "I'm really slammed with work. I don't think I'm going to make it this year."

"It's over a month away. And you haven't been home in over two years," she snapped. "If you just don't want to come home, you should say that."

I closed my eyes and took a deep breath. The mixed smell of peonies and freshly baked bread filled my nose and dulled the daggers threatening to spill out of my mouth. "I'll see how it looks closer to the date. I'll try though, I promise."

My eyes scanned over the tops of the sky-reaching sunflowers in the market and landed on the back of a familiar head. A *very* familiar head.

Oh God.

Jack.

He was turning around.

Okay, perfect. This was good. I could talk to him in person, apologize for being a jerk, and we'd go to Angelo's for lunch like we always did every Sunday afternoon.

I took a deep breath, took a step in his direction, and that's when the really pretty blonde holding the biggest sunflower I'd ever seen turned around.

Okay. Maybe a friend.

She threw her head back and laughed, Pantene-commercial style, then he kissed her on the cheek.

Okay. Maybe not a friend.

Then I did what any other self-respecting woman would do.

I ducked.

"Sunshine!" Italian Marco's booming voice pierced the air. "What are you doing on your hands and knees? Here, let me help you up."

"No, it's okay. Really. I just dropped something down here." I hugged the ground.

Cue the rom-com movie montage of unexpected and humiliating

events because *that's my life*. I crawled away from them under the flower stand, bumping my head on the wooden cradle nestled with buckets of brightly colored tulips that tipped over in slow motion. That, of course, knocked into the three-year-old standing next to it and spilled her strawberry smoothie down the front of her cream-colored linen jumper that her mother most definitely overpaid for. I clearly ruined the perfect photo op from the next Mommy Influencer and she was *not* happy. I continued to crawl on all fours past the colorful mound of petals, dragging my knees through the strawberry and milk mixture that smelled glorious, and stood up holding the garden roses to fully block my face from view, only to then run into a man eating a Magnolia Bakery red velvet cupcake that smashed into his nose before I bolted away from the market.

"You have to pay for those!" I heard Italian Marco yelling as I sprinted down the crowded sidewalk.

I ran for three blocks, turned twice, and leaned back against a brick wall, still carrying the stolen flowers in my hand.

I was a thief. Or a fugitive. I guess technically both.

And Jack was with someone else.

☀

I walked into the office Monday morning to a sticky note that read, *Glenn's office, ASAP*. He didn't even look up from his desk when I walked in.

"Go home and pack. You're catching a flight to Florida in less than three hours."

The wall clock read 8:03 a.m. Three minutes into my day and already we've hit a land mine. "I'm sorry, what?"

Glenn glared at me over his glasses and pointed toward the door. "Go home. Pack. Robby got appendicitis and has been in the hospital since Saturday. He was trying to leave against the doctor's orders and they called his emergency contact, which apparently is me, for some godforsaken reason."

"Is he okay?"

"If he keeps his hind end in the hospital he will be. He'll be sedated for a few days from the sound of it." Glenn shuffled around a few papers, then put them back in the exact same spot. "Game time substitute. Funding got pulled on the Oakstone project, so it's perfect timing. You can start the due diligence down there for the first week or so. We'll swap you out once he's feeling up to par. I pushed the intro meeting with the seller to tomorrow morning, which should give you plenty of time if you prep on the plane."

All the air was knocked out of my lungs.

"You're from down there anyway, right?"

I blinked. "Florida's a pretty large state, sir."

"Robby said you were from Rock Island."

My throat started to tighten. "The general area, yes, sir."

"Headed back home then. Good. It should take half the time if you already know the territory. Maybe it'll give you an upper hand in getting what you need from the locals."

I think my head was nodding up and down.

"Robby's assistant will shoot Ivy all the travel details that have been rebooked in your name. There's a car out front waiting for you to take you home, then to the airport. Better get moving if you want to make your flight."

"Yes, sir. Of course."

The clock on the wall read 8:06 a.m. Three minutes and my week had been shot to hell.

ME: My house. STAT.
I'm going to Florida.

IVY: with pugbug?

ME: Without PugBug.

IVY: wait y

ME: Appendicitis. Emergency surgery.
I'm going until he feels better.
Few days.
A week max.

IVY: ummmm 4 weeks
says google

ME: Google could be wrong.

IVY: google is never wrong

ME: Yeah, well Google says it's illegal to
have oral sex in Florida.

IVY: y do u know that

ME: MY HOUSE. NOW.

I stood in my apartment, which was uncharacteristically quiet. Was I really going to hop on a plane and go home for a month? A *month*.

I hadn't been home in over two years. Since I escaped for good seven years ago, I had only been back a handful of times. None went over particularly well.

But it hit me as I stood in the silence—I didn't have a choice. I wanted this promotion. I deserved it. And the best way to show I was the right person for the job was to suck it up, jump on a plane, down three first-class tequilas, and enter the seventh layer of hell for thirty days. That's all it was.

I had done everything in my power to get away for the sake of my sanity a very long time ago, and here I was, heading back.

A fist pounded at my door half a vodka tonic later (only clear liquor—it was still before noon, after all). Ivy barged in with a wardrobe of clothes with tags draped over her shoulder, two triple skinny vanilla lattes, extra hot, and a large brown paper bag.

"These will fit. Stick them in your suitcase."

My shoulders sagged. "Can I stick you in my suitcase?"

"The baggage compartment is a far cry from first class."

My typical facade of *I have my shit pulled together* must have been wavering because her expression changed into something a bit softer. "This will be good for you. Maybe the Florida pace will force you to slow down. Believe it or not, there is a life outside of work."

She had a point.

"And Jack just dumped you and is ignoring you so you might as well go," she added quickly.

"So...I saw him at the market yesterday." I paused. The tears that pooled in my eyes took me by complete surprise. I blinked them back. "He wasn't alone."

It seemed like a bigger deal once I said it out loud.

Ivy pulled me in for a hug then lowered her voice. "Jack is not your epic love story."

"I don't believe in epic love stories."

"Neither do I."

"You literally write about them in your free time."

"*Wrote*. And that's why I called it fiction." Ivy's voice was level and calm. "This is not a vacation. Like you told Snuffleupugus earlier, you'll be working so much it's not like you'll even have time to see your mom. At least, not a lot."

I smiled. That was her best name for Robby yet.

"Forget Jack for now," she continued. "That's for another day. I'll stalk him and bury his body while you're away. A little distraction from that could be a good thing right now. You need to focus on this trip, which will set you up perfectly to take over this male-run chauvinistic testosterone show we've come to know and lovingly conspire to take down."

She was right. It was due diligence for a multimillion-dollar deal. This was a huge opportunity to show I wasn't even playing in the same ballfield as Robby. If I steered this due diligence and knocked it out of the park, he couldn't take credit for it. Unlike everything else I've ever done in my entire career. I'd prove that I could severely kick ass and that there's no better choice for the next director.

It would just cost my soul in the process.

"Let's think tank this. What about sending Forrest? He's on the North Dakota project."

"I think you'd have a hard time convincing Glenn you know more about farms than Forrest, who I'm pretty sure was born in an actual barn. In North Dakota."

I thought for another second. "I could make you go."

"This isn't about me. Indulge me for a second on what our future would look like if Puganator made director over you."

I thought about it for a minute. "There'd be an office chant with foam fingers for sure."

"Team-building excursions at the gun range."

"Can you just imagine the jokes about his concealed weapon?" I cringed.

"For the love of God, please don't subject me to that. Samantha, you're the right person for this job. This isn't just about you anymore. Glenn's company will swan dive headfirst into an HR nightmare if PugDiddy makes director."

I knew *developed* cities. But there was a part of me, a small part, that perked up knowing I could come up with anything I wanted for the land. *Anything.* When I framed it like that, it almost sounded exciting.

"And you're basically saving humanity as a bonus," she finished. "What's there to lose?"

"My sanity?" I suggested.

"Overrated."

"My pride?"

"Overvalued." She reached for the brown paper bag. "And look, I brought you lots of tiny hugs to pack in your suitcase."

She opened the bag showing me thirty or so miniature liquor bottles. "I was wondering what was in that thing." I laughed as they clanked against each other. "Okay, I'll go. But will you promise you won't kill my fern?"

"No."

I sighed. "You are absolutely zero help."

"You're going to do great. Do I need to ride to the airport with you so you don't go to Hawaii and open a snow cone hut on the beach instead?" she asked.

My eyes widen. "That's such a great idea."

"Samantha." She leveled her gaze at me.

"No. I promise not to bail and move to Hawaii to open a snow cone hut. I will go to Florida and save the human race."

"Great. Then it's settled. Let's get your ass to the airport before you change your mind and miss your flight. I need a martini after all this."

I was going *home*. As I rolled my carry-on through LaGuardia security, I ran through the roster at Goodrich in my head again. I'd looked at the situation from every angle and suffice to say, I was heading to Florida unless I wanted to spoon-feed Robby my promotion.

A loud buzzer went off as I walked through the scanner, interrupting my internal debate of fighting a decision I'd already made.

"Ma'am, step aside," the very tall TSA agent barked at me.

"Sorry, I forgot I have to go through the other line. I spaced out." I reached for my medical card and stepped to the side for the one-on-one pat down party.

Fun fact—when I walk through metal detectors, it sounds like a really aggressive outdoor garden chime section at Home Depot during a hurricane.

"Is this your bag?" he asked as he plucked my carry-on from the conveyor belt.

"Yes, it is." I gave him the brightest smile I could muster as I handed over my medical card.

He glared at me, inspected the little plastic card I always carried around, and bounced his gaze to my arm like he didn't believe there were exactly twenty-three screws holding it together.

"Accident in high school. Just call me *Ter-mi-na-tor*." I rocked my arm back and forth like a robot.

"Spread your legs, ma'am."

"Not a joke guy. Got it. Too early for that stuff anyway." I held my breath as he groped me with a plastic wand that blared as it circled my arm. Once the unofficial first base had been crossed, he put my carry-on on top of the table. He unzipped the top and eyed me as he pulled out the brown paper bag.

"They're all under three ounces each," I blurted out, like that's going to explain away all the alcoholic vibes I was giving off.

"Ma'am, have you been drinking today?"

"I have anxiety with flying." *Liar.* "And I'll be gone for a whole month. To my hometown. And I'm seeing my mom and we don't exactly get along all that well. These are kinda like mini backup reinforcements. Little bottles of courage."

He didn't even respond, and walked over to his supervisor who put my carry-on into one of those little machines that test for bomb residue. It clicked green after an agonizing ten-second stare-down competition. He handed me my bag and reluctantly nodded me through.

My phone rang.

FACETIME—MOM flashed across the top of my screen. Against my better judgment, I answered the call.

"Happy birthday to you…"

"Mom—"

"Happy birthday to you…"

I turned down the volume on my phone.

"Happy birthday, dear sweat pea…"

"Mom—"

"Happy birthday to you!" She wore a pointy birthday hat and blew a tiny paper horn into the phone. "I remember the day you came into this world, screaming your head off and red as a tomato. You were *so* pissed off."

Her words had that slight, familiar slur. Not noticeable if you weren't looking for it. "Right. But, Mom—"

"You didn't calm down until your father grabbed you from that nurse and started singing to you."

My chest squeezed at the mention of Dad.

"Mom, it's not my birthday."

"Of course it's your birthday. It's the sixteenth. You think I'd forget one of the most important days of my life?"

"My birthday's the sixteenth... of next month."

She stilled for barely a second. "Well, there's absolutely nothing wrong in celebrating a little bit early, now, is there? If your father hadn't left, we'd be celebrating at Charley's tonight like we used to."

"He didn't leave, Mom. He died."

"Well, he's not here regardless. It's the same."

"There's actually a pretty big difference, technically speaking."

"Well, we'll agree to disagree on that one."

"Have you been drinking today?"

Her face pinched. "I don't see how that's relevant." She dismissed the subject like we were talking about the weather.

The intercom screeched from above with boarding announcements.

"Where are you?" she asked. "It's so loud."

I was still on the fence about telling her I was coming back, but there was no way I could avoid her for a month. It was an impossible feat in such a small town, even if I was staying at a hotel. I'd have to tell her I was coming. But I was thankful for the small things, like not having to sleep in a house that most likely looks exactly the same as it did seven years ago: boy band posters half torn off my bedroom wall, a My Little Pony collection cluttered on the dresser, and a house void of pictures of a father who was taken away too soon.

I took a deep breath. Half-truth time. "I'm actually at the airport now. I have a quick work trip, then I'm actually going to be heading to the island for a little while to scout out a new potential location for work. I'll let you know when I'm in town, okay?"

"Wait, what? My baby's coming home?!" she shouted.

"Hey, my flight is boarding. I'll call you in a few days!" I hung up quickly and leaned against the waiting area wall.

Drinking was back on the table for her. Clearly.

Granted it was after noon, and I myself was already down a drink (or two), but a birthday month swap was a pretty big oops. And it wasn't like she was having another pivotal life-changing moment plummeting her into the depths of forgetfulness.

It always got worse around holidays, birthdays, or Sundays in general. When she was good and sloshed, she brought up Dad, which tore open a wound decades deep every single time. She still carried around resentment for his illness and the swift change it made to our lives. She lived by herself, and for the last seven years the buffer of distance stood between us. But I was on my way to being up front and center with the chaos.

I needed to build the cement walls back up in my mind protecting myself from the wreckage that was my mother.

"Now boarding flight 1752 to Fort Myers, Florida," the intercom screamed.

Well. Here we go.

6
AUSTIN

Monday was busier than usual.

Over the last few years, there had been a steady increase in the number of tourists coming to visit, even in the later summer months when your shirt would stick to your back if you just dared to think of going outdoors.

The ferry schedule was tight. Tight enough that if I added any more runs, I'd be working my crew into the ground. We were already running six days a week, filling any daylight hours with runs across the water. I didn't personally like nighttime runs. The view of the island in daylight was a much better first impression but if numbers continued to grow like they were, I wouldn't have a choice but to add a few onto the schedule.

What I needed was a bigger boat. And bigger boats were expensive.

"You go see that two-hundred passenger for sale yet?" Patrick asked as he mopped down the deck between runs. A sightseeing charter in north Florida had been bought out and had a boat for sale a couple hours away. It was the perfect upgrade to my current one-boat show, and the new owner wasn't local. He wanted to get rid of it quickly, so the price was right.

"No. Ran out of time and couldn't squeeze it in."

"Want me to go take a peek? I've got the time tomorrow while you're running. Or," he switched to his Jamaican accent, "I could run the ferry, mon. Allow me to introduce your guests to the beautiful world of Rock Island—the authentic way."

I did a double take. He really did look like the Bolt.

"And what exactly is authentic about a Jamaican ferrying people to an island in Florida?"

"Similar climates. And people always love the accent, you know that." One corner of his mouth pulled up and he wagged his eyebrows. "For real though, you need to take a look and this ferry needs to keep running. I've got you, man."

Generally speaking, I'd rather do something myself and make sure it gets done right, even though I trust Patrick as much as I'm capable of. Previous experience in trusting other humans would lead me to believe it's a safer bet to rely on yourself. If something were to happen on my watch, the guests' safety would be in my hands. But if I'm not there, I can't do anything about it.

My mother calls it *guarded*. I call it *being responsible*.

"What do you say, Capt'n? You promise to go take a peek at that new boat you need to be buying, and I promise not to sink this one. Deal?"

Click-click-click.

My head shot up.

There was something about a certain *click-click-click* coming down the dock that told you the owner of that noise was going to be trouble. That sound meant one of two things—the owner had never been on a dock before and didn't realize their heels would inevitably get caught in the open slats, or two, they knew and didn't give a shit.

I didn't need the confirmation of the big floppy hat and oversized sunglasses to tell me this one was the latter.

Click-click-click.

I watched out of the corner of my eye. She halted halfway down the dock as her suitcase slammed into her leg. One heel had wedged itself into the open crack of the old wooden boards.

She mumbled something under her breath.

Well, that's what happens when you walk on a dock in inappropriate shoes—they're not exactly high heel friendly. Her oversized hat engulfed her frame as she bent down, dropping her purse to the ground as her rolling suitcase fell over to the side. She worked to get her heel out, then fell back on her butt. She took her glasses off, turned her head to the sky, and exhaled loudly.

Holy shit.

It couldn't be.

I guess technically speaking it could be, but the chances were so slim I shook my head and squinted my eyes just to make sure.

Here's the thing about our small town and the people who grow up here—there are three types. There are the ones who stay. Forever. They marry their high school sweetheart they walked on homecoming court with, have babies soon after graduation, then your mom ends up teaching their kids first grade eventually and you're cheering at the same Little League games with them. You see them every Friday night at the high school football game working concessions, then at the grocery store every Saturday afternoon, then nestled in a church pew on Sunday morning.

Then, there are the ones who boomerang—they leave for a little bit, but inevitably come back to run the family business, take care of a sick parent, or they just partied too hard in college, flunked out and have nowhere else to go so they make it work.

Then there were the Samantha Leighs—they left and there wasn't a shot in hell they'd ever come back.

Patrick's voice rang out from beside me. "You good, man? You look like you've just seen a ghost." He followed my eyeline and whistled. "Now that's a fish outta water if I've ever seen one."

She had managed to wrench her heel free and was almost to the boat, but Patrick shot up at the sight of her, always the knight in shining armor, and leaped off to help her. She was looking up at the signs on the dock, but there was no doubt in my mind she was headed for ours.

I counted how many seconds it would take for him to recognize her. She was a few years behind us but she had one of those faces that's hard to forget.

"You looking for a ride to Rock Island?"

I saw her eyebrows pull at the sight of his name tag, probably trying to reconcile a semi-familiar face with a totally bogus name. "I am. Are you with Scuttle's Ferry?"

"The one and only!" he responded. My eyes stayed glued to the deck, untying and tying the same rope for the fifth time. "Let me grab this here monstrosity for you and help you right along on board." He grabbed her suitcase, which really should have been considered cargo freight, and hoisted it onto the boat.

"Those heels there might kill you getting in. No sense in breaking an ankle." Before I knew what was happening, Patrick picked her up like a baby and hoisted her aboard.

Her breath caught and I couldn't help but laugh. Oh, he was going to get it.

Once her heels touched the fiberglass of the boat deck, she turned around and glared at him, eyes narrowed as if she could pierce straight through him with her gaze.

"I'll have you know, *Patrick*," she stepped toward him, jabbing his name tag to his chest, "I'm perfectly capable of getting on and off this boat by myself."

At the same moment, a rogue wave from a Sea-Doo splashed against the side of the boat, rocking it just a bit, tipping her barely off balance and backward. Right into my arms.

"Okay, yeah, sure." His eyes twinkled. "Maybe getting on and off, just not *standing* on the boat."

"Whoa there." I hoisted her back on two feet carefully. She smelled like expensive shampoo. "You might want to take them off just for the ride. It can get a little bumpy."

She looked straight into my eyes and I watched her eyes soften, blink slowly, then narrow. "Austin?"

"Long time no see, Scuttle."

7
SAMANTHA

The boat pulled in just after sunset with still enough light to make out the familiar shoreline I'd grown up with. Luckily, my first work meeting had been pushed to the next morning so I had the night to settle in and relive all my high school nightmares in private.

It was exactly as I had remembered it.

The Starfish Hotel faced Main Street, its brightly colored bungalows seen from any boat ferrying in. Charley's Lobster Shack cheerily greeted you from the dock, while its white awnings and picnic tables waved at you from the shore, all basked in the warm glow of the sunset. A small crowd buzzed with their mouths full, chatting over clear plastic cups of cold beer and baskets of fried food. Rosy cheeks, flip-flops and Nantucket Reds, aviators and windswept hair. Shell-paved roads lined the island closest to the water and palm trees were evenly spaced along the sidewalks.

It was charming and quaint.

And gave me a sweeping sense of nausea.

Where people saw a cute mom-and-pop pharmacy, I saw the building I would drag my mom out of when they wouldn't give her pills. Where people saw a perfect plucked-out-of-a-film-set ice cream store, I saw the metal bench she normally passed out on. This town was full of memories everywhere, and it dawned on me I hadn't brought any Xanax.

"Here, let me grab that for you." Austin reached for my luggage. His arm brushed against mine and the small dusting of blond hair tickled my skin and gave me chills.

"No, it's okay, I got it." I struggled to get the rolling suitcase, carry-on, and purse to balance as I walked along the ramp.

I shook my head, scattering the memories that were trying to pour in through the cracks of the fortified dam I had built over the years. Of course, the first person to welcome me to town was Austin.

Austin Marcs.

I had more than a few dedicated pages in my diary pairing my first name with his last—*Samantha Marcs*—written in pink glitter pen with hearts doodled around it. I'm pretty sure my mom kept the scrapbook I made for our future wedding, chock-full of red roses, puffy silk sleeves, and tulle.

Not that I would ever admit something like that to anyone. I was a lovestruck eight-year-old with a crush on my best friend's older brother, which happens, like, *all the time* so it absolutely officially belongs in the not-a-big-deal-let's-move-on column.

I made a mental note to burn the diary if I found it while I was here.

But Austin's baby face looked different, with a five-o'clock shadow that had darkened into something more rugged—closer to a seven-o'clock. His eyes crinkled at the edges and he was so *tan*. I didn't know skin cancer could be such a positive thing. He smelled like salt water, too.

I mean, we were on a dock. The water probably smelled like salt water.

Whatever.

"You're seriously going to break your ankle." His eyes narrowed. "Drop it."

I glared back at him and relented.

"You heading to your mom's?" he asked.

Right. This was going to happen a lot here. People knew things about me—where I was from, who my mom was, that I lived in the little house on Rocky Point with the blue shutters that never brought the trash cans in. There was a familiarity that existed on this island I was all too happy to give up when I left, and here I was being blasted back into it within five minutes of setting foot on the soil.

"No, I'm staying at the Starfish." His eyes flicked over to me questioningly. "I'm actually here for work. Not really to visit."

"Well, looks like she didn't get the memo," he said casually.

"Wait, what?"

"Your mom." He nodded toward the shore. "She's across the street walking over here."

"Crap. Duck!" I crouched behind a large plastic dock box on the pier.

"What?"

"Duck!" I grabbed his shoulder and pulled him down next to me so we were both out of view.

"Why are we hiding from your mom?" We were huddled so close. The gold flecks in his eyes shimmered as they widened, the truth dawning across his face. "You didn't tell her you were coming."

"Shh! She's going to hear you."

"She's across the street. She's not going to hear me. Why doesn't she know you're here?"

"Did she see me?"

"Umm, I don't think so," he said.

I peeked around the container. "I told you I'm here for work. I didn't really want to deal with her and the whole argument of staying at her place."

"So you're avoiding it until..."

"Until it's unavoidable."

"This doesn't count as unavoidable?"

"Not yet." I peeked around the container and watched in horror as she crossed the street and walked toward the dock.

Austin dipped his head to mine and dropped his voice to a whisper that shot goose bumps down my neck. "I feel like we're approaching *unavoidable*."

I couldn't tell if my heart was ping-ponging out of my chest from my mother walking toward me or Austin's lips that were *right there*.

"Go stop her," I ordered.

"And you're going to..."

"Stay here until you get her to walk the other way. The Starfish is right there. I can make a run for it."

"In those heels?" he questioned, eyeing the three-inch monstrosities I had put back on.

"Heels are like sneakers in the city. It's fine."

"You'll break an ankle."

I peeked around the storage container again. "You have ten seconds to stop her from walking onto this dock. If you don't, I will shove you into the water and somehow find a way to sink your boat."

His eyes dipped to my mouth. "You're not exactly the tongue-tied awkward teenager you used to be, Scuttle." Amusement dripped from his lips as he popped up and jogged off toward the marina walkway. I hadn't even stepped onto the dirt of the island yet and I was already hugging a dock that smelled like fish guts and hiding from my mother. It took less than half an hour for my *I have my shit together* grown-up facade to go up in flames.

Mom's eyes glittered up at him as he walked closer. She always loved Austin. Well, she loved generally any man that paid her attention, but Austin always had a way of making people feel seen.

He towered over her small frame and guided her with a hand behind her back to look the opposite way of where I was crouched. He was completely dialed in and listening intently as she spoke with her hands flying all over the place, a Leigh family trait. We both did it—like the energy we felt coursing through us needed some sort of physical outlet.

I watched as she laughed and he chuckled. She grabbed his arm. *Oh my God, did she just squeeze his biceps?*

She had put on a little bit of weight since I'd last seen her. Her jean skirt was still too short and her polyester shirt was still too tight. But she looked better, like maybe her diet consisted of more than just pills, vodka, and string cheese.

She hugged him and headed in the other direction. She walked into Charley's as Austin made his way back to me.

"Were you *flirting* with her?" I said, still crouched on my knees.

"You told me you'd sink my boat if I didn't get her to leave."

"Well, I appreciate your dedication to my anonymity, but *ew*."

"Anything for a guest." His boyish grin turned mischievous. "Give me your bags."

"As I said before, I am perfectly capable of taking them myself."

"Let's not add an ER visit to your stroll down memory lane today. I do have other plans and can't be your invisibility cloak all night."

"I don't need—"

"Don't argue with me." He stepped closer to me, his gaze towering down from above me.

"I don't remember you being so bossy." I stood up and straightened my skirt.

"I don't remember you being so violent." He leaned in and grabbed my bags from my hands without breaking eye contact. So, apparently there's a navy-blue circle around the outside of his eyes that compliments the green and the gold and all the other wonderful shades of color that I could perfectly see because he was *two inches from my face* and I forgot what I was supposed to be doing.

"You need me to draw you a map?" he asked, still way too close for rational thought.

My heart stutter-stepped. The Starfish. *Right.* "No, thank you. I'm going." I turned and walked up the dock.

"You're welcome," he sang as he followed behind me. I could hear the smile in his voice.

Bells jingled above my head as I pulled open the screen door to the hotel. The lobby was small, overrun with pale yellow and bright teal accents, trying to make up for the drab tile floor.

The woman behind the desk lit up as we walked into the lobby. Her name was Josie, according to her name tag that had a little starfish hot glued to it. "Hello there, handsome," she said, beaming at Austin, before she turned her focus to me. "Checking in, darling?"

"It's under Sam," he answered.

"It's actually Samantha."

"Great! Just give me one second." The humming from her old-school desktop computer cut the thick silence that trailed us from the dock. "Samantha Leigh. Looks like we have you for a month?" She glanced up to confirm.

Austin's gaze pierced my cheek. Busted.

"Uh, should be for only two weeks. Here on a work trip."

"Oh, wonderful! I love having a face around here a little more than a night or two. I get tired of looking at this one's mug day in and day out," she said, smiling at Austin. She looked at me again, this time holding just a tad bit longer. "You look familiar." She looked back down at the reservation. "Samantha Leigh? My goodness, Bonnie's daughter?"

My smile tightened as I nodded.

"Oh my, you have grown up! I'm friends with your mother, and I've seen about a thousand pictures of you. I can't believe I didn't recognize you. Your mother didn't even tell me you were coming into town!"

Panic set in. I forgot how small of a town this was. Luckily Austin jumped to my rescue. Again.

"How about we keep it on the down-low for now since Sam is surprising her mom once she gets settled in?" He added a wink.

"Oh, of course! She'll be tickled pink." Josie winked back and he gave her his winning smile in return.

"Thanks, I really appreciate it."

Josie beamed, fully committed to her new life mission of keeping a secret. "I'll have your bags brought around for you. You just let me know if you need anything else in the meantime."

"Great, thanks. Oh, what's the internet password for the room?"

"Oh, um, I'm afraid it's not too great out here," she answered apologetically. "A hit-or-miss kind of thing on the island, as you know. But it's *iheartseastars*, all lower case." She passed me a key with a teal starfish buoy attached to it. "I put you in 1A, best little cabin in the place. First teal bungalow on your right out the door, facing the water."

"Thanks, Josie."

We walked back toward the front door and I fiddled with the key in my hand.

"Thanks for the help with my luggage. And my mom."

"Wouldn't want my boat being sunk. Then you'd be stuck here forever." He kept looking at me with his deadpan face. Was he serious? Was he joking? Why did I question my life's existence when he looked at me like that?

"Don't forget the free happy hour at four!" Josie called out from behind us. "It's a local winery, you won't want to miss it!"

"There's a winery on the island?" I whispered to Austin as we walked out the door together.

"*Winery* might be a generous description," he muttered.

The thick wall of Florida heat rolled over me like a wave once we stepped outside. "I forgot how hot it was here." I fanned myself with the Sea-Doo rental pamphlet Josie gave me.

He stopped and stared at me, squinting his eyes just a tad as they roamed over my face. I think the last time he saw me I was in the middle of blooming teenage acne and braces. Yes, I was one of the lucky ones who got both in high school, the metal mouth addition on the back end of one of my mom's kicks to make everything around us seemingly perfect, including teeth.

I ran my tongue over my teeth out of habit. "What?"

"Good to see you, Scuttle." He smirked as he turned and walked back to the boat, not looking back a single time.

I opened the front door of the cabin into an alternate world of seafoam-green accessories and whitewashed wicker furniture. A *ding* came through on my phone.

IVY: did you make it alive

ME: Affirmative.

IVY: how's the sea anemone

ME: Starfish

IVY: same

ME: As charming as ever

IVY: sending over updated list of places for DD, per Glenn

ME: Wonderful. Is my plant alive?

IVY: we'll talk about it later

ME: I've been gone 12 hours

IVY: like i said, not really my thing

I paused. While I was a pretty private person at work, Ivy had been my assistant for two years. She unfortunately had an unavoidable front-row seat to some of the drama. My mother called my office enough (when I didn't answer my cell phone fast enough) for her to get the gist of the situation and to have a vague understanding of our dynamic.

ME: I saw my mother already.

IVY: on a scale from gizmo to gremlin

ME: She didn't see me.
I ducked.

IVY: again?

ME: Seems to be an effective avoidance strategy.

IVY: 2 for 2
get some sleep, boss
you can deal with her tomorrow

ME: Water my fern

IVY: 😑

Even though my screen was filled with numbers and Excel columns that night, my mind kept wandering back to Austin.

His Facebook was set to private so I couldn't see anything but his profile picture, which was too blurry to zoom in on. His Instagram had only three pictures. The first was a sunset. Predictable. A typical post for any human being living in Florida. The second was a picture of a picture—him fishing off the back of a boat when he was younger, maybe eight or so, facing the water with a pole that stretched out longer than him. And the last one was of him and his mom smiling underneath a SCUTTLE'S FERRY sign from a few years ago.

I related to wanting to be a virtual ghost online. I didn't even have accounts. But then I googled him and hit the jackpot. Apparently Carla1936 on TikTok had quite a crush on "Captain Handsome," who was recently identified as the one and only, Austin Marcs. My page filled with GIFs and memes of him shirtless pulling up the anchor with sayings like "I'll pull up your anchor any day."

On page three of my deep dive, I caught an article from the *Rock Island Gazette* about Ronald "Rex" Love taking over the local high school football team. It had a picture of the Marcs family standing in the middle of the field, Bill's arms draped over both Austin and Rex's shoulders, with Lexi nestled into Rex's other side. The caption called her his fiancée.

Lexi was engaged.

My heart cracked at the sight.

I couldn't help the smile that crept across my face. She got her *happily ever after* after all. But then my heart molded around the swift fist that came out of nowhere.

There was a lot of bad I chose to walk away from seven years ago. But along with that decision also came giving up some of the good.

8
AUSTIN

I walked into my house to Britney Spears's "Womanizer" blaring from the Echo. It's amazing how such a small thing could be such a nuisance. And I'm not talking about the Echo.

My feet took me straight to the fridge. I grabbed a cold beer, popped the top, turned and leaned my back against the humming steel. I downed the entire thing in under thirty seconds.

"Whoa. Rough day on the water, Captain?"

I hadn't seen Lexi sitting on the couch with her nose in a book. Beyond Sam, the last trip of the day was still on my mind. It was a little more than overcrowded, and one woman's purse fell overboard. Everything from her wallet to tampons decorated the Gulf of Mexico. It was yet another reminder we were bursting at the seams and I needed to do something about it.

"Something like that." I threw the bottle into the trash and reached for another. "How can you read with that blasting?"

"Alexa, volume two," she said as she strolled into the kitchen, hopped onto the counter, and cocked her head at me like a bird, waiting for the explanation from intuition only little sisters had.

"What?" I asked.

Lexi's apartment lease had expired a week ago, and with her getting married in a month, it didn't make sense for her to extend it.

She was crashing in between Mom and Dad's house and mine. The house felt less empty with her in it, although her obsession with talking to Alexa and blasting Britney drove me up the wall.

"All good, just a long day." Her eyes burrowed through my forehead. "What were you reading?"

She continued to stare and lean toward me, about to tip off the counter. Then she huffed. "That was a lame attempt to change the subject. Out with it."

Always so persistent.

"I had a familiar face on the charter over to the island today." I gulped down half of my second beer.

Her eyes grew wide. "She didn't."

"Nope. Not her." She was probably thinking of the *V* word.

"Thank God. I didn't feel like burying a body today."

"You remember Sam, right? From high school?"

She stilled. Then blinked. The name took her by surprise. "Ummm, ex-best-friend Sam? *I'm-moving-to-New-York-and-will-never-speak-to-you-again* Sam?" She squinted her eyes at me. "Sounds vaguely familiar."

"Yeah, so that one. She's back. And apparently it's *Samantha* now."

She took a shallow breath. "No way."

"Yes, way."

"She's back." She paused. A myriad of emotions flashed over her face at once. She hopped off the counter after a few moments of staring at me, bumped me out of the way of the fridge, and pulled out two more beers. "Like, forever? Or for the weekend?"

I'm not sure Lexi even knew what she wanted the answer to be.

"A couple weeks. Something for work."

"Huh." Lexi chewed on her bottom lip. "Tell me more."

"I don't have more. Between loading other people onto the boat and fishing feminine products out of the deep blue sea, I didn't get much other than she'll be here for a little while."

"Did she grow another head? Is she losing her hair?" It was my turn to just stare at her. "What? Cities are gross. The smog, the city pollution. It all affects your body. At least that's what I've heard."

"Does she know you're getting married?" I asked. I saw her flinch, but it was so subtle I would've missed it if I weren't deliberately looking for it.

"I haven't spoken to her since she up and left seven years ago. So, I'd go with a no on that one." Lexi was good at covering up her feelings. Most of the time. "Are you going to, like, see her while she's here?"

"No. Why would I see her?" She lifted her brow at my nonchalant attitude that clearly wasn't playing nonchalantly.

"She was still hot, wasn't she?" she teased. "You know, she used to draw hearts with your name in them."

"That's...unexpected."

"We did it with the Hanson brothers and NSYNC too. Girls do that. It's not weird."

"Debatable. But no, I'm not going to see her. Why would I? She's your friend."

"Was, until she fell off the face of the earth..." Her voice trailed off. Not many things dimmed the ball of sunshine that was my little sister, but I could tell she didn't know what to do with this bit of news.

I lowered my voice. "You can't blame her for leaving." Sam was Lexi's best friend in high school. I knew she was hurt when Sam moved.

"I don't blame her, not completely, but it doesn't change the fact that she did."

"Please don't tell me you've held a grudge against her this entire time for what happened after graduation."

"God no, not at all. I just think there could have been a way to keep our friendship, that's all. I just didn't think I was completely disposable like everyone else."

"You are not disposable." I lowered my head toward her so I was on her eye level, but I could see the hurt flicker across her eyes. I knew exactly what she was feeling. I recognized that look.

"Yeah, no, I know. It's fine." She shrugged it off and eyed me. "Is she hot though?"

"That's completely irrelevant."

"She was hot."

"Well, she's not ugly." A fact that, for some reason, pissed me off.

Lexi smiled. "Didn't you have a picture of her up in your room?" She watched my reaction out of the side of her eye as she pulled another sip.

Her memory was ridiculous. So, here's the thing. Lexi had a lot of really annoying friends. But Sam had always been the cute, funny one. But I did *not* have a thing for her. She just happened to be the friend of my sister's I preferred over all of the other annoying high-pitched teenage lovestruck friends, that's all.

More importantly, I was happily in love at that point with my evil conniving cheating girlfriend prior to her turning into an evil conniving cheating fiancée.

And Sam was four years younger than me so I barely saw her or had anything in common with her anyway. They were focused on making student council poster board signs with puff paint and glitter, and I was focused on graduating and becoming an actual adult.

"I had a group picture, which she happened to be in, hung up in my room fifteen years ago." That's not a *thing*.

"Seven years. But, same," she said. "Well, make sure you admire her from afar. I don't want you getting caught up in whatever drama she has going on."

"Lexi, she's not my friend. I'm not going to see her." She crossed her arms and leaned against the counter. "But if you think *you* should see her..."

"Definitely not. I just don't want you getting your heart broken, that's all. Again."

"Lexi, stop."

Turning the volume up to level seven.

"No, not you, Alexa!" I shouted.

Turning the volume up to level ten.

Britney's voice rang out "I'm a Slave 4 U" from the tiny device.

I yelled over the music. "You really don't want to change that thing's name?"

"Never in a million years." She doubled over in laughter. "Alexa, stop."

The screeching abruptly stopped.

"How come she only listens to you?"

"Must be my Southern charm." She gulped the last of her bottle, wiped her mouth with the inside of her elbow, then belched.

"You're gross. And I've got an early morning." I threw my bottle into the trash can and squeezed her shoulder as I started toward the back of the house.

"So you're really not going to try and see her?" I was almost out of Dodge and into the hallway when I heard her. The thing was, Sam was the same type of local that Vanessa was—the type that leave and never come back—except that Vanessa didn't leave. Because of me. And it came back around to bite me in the ass anyway.

Sam belonged in the city, and there was no point in playing with fire if you knew the end result would be a trip to the ER.

I turned around to face her. "Are *you* really not going to try and see her?" She didn't respond. "I work this whole week anyway. I highly doubt I'll see her around."

"Yeah. Totally. Plus it's, like, a super big island." She bit her lip again. She was scared. I'm not sure if she was scared of running into Sam, or scared of her being here and not seeing her at all.

"Good night, Lexi," I called out as I strolled down the hall.

Good night, Austin, sleep tight. Don't let the bedbugs bite.

The electronic voice rang out as I walked down the hall, but it wasn't louder than Lexi's giggling.

9
SAMANTHA

First thing in the morning, I was on the dock with my phone held over my head as far as I could. With my one cellular bar, my phone displayed Robby's swollen face, complimented by a backdrop of white hospital sheets and beeping machines.

"Well, don't you look chipper for a coworker gunning to steal my spot as director," he said in greeting.

"Please tell me you're joking. You can't seriously think I somehow gave you appendicitis."

"No, Leigh, I don't think you somehow blew up one of my organs. I should be thanking you if you did though. I've already got a full roster of dates once I bust out of this joint. The nurses are lining up like I'm a spigot in the middle of a desert."

"I'm sure you're their definition of a dreamboat. When are you clear to leave?"

"They said another two weeks in the hospital."

"Two weeks?" I repeated slowly.

His face froze for a moment. "Something leaked that wasn't supposed to. Again."

"Were you listening to them when they said to lie still and rest?" I gritted my teeth.

"You know how I feel about rules, Leigh. Personally, I think they just like looking at me, so they're holding me hostage with hospital jargon."

"So, you're definitely not going to make it to Florida."

"Let's wait and see, sugar. I wouldn't want to leave you there all alo—"

Robby's face froze. The signal was gone. And Wi-Fi was out at the hotel.

"Can you hear me?" I repeated over and over, trying to snag a single bar of service to unfreeze Robby's mid-word face on my screen.

"How about now?" His face stared back at me while I heard bits and pieces of static coming through. "Robby?"

I got to the end of the dock and just as I hit the railing at the farthest point, my heel slid through the dock at the exact same time a bar popped up.

"Wait, don't move! I mean, I won't move! Can you hear me?" I was half bent over with my phone over my head as high as I could reach, trying to balance as the wooden planks ate half my heel.

"I said…I really thought I'd at least get to see…bikini…down there…"

"Yeah, so I can't hear you, but everything's going great! I'll email you preliminary financials later!"

"…one more shot…"

"Right, okay, byeeee!"

"You better…"

I pushed END and looked up at the sky. *Why me?* I collapsed down on the dock and tried to tug my shoe free from the world of splintered wood. "Freaking Pugsnout and his stupid appendix and his stupid—"

"Interesting nickname for your boyfriend."

I craned my neck around and almost dropped my phone. Austin was behind me on his boat mopping up the deck. Shirtless.

"Oh my gosh, no. He is *not* my boyfriend."

He raised his eyebrows. But I had a hard time paying attention to his eyebrows when his body looked like it was cut from actual rock.

"No, really. It's nothing. It's less than nothing actually, if that's possible. He's my coworker. My cocky, overly confident, good ol' boy coworker who unfortunately is very good at his job but also likes to make inappropriate sexual comments to me and everyone else on the planet."

"Pugsnout?"

"He snorts like a pug when he laughs," I answered. "Hence, the pug reference. My assistant, Ivy, is way more creative when it comes to nicknames for him. Pugsnout is about as creative as I get."

He nodded, turned, and went back to his mopping, a signal he was done with this conversation. But, seeing as how New York City had a billion people on every block, I wasn't used to such limited human interaction on a daily basis. I was clearly going through verbal withdrawal, even though I had spent only one night back on the island so far. Also, there was this tiny muscle on his very tan arm that kept waving at me that was extremely distracting. So, I kept talking.

"Technically Robby's the one who should be down here performing the due diligence on this project. I'm just stepping in while he's recovering from a universe-induced sentence of appendicitis."

He kept mopping.

"You know, when the universe steps in on your behalf and does something you wish you could do but don't actually have the ability to do. Like blow up someone's organ."

Still mopping.

"He definitely deserves it, in case you were wondering. I would've chosen different timing, but you know, I don't run the universe. And all that."

I leaned back on my hands. My heel popped out at that exact moment, rocking me backward.

He eyed my shoes and went back to his business, throwing a coil of rope next to me on the dock. He checked a few knots here and there and threw the remaining bucket of water over the side.

"Didn't need to mop it a third time?" I joked. Not funny. Ugh, clearly I forgot how to have a normal conversation with a human being. *Pull it together, Samantha.* I didn't need to impress him by trying to be funny. I was not an awkward thirteen-year-old anymore.

But he hadn't even cracked a smirk yet. I didn't remember Lexi's brother being such a stick-in-the-mud when we were little. Although, he really wasn't around much. What was with this guy? Clearly not a morning person.

"You working today?" I asked.

"Why are you here? Shouldn't *you* be working?" he asked, turning around.

"I still can't get service at the inn. Or in the coffee shop. Or at that park bench over there. Or on any street, at all, on the entire island. Except for this spot right here just now that happened to work for one point seven seconds."

"Walk to the end of the fishing pier."

"Already tried that."

"The right side of the pier. It's the closest point on the island to the mainland."

"Is there a secret wireless gremlin stashed under the right side of the pier I'm unaware of?" No reaction. Absolutely nothing. "I feel like you smiled more when you were younger."

"What?" He looked at me with what I interpreted as a genuinely disinterested expression.

"Smile. That thing where the sides of your mouth go up at the same time and is kind of like a moon shape but on its side."

"If I think something's funny then yes, I smile." He was stone-faced. But there was a little spark in his eye.

I turned and started walking, hoping to salvage at least a shred of my dignity. "I didn't realize the locals were such a rough crowd."

"Aren't you technically a local?" he asked.

"Thanks for the pier tip!" I called out over my shoulder.

People in small towns were supposed to be friendly by some cosmic rule of nature. Clearly, rules didn't apply to him. I walked halfway back up the dock and of course, my heel got caught in the deck. Again.

"You should try wearing some different shoes," he called out.

I turned around and glared. "Well, you should try wearing a shirt!" I shouted back.

The corner of his mouth pulled.

I narrowed my eyes, unstuck my heel, and turned back around.

I didn't look back.

10
AUSTIN

Patrick and the crew were cleaning on our lunch break, picking up evidence of a business busting at the seams. The ferry overflowed with people on every run in and out. Water bottles scattered the floor and candy wrappers stuck to the cushions. There was even a kid's sock stuffed in the bilge. What I should have been thinking about was trying to figure out a way to meet the increased demand for the island.

But I wasn't.

I tried to ignore Sam when she walked down my dock earlier this morning. She wasn't a cute, innocent, chubby-faced thirteen-year-old any longer. I didn't have time to be paying attention to the way her dress shifted when she bent over the railing trying to find cell service. I didn't have time for eyes like hers. They were black holes, so intense they just sucked everything in the vicinity toward them.

She was the kind of trouble I didn't need to get myself wrapped up in. I got the occasional proposition from the fearless leader of a weekend warrior girl trip looking for some local fun for a day or two, but it wasn't my style. With a woman like Samantha Leigh, though, the day they decide they want to walk out, they don't just break your heart: they turn it into dust and sprinkle it on their pancakes the next morning. They leave behind a kind of destruction weathermen haven't come up with a name for yet.

Besides, the fact she held the former title of *Lexi's best friend* meant drama. Those two were inseparable for years. I didn't need to muddy that water. I needed to steer clear of her for Lexi's sake. And my own sanity.

"You done anything interesting lately?" Patrick asked as he tied up the last trash bag and threw it on the dock.

"No."

"Okay, okay." He paused for a few seconds. "You see anyone interesting lately?"

"Nope."

"Okay, okay." He paused for a little longer this time. "You don't wanna talk about it, I get it."

"Nothing to talk about."

He paused so long I looked up to a shit-eating grin spread wide across his face. "You think she's pretty, don't you?"

"Who?"

"Don't you be playing dumb with me. I saw you chitchatting with Sam this morning."

I ignored his comment and kept my head down, working.

"You've tied that knot twice already."

I glared at him. I had only seen her two times, but Sam was on a loop in my head since she'd set foot on the island. Patrick's questioning was bringing her front and center. Not like she wasn't there already anyway. But I knew the high-maintenance, secret-keeping, heels-wearing, *clickety-click* kind of girl wasn't my thing. Vanessa was a *clickety-click* girl and nothing good came of that.

He started singing under his breath. "Austin and Sam, sitting in a tree..."

"You're about to get your ass thrown off this boat."

"Alright, alright, I surrender. No more you-know-who talk. But just 'cause I stop talking about her doesn't mean that's going to help get your mind off her, Capt'n. You know that ain't how it works."

"You mop that deck yet?"

"Yeah, yeah, I hear you." He picked up the bucket, but made one more quick turnaround to face me. "One more thing though, I'm glad to see you a little riled up. It's about time. And stop thinking it's such a bad thing. They don't all leave you gasping for air in a bad way, you hear me?"

I ignored him and walked to the bow of the boat, hoping he'd get the hint to leave it alone.

"What'd you think of that two-hundred passenger?" he called out as he followed me. I told him I hadn't made it out yet to see it. The owner gave me first dibs on it and said I had until midweek to get up there.

"Why don't you go today? I can man the rest of the day."

"I can't today. I've got something to pick up."

"Where you goin'?" He narrowed his eyes on me.

"You're full of questions today, aren't you?"

"Just curious what's more important than a two-hundred passenger." He had that tone that told me he knew exactly what was more important than a two-hundred passenger.

"Josie's internet is spotty at the hotel. I'm picking up a booster for her."

"Well, look at you, a modern-day knight in tech armor."

"I'm just helping her out."

"Helping Josie out?" he asked. "Or helping Sam out?"

"Don't even start."

I was just doing what any nephew would do if his aunt needed his help.

The water was smooth like glass for the rest of the day.

Watching guests during the sunset run on the last ferry was always the highlight of my day. The sun setting in the background over the water could make anyone feel like you happened to stumble upon something amazing that wasn't meant for you. You were just lucky enough to be in the right place at the right time. It typically turned the water a blend of orange and pink and every single passenger would inevitably head to the stern of the boat to pull out their phone and take their new profile pic against the sherbet of my hometown sky.

"Ethel, you just jut your neck forward. It's not rocket science. Turtle, like this."

I watched out of the corner of my eye as a group of three little old ladies argued, one trying to teach the others how to "turtle" for a picture, which apparently involved doing something that looked painful with your neck.

"Here, watch me," the lady barked again.

"Oh, Gail, stop it," said another lady with a short silver bob. "I don't think turkeying is going to hide any of this flapping off our necks."

"It's called *turtling*. Just try it," Gail said. "I read it on the Google last week and I swear the difference in pictures is amazing. Here, let me help you," she shouted to the oldest lady of the group, who I assumed was Ethel, as she gripped her head and pulled it toward her.

"You leave her alone, Gail." Silver Bob Lady swatted at her arm. "You're about to tear her head clear off her neck and she can't hear you anyway. She has no idea what you're doing."

Gail let go and placed her hands on her hips. "Well, you're both going to look like old hags in the picture."

Silver Bob Lady leaned over to Ethel and shouted in her ear. "Has anyone told her we *are* old hags?"

Ethel took out a tiny silver flask and took a hefty swig.

Well then.

Gail took her assertive posture and turned it in my direction. "Captain Handsome! Can you please come take a picture of the three of us?"

"It would be my pleasure, ladies."

"Ohh! I thought that was him from Tripadvisor!" Silver Bob Lady swooned. "We've read all about you."

This happened about once a week. A guest nicknamed me Captain Handsome on a review after a particularly flattering shirtless picture of me pulling up the anchor was posted and it caught on like wildfire.

"You're on our bucket list." Gail beamed from ear to ear.

"And so is Usain," Silver Bob Lady piped in. "We were hoping to get Ethel here to dance with him."

"Her husband was a ballroom dancer," Gail said. "They took Senior IV titles back-to-back for five straight years. No one could touch them."

Ethel's eyes sparkled. "Love me a good dancer."

"Well, I'll be happy to take over his first mate duties so he can make his stellar dancing abilities available to you ladies."

"Is he married?" Ethel asked.

I coughed. "Nope, he's as single as they come."

"Well, I can't help what happens when my feet start moving. I don't want some whippersnapper falling in love. I don't have the energy to keep up with these young ones anymore."

I'm pretty sure she was serious. She also had to be seventy years old.

"Are you married?" Ethel asked.

"No, ma'am."

"Well, what are you waiting for?"

I paused. I typically skirted relationship questions from strangers. Hell, I skirted them from folks I knew too. People were just busybodies with too much time on their hands meddling in my business. But for some reason, these ladies seemed harmless so I gave them the real answer. "The right woman."

Gail interjected, "Well, at least he's got a good reason."

Silver Bob Lady snorted. "Oh please, the right one may or may not come along. Live a little in the meantime, Captain Handsome."

"You leave him alone, Shirley," Gail said. "He's too young for you. And he doesn't need to be spreading his seed to the whole island either."

"Age is just a number," Shirley with the silver bob protested. "I have a young soul."

"You may, but pretty sure your soil's as dry as desert dust."

That one got a chuckle out of me.

"Well, I wouldn't argue with you there," Shirley laughed as she grabbed the flask from Ethel and took a swig, draining it. "We're out! I'm going to fill up from our reserve." Shirley and Gail walked over to their bags and pulled out a bottle of Wild Turkey.

I turned to Ethel. "Where are you ladies visiting from?"

"New Hampshire. Ever been?" Ethel asked.

"No, ma'am. Have pretty much stayed here in Florida my whole life."

"We're taking a very much needed girls' trip. We should have done this in our twenties, our forties, hell our sixties, but we always found excuses not to."

"This one's single for the first time in a decade," Shirley walked over, pointing to Gail with her now full flask of bourbon.

"I'm sorry to hear that," I responded, assuming her husband passed away.

"Oh, please," Gail replied. "It's not like he's dead or anything. He just moved to Kansas to become a farmer. Developed a weird thing about goats. I was fixing to get rid of that one for years anyway."

Ethel leaned over to me and lowered her voice. "Pay her no mind. That was her fifth husband. And he always had a thing about goats, she just ignored it. Nothing worse than being in a relationship that's not right, convincing yourself it's better than being alone." She looked back out at the horizon. "You know, this is the first time I'm looking at a body of water I can't see the other side of. Makes you feel small, doesn't it?"

I nodded as she turned her eyes on me.

"If you've got other things on that bucket list besides driving this boat," she continued, "don't wait until you're over seventy like me to start checking them off. This was worth seeing decades ago."

Yeah, I had a bucket list.

When we were kids, Patrick, Tom, and I talked about building houses next to each other. Then we decided we'd just live in the same house—but make it a big one. Three stories tall. I'd captain our fishing charter, Patrick would be first mate and entertain the guests, and Tom would run marketing. He could sell ice to an Alaskan. We'd take over the island, three brothers separated at birth.

My mind still drifts back to that sometimes. Life as it was supposed to be. The three amigos, instead of two. And a life with Vanessa. If I'd seen the signs earlier—the subtle looks, the lingering stares. If I didn't care so much about being around the damn water. If Vanessa didn't hate Florida. If I had told her I'd move before everything fell apart. If Tom had a shred of decency and said no instead of yes.

Sometimes life tips the bucket list over and dumps it all on your head, leaving you standing there soaked in all the things that didn't go as planned. My bucket list had the usual—white picket fence, two kids, a Labrador, and a happy wife. What it didn't have was a best friend—the guy who taught me how to play checkers and who had a toothbrush at my house—slipping into my fiancée's heart. And bed.

My bucket list didn't include losing two of my best friends in one shot.

Gail thrust her camera into my chest. "You know how to use this, Captain? It's not one of those fancy schmancy phone cameras. It has a button. You gotta push down."

She shuffled the ladies together by the edge of the railing. "Now, make sure you get a good view of the sunset behind us."

I nodded and smiled.

"Remember to turtle, girls!" Gail reminded them.

"Say, Captain Handsome!" Shirley called out.

"CAPTAIN HANDSOME!" they all sang in unison with their hands raised.

Normally that name irked me, but a grin crept across my face as I snapped a few photos of them.

"I'll see if I can wrangle Usain for you ladies before the end of our trip. Sit down, relax, and enjoy the rest of the ride over."

I filled Patrick in and pointed out his fan club. Attention from little old ladies was like catnip for him. On my way back around I caught Gail in a moment by herself silently staring out onto the horizon, watching the last bit of sun sneak underneath the waterline.

"I'm used to New Hampshire sunsets. This is something else."

"You'll have more of these while you're here," I promised. "But in all the years I've called Rock Island home, I've never seen the same one twice."

Everyone's seen a sunset, but not everyone's seen a Florida sunset.

I filled her in on the best of the island, including the lobster roll at Charley's and the sunset view at Harpoon's. "Captain Harold runs the inshore fishing charters out here too if you have the yearning to catch a fish or two. He'll even fillet it up for dinner on the boat."

Just then, Justin Timberlake's voice burst through the speakers above us. Ethel's eyes went wide as she spotted Patrick doing his famous shuffle-shuffle-wiggle toward her to "Can't Stop the Feeling!" from the front of the boat. He made his way over and bowed to her.

"I heard someone's in the mood to get down." He bowed cordially and thrust his hand out. "May I have this dance, madam?"

"Only if you promise not to call me *madam* again." Ethel didn't miss a beat.

I made my way to the helm to take the wheel as Patrick danced Ethel around in a circle, a smile plastered on her face that lit up the whole boat and had all the other guests cheering and whipping out their phones. Gail took pictures and Shirley danced along, throwing sunshine out of her pocket along with the lyrics.

I've known Patrick for twenty years and he's always had this rare ability to make everyone in the room feel ten feet tall. I looked back to the water and couldn't help but smile. Today was a good day.

11

SAMANTHA

I walked into the bungalow and found a note on the dining room table.

> *Installed a booster for the internet. Should take care of (most)*
> *of the internet issues.*
> *Network: DockGremlin*
> *Password: Pugglestiltskin*

Well. Maybe he wasn't a total stick-in-the-mud. I looked over at the small black box humming away underneath the desk, highly doubting it would solve all my problems.

One thing that *would* solve my problems would be Robby getting his butt down here like he was supposed to, so I tried Face-Timing him again. He picked up on the first ring.

"Why are you standing up?" I asked when his face came into view, the crisp white sheets of a hospital bed missing from frame.

"I'm just stretching my legs."

"And by that, you mean you're not listening to their instructions about staying in bed."

His eyes went wide as he pulled the phone closer to his face. "I don't understand what they want me to do all day. They won't let me have my laptop in bed. I can only stare at my phone so long before I go cross-eyed. The spreadsheets you're sending are way too small to look at on a phone screen. I'm going crazy."

"Well, the longer you stay there, the longer I stay here. So, let's make a plan that you stay in bed and do what they tell you, and I won't kill you myself. Deal?" I hung on to the small possibility that if Robby acted like the model patient, we'd still have time to switch places. A couple weeks on Rock Island was better than a month on Rock Island.

"What, not loving the scorching Florida sunshine and barefoot policy?"

"For your information, people do wear shoes here. And, while I'm thoroughly enjoying the Florida sunshine, I'd much rather enjoy my real life in the city." I missed conversations with people who actually responded.

"You're not fooling anyone, Leigh. You don't have a life."

I closed my eyes and exhaled. I'd forgotten how charming the normal Robby could be. "That's an incorrect and rude assessment."

"I highly doubt you're traipsing around the beaches with a strawberry daiquiri in your bikini."

"Unlike you, I don't drink on the job. And I'm not a bikini person." His eyebrows shot up. "Not that it's any of your business."

"I wouldn't have clocked you as a nudist."

"That's not what I said."

"Don't you ever lay out in Central Park?" He shoved an orange glob into his mouth.

"Are you eating Jell-O?" I asked.

"Don't change the subject."

"What are you, five?"

"You're one of those people who count the walk to work as your daily dose of vitamin D." He scraped the bottom of the container.

I don't know why I felt deflated at the fact he nailed it. I didn't consider my lack of outdoor playtime to be a bad thing. It's a widely known fact that too much sun causes skin cancer. And, in just a few short years *because* I'd worked so hard, I was up for a promotion that was typically given to people five years my senior. So clearly, it paid off.

"On another note, you look pale."

"Glad to see your observational skills haven't melted in the sun."

"Only my soul," I deadpanned.

He chuckled, then his face fell just the tiniest bit. "They only serve room-temperature mashed potatoes and mystery meat. I haven't eaten much lately."

I hated the tiny pull in my stomach that felt sorry for him.

"Want me to get Ivy to bring you real food? I can have her sneak it in."

"If I didn't have every nurse in this place watching me like a hawk, I'd say yes."

"Known for breaking rules already?"

"Only hearts, Leigh. Only hearts. Speaking of, run into any of your high school haters? I've been lying here thinking of revenge tactics for the mice windup thing."

It took me a second to remember I told him one of my deepest, darkest secrets. And I was shocked he remembered. In a good way. He thoroughly piqued my curiosity at *revenge tactics*.

"Luckily I've been able to avoid most interactions with the local species," I answered.

"I found a place that sells tiny mice. In bulk. Apparently there are quite a few people in Florida who think owning snakes counts as an *indoor* pet option. And get this—you have to feed them. With mice."

"While I'm simultaneously confused and warmed by the thought of you buying me mice as payback, I'm not sure I'm following your train of thought."

"I'll totally fund the purchase if you'll be the boots on the ground." His eyes darted around, checking for the nurse's ever-watchful glance, then reached for his computer on the bedside table. "Maybe she owns a place. What's her name? Is she married? I'll google her."

Was he thinking I'd let them loose in her house or something? Or her car? I imagined little mice running in and around every piece of furniture she owned. The thought of one poking its head out of her car tailpipe made me laugh out loud.

"You're imagining it, aren't you?" he asked with a devilish grin.

I smiled but didn't give him her name. "As hilarious as that seems, I'm not sure if that's the right path of retribution."

"Well, you just let me know when you're ready. I've got my credit card handy."

I closed my eyes to reset. Here he was, acting like this normal human being again. Well, a normal human being who would buy mice in bulk to infiltrate someone's house. It was quite charming actually. But I'd never seen him so pale. Tiny dark bags clung to the bottom of his eyes and even though he cracked jokes, they didn't have the bite they normally did.

"On a serious note, you really need to listen to your nurses. I've got a few places on the docket to grab pictures of tomorrow but a team brainstorming meeting would be great in a couple days if you're up for it. I'd love to start pitching a few ideas and thoughts I had on what's missing here, but also cover what's working really well."

"I will, I will. Scout's honor I'll keep my butt in bed." The hospital bed squeaked as he crawled back in it.

"*And* believe it or not, I would like your opinion on a few of the financials I'm sending over later tonight. While I don't want to encourage patient disobedience, if you can sneak your laptop for a little, let me know if I'm missing any major line items for the new development."

"Aw, are you requesting my help, Leigh?" he asked.

"You mean, your help on the project you're supposed to be heading up? I would never."

"I will if you say *pretty please*."

"Not a chance in hell."

He gave a hearty laugh that rolled into a coughing fit. He sounded horrible. "I'm sure I can take a peek. My night nurse loves me. I've already bribed her with a date when I break out of here in exchange for the red Jell-O. The orange is gross."

"You're predictable."

"You're jealous. Hear from Jack lately?" he asked.

"Goodbye, Robby."

I hung up the phone and against my better judgment, I let myself laugh.

12
SAMANTHA

Three days of poison from the one-pot Mr. Coffee was all I could stomach. I was shriveling away from lack of human contact and hadn't ventured out much yet, and it was only a matter of time before I ran into someone I knew. But I was desperate.

I had somehow gotten through my first big meeting. Even though the call with the owner of the land we were buying had gone a bit haywire. At the last moment he'd backed out citing a stomach bug, but connected me with his daughter, who apparently was dealing with the sale for him. She lived in Chicago. She was whip-smart and super organized and knew every single answer to any question I had and was more than happy to be accommodating with requests from my end.

Her father had owned the land since he was in his early twenties, inherited it from his grandfather. He used some of the land to construct a little fishing post on the northernmost corner of the island. It sat next to the lighthouse his grandfather had built with his own two hands. Her father was a bit of a hermit, she said. He had no desire for building or managing anything that would lure more people to his sacred spot, so he just held on to it. But he was getting older, filling his days with shuffleboard in a retirement home on the other coast. She had no desire to move to Florida and wanted to sell. He hadn't even seen the property in over ten years and had no idea what was still standing or not, so he gave her his blessing.

Somehow I got through that meeting bushy-tailed, but I was wearing down. I needed espresso. I put on my best incognito outfit and walked the two blocks to the Mug. It had changed ownership since I had visited last, and what I walked into completely surprised me—white walls filled with subway tile, rustic natural wooden beams, and an exposed black ceiling with huge windmill fans slowly whirling around. The baristas wore gray linen aprons with little embellishments of brass and worn leather. I walked into a little haven protected from the outside world of palm trees and starfish. I was in heaven.

And I smelled espresso.

The girl behind the counter looked like she had stepped right out of *Barista Magazine*, beaming at me through vintage wire frame glasses. There were little cups of coffee painted on her green headscarf.

"This your first time in here?" she asked after I gave her my order for a triple vanilla latte, extra hot.

"Yeah, just visiting for a while."

"Cool, cool. First one's on the house. What's your name?"

"Sam." A woman's voice came from behind me. "Oh, but apparently it's Samantha now, right?"

My stomach somersaulted. I'd know that voice anywhere.

Being back on island, there were two major things I was dreading. One, my mother in any and all forms, who I'd barely avoided thus far. And two, Lexi.

I turned around slowly, some unknown organ in my throat with no idea what to expect.

"Hey."

She stood there and blinked. This person who knew every bit of my life *before*. The braces, the bang phase, and the immediate regret of said bang phase. She was there to witness the acne that bloomed on my face overnight when I was twelve and didn't go away for years. I was there to witness the fallout when Travis McGlowen lost his virginity to Tiffany "Doormat" Dornment in her dad's Volkswagen, and the love of her life was officially taken off the market. She rode sidecar to my obsession with wearing different color tube socks. She was the rock when my dad was diagnosed. And when he was no longer there. And when Mom was no longer there, either.

Then, there was the bang phase, again.

"Austin told me you were in town. I almost didn't believe him, but then I walk in and here you are, Samantha Leigh, in the flesh."

"The rumors are true." She looked exactly the same. A pile of messy blond curls sat atop her head and she had the same hazel eyes as her brother, but hers were more brown than green today. Seven years hadn't done a single thing to dim the aura that surrounded this ball of sunshine. I hadn't realized how much I missed this woman.

"I was going to grab a quick drink. I have a few before my fitting."

"Fitting?" I asked. I didn't want her to know I'd been cyberstalking her and already knew about this monumental change in her life.

She held up her engagement ring.

"Oh my gosh, congratulations!"

"Thanks. It's next month, which you would have known if you had returned even a single call or text I sent over the last seven years."

I blinked. My smile wavered.

She cocked her head. "Actually, it was more like three years. Had to give up at some point. Didn't want to look desperate, you know?"

I didn't know what to say. But I braced myself for the swift kick I knew was coming and that I deserved.

"You walked away without saying goodbye." Her voice was clear and strong, like she had rehearsed this a hundred times over. "You didn't return calls, or texts. The least you could have done was tell me you needed space. Hell, the least you could've done was just texted me back saying I was a reminder of everything you were trying to leave behind and you needed time."

"I know th—"

"I'm not done yet. I would've given it to you. Do you get that? I would've given you whatever space you needed. I spent years wondering if there was something else I could've done. Or said."

"You didn't do anything wrong."

"Oh, I know, trust me." A forced laugh made its way out. "I went through years of therapy just to make sure I didn't. You were the one who was selfish. You set off a bomb when you left and didn't look back. Just like your mom always does."

Tears stung my eyes. My mother was the last person on earth I'd ever want to be like, but I was never going to be anything but somebody else after that day. "I just thought it was better if I walked away."

"You didn't just walk away from your mom and the accident. You walked away from eighteen years of friendship. You walked away from me."

The hurt in her eyes crushed my already shredded soul into even tinier molecules.

"You took away the choice for me. That was my decision to make whether I wanted to be there for you or not. And I did. I would have a thousand times over. That's what best friends do. And you didn't give me the chance."

Of course, I didn't give her a chance. She was a reminder of everything I was leaving. And to put so much energy into keeping that one little string tied when it would end up breaking anyway didn't seem worth it.

"Are you done?" I asked quietly. "Because if you are, maybe I can finally tell you that I'm sorry. I'm sorry that my mom is a raging addict and I didn't know how to handle it other than to walk away. That I'm sorry there was wreckage left that I couldn't face. That I was too scared to face. That I didn't know *how* to face because I was *still a kid*. Survival mode meant taking care of me. And I'm sorry that I couldn't handle that more like an adult."

My hands were shaking.

"For what that's worth, I wish I could go back and do things differently, but I don't know if I'd be able to."

She looked down, nodding her head.

"I never wanted an apology." She wiped the tears that slowly leaked down her face. "I just wanted my best friend back."

The floor swayed. So this is what it felt like to have a sinkhole swallow your heart.

"That person is gone."

The moment hung, the world waiting for a bridge to build, or a stick of dynamite to go off.

"Well," she said softly, "then can I get to know this one instead?"

I blinked. I wasn't expecting her eyes to fill with little pools of water, and her to smile at me. I nodded, and all of a sudden, seven years of not speaking evaporated. She lunged forward and hugged me, nearly spilling my latte all over her and the floor. I didn't even mind that when it felt like it was time to part, she held on tighter like she always used to.

"Do we both get to fall apart now?" I asked.

"I don't see why not."

Twenty minutes flew by reminiscing about high school and catching up on more recent life changes, including scandalous bartending stories that should absolutely be made into a coffee table book.

Lexi's eyes sparkled when she talked about the wedding. "We're doing it out back at Mom and Dad's on the water. It was supposed to be low-key, but you know how Mom is."

"So, it's looking more like *Southern Living*'s Celebrity Edition version of low-key?" I asked.

"Exactly. And you'd love the restaurant catering the rehearsal dinner. It's a new place on the island. More of a city vibe. The food would blow your mind."

"It feels like a lot's changed, but it's all still weirdly the same. Like this place. It doesn't feel like it belongs on the island. It's so..." I searched for the right word.

"Amazing?" Lexi asked. "Yeah, I know. A lot of places have gotten a makeover like this in the past few years. It's starting to look like something out of a movie, each place getting more trendy as the younger generation takes over. Do you remember when this place was called First Cup?"

"They sold Folgers as their special brew. How could I forget?"

"That was the barista's grandma. She took over about three years ago and has completely revamped the place—the menu, staff, everything. She's even been written up in one of those magazines for baristas. Apparently, it was a pretty big deal."

I was so thankful we could fall into a comfortable rhythm. It felt familiar, yet something was different. That's the thing about best friends, right? You can *not* speak for years, but pick up right where you left off, like no time had passed at all. Being with her was so easy, but there was a hum of uncertainty pulsing through my veins as we talked. A low electric current of self-doubt. I kept wondering when she was going to get up and walk away, done with walking down memory lane once she remembered the moment where I left her and didn't look back.

"So, tell me about this guy," I asked, hoping to keep the conversation going. "What's he like? How'd you meet him? Tell me all the things."

"Rex is one of the good ones." Lexi's cheeks grew rosy. She told me about his job as an assistant football coach at Mississippi State, but how he wanted a head position. He's always loved high school kids, so when a position opened up to coach Rock Island's team, he applied. The school flew him down for the weekend and on his last night in town, he sat down in front of her at the bar. He said it was love at first sight.

"I'm sure your dad loves him."

"I think he likes Rex more than me. Like, for real." She laughed. "He's a total gentleman. Completely swept me off my feet."

She held out her hand. "Turns out his grandmother liked to collect expensive jewelry and left him this."

"It's stunning."

"Thanks." She looked down at her ring and smiled, like she was seeing all of its captured memories play out before her. "So, what about you? Are you dating anyone up in the city?"

"Was. But not anymore." I took a long sip of coffee. I'd texted Jack (and emailed, just in case) letting him know about Robby's situation and that I was leaving for a few weeks. I told him I wanted to touch base and at least clear the air but I hadn't heard back from him.

"Was it serious?" she asked.

We always had this type of friendship between us where she knew what I was trying to hide anyway, regardless of what I said, so it never helped to put off the inevitable. But the truth was, I didn't really know how to answer the question. Six months in terms of my average dating time wasn't short. But did I ever really see myself marrying him someday, owning a house with a white picket fence, a dog, and two and a half kids? No.

But I didn't see that for myself, period.

"I guess it was an answered prayer in a way then," she said tentatively.

"Yeah, I guess so. And he chewed with his mouth open."

"Ugh, I *hate* when they do that," she gagged.

My gaze traveled out the window down Main Street and started walking the docks of the marina.

"So," she continued, following my eyeline, "I heard my brother brought you over. I bet it was a blast from the past seeing him and Patrick again."

"He seems to be doing really well with the whole ferry thing."

"I can't tell if having Rex as the head football coach has made things better or worse for Austin. On one hand, it took some of the heat off him, but on the other, it's like Dad's watching what could have been, play out right in front of him. But with someone else. The ferry thing has worked out for him so far, but it isn't what he wants long term." She started to smile and leaned in. "Do you remember when we used to sneak into his bedroom and look for his money?"

I laughed. We used to slip into his room when he was gone and dig around his closet. We would flip a coin to see who would get stuck looking in his underwear drawer, but then we'd giggle so loud, we'd always get busted by their mom.

One time when I was poking around his desk, I swiped a picture of him and his girlfriend posing on the field for homecoming. He was in his football uniform, his shaggy hair damp from sweat with dirt streaks smeared across his football pants. They had just been named king and queen, and his crown was crooked on his head. It matched the smile plastered across his face.

"His girlfriend used to be so mean to us."

Lexi scrunched her face. "Ugh, *Vanessa*. She was the worst."

"She was. They were together forever. Whatever happened to her?"

"Long story. She's not worth the time."

Every girl at our high school was scared to death of Vanessa Worthington. Probably because, even after she graduated, we were all still doodling Austin's last name in our notebooks and terrified she'd find out. Austin was the tight end of the football team and happened to be a really nice guy, too. I would head to Lexi's after school and we'd watch *The Little Mermaid* almost every day. He said I reminded him of the seagull Scuttle, Ariel's little sidekick. He called me that one afternoon and it stuck. Now that I'm older and have realized Scuttle is the weird uncle character in the story, I'm not so sure it was a compliment. But back then I melted every time I heard it—he didn't have a nickname for everyone.

She started clinking her ring against the wooden table. "Just so neither of us stays up wondering about it later, I want you to know that I don't blame you for leaving."

I turned the brown paper sleeve on my coffee cup around and around.

"It doesn't mean it didn't sting," she continued, "and that I wasn't hurt by you falling off the face of the earth. And for the record, I wouldn't have done it the same way. But I get why you did and I would never, ever be mad about what happened to you or hold any sort of grudge against you because of it."

The sting of tears hit my eyes and I looked toward the ground, tracing the outline of the black-and-white tiles beneath my feet. I didn't realize how much I needed to hear that from someone. Anyone. But coming from her, it meant the world.

"Thank you." It was too hard to keep any sort of tie to my life here after graduation. All I saw was pity when people looked at me. All I felt was complete embarrassment. I couldn't hide from it. The only way to escape it was to literally leave town and give up everything that came with it. Including her. I had almost called her a million times but when it came down to actually doing it, I just didn't.

"I wish it could've been different." And I meant it with every single cell in my body. "I just wasn't the same person after that."

"It wasn't your fault."

"It doesn't make it untrue."

She squeezed my hand. "I have to run, but while you're back, if there's anything you need, like with your mom or whatever, you can always call me. Here, put your number in." She handed me her phone. I programmed my number into it and slid it back across the table.

"I haven't even told her I'm here yet."

"Are you going to?"

"Eventually."

"For real, I'm here. So is Austin."

"Thanks." And for the first time since I'd set foot back on the island, my heartbeat slowed just a tad.

My feet were lighter on the way back home. Whether it was the sweet feeling of potential reconciliation or the triple espresso, I'd take it.

My phone rang and my face fell. Cue the disaster. It was time to face the music.

"Hey, Mom." I weaved my way down Main Street back to the cottages.

"What city are you in? I saw Josie and she was acting all weird and asked if I had seen you *yet*. What does *yet* mean? Where are you? What's going on?"

She was getting more animated and hyper the more she talked. I knew my secret wouldn't be kept for long but I was hoping to get a few more days under my belt before it all came crashing down.

"I just got to the island. I had some crazy work deadlines right away and was going to pop over tonight to say hi and surprise you," I lied.

"Well, I'm not on the island right now. I wish you would have told me sooner. I could have planned around you being here. But I've already cleaned your room for you. You have fresh sheets. There's a key under the mat. It would have been nice to get a *little* more notice—"

"Mom, I'm not staying at the house. I have too much to do for work and it's easier to concentrate at the hotel." The line went silent. "I have lots of calls also. All day. I didn't want to intrude on your schedule and my boss is pretty particular about distractions on calls. The company's paying for it too. I just thought it'd be easier."

"Easier for whom, dear?"

I forgot how that tone of voice crawled up my spine and stuck a needle in the back of my neck.

She bulldozed ahead. "Easier than staying here and letting me take care of you?"

Right, because that ever happened in the last ten years.

"Are you free tomorrow?" I asked, shoving the back talk down my throat.

"I'll be back on the island tomorrow, yes. Make sure you steer clear of Mr. Crenshaw downtown. The old man's been pulling out his privates and showing everyone lately. It's really become quite a distraction on the street."

"I'd imagine so." Every call with her was a roulette wheel spin but I couldn't help but chuckle.

"Don't touch it," she continued. "There's a rash or something on it. Apparently, he's been fooling around with another patient at the assisted living—"

"Hey, Mom, I have to jump on a call real quick. I'll stop by tomorrow," and I hung up. Why in the world would I touch Mr. Crenshaw's wiener? I really never knew what my conversations with her would be like.

I walked up the steps to my bungalow and plopped down in the wicker chair. I took a deep breath. The air felt just a little bit damp no matter what time of day it was.

My phone dinged.

> **LEXI:** Hiiiiiiii, it's Lexi
> Any chance you're free to hang tomorrow night?

> **ME:** Mom said she'll be here tomorrow.
> I have to go say hi. 🙂

> **LEXI:** Perfect timing.
> You can say hi, then I'll come rescue you.

> **ME:** I prolly shouldn't commit just in case.
> You never know what could happen.

LEXI: I'll be your scapegoat.
You could use a distraction after the fireworks.
Just for a few hours.

                                                          ME: Maybe?

LEXI: I won't take no for an answer.
I have an idea.
I'll pick you up at 6.

13
AUSTIN

"You want me to go where?" I asked Lexi over the phone, positive I heard her wrong.

"Putt-Putt golfing." She was exasperated, like I was severely putting her out by confirming her harebrained idea just one more time.

"I thought that got shut down by the city years ago."

"I'm seventy percent sure it's still open."

The last time I went Putt-Putt golfing was in high school, when pimple-faced kids downed Mountain Dew and Pixy Stix. The old course was on the south tip of the island. The whole island was beautiful, but if you were forced to pick an area that needed a coat of paint and a tiny exorcism, that would be it.

"Sam needs a distraction. She's seeing her mom this afternoon so we need something that'll drag her out of the inevitable slump her mother will put her in."

Lexi told me she had reconnected with Sam and all was water under the bridge, which was great. But I didn't feel the overwhelming desire to aid in the distraction.

"And drag her into what, exactly?" I asked.

"Something different."

"And you want me there because..."

"I refuse to go down there alone. It's not safe."

I laughed. She was kidding, right?

"Don't mock me. Anything can happen in the south tip. We're picking her up at six p.m."

As Sam walked out of her bungalow, I tried to ignore how her dress clung to her waist and how the fabric swung in a way that made everything seem to go in slow motion.

Lexi caught me staring.

"What?" My voice carried a little too much aggression.

"Nothing, geez. Chill."

My truck door swung open. "You do realize we're going to a *miniature* golf course, not an actual golf *club*." Sam and her high heels climbed into my truck.

"They're kitten heels." She looked at me like I knew what that meant. "They don't even count as high heels."

"Leave her alone." Lexi turned to Sam. "He's just grumpy that we messed up his nightly loner routine. So, do we want to talk about what went down with your mom or are we pretending like it didn't happen?"

"She never showed. But she eventually texted that she was *off the island* for one more night and isn't coming back until the morning." The relief in Sam's voice was palpable.

"So we're celebrating dodged bullets tonight! In *kitten heels*." Lexi flashed her biggest over-the-top smile as her phone dinged. "Oh, it's Rex. He's going to meet us there too."

"The more the merrier." I eyed her.

"I guess you can both chaperone us."

I could tell she wasn't ecstatic about the unintended double date setup. She wanted me to stay far from Sam when it came to dating.

I drove south about twenty minutes past all the familiar landmarks. Most of the streets leading to the water on the island were lined with small beach cottages, one right after the other, passed down through generations. Front doors were usually open, only a screen standing between the family living there and every other neighborhood kid who threatened to bombard the house. Moms could look down the street at any given time to see which house had a pile of bikes in the crushed shell driveway, a sign of where the kids landed that hour.

I drove until a large neon sign poked into the sky. The lights were blown on a couple letters so it read PIRATE'S BOOTY UTT- UTT. A few of the streetlights flickered. It looked a little more like something out of a thriller than the miniature golf park I remembered.

I drove up to a half-lit parking lot. "Lexi, I don't think this place is still in business."

"There's a light on over there." She pointed to an old, dilapidated palm hut. A CHECK-IN sign hung crookedly off the roof. I parked a healthy distance away from the one brown Crown Victoria parked in the lot.

Sam closed the door to my truck and looked out over the empty lot. "This is definitely the beginning of a horror film."

"Huh. I really thought other people would be here. People still play miniature golf, don't they?"

"In general, or at this establishment in particular?" Sam asked.

I chuckled.

There was a large fake mountain in the center of the course, with little putting greens throughout. At the top, a large pirate ship sat in the middle of the course, a ripped skull-and-crossbones flag sagging straight down. A life-sized plastic replica of Captain Hook stood at the front of the ship pointing to a huge open-mouthed crocodile below. Although the crocodile was more of a faded avocado green from years of being hammered by the sun.

A small turnstile squeaked as we walked through the entrance and up to the hut. A wooden sign hung above us with a huge bite out of the corner—ENTER AT YOUR OWN RISK!

"We're positive we're doing this?" I asked.

"We are *so* doing this," Lexi replied as she walked through.

Sam looked at me and stepped closer. "Don't you dare leave my side," she whispered. "If there's a sacrifice demanded, she goes first."

"Deal." I focused 100 percent on not looking at her cleavage.

Lexi rang the bell on the counter.

Thump. Shuffle, *thump.* Shuffle, *thump.*

"What do you think that is?" Sam whispered. I caught a whiff of her strawberry scent again.

"A dead body would be more of a *shuffle, shuffle* thump," I whispered back. She cracked a smile and a small victory curled in my chest.

The sound grew louder and the wooden door swung open to reveal a very old, frail man decked out in a brand-new shiny polyester pirate costume. The smell of bourbon, cigarettes, and plastic followed him.

"Ahoy, mates!" His voice was scratchy and surprisingly loud, like he was greeting the audience opening night of a Broadway play. I looked behind me just to make sure we hadn't missed a Greyhound bus of patrons walking in after us.

"Welcome to Pirate's Booty Putt-Putt. How many of ya will be walkin' the plank tonight?"

"You're open for business?" It poured out of my mouth before I could stop it. The pirate narrowed his eyes on me.

Lexi jumped in to try and save me. "Oh, we just weren't sure if you were open or not. With the parking lot. And the lights."

"And the general lack of humans," Sam finished out of his earshot and I chuckled again. She was funny.

"Well, consider yerselves lucky tonight. Ya've got the place fer now. Watch out fer the crocodile on hole eight. He'll snap at yer barnacles if ya get too close."

"Aye, aye, Captain." Lexi saluted him.

"Sticks and stones are around the hut. If ya finish the course, I'll have some grog waitin' fer ya when yer done." He motioned us through the back door and disappeared.

Sam looked down the hall to make sure he was gone. "I'm not drinking a single thing he's offering."

"Sticks and stones?" I asked as we walked through the back of the hut to the course.

Lexi laughed. "Golf clubs and balls. C'mon, Austin, get with the lingo."

"What exactly are my barnacles?"

"Now that, I can't help you with."

"I don't think you want to know." Sam led the way as we headed toward the first hole, stepping over a small stream of water trickling its way in and out of the pathway.

"You guys never came here in middle or high school?" I asked.

Sam lined up her teal ball on the green. "Absolutely not."

"I did once. But I don't remember it looking quite this…charming."

"I came here on a date once." They both whipped their heads toward me.

"Eleventh commandment." Lexi narrowed her eyes at me. "Thou shalt not say the *V* word out loud."

I rolled my eyes at her. Of course, it was Vanessa. I took her here for a date and bought her a round of golf and a soda pop. It was the summer after tenth grade when I could finally drive. It was our first real date, since our parents had always driven us before that. It was packed. Everyone who was anyone wanted to be seen here. And there's nothing like shooting a ball into the mouth of a crocodile and watching it roll out its butt, only to be dropped six feet below onto a deckhand's head.

Sam craned her neck around me. "Is he watching us?"

I looked over and sure enough, there was a pirate peeking through the palm fronds by the ship, which immediately flapped together again once I caught him.

"If I've survived seven years in New York City just to be kidnapped and skinned by a pirate wearing polyester on a rundown Putt-Putt course, I'm going to be really pissed off." Sam swung her club and sunk the first hole-in-one of the night.

Lexi's phone dinged. "Rex is going to meet us after actually. His practice ran late. You guys cool to grab a drink after this?"

"If we make it out alive, I'll buy."

"I think I'm going to need more than one after this." I turned away and smiled.

~~

"And then," Lexi laughed so hard she could barely get the rest out, "she falls into the moat surrounding the pirate ship!"

"Wait, there's a moat?" Rex desperately tried to keep up with Lexi's storytelling abilities.

"It wasn't a *moat* moat." Sam laughed as her entire body shook. "It's only two inches deep, but it was freezing and the crocodile took me by surprise."

"*Mechanical* crocodile," I corrected.

"To be fair, there weren't any signs," Lexi added.

Rex nodded toward Sam's shirt. "I was wondering if the whole *man's-work-shirt-and-kitten-heels* thing was a city fashion trend I wasn't aware of."

Sam's half-soaked dress was hanging off the bed of my truck while she donned one of my large work shirts I had in the back. And my mind was not behaving. I kept telling myself it had nothing to do with Sam, and just the fact I had never seen a woman wear one of my Scuttle's Ferry work shirts before.

"Did you just call them kitten heels?" Sam's eyes shot up.

"I have four sisters." Rex brushed it off nonchalantly.

"Ah. Makes sense. Well, Creepy Pirate Guy knew exactly what he was doing. He clearly sent the alligator after me."

"It's amazing how realistic it was too," I joked. "The sun-bleached avocado green is probably really close to its natural color."

"And those teeth! Like miniature marshmallows, all perfectly square and lined up." Lexi was laughing so hard, tears were gathering in the corners of her eyes. "Totally believable."

"You guys are miserable together." Sam flicked condensation from her beer at both of us. "Kudos to you, Lexi. Getting pushed into a freezing cold moat by a *mechanical* crocodile and being stalked by an old dirty pirate certainly checks the box of something to distract me."

Sam's eyes were locked on mine. I liked being around her. I liked hearing the sound of her laugh. She brightened everything near her.

"She would have been a goner if Austin hadn't jumped in and saved her." Lexi batted her eyes at me.

"Just doing my part."

I couldn't take my gaze off Sam. Her eyes were so brown they looked black and they could swallow me whole.

The beer bottle paused on her lip, barely hiding a smirk.

Lexi leaned across the table like she was spilling a deep, dark secret. "You know Creepy Pirate Guy was watching from somewhere too. Probably lurking around, loving every moment we looked behind us."

Sam finally took a drink from her bottle. She did this thing where she barely bit the glass and smiled into it right before she took a sip. Her eyes flicked up at the last second and caught me staring at her.

"You're turning into a grog blossom!" she cried as she grabbed my face and turned it toward her.

"A what?" My ears immediately heated at her touch and a warmth crept up my neck.

"A grog blossom! Someone whose nose turns red after they've been drinking."

I stared at her. I had no idea what she was talking about.

"What? I looked up some pirate lingo. Don't be a hater." She fist-bumped Lexi.

My cheeks tingled from where she touched them.

"On a more serious note," Sam piped in, "thank you, Lexi. This was a perfect distraction to what was supposed to be a swift kick back into reality for me. And honestly, the course wouldn't be that bad if it underwent a few cosmetic changes."

"And a change of ownership," Lexi added.

"It would be cute with a little diner or soda shop attached to it. Oh! And a little gelato hut."

Back in the day, it was packed with families on the weekend. It was the most fun a kid could have without getting into too much trouble.

Sam chewed on her bottom lip, the same habit Lexi had when she was deep in thought.

"Not sure I love the pirate theme, or Creepy Pirate Guy running it, but something more native to the island could work really well. Like coastal, but chic, upscale coastal. And no starfish."

Rex piped in. "Alexandra was telling me what you do for work. It sounds pretty fun."

"It is. I love reimagining places." Sam's face lit up as her foot jiggled under the table. "It's crazy this land sat here for years undeveloped. Usually I work with places that are already established but out of date and not pulling in revenue for the city like they used to. But this one here is from the ground up, so I get to pitch whatever I want."

They continued to talk about her work for a little, brainstorming Putt-Putt golf course themes and ideas from starships to an underwater bubble. It didn't surprise me that Sam and Rex got along. Rex could get along with anyone. But this relaxed and casual Sam was fun and flirty, and felt like she belonged so easily.

She was still trouble, but now, a different kind of trouble.

"Not that I want to turn it into some crazy tourist trap or anything," Sam continued, "but there's a lot of potential."

"Well, the crazies on the town board wouldn't let you get away with that anyway, but when the time comes, we can help pay them off for you." Lexi giggled into her drink.

"Town board?"

Only the complete bane of my existence. "Just a group of retired busybodies who take rules way too seriously," I explained. "They banded together a few years ago and now God forbid anyone do anything without their approval."

Lexi jumped in. "They've got their panties in a wad about Austin's request for extended hours at the marina. There's a meeting tomorrow he has to attend. You should go. It'll be good for your research to see what everyone's doing around here."

"*Trying* to do around here," I corrected.

"I can't. I've got a team video meeting in the morning."

"Perfect," I said. "The seashell mafia convenes at three p.m. Buckle up. And bring snacks."

A lot had changed on the island. It wasn't the same place as when she'd left. "So what's your initial diagnosis?" I asked. "Is our little island doomed or are we the next Disneyland?"

"Doomed." She bit her glass again and stared at me over the rim. "For sure."

~

Three rounds of darts and four pints later, a giggling Sam was trying to crawl into my truck. Lexi jumped in with Rex, and I was stuck with a woman I didn't exactly hate. Who was still in my work shirt.

"It'd be easier to get in the truck with your heels off."

Her foot slipped off the running board and back onto the ground. "I don't want to take off my shoes."

"Clearly. The horror."

She gave me an amused look. I was beginning to keep these little expressions in my pocket, trying to figure out ways to make her laugh or smile.

"Take me home, Capt'n," she sang as I hoisted her up on the passenger side. A vision of me lifting my oversized work shirt over her head crashed into me without warning.

"Austin?" She sat looking at me, her mouth barely open.

I shook my head to try and focus. "Yeah. Let's get you home."

14

SAMANTHA

The morning rays were peeking in through the horizontal blinds as Ivy's dark eyes squinted at me on my computer screen.

"Look at you. You look like you've seen the sun. Nice to see you finally have internet that works."

"Austin dropped by a booster earlier."

"Austin?" Her eyebrows perked up.

"Yes, Ivy." My stomach tumbled. "The older brother of a childhood friend I have absolutely zero interest in. Yes, he's cute. No, it doesn't matter. He's a ferryboat captain. Hazel eyes, but more green than brown. Shaggy blond hair. Actually, it's more of a light brown. And no, I won't change my mind."

She smirked. "You sure?"

"We're not all characters in a romance novel, Ivy. Moving on. What's the temp on Glenn?"

"That's why I needed to talk to you first. Robby busted out of the hospital. Clean bill of health. He and Glenn have been holed up talking about waterslides all morning."

"Waterslides?" I asked.

"Apparently Glenn's adolescence didn't include enough of them and he's trying to stick them everywhere he can now, including the new resort. You've officially been warned. Anything you want me to tee up?"

"Not yet. I dumped all the pictures I have of Rock Island into the Google Drive already, but I haven't been able to get my hands on a lot of the financials yet. Businesses are being pretty tight-lipped."

"You'll get them to warm up. Schmooze them."

"I am schmoozing them."

"I know. But, like, SparkPug-schmooze them. Sidenote, I love the starfish on your coffee cup."

"I never want to see another painting, statue, ceramic, or metal reproduction of a starfish in my entire life."

"So, no sea creature theme for your new corner office decoration. Noted."

"I've missed you."

She smiled. "It's five till nine. Let me get in there and conference you in."

"Glenn here." He nodded to the camera.

He always did that even though I could literally see his face on my computer screen. They were set up around the conference room table, remnants of breakfast scattered about. It looked like they had been there a while. There was a huge screen on the back wall that I knew showcased my face at the moment.

"Good morning, Glenn. Robby, good to see you vertical." He flashed his golden boy smile at half-mast. "I figured we'd jump right in and go over some of the information I've been able to gather so far."

"Good plan, but we'll show you our ideas first." Glenn nodded to Robby.

Why did I even bother? It'd be the same buddy-buddy back-and-forth with the two of them propping each other up, Robby encouraging Glenn's ideas, regardless of what they actually were. I'd sit and nod my head, internally screaming at both of them while my smile tightened and froze until I felt like the Joker.

Ivy warned me, but nothing could have adequately prepared me for the monstrosity on-screen. Robby stood up and held out a three-foot-long printout of a waterslide—a neon-green hunk of plastic that looked to be over a hundred feet tall scaled down.

Glenn's eyes brightened.

"It's quite... bright." How could I possibly spin something positive about this horrible idea and hold in the rising bile at the same time?

"Shoots you out going up to sixty miles an hour," Robby said, beaming. "Would be great to erect this puppy at the main pool."

Ivy coughed.

"It's definitely something," I mumbled under my breath.

Glenn nodded so hard that his brain had to be jiggling. Of course he did. They'd probably been looking at pictures of stupid waterslides for hours together as they ate breakfast, giggled like schoolgirls, and ordered matching best friend necklaces online. *Ugh.*

I heard shouting in the distance. Then singing. My eyes gazed across the screen looking to see who'd be singing in the conference room.

"Honeyyyy!" a woman's voice sang through my front window. "Are you here, baby girl?"

Oh, no, no, no... It was coming from my side, not theirs.

Mom only called me that when she was good and sloshed. Last night's *off the island* must have been code for *binge drinking*. Did I tell her I was staying at the Starfish? I couldn't remember.

Please tell me I locked the door.

Singing drifted in through my cracked window. *"...yellow polka dot bikini, that she wore for the first time today..."*

Dear Lord above, if you exist, please don't let her— My front door burst open and there she was: my mother, sporting the tiniest yellow polka dot bikini ever made, giant pink sunglasses, and a straw hat big enough to have its own zip code.

"Baby girl!" she shouted across the room throwing her arms up like she was accepting an Oscar.

I shot out of my chair and lunged for my laptop, trying to slam the screen shut, but my elbow hit my coffee first spilling it across my keyboard. I yanked my shirt down to soak up the mess, which did absolutely nothing but smear coffee all over the keys.

Mom sauntered across the Berber carpet, but tripped in slow motion before dramatically laying out on the couch beside me. "Whoa, it is a hot one out there today. I need lemonade."

I looked back to the screen. Ivy's eyes were wide, her hands flapping in a silent panic, miming for me to pull my shirt up. I looked down and I had tugged my shirt so far down that I was giving the entire conference room a front-row seat to my girls. I reached for the laptop again but Mom wedged her hand in and pried it back open.

"Your friends! Oooh, let me see!" She swatted my hand away.

"Hi there!" She waved into the camera. "Oh, look at that! I can see myself!" She puckered her lips and posed, watching herself in the little box nestled in the bottom right-hand corner of my screen. "Not too shabby."

This couldn't be happening. This had to be cosmic punishment— for the goldfish I forgot to feed in sixth grade, for that tinted ChapStick I accidently stole from Target, and for kissing Max under the bleachers when I was dating his brother. And basically every other morally questionable moment of my entire life had led to this.

"Mom, I'm in the middle of a work call."

She leaned closer to the computer and winked at the screen. "Well, you're fun to look at."

"Oh. Umm, okay." Crimson creeped up Glenn's neck.

"Oh, I didn't mean you. You're much too old for me. I was talking to him." She pointed straight at Robby.

Oh my God.

"I'm so sorry, Glenn, let me give you a quick ring back." I angled my laptop away from my mom's face.

"No need, no need, you all get back to *work*," she slurred as she finger-quoted *work* like it was a joke. "But don't work all day, you could use some color, baby girl." She squeezed my cheeks, turned, and threw a "see you later tonight" over her shoulder.

I looked at the screen, scanning faces trying to gauge the amount of damage control I'd need to do when Glenn's face went fire-engine red. Ivy's normally perfect composure slipped. Her eyes went wide and her mouth was slack. I looked on the screen at my little face in the bottom right-hand corner just as my mother opened my front door to leave, revealing that her tiny little yellow polka dot bikini was, in fact, a thong.

Do you know that part in a movie where the scene's sound cuts out and it's just an instrumental track playing over total devastation in slow motion? This was that moment. The blood drained from my body. The fading singing was the only sound for a solid five seconds after the screen door slammed shut behind her.

"Well, she's certainly lively." Robby's voice broke the awkward silence, bringing me back to reality. "And in pretty good shape. How old is she?"

Ew.

"She'd make a great activities coordinator. Very friendly," Ivy piped in, clearly trying to help. "But probably not the type of resort we're really going for," she added quickly, apology in her tone.

"The waterslide sounds great." My voice wavered, trying to pretend the last three minutes never happened. "Let's table it for now though and I'll get with Robby one-on-one to chat after I've sent everything I've got. We'll touch base again later. Anything else for me?"

"Nope, I think we're all set here." Glenn bolted from the room, his face the color of a plum.

Oh my God, Ivy mouthed from her chair as she got up.

I ended the call and sat there staring at the black screen, which was also ironically a representation of my soul at that moment. I closed my eyes.

Welcome home.

15

AUSTIN

Sam was already waiting outside the community center when I pulled up. The parking lot was packed with golf carts, not a single inch of pavement left.

"Wow, people are really serious about this, huh?" she said as I walked up.

"Very."

We tiptoed in and slid into two chairs in the back.

"Are we late?" she whispered.

"No, these things go for hours. People come and go the whole time."

The meeting was already in full swing and it was only 3:04 p.m. At the front of the room, a wobbly folding table held the weight of local democracy with Bob, the board president, half listening, and Donna, the board secretary, furiously scribbling notes. The twenty white plastic chairs lined up facing the table were mostly filled. A wiry man in a faded Tommy Bahama shirt was already standing, mid-rant when we walked in.

"It's July, Bob. Christmas lights shouldn't be allowed to still be hanging in *July*."

"Your Honor," a woman across the room piped up, her Christmas lightbulb earrings jingling as she spoke. "They're festive. And they're not on Ricky's property. So this entire conversation is irrelevant."

"You don't have to call me *Your Honor*, Rita," Bob muttered, like it was the hundredth time he had told her.

"The lights are distracting," Ricky fired back.

"They're joyful."

"It looks like a disco in my house, Bob."

"Can't you just close your blinds?" he asked exasperated.

"I shouldn't have to close my blinds. That's the point!" Ricky's arms flailed. "It's my house. I should be able to leave the blinds open without it turning into Studio 54 in there."

Rita smirked. "What's wrong with Studio 54? That was one of the greatest eras of all time."

"If I wanted Studio 54, I'd turn on my TV. Or, I'd set foot in your house where I'm sure I'd find a *plethora* of Lycra and spandex."

Sam giggled beside me. "Is it always this entertaining?"

"Only if you're lucky," I whispered back, trying to contain myself.

She kept her voice low. "What does Ricky do?"

"He runs the general store on the island. Ironically, he probably sold Rita the Christmas lights he's mad about."

Bob rubbed his temples, looking like he'd rather be anywhere else. "Rita, it's seven months past Christmas."

"Technically, it's only five months *until* Christmas," she corrected with a grin.

"Maybe you could at least get rid of the reindeer," Bob suggested.

Samantha straight up laughed, and a few people turned to glare at us.

Rita folded her arms. "You show me where in the city bylaws restrictions on lawn decorations are mentioned, and I'm happy to take them down."

Bob sighed, utterly defeated. "She's got you, Ricky. There's nothing I can officially do here."

"And, Your Honor," Rita jumped in, "I'd like to formally request that you make Ricky give me back my five-foot plastic Santa."

"I didn't take—"

"Yes, you did!" She pointed an accusing finger. "Don't you lie, Ricky!"

Bob groaned. "Ricky, did you take her Santa?"

"Bob, this is ridic—"

"I know it's in his garage, Your Honor. I'd like permission for a rescue mission; anything it takes to free it from captivity."

"Ricky, did you take her Santa?"

Ricky hesitated. "I plead the Fifth."

"You can't plead the Fi— You know what? Ricky, give the Santa back. And close your blinds. Rita, get rid of the reindeer. At least the one with the broken antler and missing eye—that thing scares my grandkids. And no Christmas lights after ten p.m." He took a deep breath. "Alright, next up, Austin Marcs."

"Buckle up," I whispered to Sam as I stood.

"Just here to request permission for extended ferry operation hours, Bob. I need to schedule a few more runs to the island."

Ricky shot to his feet again. "Why? Are we bringing more people to the island? Do we really need to do that?"

Sam pulled on my arm and mouthed, *What is he doing?*

"Yes, we do. It's tourist season and we have the typical influx of visitors. But I'm already sold out for the month. I need to extend hours to get a few more runs in. Early morning doesn't tend to go over well with guests, so I'd like to request evening hours."

Ricky pursed his lips and crossed his arms, looking to Bob like he expected an overwhelming agreement.

"Yes, Austin, we've discussed and the board agrees, extended hours are fine."

Ricky huffed. "What about city noise ordinances? He'll be in direct action against them."

Samantha stood up beside me.

"Ricky, is it?" Sam asked, her tone polite but sharp enough to turn heads.

Ricky squinted at her, suspicious. "Yeah?"

Sam smiled sweetly, but there was an edge to it. "I'm sure you know that the noise ordinance doesn't apply to marine vessels on the water after sunset. It's covered under section twelve, subsection C of the city code."

Ricky's expression faltered, his arms dropping to his sides. "Well—uh—"

"And," Sam continued, not missing a beat, "even if it did, the ordinance allows for exceptions when the noise is connected to public transportation or tourism-related activities. Which a ferry service qualifies as. Isn't that right, Bob?"

Bob blinked, a little stunned, then nodded. "That's...correct."

Samantha tilted her head, all charm. "So, technically, unless there's another complaint you'd like to file—maybe about the city's support of small businesses?—I don't think Austin's request goes against sound ordinances."

I stared at her, impressed. I didn't see that coming.

Ricky fumbled for a response. "I just—I don't think—"

"You own the general store on the island, right?" Sam asked, raising a brow. "Seems to me, more ferry runs would only bring more people through your door."

A few people around the room murmured in agreement, and Bob took the opportunity to slam his hand lightly on the wobbly table. "Extended ferry hours approved. Wrap it up by ten p.m., Capt'n."

Ricky sank back into his seat with a grumble. "Guess I'll just have to stay open till midnight, then."

Rita leaned over and whispered loud enough for everyone to hear, "I'll leave the lights on for you, boo."

Sam sat down gracefully, the corners of her mouth tugging into a smile.

I chuckled, low and appreciative. "That was impressive."

She gave a playful shrug. "It's just good business. Someone has to know the rules."

For a moment, I just stared at her. Sam was smart, sharp, and a step ahead of everyone else. And damn, if it wasn't attractive.

"Alright, moving on," Bob sighed, shuffling his notes as the room dissolved back into bickering.

I grabbed Sam's hand and we made for a quick exit. As we walked outside, I was still in awe of how effortlessly she'd stepped in and shut Ricky down, and how she made it look so easy.

Maybe this girl from my past wasn't just someone to catch up with. Maybe she was someone to keep up with.

16

AUSTIN

Her text dinged as I pulled in from a midday run the next day. When I looked, the memory of her legs poking out from under a Scuttle's Ferry T-shirt took over my brain.

    SAM: Busy?

Heat raced down the back of my neck, even though the thermometer outside already read eighty-nine degrees.

I ignored it, telling myself I was putting a little distance between us. It had been a long time since a woman had taken up so much real estate in my mind. Her face seemed to be hovering over every single thing I looked at. But when her name popped up on my phone as an actual *call*, I picked up. People like Sam don't call other people unless someone died or something was on fire.

"So, quick question for you." Her voice was an octave higher than normal when I answered.

"Oh-oh, what happened?"

"Let's just say, hypothetically speaking, a washing machine was producing a voluminous amount of foam and won't stop."

"Okay."

"What would be something you could try to get said washing machine to stop decorating your floor with bubbles?"

"Did you turn it off?" I asked.

"Hypothetically speaking, yes."

"And it's still spinning?"

"Violently."

I could hear a whirring sound in the background reminiscent of a tornado. "Can you get to the wall outlet to unplug it?"

"I tried and it's really heavy. I don't think this thing has been moved in about thirty years. It's stuck to the floor."

"I'll be right over." I didn't think twice about it. Maybe seeing her would help kick her out of my mind. Like when you have a song stuck in your head all day, you're supposed to listen to it and it works its way out of your system. Maybe I just needed to work her face out of my system.

I hung up and Patrick side-eyed me. "Not a peep out of you."

"Knight in shining armor looks good on you!" he called out as I hopped off the boat.

"If I'm not back in thirty, run the two p.m. solo. You think you can handle that, Lightning Bolt?"

"It would be my pleasure, Capt'n." He winked and bowed to me.

I sprinted down the dock and up the street to the Starfish. I could hear the howling from outside the front door. I turned the knob and it was locked.

"Sam?" I yelled as I pounded on the door. It sounded like someone with a jackhammer was right inside having a heyday. I looked down and tiny bubbles were oozing out under the door.

Uh-oh.

"Sam!" I yelled again.

"Coming!"

The door opened and her face filled with relief the moment she saw me. Her hair was piled up on top of her head with little bubbles attached to it and her face was flushed. The left side of her shirt and jeans were completely soaked and suctioned to her skin. *Jesus.* So much for working her out of my system.

"Here, watch your step."

"Why's your door locked?"

"Because I want to keep the bad guys out. Obviously."

"This is Florida. People don't lock their doors here." My attention was ripped from her as I looked to the ground, where the floor was completely covered in soapsuds three inches high. As I walked through the living room, it felt like little suckerfish popping up against my shin.

"Wow. You could have called me sooner."

"I texted you." She wiped her forehead, knocking loose a flurry of bubbles that started floating toward me. I held in a laugh. "Don't give me that look. It happened really fast."

The room was small so it didn't take long to get to the back closet where the washer and dryer sounded like they were keeping a gremlin hostage. I tried to pull the unit straight out but it wouldn't budge. I shimmied myself between it and the wall and pushed. My feet skidded out but I caught myself.

"Oh no, is it slippery over there too?" she asked innocently, looking at me with her arms crossed and her hip jutted out to one side. Such a pain in the ass.

I was able to move it a few inches forward and reach behind to unplug it. The gremlin slowly quieted as I eased myself from the wall and turned toward her.

"See? Not that bad—"

A sound popped behind me and the machine started rocking back and forth. My feet went flying out from under me and I landed flat on my butt, a snowstorm of bubbles floating up all around me, covering me as I landed. I turned on all fours and scrambled to get back to the washer but my hands kept slipping out from under me, sending me face-first into the foam. I managed to scoot a few inches, pulled myself up on the washer and unplugged the dryer too. It slowly came to a halt with one last pop for good measure.

We both stood staring at it for a moment, waiting for a possessed demon to poke its head out the top.

"What in the hell was that?" I asked, more to myself than to her.

When a good five seconds passed, I looked over to her. She gave me a once-over, then cracked up. I was soaked from head to toe. I plopped onto the floor, soapsuds covering every inch of my frame.

She crawled over toward me, grabbed a fluff of bubbles and rubbed some on my cheeks and around my chin. My skin buzzed where she touched me. I took a handful and put them on my head in the shape of a mohawk.

"You look like George Washington." Tears hung from her eyelashes.

"Yeah, well, you look like a wet cat."

She tried to get up but slipped back down on the linoleum. Half her face was covered in foam. She tried to get up again but her arm slipped out from under her and she fell face-first into the bubbles. She looked completely absurd, trying to get up and falling right back down, a new spray of white puffing up every time she thudded back to the ground. My side squeezed a little more with every slip from laughing so hard. I hadn't laughed like this in a long time.

I tried to crawl closer to help her and my knees skidded out from under me and my hands slid forward. I was completely laid out. She roared next to me. I blew a huge breath her way as a wave of white flew toward her. We looked utterly ridiculous.

"What the hell happened here?" Our heads snapped to the door as Josie stood in the doorway with her hands on her hips. It felt like we were two kids who got caught with our hands in the cookie jar.

I cleared my throat and tried my hardest to keep a straight face. "Washing machine was acting up just a bit. I came by to help. I think we stopped the bubble production, but there's just a bit of a cleanup needed now."

Sam burst into laughter beside me but slammed her hand over her mouth.

"I'm so sorry. The, um, *bubble production*, was my fault. I think I put too much soap in the dispenser."

She held her breath and glanced at me. And we both fell into hysterical giggles again.

Josie looked at me from the door with a sly smile and narrowed eyes. "It's been acting up a bit lately. I'll tell Harold. In the meantime, let me check which room I can switch you over to temporarily, Ms. Leigh." Josie winked at me as she turned and walked back out.

"What'd you do, put the whole bottle in there?" I joked.

She paused. "Was I not supposed to?"

"Wait, you seriously put the *whole bottle* in there?"

"It was super tiny!" she yelled. "I thought it was one of those things like the shampoos they give you in hotels."

"Those last a couple days!" I yelled back.

"Well, you don't have as much hair as I do!"

"Why are you yelling at me?!"

She burst into a fit of giggles again.

"I don't understand," I eked out in between breaths. "Do you not do laundry at home?"

"No. You send your laundry out in the city. People come to your door, pick your dirty clothes up, and drop it off clean the next day, folded all nice in these little stacks that all match."

I had no idea something like that even existed.

"Most apartments in the city are too small to have a washer-dryer. It's big business up there."

Little did I know, laundry fairies were real.

"I haven't done my own laundry for years." She tried to wipe some of the suds off her.

"I didn't do laundry until I was forced to as a full-grown adult."

"Yeah, well, when you run out of clean underwear as a teenager and your mother can't get off the couch, you figure it out." She laughed through it like it was such a normal thing to say. "Although I will say, I avoided this particular situation happening somehow throughout my early years of domestication. I guess it's been a while."

Lexi and Sam are four years younger than me. When she was a freshman, Vanessa and I were riding high on life after having graduated, talking about marriage and kids and what it all looked like long term. I technically had a room at our parents' house still, but I didn't ever stay there. Vanessa's parents were never home, so I practically lived at her house. I remember Mom talking about how Sam's dad got sick. Really sick, really fast. He passed quickly. Her mom didn't take it well, not that anyone would take an unexpected death well but she turned to pills, then alcohol.

Sam was over at our house a lot after he died, especially as her mom's drinking ramped up. She was a staple at family dinner nights, but I wasn't anymore, which was yet another reason Mom didn't love my fiancée. Vanessa couldn't fathom having dinner with family every single week so I wasn't around a ton. I was working a lot, saving up money at the time to buy a house.

"Have you seen her yet?" I asked as I made my way on all fours to the small dining table in the middle of the room. I eyed the chair, hoping to use it to gain a fighting chance of standing up.

"Well, she made a spirited appearance on my Zoom call with my boss and the rest of the due diligence team in her thong bikini yesterday morning."

My jaw dropped. "She didn't."

"Oh, she did. I'm still waiting for the fallout. While I think she's doing better than I expected her to be, she single-handedly may have cost me my job."

I pushed up and braced myself against the chair.

"You good?" she asked from the floor.

"Of course." I stood straight up too fast and the chair slipped from under my palm. I crashed onto the floor, my head making contact with the side of the table as I went down.

And then, everything went black.

~

"I really don't think we need to call an ambulance," I heard a faint voice say. It was velvety and made me feel warm all over. I heard some shuffling.

"Patrick just took the boat out. I say we give him a few minutes and if he doesn't wake up, I'll call one for him."

I blinked my eyes and stared up into the most beautiful eyes I'd ever seen. They kind of sparkled. Had they always been that color?

"Yes." She smiled.

Was that out loud?

I tried to sit up.

"No, no, no, stay down. You hit your head pretty good." She was cradling my head in her lap.

She was so pretty. And smelled so good. She giggled and leaned down toward me, "I think you hit your head harder than we thought."

I whispered back, "I think you're prettier than you think."

"You're quite charming after a head injury. Does it hurt?"

"Your eyes are glittery."

"Glittery? Oooh, that sounds fun."

"And your eyelashes are really pretty," I whispered.

"Well, that's a new one, Casanova." Josie's face appeared above me. "How many fingers am I holding up?"

"Two. And the president doesn't matter."

"Great. You stay down," Josie ordered. "I'll be back with a mop."

"I'm fine, really."

After she walked out the door, I tried to sit up.

"Samantha, don't let him get up," she called from outside. "He could have a concussion."

"Well, since I have you captive in my lap, let me take this moment to thank you profusely for coming to my rescue."

"You were in grave danger. You were lucky I was so close." My eyes felt heavy again.

"I would have been sucked into the bubble vortex, never to be seen again, if it weren't for your quick bubble production exorcism skills." She bit her lip, holding back a smile.

"I would've been sad. If you got sucked into the bubble vortex, I'd come with you."

"I think I'd like that," she whispered as I closed my eyes.

17
SAMANTHA

IVY: so did u kiss him

> **ME:** He was incapacitated on my floor. Highly inappropriate.

IVY: just asking if you took advantage of the situation

> **ME:** It's not like that

IVY: ok

> **ME:** It's not.
> He's my friend's older brother

IVY: that matters in high school
for some people
age is just a number

> **ME:** That's what old people say when they want to seem young.

IVY: also true

                ME: Any word from Glenn or Robby?

IVY: nothing

                ME: Maybe they're conspiring on all the ways
                      to fire me without legal retribution.

IVY: maybe
or maybe they're getting matching
tattoos on their lower backs

                              Me: Maybe.

18
AUSTIN

SAM: Any chance you're dying to show off your knight in shining armor capabilities again?

ME: Another bubble incident?

SAM: Something like that. Don't wear nice shoes.

ME: ?

SAM: Need help with mom if you're okay with it.

ME: Of course. Whatever you need.

SAM: Are you sure? I don't want to interrupt your night.

ME: Sam.

SAM: OK. I'll pick you up in five.
Won't take long.
Promise.

She pulled into my gravel drive ten minutes after midnight. I climbed into her rental car and she was silent as she backed out. She wore an oversized sweatshirt that made her look like she was thirteen again. Her gaze bounced around the road and the surrounding street, and she hadn't looked at me yet. Her knee jerked from side to side.

"So." She laughed awkwardly and wiped her hand on her jeans a few times. "How's your head?"

"Feeling much better, thanks to you." She was still nervous, biting her lip and looking anywhere but at me. "So, want to fill me in or is this a surprise?"

"Apparently the Zoom call was the *hey-welcome-back-to-reality* opening scene. You said earlier I could call you for anything, right?"

"Of course." I wondered what the hell I just agreed to.

"Mom apparently passed out at some house. A man called me from her phone and since I didn't recognize the address, I figured backup couldn't hurt. Wouldn't want to voluntarily walk into a kidnapping situation."

"There's a lot of those around here."

She gave me a shrug and a small smile. "I can't lift her by myself when she's completely passed out like this."

Something in her voice gutted my soul.

During the rest of the drive, she kept her eyes on anything but me. To think she dealt with these little bombs all throughout high school made my stomach twist. Every family has their shit but mine didn't include picking my drunk mother up from strangers' houses after my father died.

We pulled into a small quiet neighborhood with tiny shell lawns and colored shutters. She parked and waited for me to walk her to the door. A man was waiting in the shadow of the front alcove.

"Mr. Johnson?" she asked. Her voice climbed an octave as she walked up to the open door that was waiting for us after we pulled up. It was our old high school principal. "God, what is with her and this teacher fetish?" she said under her breath to me. *Later* was all I got when I gave her a questioning look.

"Well, I'll be damned. Good to see you, Marcs." He reached for my hand. "I've been following the Mariners. You know, I had my money on you taking over the helm but Rex is doing a fantastic job." I stood there awkwardly not quite sure of the best route to take.

"You remember Samantha Leigh?" I put my hand on the small of her back.

"How could I forget." His voice was sincere, but laced with pity. She flinched under my fingertips. "It's a miracle to see you up and walking. I retired a few years ago."

"Oh, that's nice," she replied.

Cue the awkward silence.

"So, Sam's mom?" I asked.

"Ah yes, right there on the couch in the living room. Good and passed out."

We walked into the living room where Sam's mom was face down on the couch, a drool stain puddled on the fabric near the corner of her mouth. There was a blanket draped over her, tucked in at her sides.

"Don't worry about that, it'll disappear in a few minutes," Mr. Johnson said from behind me, like this was a normal weekly occurrence. "So," he directed his attention back to Sam, "your mom told me you're in New York City. Not a surprise there, you were always such a great student. Landed on your own two feet. Like when you throw a cat."

She looked like she wanted to crawl into a hole and die. Mr. Johnson was a good guy, just lacked a bit of social intelligence. "I'm doing well. Thanks. Yeah, I landed in New York City."

"Big city corporation or something like that, trying to take over the world? How do you like it?" he asked as I picked up Sam's mom like a baby with her head resting on my chest. She snored loudly on my shoulder. She was definitely drooling on my shirt.

"Umm, so sorry about this." Sam awkwardly turned toward the door. "I don't think this is really the best time to catch up fully, but thank you for calling about her."

"Oh, of course, you should get her home, but don't worry, she'll be fine in the morning. It was nice seeing you!" he called out as we walked down the driveway back to her car. "Go Mariners!"

"Isn't he married?" she asked me as she opened the back seat door.

"Divorced a few years ago," I answered. "And unofficially voted most eligible bachelor on the island last year. He's a bit of an awkward dude but he means well."

"This obsession with my former teachers is *so* weird." She pulled out of the driveway with her mother fast asleep lying across the back seat.

It was after 1:00 a.m. before I laid her mom down in her own bed. Sam led me back out to the living room.

"Here, you take these," she said, handing me her car keys. "I'm going to stay here on the couch just in case she needs anything. And you know, doesn't randomly stop breathing on me."

She kept looking at the floor like she wanted to pull up the carpet and burrow underneath. I could see water pooling in the corner of her eyes but she kept blinking it back. "Thank you, by the way.

I didn't know who else to call who would actually be able to carry her."

Her laugh was small. She looked like such a kid in her oversized sweatshirt. This was the first time she felt familiar to me, this shy awkward girl unsure of herself. I wanted to shelter her from this, take away whatever was making her shrink into herself.

"Are you saying you think I'm buff?" Her laugh was just a breath of air. I kicked myself for trying to lighten the mood a little. *Now is not the time.* "Seriously, it's no problem."

Her keys weighed down my hand like they were made of lead. I walked to the fireplace, where a row of pictures lined the mantel. There was one of Sam and her mom at her high school graduation. Sam was still in a wheelchair but her mom was hugging her, squishing her face to the side. There was one of a little blond girl in pigtails on the beach, rosy cheeks and nose, squinting into the camera lens holding a shell out.

"This little blond thing you?" I asked.

"I had blond hair up until fifth grade, then it turned dark overnight, to my mother's dismay."

I walked down the row of pictures. They were all of Sam at various stages of life—baby pictures, Halloween costumes, Christmas morning. Another frame held a young teenage Sam posed next to some boy band icon, her smile so big it forced her eyes into tiny slits.

"First boyfriend?" I teased.

"Please tell me you know who that is." She stared at me in disbelief.

"I have absolutely no idea," I responded, trying desperately to hide a smile. Her jaw dropped.

"Taylor Hanson," she snapped.

"Is he a cousin?"

The shock on her face was fantastic. Lexi's room was decorated with life-sized posters of the Hanson Brothers during her high school years. And I'm pretty sure she blew out speakers from two different boom boxes I bought with my own money because she blasted "MMMBop" so loudly. So yes, I was fully aware of who Taylor Hanson was.

"I'm totally kidding. Of course I know who the Hanson Brothers are. Only the most iconic family boy band trio, like, *ever*."

"Do you want to see something fantastic? It better still be hanging on the back of my door," she asked, eyes alight with excitement.

"Wait, what's still hanging on your door? Please tell me you're not a weird mega fan that has a lock of his hair tacked above your doorframe in a plastic bag."

She ignored me and took off down the hallway into what must have been her childhood room. The door squeaked open.

"Come here," she called out.

I looked above her at the doorframe and hesitated.

"Oh stop, there are no body parts warding intruders away. In. Now."

When I cleared the door I was greeted with Pepto Bismol–pink walls and a fluffy white duvet with *lots* of stuffed animals on the bed staring at me.

"Now *this* is like something out of a horror film." I walked slowly into the room.

"Mom refuses to change anything in hopes it'll entice me to come back. Okay, ready...look." Her voice came from behind me and I heard the door click. I slowly turned around and a life-sized cutout of Taylor Hanson was taped to the back of the door.

And he was winking at me.

It took me a second to find my words. "I'm not sure what to say here."

She was looking at the door, absolutely beaming. "Isn't it great? My dad bought it for me before my freshman year of high school and I refused to take it down. He said I had Taylor, so I didn't need a real boyfriend. It was his last ditch effort to ward me away from teenage boys." She stood there soaking in all the cardboard glory. "It was one of the few things that survived the purge."

"The purge?" I asked.

She paused just long enough for the room to feel heavier. "He got sick my freshman year."

She turned away from me and began to circle her room, her gaze brushing over the dust-layered trophies, the faded place ribbons tacked to her mirror, and the team photos that were probably still sticky-tacked to the wall. Her movements were slow, deliberate, like she was measuring the distance between herself and the memories she wasn't sure if she wanted to revisit.

"They gave him six months to live," she continued, her voice steady. "It was a brain tumor. An inoperable one. He was gone in less than two."

She picked up a little ceramic statue of a kitten off the shelf, revealing a perfectly clean circle of wood underneath it. It made her pause, like she wasn't expecting anything to be protected against time. She put it back, covering the treasure she'd found, and made her way to sit on the bed. "Mom took down everything in the house that reminded her of him—knickknacks, coffee mugs, it all went. She even threw away his recliner—anything that even hinted of his existence was put in a box in the closet or in the trash. But Taylor survived."

That's what was missing from the mantel.

Her dad.

I hated that I hadn't noticed right away. It felt wrong, like I failed to notice something so important. I was never in high school with

Lexi and Sam at the same time so I didn't know much of the news around her class. Even though it was a small town, the age gap proved enough for me to keep a distance from most stuff that was happening in my little sister's world.

"I didn't let her touch my room though. He gave me this poster sometime before his diagnosis that year, then he was gone in two months." Her eyes flicked toward the wall where it still hung, faded but defiant. "I wouldn't let her take it down."

"I didn't realize it happened so fast." I slipped my hands into my pockets. I couldn't imagine a world where one season your dad was there, and the next, he was just gone.

"You hear all those horror stories about watching the people you love wither away but that wasn't him." She walked over to a white desk where Polaroids of friends and landscapes were taped up. Random beaded necklaces draped over the corner of the mirror. "One day he was here, the next he wasn't." She opened the top drawer, reached to the back, and pulled out an old Polaroid.

She handed it to me. "Lexi took this with that little camera she carried everywhere."

It was a faded Polaroid of her and a man. Dark eyes, dark hair, tanned skin. She was the spitting image of him.

Her eyes stayed glued on the fuzzy picture. "His eyes smiled like that all the time."

I leaned over her shoulder at the familiar face staring back at me.

"Yours do that too," I whispered without a beat. She barely turned her head and held my gaze for a second before turning away. I never really understood that phrase until she said it, but that's exactly what her eyes did.

I couldn't just leave. She had spent her entire life dealing with her mom by herself. Lexi had seen this play out a hundred times, and she would know what to do. But Lexi couldn't be here at the moment. So I decided I would be.

"Hey, so I actually have extra hands on the boat tomorrow, so it's not like I need a ton of sleep tonight. I'm going to stay here if you're cool with that. You know, in case you need help or something. I'll sleep on the couch." Part of me wanted to make sure I was here in case her mom took a turn south for some reason. But a bigger part of me just didn't want her to be alone.

"No, you're good. Really. She probably won't move all night. Plus, I really don't want to sleep in here, it totally freaks me out, so I was going to take the couch."

"Sleeping with Taylor winking at you doesn't do it for you anymore?"

"Sadly, my tastes have evolved," she responded. "And I'm kind of wired at the moment. I wasn't planning on going to bed anytime soon anyway."

"Me either. I feel like lying down would be pointless at the moment for either of us." I really didn't mind. All I was going to see was her face when I closed my eyes anyway.

"We could stick in a movie?" she suggested. "But I think the only movies we have are my mom's old chick flicks."

"Perfect."

"You sure?" she asked. "You really don't have to. I'll be fine by myself." She looked so scared all of a sudden, like I might back out and change my mind.

"Yeah, I know you would be. But your mom lives right by the marina. I can wake up tomorrow and literally walk on the boat. It's closer than my house, and all my stuff's already on board. That way if she wakes up or you need help with her before she's able to actually walk herself, I'll be here."

"And you're okay staying in here? You're sure all *this* won't give you nightmares?" she asked, waving her hands in the general direction of "MMMBop" royalty.

"Yeah. Taylor's actually pretty cute. It's all the stuffed animals I'm more freaked out about."

And she cracked a smile—the first real one of the night.

※

"How do you think they got all those ducks to stay in the water while filming?" She lay back on the couch wrapped in blankets, eating popcorn.

Ducks?

"What? It's a logistical question. Everyone knows you don't shoot movies with kids or animals. They're difficult to work with."

"That's what you're thinking when you watch this scene? Not, how romantic it is that Noah took Allie out on a canoe and is paddling her through, like, a whole other universe?"

"I'm thinking it probably smells really weird and somehow they're all quiet at the same time."

She had a point.

"I guess every romance has to suspend real life to some degree," she continued. "Nothing like that would actually happen. But I still don't understand how they pulled it off."

"Okay then, since you're such a movie romance expert—enlighten me. What would *actually* happen?"

"First of all, there's no way they could hear what each other was saying because there would be way too much quacking. When have you ever heard a duck be quiet? Let alone four hundred of them at one time."

I fought back a smile.

"And look, she's holding that little loaf of bread," she went on. "No way she doesn't get ambushed by all of the ducks once they realize she's got it. Have you ever fed ducks?"

"Yes," I answered.

"They're ruthless. They come *to* you when you have bread, right? Isn't that the whole point of feeding ducks? She'd be eaten alive in two seconds. The males can get very aggressive."

"I didn't realize you were such a waterfowl expert," I teased. "But I think there's just one tiny flaw with your whole duck theory."

"Try me." She leaned back like her argument was completely foolproof.

I grinned. "I'm pretty sure they're swans."

She blinked, turning to the screen, then back at me.

"Well, most of them are swans…and maybe a few geese. But most of them aren't ducks. Not, like, *duck* ducks."

The realization slowly crept over her face and it was priceless. I tried my absolute best to just sit and not move but I couldn't hold it in any longer. I burst out laughing and couldn't stop. I couldn't catch my breath. When I glanced over, she had her face buried in the pillow, laughing just as hard.

When she lifted her head, something in her had shifted. The heaviness she'd been carrying from the night—and from her mom—seemed to lift, if only for a brief few seconds.

Sitting there, her face lit up with laughter. She was so radiant, it almost hurt to look away. I couldn't remember the last time I'd been so reluctant to tear my eyes from something.

19
SAMANTHA

Austin was already gone when I woke up. My side still hurt from last night. He had me in stitches. After half an hour of deep dive googling ducks versus swans in *The Notebook*, we eventually passed out on the couch foot to foot with *Serendipity* playing in the background. A horribly embarrassing night turned into one of the best nights I've had in a long time.

There were two piping hot lattes on the kitchen counter. How he snuck them in without waking me up is a feat of magic. I'm the lightest sleeper known to humankind.

I looked around for the first time as I sat at the little kitchen bar counter with my coffee. The counter was perfectly spotless and wiped down. A fresh vase of flowers sat on the windowsill. Not a single dirty dish in the sink. One clean coffee mug sat by the single cup coffee maker. A cheery yellow and white striped Williams Sonoma dish towel draped over the sink edge. Perfectly put together and tied up, the way it's always seemed.

"Well, look who the cat dragged in." A raspy voice pierced the air from behind me followed by the flop of her slippers.

I took a really deep breath and bit my tongue. "Good morning, Mom. How are you feeling?"

"Wonderful, actually. To what do I owe this special morning visit?"

Was there really a possibility she didn't remember the night before? From the time we left Mr. Johnson's house to the time Austin laid her in bed, she was completely and totally passed out. She never woke up. In all the chaos (and unintended distractions) of the night, it didn't dawn on me she could have no recollection of the evening.

Well. This should be fun.

"The house looks nice."

"It looks exactly the same as when you lived here. Is this for me?" She held up the latte.

"It is. Compliments of Austin Marcs, actually." She turned her back to me. "Need some ibuprofen to go with it?"

She completely ignored my question and turned on the faucet. "Well, that was nice of him."

I raised my voice over the stream of water. "I saw Mr. Johnson last night."

No response.

"Did you hear what I said? I saw Mr. Johnson."

"Oh yeah?" she called over her shoulder.

"Yeah, I got to see him at his house last night. When I picked you up."

She stilled, but for just a second. "Really? Huh. He was always such a fan of yours. He asked how you were doing. Asked if you liked New York. He always follows his favorites."

"So which part do we want to dive into first? The fact that you're sleeping with my old principal or the fact that you passed out on his couch at midnight from mixing too many substances?"

She turned around abruptly. "The first is none of your business, young lady. And the second, I didn't feel well. I've been having a stomach thing the last few days and it must have taken me out last night."

"You were not sick. You were passed out drunk. Or high. Or both."

"That's absolutely not true." She puttered around the kitchen wiping the clean countertop off again and again, avoiding eye contact.

"I had to call Austin to help me carry you since I can't actually transport your dead weight by myself."

Anger flared in her eyes. "Austin carried me?" She looked absolutely horrified.

"And tucked you into bed, safe and sound," I sang as I brought the latte against my mouth.

"Samantha Leigh, how dare you bring a grown man into the house to see me in that state?"

"You mean your stomach bug state? I didn't have a choice, Mom. A random guy calls me from *your* phone, tells me you passed out on the couch and he can't wake you up. I don't recognize his first name, don't know the address, but I know I can't actually carry you by myself. What other option did I have exactly?"

"How long did he stay?"

"He spent the night. Just in case, oh I don't know, you stopped breathing in the middle of the night again, and I needed someone to help me get you to the ER."

"You're blowing this a bit out of proportion."

"Am I? You were completely unresponsive. We probably should have taken you straight to the hospital to have your stomach pumped."

Having sensed my anxiety building, she deployed her first tactic. She'd try her best to swing the pendulum the other way. She came over and placed one hand gently on my shoulder as she slowly stroked a piece of hair behind my ear with the other. I hated how my body responded to that small display of maternal affection.

Regardless of what she put me through, what she continued to put herself through, when she fell back into the mother role I felt myself curl underneath her, desperately wanting her attention, approval, love—whatever you want to call it.

"I haven't been feeling very well." She slowly stroked my back. "And I shouldn't have mixed my medicine with wine last night. It was my fault. I'm sorry you had to deal with that. I really am. No more drinking on medicine. I promise."

"How about no more drinking, period?" I countered, which she ignored as she went back to wiping her clean counters.

She smiled to herself after a minute. "Mr. Johnson's pretty cute, isn't he?"

"I'm serious, Mom. I think it's time we had a real conversation about this again."

"Samantha, I don't need you meddling around in my personal life for the few weeks you've decided to grace me with your presence."

She knew every button to push that would send me over the edge. I saw it coming and wasn't going to lose the war on this one.

"And you refuse to even stay here, in your own home, when you *do* come," she continued. "You'd rather pay money out of your own pocket to stay at a motel. It's ludicrous."

"The company pays for it, Mom, and I need a place to *work*," I answered. "Should we address the Zoom call that you decided to crash in a bathing suit that has the real possibility of getting me fired?"

"Oh please, those tight pants needed a little levity. They should be sending me a thank-you note for the show. It was probably the most exhilarating part of their day."

I had learned over the years if I poked at the small details, she'd almost always justify her actions like she was doing a favor for the general public. I took a breath. This was much bigger than my job. Or the latest teacher she was dating.

"I'm sorry I haven't been around more," I said, treading carefully. "But I would hope that you of all people would understand my severe hesitation in coming back considering what happened graduation week."

She turned, looked straight at me, and threw her dish towel on the counter. "We are not getting into this again."

"You never even apologized." My voice came out even and controlled, the exact opposite of how I actually felt.

"It was an accident. Don't be so dramatic."

"Dramatic? I have twenty-three screws in my arm. I think I earned the right to be *factual*."

She turned away from me and started to walk back down the hallway to her room.

"I was in the hospital in a coma, Mom. For three days. You don't think that deserves an apology?"

"Well, if your father hadn't left—" she started over her shoulder.

"He didn't leave, Mom. It wasn't a choice," I called out after her. "It's not like he packed up a suitcase one day and said he didn't want us anymore and walked out the door."

This was the argument I walked away from every single time, but I wasn't going to walk away this time. I was tired of being scared to pick up the phone, terrified of getting the call where she did something irreversible. Again. And maybe this time, they didn't get to walk away with just a few screws.

"He wasn't here anymore and that's not what I signed up for."

"Taking care of a drunk while I'm trying to deal with losing my dad isn't what I signed up for either. You think that was an easy thing to do? You think that's a fair weight to carry for a teenage girl?"

"He left us, Samantha."

"Yeah, well, you left too. Your body just hung around a little longer than his did."

She looked at me like I had slapped her across the face.

"It's time for you to leave."

"I'm tired of ignoring the fact there's no oxygen in the room. It's suffocating both of us. I can't live with this on my chest anymore. Something has to give."

"How about you do what you need to for work, then run back off to New York again and pretend like I don't exist down here. That's been working well for you for the past seven years. I don't see a need to change that now."

"You didn't give me a choice in leaving, Mom. I was out of options."

"You always have a choice."

"Ironic advice coming from you."

"Out," she ordered.

"If you're not up for talking about this now, fine, but this conversation isn't over." I pushed myself up from the counter. "Oh, and you're welcome, for coming and getting you last night so you didn't puke all over cute Mr. Johnson's couch and floor. I'll tell Austin you said thanks for the coffee."

I walked back to my room to grab the few things I had brought for the night.

I hadn't noticed it the night before, but the air in the room smelled stale, like it hadn't moved since I left seven years ago. Third-place dance trophies stuck in time sat on a shelf collecting dust. Pictures were frozen on the mirror dying to grow older. My bedspread reeked of that unmistakable mustiness of mismatched linens forgotten in the back of a closet that didn't belong anymore but never got thrown away.

I opened the top drawer of my desk, and underneath the stacks of handwritten poems and papers, school announcements and homecoming court pamphlets, I knew was the folded newspaper article.

I pried open the top of it: LOCAL HIGH SCHOOL SENIOR IN COMA AFTER MOTHER'S ACCIDENT SHAKES SMALL COMMUNITY.

Most people say they don't remember the first few days after losing a loved one. I'm not one of those people.

I remember every single moment after my dad died.

I remember the way the slices of bread I would leave beside my mom's sleeping body on the couch would get stale.

I remember the smell of rotten casseroles piling up in the garbage—too many, too quickly—and taking out the trash took energy I didn't have.

I remember crawling into their bed when she refused to leave the couch and smelling every single inch of fabric, trying to find a trace of my dad.

I remember screaming into his pillow as loud as I could, hoping my mom didn't hear me because I was so embarrassed that I just couldn't keep it in and quiet like she did.

Then, I remember years of watching her waste away, pound after pound.

I remember watching her pour vodka into her coffee in the morning when she thought I wasn't looking.

I remember opening the refrigerator to find only string cheese and yogurt past its expiration date.

I remember getting into her car after the senior graduation pep rally, turning to wave goodbye to my friends, calling out to them that I'd see them later at the game.

I remember riding in the front seat, reaching down to get ChapStick out of my backpack, and not opening my eyes again until I heard the beeping of a heart monitor three days later.

LOCAL HIGH SCHOOL SENIOR IN COMA AFTER MOTHER'S ACCIDENT SHAKES SMALL COMMUNITY

May 31, 2016—Rock Island, Florida—Rock Island citizen's car crash puts daughter into ICU.

The small community of Rock Island is still shaken from the news of local Rock Island High School upcoming graduate Samantha Leigh in the hospital. Leigh remains in a medically induced coma after her mother, Bonnie Leigh, veered off the road and impacted a streetlight after traveling southbound on Main Street in her 1996 Honda Civic at a high rate of speed. Witnesses report the car was going far over the speed limit, although that has yet to be confirmed by the local authorities.

Dr. Neal Nguyen, head trauma surgeon at Tampa Medical Center, who is not treating Leigh, told us a medically induced coma is sometimes necessary to decrease swelling of the brain. "Inducing a coma allows the brain to rest and decreases the brain's activity and metabolic rate," Dr. Nguyen said. "Ultimately, this state helps decrease brain swelling and protects the brain from further damage."

"Sam [Leigh] is the perfect student," a close, personal friend of Leigh's said, also a senior at Rock Island High School who has asked to remain anonymous. "But her mom's had a problem for a while now. It was just

> a matter of time before she hurt herself or
> someone else. I just can't believe it was Sam
> in the end."
>
> Bonnie Leigh's toxicology report has yet
> to be confirmed.

I smoothed out the creases, laid it carefully on top of the desk, and walked out the front door without saying goodbye.

20

SAMANTHA

When it comes to the friendship communication tier, texting is considered the acceptable norm. Email is saved for when you know you're going to piss someone off but want it to look like you've really thought about it and it typically includes bullet points. Actually calling someone is reserved for when something's on fire or you're being abducted.

So, when Ivy's name flashed on my screen as a caller, either her apartment building was going up in flames or aliens were luring her into their mother ship and I'd be interviewed for the next *Unsolved Mysteries* case as the last person to speak with her.

"What's wrong?" I answered.

"It's about Robby."

My stomach dropped. "Did you just call him Robby? Wow, this must be bad if you're using his real—"

"The Oakstone contract came back around."

I paused. "Isn't that good news?"

"Glenn put Robby on it."

I sunk into the wicker couch covered with stamped starfish. "I'm sorry, could you say that one more time? I could have sworn you just—"

"Glenn said you were already deep into the due diligence in Florida and he didn't want to pull you."

Warning bells went off.

"But that doesn't make any sense. Oakstone is my project. Robby doesn't do developed cities. He does blank slates." My voice rose a little. "He doesn't do local restaurants and breweries and city councils with art festivals and dog parades."

"Not usually, no."

Oakstone Springs was as high profile as we had run into. And I had been the lead on the project just the week before last. My history of city revitalizations was impeccable. My ideas were specific and unique to the groups of people I studied in these areas, not only the locals and what was important to them, but the transient traffic the city received. I knew how to capitalize on the wants and needs of both parties to elevate the whole. I was hired for that sole reason.

This didn't make sense.

And now Robby was going to convince them of that instead? How could Glenn possibly think Robby could do a better job when I had made it my life's mission to do exactly that for every project we'd run across? And had a successful track record of doing exactly that. This was just on a much bigger scale.

Robby should be the one stuck down here with wicker couches and spotty internet, and I should be on a plane to Oakstone Springs, meeting with the mayor, talking about the reconceptualization of the city.

"Robby doesn't have any experience whatsoever with cities like Oakstone. There would be no sound reason he'd put him as lead on that project, unless…" My voice trailed off.

"It gets worse."

"How could it possibly get worse?"

"Robby's coming to Florida."

Something didn't click. *Why would he be in Florida?*

"I thought you just said Robby's on Oakstone." My words were slow and steady.

"He is. But it doesn't start for another six weeks. That's when the city approved funding. Glenn's sending him down to...help you out."

"*Help me out?*" She was silent. "As in, *supervise* me?"

She spoke slowly and carefully. "While what happened on the company Zoom call will make for a great story once this is all said and done, Glenn's got twenty million riding on this."

"So he thinks I'm jeopardizing the contract because my mother interrupted a call in her bikini."

"Not in so many words, but yes. If that had been a client call, or someone from the board had been present, it wouldn't have been as entertaining. And there's one more thing."

"Just stop talking," I pleaded.

"He's staying with you."

The line went silent. I looked over at the single queen bed with the sand dollar–printed duvet that sat in the middle of the room. This had to be a joke.

"Before you ask, I already called the Starfish and they're completely booked up. So are all of the other hotels and rentals on the island I've checked so far. Apparently there's a *national high school football showcase*, or something equally absurd, happening this weekend."

"He cannot stay in this room with me."

"The lady at the front desk assured me the couch is a pullout."

"This is completely inappropriate."

"Obviously. Can you stay with your mom?"

"After this morning's pleasant interaction, most definitely not." I was not about to turn around and ask my mom for a favor. "I'll figure it out."

The pieces all came together at once. I knew what this meant. Robby got pulled onto the Oakstone Springs project over me, when I'd already worked on it for weeks. It didn't even start up again for over a month, which meant I'd be done with the DD in Florida in time to jump back on it. Robby being sent down to chaperone me because my boss thought I wasn't being as responsible as I should be with the project could only mean one thing.

"He already knows, doesn't he? Who the promotion is going to?" The words stuck like syrup coming out of my mouth.

"Don't let your mind go there," she warned.

"The decision's already been made and he just hasn't told me." The thing I had been chasing, that I had been enduring the entire state of *Florida* for, was gone.

"I haven't been able to confirm anything."

"But you thought the same thing."

"No announcement has been made, but it crossed my mind." She paused. "The board still has to vote. It's not solely Glenn's decision, and to my knowledge, they don't know about the yellow polka dot bikini call." I leaned back on the couch and closed my eyes as Ivy continued. "I know Glenn is smarter than that. I think it was a 'right time, right place' kind of a decision. It really doesn't make sense to pull you off the Rock Island DD when you're already halfway through, right?"

"You're not convincing me."

"He's just a safety net, Samantha. Glenn has seen your reports so far. You're doing a great job. A better job than what Pugglepuff would do. Rock Island is a bird in hand for us and he probably just wants to make sure it stays that way. Oakstone Springs is still a bird in the bush. They've already flaked out once. Doesn't make sense to pull you from something that's a sealed deal to put you back on a project that may flake out again."

I heard half of what she said. All I could think of was that Robby was going to get the corner office and the title. And I wasn't.

"Let me do some digging. Just because Glenn put him on Oakstone doesn't mean he's already made up his mind. It could be a test. There's got to be something else here."

There wasn't anything else here. My boss was giving my work nemesis my project, *and* my promotion, and I was stuck in Florida for two more weeks.

"Are you still breathing?" she asked.

"Barely."

"Give me the weekend and I'll find out what's going on and call you Monday."

"Great. Don't mind me, I'll just be sitting here on my wicker couch that has blue starfish screen-printed all over it."

"Oh, God. It does?"

"Only in hell."

I hung up and closed my eyes. As much as I tried to find a workaround in my head, I could only land on one sure thing. There was no way Glenn would use Oakstone Springs as a test for Robby. It was too high stakes and too high profile a case to gamble with. Glenn had already made up his mind about the promotion and he was showing off his new shiny toy to the largest client we've ever had.

I needed some air. I pushed the screen door open and walked out onto the patio. The sky was starting to lose its blue hue, turning into a hazy honey color as the sun set.

I needed a distraction. Bottom line.

ME: Feel like going out tonight?

LEXI: Ugh I wish! Plans with the in-laws. ☹
Everything OK?!?!

ME: Yeah. Rough day.

LEXI: I'm sorry. I'll call you later!

There was only one other person on the island I could think of that would be the perfect distraction.

ME: How do you feel about a plus one for tonight?

AUSTIN: you down for harpoon's

ME: If they still serve alcohol, yes

AUSTIN: pick you up in 20

ME: 👍

21
AUSTIN

A zing shot through my chest when her text came in even though I stood ankle-deep in puke. On the last ferry over, someone got sick and spewed on someone else's suitcase. It was a mess. It happened more frequently than one might think. I was inclined to just head home and get ready for the early morning, but I wanted to see her again. I warned her my typical Thursday night probably didn't look like hers. After the last run, Patrick and I usually head to Harpoon's to celebrate the slew of tourists who would make the trek to the island to start their weekend.

"It's just Harpoon's," I said to her as she hopped up in my truck in a tight gray dress. She said she felt like "celebrating freedom from the constraints of corporate America," whatever that meant. My radar was up. I wished I had a random sweater in the car to throw over her.

I walked into the bar holding my breath. Sam would stick out like a sore thumb in this town on any given day, but especially in two square feet of fabric. And she had a confidence about her that was intimidating. Not a lot of women walked around like that here. I didn't think she actually knew how objectively pretty she was. I couldn't stop looking over at her. It felt like I had a ticking time bomb sitting on the truck bench next to me and if I hit a pothole, she'd explode.

The bar was packed as usual. All the locals poured in right from the docks after a day on the water, and the smell of sea salt and sunscreen filled the air. And just like I thought, the entire bar swiveled their heads around like a two-headed dragon had just walked in.

A two-headed dragon in heels.

I stepped closer to her and put my arm around her waist to guide her to the bar. I told myself I wouldn't take my eyes off her all night, just in case. But apparently neither would every other set of eyes in the room based on the low catcalls that came clawing across the floor. I stepped closer to her. I didn't want anyone getting the wrong idea—she wasn't some prize up for the highest bidder. Not that I had the right to be upset about it. She wasn't mine either.

She walked right up to the bar, ordered four shots of tequila from Becky, who gave me a side-eye look, and slid two over to me.

"To Florida."

"I thought you didn't like Florida."

"I *love* Florida." She threw back the two shots without even waiting for me.

So, it was going to be that kinda night.

There are little wooden triangle games that sit on the table of some restaurants and bars. Harpoon's has them all over the place. By the end of the night, grown men are arguing over rules and threatening to throw punches over whether a plastic golf tee moved when it shouldn't have.

"Bet you I can get it down to fewer than you can." She handed me one and kept one for herself.

"Next round on the loser?" I asked.

"Deal." A smile slowly crept across her face.

I let her take the bait. She hadn't been coming here for the last seven years practicing like I had. In a handful of moves, she had three tees left. She smirked and took a long drag off her vodka tonic—two lemons, one lime. In five moves I had two tees left. I didn't want to completely obliterate her on the first try.

"I think that means next round's on you," I loudly slurped up the last of my Jack and Coke through the small straw.

"One question for every tee left." She pulled a little white tee out of the triangle.

"That seems unfair." I narrowed my eyes at her.

"So is the way of the world, my dear Austin," she responded. I didn't want to press her, but there was something different about her. And not in a good way.

She wiggled one of her three tees up in the air. "What's your middle name?"

"That's your question?" I asked. Of course, it would be. "Of all the questions in the world you could pick?"

"Absolutely." She pursed her lips together. This was a setup.

"Francis." I cracked a smile and she burst out laughing. "Don't you dare! It's a family name. Mary Kay would be highly offended."

Her whole body shook. Her eyes twinkled when she laughed like that. That reckless feeling I had just the second before vanished and she was absolutely beautiful. It caught me off guard.

"Why are you staring at me like that?" she asked with tears in her eyes. "You're the one with Francis as your middle name."

"Okay, Giggles, my turn. What's the weirdest thing about you? Something people would be surprised to learn."

She bit her lip as she thought. "I have an alarming addiction to sweets, but especially cotton candy. If I'm at a carnival or fair, I can't pass it up."

"That's not weird," I countered.

"But the fact that if I'm at a gas station in the middle of the country and I know the bag that's hanging on the hook for three forty-nine has been sitting there for a year, I'll still buy it, is."

"Eww, really?"

"Definitely. My turn. I'm stealing your question. And your cherry." She reached across me and plucked the cherry out of my glass.

"I love romances. I'd rather stay home on a Saturday night and watch Allie admit she loves Noah just as much as she used to over practically anything."

"I already know this about you," she drew out.

I leaned closer to her and whispered. "But what you don't know is that I currently own thirty-four VHS tapes of romances from the eighties I refuse to throw out."

Her eyes grew wide. Her smile, wider. "No."

"Yes. I'm a total sucker for them."

"You're lying." She squinted her eyes at me. "What's your favorite of all time?"

I leaned in closer. "I think it's my turn."

She laughed again and threw her head back. It was the kind of laugh you felt curl deep in your stomach and snuggle down. She was stunning. And I was feeling very warm. There were fifty people in the bar but all I saw was her. Starting something with my sister's childhood friend who was leaving in less than two weeks was a very bad idea. I did not have time for it. My life was simple and drama free.

Sam was not.

"Why do you hate coming home so much?" I asked.

Her smile fell a fraction. She plastered a fake one over it but I could see the light dim a bit in her eyes and it knocked the air from my chest.

"You know about my mom, obviously." It wasn't a question.

I nodded my head.

"When she calls I never know what I'm going to have to deal

with. And there's so much time to fill with worrying about her when I'm here. In the city I have my job. I work all the time. I can remove myself from her issues more than if I'm physically here. Her emergencies don't seem as catastrophic when I'm three thousand miles away."

"I get that."

"And there are the mean girls from high school that I randomly run into at the gas station. That's always fun."

"I remember a few of those."

"Lexi and I used to make it a game. We'd find other ways to get to class just to avoid them. God, it was awful." She sipped the rest of her vodka tonic and signaled another round to Becky.

"They were just jealous of your boobs."

Bingo. A fountain of liquid sprayed from her mouth across the bar. I got an alarming amount of satisfaction from wiping the sad eyes off her face.

"What?" I laughed, wiping the residual off my face. "They were probably jealous of everything about you. It's not really fair to be this beautiful *and* smart simultaneously."

"Oh my gosh, I can't believe you just said that!"

It felt good to make her laugh. I wanted to do it again.

A wave of red crept up her neck. "Moving on, last question."

I looked over her shoulder as the front door swung open behind her.

I froze.

"Why does your face look like that?" she asked, but her voice sounded far away. Everything sounded muffled and moved in slow motion.

"And that's not my question by the way!" I barely registered her talking as Tom McCormick walked through the wooden door.

Former state championship senior quarterback.

Former town golden boy.

Former best friend.

Current husband to *her*. Vanessa, my ex-fiancée, who happened to walk in right on his heels.

Lucky for me, when the crap hit the fan years ago and all hell broke loose, they moved away almost immediately. Tom got a job in Boston. Vanessa's family moved shortly after to follow, so it's only the rare occasion he decides to come home to visit his side that I have the potential of running into him.

But he's never brought her home with him.

"Did you hear me?" Sam asked again.

"No, sorry. What?" They were greeting someone by the door, slapping backs and shaking hands, with *where have you been*s floating through the air.

"I said, do you want another?"

"No, I'm good, actually. I'm ready to leave if you're cool." The last thing I wanted was to confront them after I'd had more than a few shots. And Sam was quite liquored up at the moment as well. It wasn't a good combination.

"Leave?" she asked. "Where are you going?"

"I mean, we can still hang out if you want to. Maybe we could head to Charley's for a nightcap?"

"Oh yes! I love those little mini forks they give you." She grabbed my arm and hopped off the barstool. "But I have to go to the ladies' room first."

"I'll come with you." The bathrooms were next to the back exit so we could sneak out easily.

I slipped off the barstool just as Becky gave me *the look*. I hadn't had one of those in a while, and that's what I hated most—the stares full of pity where everyone in the room looked at me as the guy who was hoodwinked.

On my way to the restrooms I noticed a few more eyes turning my direction.

I splashed cold water on my face and looked at myself in the mirror. I was a little pale. I didn't even mind seeing Tom and Vanessa so much, although seeing them walk through the front door tilted my reality a degree. What bothered me were the assumptions I was still pining away and distraught over something that happened so long ago.

I wouldn't deny it was a tragic story—my best friend for over eighteen years walking in with the woman who I was supposed to spend the rest of my life with—but people move on. I had.

Looking in the mirror, the conversations came crashing back and played over in my head. *It just happened... We didn't mean to hurt you... We never meant for it to happen like this... Dude, you know I would never betray you like this if she weren't the one...* The excuses went on and on until I was the bad guy standing in the way of soulmates. Because God forbid I be pissed that my best friend swooped in and stole the future mother of my children. That he used every argument or discussion that I told him about as ammunition to get on her good side. Every preference I told him he used to his advantage and swept her off her feet.

Unintentionally, of course.

I took a swig from the sink. I walked out a minute later and leaned up next to the women's restroom door.

"Earth to Austin. Didn't you hear me?" Sam stood in front of me. "You look like you've seen a ghost." She placed the back of her hand on my forehead. Her skin was warm and her breath smelled like cherries.

"Kind of accurate."

"Maybe you should do a shot of Jäger," she whispered as she leaned in and cupped my face. I couldn't help but laugh at how intense she was, like she had just found the cure to cancer. She was more vibrant tonight than I'd ever seen her and it was quite entertaining. Probably had nothing to do with her being four vodka tonics deep.

"No one does shots of Jäger anymore," I whispered back.

"Well, don't look now, but there's a lady friend staring daggers at you at the moment."

"Does she have black hair? Small frame?"

"Affirmative."

"We've been spotted. We really should go. I'll explain later." I grabbed her hand and turned her toward the back door.

"Weirdo stalker?"

"Ex-fiancée." I tried to pull her down the hallway but she pulled back.

"Wait, *that's* Vanessa? I didn't even recognize her." She paused. "She's with Tom McCormick."

"Yep."

She stopped in her tracks and her eyes went wide. "Wasn't that your best friend from high school?"

"The one and only."

I watched the realization dawn over her face, replaced by disbelief and anger. "You're kidding me."

"I wish I was."

"What a piece of crap," she spat out.

"Which one?"

"Both."

"I couldn't agree more," I answered.

"Huh." She glanced back to them, then turned to face me with a wickedly playful smile. She grabbed me by my shirt and pulled me to her with her back against the wall. She snuggled close to me and I felt her head tilt up.

I swallowed. "What are you doing?"

"Making her even more jealous," she whispered into my neck. Her lips felt like a branding iron on my skin. It took everything I had to remain standing up straight instead of melting into a puddle on the floor.

"I don't think she does the jealous thing."

"Oh, trust me. Every girl does the jealous thing."

I cleared my throat. "Trust *me*, she couldn't care less." I braced my hand on the wall behind her head to keep myself from being flush against her.

"The way her eyes are lasering through your back at the moment, I'd beg to differ."

A shiver shot through my body. Were those teeth on my ear? *Good God.*

"What are you doing?"

"You already asked me that."

"Right."

She chuckled softly and I felt it shoot down my legs.

"I'm telling you this isn't going to—"

"Shhhh."

Did she just shush me?

Her lips found their way to mine, brushing just the corner of my mouth. A riot of sensations rocketed through me, a confusing mix of excitement and shock and *God, why is it so hot in here?*

It had been a really long time since I let anyone this physically close to me. I forgot how warm another human body could be, how soft, and how it could perfectly lean into all those places my body was built for.

"Kiss me," she breathed into my mouth.

My anxiety flared. I didn't just go around kissing people to make other people jealous. That isn't the kind of guy I am. My eyes dropped to her lips, and I caught her tongue wetting the corner of her mouth. I didn't want to kiss her to make anyone jealous. I wanted to kiss her because if I didn't, I might break apart into a thousand pieces.

She was sexy. Sexy, and funny, and bossy, and had become such a beautiful pain in my ass.

Apparently, I was taking too long with the conversation in my head because the next thing I knew, her lips were on mine. They were soft and smelled fruity. I stared at her with wide eyes as she pressed her mouth to mine. And I was a statue. Nothing moved—not my lips, not my hands.

I had forgotten how to kiss.

But I couldn't kiss her back. She didn't want to kiss me, she was just doing this to make Vanessa jealous and I couldn't bring myself to play the game. She pulled back, and her eyes dropped to my lips, and her mouth curved up on one side.

Then she bit me.

22

AUSTIN

I'm pretty sure she drew blood. But I can't remember because at that moment everything went white-hot. My body leaned into hers without even thinking. The chatter in the bar disappeared as the heat from her lips radiated through me.

I wasn't still anymore.

My whole body woke up as I slammed her up against the wooden planks of the wall and kissed her. The world melted away. It felt like coming up for air after almost drowning.

My hands grasped her hips and lifted her off her feet, balancing her small frame between me and the wall.

I tilted my head deepening the kiss and moved a hand around the back of her head, loosening the tiny hairs around her neck. I let myself curve and push into her. She was so soft everywhere. A tight shudder rolled through me as teeth pulled on my lip again. I could taste my cherry on her tongue. I'd never look at another cherry and not think of this exact moment ever again.

I pressed my fingers into the skin of her thigh as a small groan escaped her mouth into mine.

I was only vaguely aware of hoots and whistles and a slamming door somewhere in the background. The sound sent a wave through my conscious thoughts and I paused, enough to break the momentum for only a second. I took a deep breath only millimeters from her lips, my fingers still laced through her hair, my forehead pressed to hers.

My eyes stayed glued to her lips, now swollen and a deep berry, as they slid up into a wicked grin.

"Follow me."

"Where are we going?" I asked, not recognizing the husk in my own voice.

"We're making an escape."

She wiggled down, grabbed my hand and we burst out the back door of the bar, which looked out over the old marina. The moon lit up the water in between the boats like mercury and stars littered the sky.

"Well, that was convincing." She cleared her throat. "Clearly you learned a thing or two from your obsession with romance movies. I think it worked."

"What worked?

"She's gone."

Oh, right. *Right.* That's what we were doing.

She leaned against the outside of the bar and closed her eyes. The water slapped the docks and the buzz of voices from inside were the only sounds around us. My heart was still slamming against my chest.

Then we heard it.

"What was that?!" she screamed as she jumped into my arms.

I traced the foreign sound with my eyes to a dock piling, where Mr. Crenshaw was curled up, fast asleep, snoring against the wooden post.

"He really does just sort of pop up everywhere, doesn't he?" she asked.

"Yeah, but stay clear of him. Especially when he's awake."

"Oh, don't worry, I've already been warned," she whispered into my neck.

Heat was radiating from every inch of her legs wrapped around me. She slowly unwound herself as my gaze dropped to her mouth.

Screw this.

I wanted to kiss her again. I hadn't felt this awake in years and wanted more.

I took a deep breath and locked my eyes on hers.

"Hi."

"Hi." She gave me that small smile that had demolished my walls.

I took a deep breath, ready to thrust my hands through her hair again as she turned her head to the side and puked all over the ground.

23

SAMANTHA

I woke up to the smell of bacon. *Am I in heaven?*

I moved my head.

Nope. Definitely not in heaven.

"There's water and Tylenol on my nightstand." Austin's voice seared through a pounding headache.

I opened one eye and looked at him as he stood in the doorway.

"Are you wearing an apron?"

He stood in front of me holding kitchen tongs and wearing a chambray apron with white lace lining the front pocket.

"Wouldn't want to get bacon splatter on my limited edition Guy Harvey, now would I?" He winked and turned around.

Memories of last night flashed through my head and I flushed. I bit him. *Oh my God, did I seriously bite him?* What was wrong with me?

Four vodka tonics and three shots was what was wrong with me. I can't even remember what happened after that. I sat up and looked around. I was in a king-sized bed that felt like a cloud. A few pictures hung on the wall—one of Austin and his dad on a charter boat with a huge fish and one of the whole Marcs family out on a dock.

I was in his room.

I looked down at the huge tarpon screen-printed across the shirt I was wearing. *Oh my God, he changed my shirt! Did we have sex? Oh God. Oh God. Oh God.* I didn't randomly sleep with strangers after a few too many beverages.

Well, he wasn't a total stranger.

"You going to throw up?"

"What?" I didn't realize he was still standing at the door again.

"You look a little queasy. Are you going to get sick again? There's a trash can on the other side of the bed."

"Again?" Shock rang through my body. "I threw up last night?"

"You vomited quite aggressively."

My body broke out in chills. "Ew, don't say that word."

"What word? *Vomit?*" His eyes danced as he leaned casually against the doorframe.

"Stop. Seriously. You're going to make me puke."

"I'm not sure you have anything left to offer."

I buried my head in the pillow but popped up as a thought crossed my mind. "Oh no, too fast— Wait, so if I was incapacitated all night, did we… Don't laugh at me, I'm serious!"

"Puking drunk girl who can't hold herself up really isn't my style."

I swallowed cotton and whispered. "I was that bad?"

He nodded.

"Don't ever let me do that again."

"There are clothes on the chair that'll probably fit. Take your Tylenol. Come out when you're ready."

"Yes, sir, Captain." I gave him a salute, one that immediately made my head spin.

"And no quick movements," he added.

I gave him a thumbs-up as I turned over and buried my face in the pillow. The covers were wrapped around my legs and the heat was stifling. I slowly kicked at them, sighing at the feeling of cool air rushing to my legs. I opened my eyes to Austin's flushed face, his gaze fixed on my lower half. My fire engine–red lace thong practically screamed a bright and cheery *good morning* against his white sheets.

"I'm going to go flip the bacon," he muttered, his ears turning crimson as he bolted from the door.

The clothes on the chair weren't his, unless he was into dressing like a woman three sizes smaller than him. Vanessa flashed through my mind. Would he give me clothes his ex-fiancée wore? And even weirder, would he seriously keep them this whole time?

No, thank you.

I pulled a pair of way-too-big gym shorts out of his dresser and used the bathroom. After splashing my face with cold water a few times I felt more awake, but still seemed a little green around the gills.

I walked into the kitchen and he looked me up and down.

"They didn't fit." I had a little more attitude than necessary. He smirked as he handed me a mug of steaming coffee.

I slowly gazed around his house. It was clean and tidy but simple, with a dark gray couch in the middle of the living room and a small entryway table. "What's that?" I asked, peering over to the table where a little plate held his keys.

"It's a key dish."

"A key *what?*" I asked, chuckling.

"A key dish. You put your keys on it."

"Why don't you just put your keys on the table *underneath* the key dish?"

"But then what would I do with my key dish?" I couldn't tell if he was trying to be funny or if he was serious.

I inhaled the coffee. It may have been the best smelling coffee I'd ever had in my hands.

"So," he continued, as I perched on a barstool, "what was up with last night?"

"What part of last night?" I asked, trying to play it cool as I busied my mouth blowing on my coffee.

"The mission to get wasted and forget your day." He put four pieces of toast into the toaster.

I could still hear Ivy's words rattling around in my head, even though it was all a little foggy. "Do you remember that guy I was telling you about? My work nemesis who sounds like a certain breed of canine when he laughs?"

"Your Pugentine?" He gave me the side-eye.

"Nope, still not my boyfriend. But my assistant, Ivy, called yesterday and told me he was put on the highest profile project our firm has ever had—the one that I was managing before I came down here. I would have been put in charge of it, *should* have been put in charge of it, but wasn't. Because I'm here."

He grabbed a plate down from the cabinet.

"We're both gunning for this big promotion. The fact my boss gave this other project to Robby is pretty much a flare gun with the news that Robby's getting it over me."

"Have they announced he got it yet?" He caught a slice directly from the toaster as it popped up.

Well, that was surprisingly hot.

"Not yet." I watched as he spread butter over the entire piece. "You're being very intentional with your buttering skills. Most people just put a blob in the middle and call it a day."

"I'm not most people." He poured himself more coffee and leaned against the counter. "I'm sorry."

"You're not going to try and convince me I'm crazy for reading into it?" He shook his head. "It gets better...He'll be here at five o'clock."

"Here, like in Florida?"

"Yep. Apparently while my mother's little bikini incident garnered quite a few laughs, it also demonstrated I may have some other priorities while I'm here that may be distracting me from my job."

"So your boss is sending him down here to chaperone you?" he asked. "I'm all about looking for the silver lining but that seems pretty crappy."

"I don't know whether to dump my coffee on your head or thank you for your honesty."

"I get that a lot." He slid a plate of toast and bacon in front of me and filled up my coffee again. "Hangover cure. Half a pound of bacon, buttery toast, and black coffee. Eat."

He sat next to me, coffee full and plateless.

"You're not going to eat?"

"I don't do breakfast."

"But it's the most important meal of the day."

"Doesn't do it for me."

He turned his coffee cup a quarter around every few seconds. He waited until my plate was half empty before he spoke again. "So, if it is true, about Pug Nugget and the promotion, what's next?"

"You mean besides drinking myself into oblivion for the next couple weeks out of misery? I stay here for another week or so, finish out the due diligence on the island and head back to New York. Probably jump on board his Oakstone Springs team, plaster a big ol' smile on my face and pretend like I won't pull the majority of the weight for him when I know I will. Again."

"And what if it's not true? What if the promotion is still up for grabs?"

I stuffed a piece of bacon in my mouth. Heaven in food form. I wasn't used to this many thought-provoking questions at once. His voice sounded whiskey soaked and raspy in the morning. It was distracting. And he was hardcore staring at me.

"I'll still stay here for another two weeks regardless I guess, then head back to New York, and…" I paused. I didn't know the right words to finish the sentence. What *would* happen? Keep working my ass off to hopefully get the promotion? There wasn't a specific timeline necessarily, but the general assumption was that by the end of the month, an announcement would be made.

"And keep busting your ass for a chance at this promotion."

I took a long sip of my coffee. "I guess so."

The thought felt strange for the first time. It felt less important all of a sudden. I spent the last handful of years grinding my life away to climb the corporate ladder and I didn't see it changing anytime soon.

He was staring at me, trying to read something on my face.

"What?"

"It just doesn't seem like you're all that excited about going back and working yourself down to the bone. And either way, it looks like that's what you're going to do, promotion or not." Work was the last thing I wanted to talk about. My head still hurt and I wanted more bacon.

"You're being way too intense to be wearing that apron." His eyes were so green in the morning. "So, about last night…"

"Sam?" My head whipped around way too fast at a female's voice. Lexi padded in the front door, well, more like skipped in, to the kitchen and side-hugged me really hard.

"Careful, she might puke on you."

My head spun. "What are you doing here?"

"Mom and Dad are at one of her little flower show thingies and staying in the house alone all day freaks me out."

"She thinks sea monsters are going to crawl up out of the ocean and kidnap her," Austin teased.

"You're still afraid of that?" I asked.

"That nightmare I had when I was six changed my life." She made her way to the coffeepot and poured herself a mug. "I keep a bunch of stuff here just in case they decide to bail on me last minute for a hydrangea trade show."

Ah. The clothes. I saw Austin smirk out of the corner of my eye.

"What do you have planned for today?" She looked at her brother's clothes hanging off me and pursed her lips.

"Looking for a place to move to for the weekend, actually."

"What's wrong with the Starfish?" Austin had somehow refilled my coffee without me noticing. "I thought Josie had you down for the whole month."

"She did, but the rest of the rooms are sold out for the weekend for the showcase, as well as every other hotel on the island. With Robby coming down today, the assumption is that he would crash with me."

"You're kidding." Austin sounded kind of pissed. "Isn't that against some HR code or something?"

"Not when you work for Glenn. And I'm sure Pugster did everything in his power to convince our boss it'd be no big deal." I could see it now, Robby telling Glenn he'd *make it work* for the sake of the company.

"Who's Pugster?" Lexi asked.

"Her coworker who sounds like a pug when he laughs," Austin chimed in.

"He kind of looks like a more attractive, younger, less creepy brother version of Perez Hilton," I added.

"Who's that?" Austin asked.

"Pop culture is not his forte. Don't hold it against him. He doesn't even know who J.Lo's married to this year."

"Yeah, I do," he argued. "One of her dancers."

"See?" Lexi chuckled. "So, assuming your mom's place is out?"

"Considering our fight yesterday morning, and well, the last twenty-six years of my life, not an option." I rested my head on the cool granite of the kitchen countertop. My mind replayed the argument again. That, along with the tequila shots I'm pretty sure we had last night, made my head spin.

"And he's getting here today?" Lexi asked.

I nodded. An awkward silence filled the space. "For the record," I blurted out, "we didn't sleep together." Lexi coughed into her coffee mug. "I just had too much to drink and Austin let me crash here."

"Okay." She gave me a small smile once her coughing fit passed.

"Why don't you just stay here?" Austin said.

A spoon hit the counter. I peeked my eyes up just in time to catch Lexi's deer-in-headlights look at Austin.

"What? I have a spare bedroom. And didn't you say it was only for a couple nights?"

"Just the rest of the weekend," I confirmed.

"Okay. And it's not like I'm here much anyway."

"Yeah, he'll be gone... working," Lexi repeated, clearly not loving the idea. "Hey, maybe she can pick out some throw pillows too, while she's here. It's all gray and manly and mopey in here."

"It is not gray and mopey." Austin nodded to me for some confirmation.

I looked around. "It'd be super cozy for Eeyore."

He pulled my empty bread plate across the counter. "That's the last time I butter your toast like that."

Lexi's eyes went wide. This was clearly too much for her to handle. "I'm going to go for a run. I'm assuming you don't want to join me?" she asked me as she filled her water bottle. "I'll let you two get back to your morning chatter."

I watched her flutter out the door. "She just poured coffee into her water bottle."

"Yep," he nodded.

"She definitely thinks we slept together."

"Definitely."

I looked at him and we burst out laughing.

24

AUSTIN

She didn't remember a single thing from last night after we left the bar. I wasn't going to tell her I carried her all the way home—or that she caught a second wind the moment she stepped into my kitchen and raided my pantry of every carb I had. Or that as much as I wanted to climb into bed with her, I slept on the couch but got up every hour just to make sure she was still there, sleeping soundly wrapped up in my sheets.

It was Saturday. It was one of the busiest days for the boat, but I didn't want her to leave just yet. I texted Patrick and asked if he could handle the runs across the water for half the day with our normal crew. It was a well-oiled machine, and he'd been asking to give his cousin a shot at helping run the boat. I figured today was as good as any. Once I confirmed I was *not* in the hospital and that I, in fact, had *not* lost my mind, he enthusiastically agreed.

"I want to take you somewhere," I told her after she was finished with breakfast.

"I don't think I'm in the best shape to be going anywhere." She put her forehead on the counter again, but was starting to get a little color back.

"Trust me. The fresh air will be good for you."

"Fresh air sounds miserable. And I don't have the right shoes."

"I'm going to run you by the bungalow to get some clothes on the way."

She looked up at me. Her ponytail had started to shift over to the side of her head and pieces were loose around her face. Her mascara had run a bit under her eyes. She looked perfect. "Do I have a choice?"

"You don't." I lifted her off the stool.

After a bit of a touch-and-go boat ride, we pulled up onto Birchwood Beach. She looked around completely mesmerized, like I knew she would.

"I've never seen anything like this in my entire life. How did I not know this was here?"

"It's still a bit of an unknown treasure. And it only shows up at low tide," I answered.

I watched her walk down the beach and up to one of the mammoth driftwood branches that towered above her head. The trunk was on its side and still stood taller than her. She ran her hand down the length of the old gnarly wood, tracing the cracks and breaks along the trunk. Warped branches jetted out like they were desperately trying to reach something but time froze them in their effort.

"If you come during high tide, the water covers all of the branches completely so you'd never know they were here."

"So you could boat over all this and never know these were underwater, just sitting there?" she asked.

"Yep. There are a few tiny branches that stick up, but not enough that would make you look twice. Most are below the surface."

"They're so sad looking. But they're beautiful."

There wasn't a soul in sight. The only sound was the waves rolling onto the beach. The trunks and stumps littered the shore. You couldn't walk more than ten feet without running into a skeleton of one that rivaled the size of the last.

"I feel like I'm walking through a graveyard." Her words came out small and hushed.

"This whole beach used to be a forest that protected the island, but with time, the water and storms eroded the whole thing, leaving all these driftwood husks behind."

"How far do they go?"

"They line the shore for about a mile down the beach."

She climbed up one that dwarfed her small frame and sat on top. "Can you take a picture of me?"

Something unfamiliar bloomed in my chest as she smiled at me, hanging off the branch like a kid.

I took out my phone to take a picture and saw a text from Lexi. She said to call her when I had a sec. It was about Sam. I'm sure she wanted a complete download on the morning shenanigans, which she wasn't going to get just yet.

"I can't stay up here all day you know!"

"Hold your horses." I snapped the picture and she jumped down. I led her to an open patch in the middle of the beach forest. She was going to start getting queasy if she didn't keep her stomach full. I laid out a blanket I brought and pulled out cheddar and apple grilled cheese sandwiches from the Corner Shop.

"Did you steal this from one of your movies?" she asked.

"No, but it would make a pretty iconic scene in one, don't you think?"

"What's your favorite?" she asked.

"Movie or scene?"

"Couple."

"Yikes, that's a hard one. Allie and Noah are the clear front-runner, but second is rough. Probably Meg and Tom in *Sleepless*."

She laughed so hard she started choking. I handed her a water bottle.

"You really are serious, aren't you?" she asked.

"Dead."

"I always thought your parents stepped out of an old-fashioned romance. When Lexi and I were in high school and your mom would cook dinner, your dad would walk in and wrap his arms around her as she stood in front of the stove." She looked down at her hands and shook her head. "I have no idea why I remember that so vividly."

"They were very much in love. They still are." I opened her bag of chips and handed them to her. I wanted to ask about her parents, but I wasn't sure if she felt comfortable talking about them. I didn't know them when we were younger. I saw Sam's mom around town now more than I did back in high school and I couldn't really place her dad. But I wanted to know more about her. "Were your parents ever like that?"

"My dad was this happy bubble that walked around making other people shine brighter because of him. My mom was not," she said with a laugh. "But when he was with her, he turned a spotlight on her and she came alive." She shook her head. "You okay after last night? Seeing Vanessa?"

I nodded.

"Do you mind if I ask what happened?"

She was probably the only one left on the face of the earth who didn't know what happened. "She fell out of love with me, I guess. There were signs I should've seen that I didn't. We worked for the most part. We'd been together so long."

"You were homecoming king and queen."

"We were." I remembered how completely ridiculous I felt walking around the football stadium with her. She lived for that kind of thing—the attention, the buzz of it all. I didn't. "For the most part it was great. Really great, I thought. But looking back now, the big stuff didn't fit and we just kept ignoring it. She wasn't sure she wanted kids but I definitely did. She never saw herself living on the island her whole life. I couldn't ever see myself leaving."

"Never?" she asked.

"I'm not the type that leaves the island."

She nodded, and traced little divots in the sand at the end of the blanket. "When did you notice something was going on between the two of them?"

"That's the funny thing, I didn't for a long time."

I told her about how it was our second year in business with the ferry and we were still doing overnight trips to the mainland. Things were really busy. We were spread pretty thin. One day I was supposed to be out on a run for the night and it got canceled last minute—some engine malfunction we couldn't fix until the morning. Tom kept ragging me that I wasn't spending enough time with my best friend, always with her instead when I wasn't out on the water. So, I drove by his house to see if he wanted to catch up. I felt guilty and wanted to make it up to him. I saw her car in his driveway. I went up to the door to walk in but the curtain was barely open and I saw the two of them on the couch together.

"He was your best friend?" she asked.

"Since elementary school."

"I'm so sorry." Her eyebrows pulled together.

"I have no idea why but I walked right in." It was so unlike me to confront them like that. I don't know what came over me. I didn't knock or anything. I wanted them to know I saw them. That they got caught. I didn't want any explanations for what I saw—no justifying or denying.

"He tried like hell to explain things but as far as I was concerned I didn't need to hear a sob story about how he'd messed up and he was sorry, but he loved her and they were soulmates."

"I don't believe in soulmates. The idea just seems completely preposterous to me."

"Why do you say that?"

"The idea there are millions of people in this world, and somehow there's one specific person who perfectly fits with you, seems mathematically unrealistic. And if you're lucky, but only *really* lucky, and happen to be in the same town and place, oh and also even the right decade at the same time as they are, you find them. It just seems a bit far-fetched. Like a cruel joke the universe is playing."

"Well, when you put it that way…" I wasn't surprised at her lack of faith in the whole concept.

"Wait, you believe in the idea of soulmates?" she asked. "Even after what happened with Vanessa?"

"I guess I still have hope that maybe she just wasn't the right one and I thought she was." I'd seen examples of it in my lifetime through my grandparents and my parents. It was possible, even though it took me a while to circle back to that thinking.

"So what happened then? After you caught them?"

After it all went down, I remembered when people would ask me questions and I'd clam up. I'd get angry. I'd shut down. But talking to Sam felt different. She made it easy for me to open up.

"He got a job in Boston and they left."

"And last night was the first time you've seen her since?" she asked.

"Not exactly." She was staring at me obviously waiting for me to continue, but I was done wasting time talking about the disasters of my love life. I wanted to know more about her, like why her last relationship didn't work. "What about you? Any tragic love stories to affirm your hopeless outlook on love?"

"Ha! Plenty. My last boyfriend lasted six months, and I don't think he even knew my favorite color."

"Isn't that kind of a basic fact?"

"Exactly. And it's green, in case you were wondering. But more of a dark green, like a forest green. Now you officially know more about me than he did." She paused. I could tell she was considering whether to continue or not. "And, I think he may have had a few dalliances behind my back."

"Dalliances?"

"*Fancy* for he was an asshole. Apparently *exclusive* doesn't mean the same thing it used to."

"I don't think it *used* to mean much anyway, for what it's worth."

She smiled. "Speaking of, the look on her face last night was priceless."

"Oh, so you *do* remember something from last night?"

She blushed.

"Ugh, I can't believe I puked everywhere." She cradled her head in her hands, laughing.

"It's okay you vomited. Vomit doesn't bother me. Whether it's vomit on the street, vomit on the driveway…"

"Ew! Stop it with that word!" she laughed.

"Vomit on my sheets…"

"Oh my gosh, I did *not* puke on your sheets, did I?" she asked horrified.

"Not a lot," I answered. Making people laugh was not something

I did. I wasn't considered a funny guy, but every time I made her laugh, I felt this primal need to do it more. This beautiful sound sparkled when it reached her eyes. It made her whole face light up.

"I can't imagine staying in the same hotel as Robby, let alone the same room. It'd be worthy of a twenty page HR report. But I promise, you won't even know I'm there."

I highly doubted that. My phone dinged again.

LEXI: SOS for Sam. It's about her mom.

"Hey, have you heard from your mom?" I asked.

"No, why?" Her eyebrows creased at the quick change of topic.

"Lexi just texted me. She said to call her when you have a sec. It's about Bonnie."

She fished out her phone, looked at the screen, and a darkness swept across her face. She stood up and started to walk away.

25

SAMANTHA

Seven years later, I can still tell how far away someone is by the squeak their shoes make across the linoleum floor.

Seven years later, and my heart still pounds when the machines beep faster.

Seven years later, and the hospital still smells exactly the same.

Seven years later, but this time I was waiting to see if she was going to make it through instead of her praying that I would.

The waiting was always the hardest part. The clock on the wall ticked louder. The crinkle of the cough drop wrapper from the receptionist sounded like she was duct-taping it to the inner wall of my ear. Every time a page turned from the 2004 magazine someone was pretending to read, it felt like a jagged saw against the side of my neck.

And her heartbeat could stop at any second.

Any second.

"I'm serious. You really don't have to stay." It was the fourth time I'd told him. The plastic of the waiting room chair kept sticking to my thigh. Austin had driven us to the hospital straight from the beach. For once I was having a really nice time until Lexi texted me that Mom had been admitted to the hospital. She didn't have many details, but said I needed to head there as soon as I could.

"Patrick's got the boat. I'm good."

"You forget this isn't new to me." I gave him my best fake smile but I don't think he bought it. "I'm fine. Really."

My phone dinged.

> **ROBBY:** AIRBORNE IN 5!
> DID YOU BUY A MOSQUITO NET
> FOR OUR BED YET?

Fabulous. Another headache to layer onto the mounting disaster the day was quickly turning into. I really wasn't in the mood for exclamation points.

Austin stood up slowly but didn't turn to go. "She's been doing really well lately. Don't be too hard on her."

"Remind me again of your definition of *well*," I snapped, wondering if he'd already forgotten that he carried her limp body to her bed the other night.

"We all make mistakes sometimes."

"Like mother, like daughter, right?" The irony hit me—hungover and sitting outside my alcoholic mother's hospital room.

Austin's jaw tightened. "You are nothing like your mother."

"Because you know me so well, right? You have absolutely no idea what you're talking about."

He took a breath, steadying himself. "I'm just trying to help."

"And like I said before, I don't need your help."

He recoiled a bit, then nodded, backing away. "Understood. Call me if you change your mind."

The familiar scenario was playing itself out. My mother brought out this anger in me every time this happened. *She's* the one who deserved the arrows, but somehow, someone else took the brunt of it.

I sighed and tried to soften my tone.

"It's going to be a long time. Really." I ran a hand through my hair. "I'm just not used to all *this* again. I'm going to stay until she sleeps it off and take her home. I'll be fine. And nice. I promise."

He nodded but hesitated for a second. Part of me wanted him to stay so I wouldn't face this alone, but a bigger part of me didn't want a single witness for what was to come.

He finally gave me a small smile with a hint of pity, just like everyone else always gave, then walked out.

I was so tired of people doing things out of obligation or guilt for my mom. It was bad enough that he took care of me last night. I felt like a complete idiot and wanted him as far away from me as possible at that moment. I never had a problem with alcohol before, and here I was, sitting in a hospital completely hungover with my mother checked into the ER because she was found passed out. Great look for both of us.

This is what I'd been missing at home. Endless calls of "we found your mother." Town gossip about who she was slobbering over at Harpoon's, or who she stumbled home with.

I needed to get out of here. The promotion was gone. Robby was on his way. Maybe I'd just quit, or look for a new job. Or maybe some other monster project would sign on once wind of the Oakstone Springs project went public and I'd get that one. I just knew I needed to get the heck out of Dodge.

A nurse walked up to me and handed me two Tylenol and a cup of water. "Here you go."

"Oh, I'm not a patient here. I'm just waiting for my mom."

"Doctor got pulled into an emergency real quick, but said to let you know she's up and doing alright. You can go on in and see her. He'll be back around to talk to you soon."

I let out a shaky breath but didn't move.

She paused, then slowly eased herself down into the chair beside me with a soft sigh. "This old back gets more and more bent over the more weight it's got to carry." Her voice was smooth and steady. She glanced over at me, her smile warm and familiar, as if she'd known me my whole life. The faint scent of baby powder lingered around her, and the crinkles etched across her face—evidence of a lifetime of joy or pain—deepened when she smiled. She held out the Tylenol again. "Austin said you might need this."

"Oh, um, okay. Thank you."

"Patrick's my son." She patted my knee as she leaned her head back on the wall and closed her eyes. Her name tag—MABEL—pulled against her snug cotton scrubs.

"Oh, I see," I said, the realization of where the familiar smile came from finally dawning on me. "Gotta love small towns."

"It had just been me and my boy our whole lives, then this little boy with shaggy blond hair comes home one day with Patrick like a lost puppy. He says to me, 'His name's Austin, can we keep him?' Haven't been able to separate them since."

I smiled, thinking of Austin as a kid. I knew that shaggy mop of hair she was talking about.

"So I heard Patrick changed his name?"

"Oh Lord, don't get me started, catering to those tourists with that silly accent. He's a closet comedian, that one, always thinking he can make a buck with his jokes and his acting skills."

"He is pretty funny."

"He is, isn't he? But don't you go and tell him that. You'll just encourage it. But he's a hard worker too, even if he drives me crazy." She looked at me again, and I noticed her smile didn't have a single trace of pity in it. "She's up if you want to see her."

I looked toward the door and exhaled slowly.

"Family ain't who you choose," she continued. "They're who God gave you to love. There's a big difference."

"Well, I have no idea what I did to deserve this, then."

"She lucked out getting you as a daughter. Lots of people don't have someone who'd sit outside their hospital room after so long."

"I haven't been here in a long time." Even though it felt like only yesterday I was in these halls.

"Doesn't matter. You're here now."

"Does it count even when I don't want to be?" I asked, guilt gripping my throat.

"That's when it counts the most," she said, easing herself up. "Take that Tylenol and stop by the desk and see me on your way out." She shuffled down the hall as I stood up.

The smell of cleaner stung my nose as I walked into the small room. The curtain was drawn back, letting far too much light in, and she was lying back on the bed with her hands clasped in her lap.

She waited until I closed the door to speak.

"I know you're angry." Her voice carried that familiar grit from the friction of a tube being shoved down her throat. The bed swallowed her tiny frame. "I was doing so good."

"Yeah, until a guest called 911 because they thought you were dead after finding you topless on the dock barely breathing."

"Don't exaggerate."

"I'm being factual."

"I messed up."

"I'm aware of that." I braced myself for what would come. The litany of justifications, all the reasons why it wasn't her fault she lost control and she'd never do it again. All words that had been so familiar for so long played through my head. But being so far removed from it softened my calluses toward the excuses. My anger bubbled under the surface. I didn't have as much of a wall as I normally did.

My patience had already run out and I was only thirty seconds into the conversation.

"It's been a really long time since something this bad has happened."

I held my tongue. The less words I spoke the better.

"I really thought I had a handle on it. And I have been good, I swear. But after I found that article laying right out on your desk like you—"

"Are you really going to blame this on me?"

"I just needed to get my mind off it, that's all. I'm not blaming you. But a couple of the younger girls went out after work and I thought I could go and just hang out. It was so nice to be invited and I needed a distraction." The blame sat there heavy in the room, whether she pointed it at me or not. "You should see what they're wearing out these days. Nothing is left to the imagination anymore. They look ridiculous, and that's what I told them too. When they came back with pink shots, I didn't think it'd hurt since I was the grown-up."

"What exactly is your definition of a grown-up?"

She took a breath. "It was just a little vodka and tons of pink lemonade. It wasn't anything hard and I thought I could handle it."

"Right, because a shot's totally doable for an alcoholic," I spat.

"Don't mock me."

"I don't understand how you think because you're sober for a minute, you all of a sudden don't have to play by the rules anymore. You don't get to drink. Period."

"I realize that, Samantha." She picked at a nonexistent thread on the bedsheet. "You look awful by the way."

"This isn't about me."

"Were you drinking last night?"

"Oh, this is golden, you asking me if I was drinking."

"You're prone to alcoholism. It's genetic. You need to get help."

"Are you *kidding* me? *I* need help?"

"No, I am not kidding. This is not something to joke around about."

I stared at her. She was absolutely out of her mind. "That's it. I'm leaving. I can't believe you would have the audacity to lay there in a bed, hooked up to fluids after having your stomach pumped, and tell me *I'm* the one who needs help." My blood was boiling, hot and unforgiving. This was it. The last time I'd put myself in this position. The last time I'd sit outside a heavy hospital door, waiting. The last time I'd let her twist my emotions and wish it could be different. "I didn't come back here to take care of you. I came back for a *job*—one that is over in less than two weeks. And after that, I'm going home. You can go back to calling whoever it is you call when you wake up on docks, in alleys, or wherever else you end up when I'm not around."

I turned to the door and heard her small voice behind me.

"I'm ready to go somewhere and get help."

I froze. I turned slowly, half expecting her to be joking. Those words—words I had begged to hear for years—had never come out of her before. Not once. No matter how much I urged, pleaded, or fought with her, she would never even consider it.

"No, you're not." My voice was thick with disbelief and hope at odds.

"Yes, I am, Samantha." She sat up a little straighter against her pillows, eyes locked on mine. "I know why you don't come back home. Believe it or not, your mother is actually quite intelligent, though I don't display it quite as often in certain situations."

I didn't move. I stood there staring at her, hating myself for the little glimmer of hope I thought I'd buried long ago that simmered underneath the weight of so many years of anger.

"I'm serious. I want to go somewhere and get clean. For good."

I crossed my arms, my defenses fighting their way back to the surface. "You're just saying this so I don't walk out right now."

"No. But I understand why you'd think that."

We'd been here so many times. Well, not *here*, because she was admitting she needed help which she had never done. But we'd been to this point where my heart beat a little faster, and I felt a tiny seedling of hope trying so hard to poke through the surface of so much *shit*. This little sprout was timid and scared that it'd be stomped on again, but it was there, barely breathing.

"I'm leaving in two weeks." The words came out sharper than I intended. "Regardless of what you do."

Her eyes flickered with something. Regret, maybe. "I wouldn't expect anything different."

"You realize you'd have to leave straight from here once you've detoxed."

"I know." Her voice wavered, betraying the conviction she'd started with.

I let the air sit between us for a moment, my mind racing. After all this time, all these years. I wanted to scream, but instead I asked quietly, "Why now?"

"Do you remember the year I put you in dance lessons?"

I had a hard time hiding my annoyance at her sudden change of subject. "Vaguely."

"You were maybe six or seven, and you practiced that recital dance a hundred times. But you walked out, smack-dab in the middle of the stage, and looked like you had just seen a ghost. You looked out and saw all these people staring at you, just waiting for you to perform, and your face drained of all color. Your dad was there. Do you remember that?"

"I do." A tightness rose in my chest at his memory.

"You just stood there while everyone else was dancing. You completely forgot the routine. But after about ten seconds, you lifted your chin up and started dancing. You made up an entirely new routine and did your own thing all over that stage, weaving in and out of all the other girls."

I rolled my eyes at the memory. While I didn't remember the actual recital, most likely subconsciously blocking it out of my memory, I had seen enough pictures and heard enough stories to validate the ridiculousness of it.

"When I asked you what happened, you looked at me and said, *Well, I couldn't just stand there. I had to do something.* And we all burst out laughing." She wiped her eyes once her laughing subsided and looked at me dead-on. "I can't just stand here. I have to do something."

Tears welled up in my eyes. I was just so tired. Tired of running around trying to prove to everyone that I had it all together when I was so scared that I was just like her, barely keeping my head above water and hoodwinking the entire world. I had clean countertops and not a single dirty dish in my sink. My fate sat staring at me in the face, someone who pretended to have it all worked out who was finally saying maybe it wasn't all working out the way she pretended it was.

But she was going to try. And she was willing to do something different this time.

And that was something.

"Okay."

"I'm going to get some rest. You get out of here. Go back to the hotel and take a nap. You look horrible."

"Right."

"I'll have them call you when it's time to leave."

"What about where you'll go? All the details? What do you need from the house? I can grab it for you." I wiped my cheeks with my shirt.

"Don't do that, you'll stretch out the neck." She smoothed out the nonexistent wrinkles on her bedsheets. "I'll figure out the details. I'll take care of it for once. Sound like a plan?"

I nodded. There was this part of me that desperately wanted to walk over to her bedside where she looked so frail, grab her hand, and crawl up next to her in her hospital bed. But there was a bigger part of me that didn't.

"I can't promise you this is going to fix everything. But I can promise you I'm going to try as hard as I possibly can to make you proud of me."

My throat felt like a fly trap for words, so I just nodded and gave her a small smile, opened the door, and walked out.

I walked to the nurses' station where Patrick's mom was sitting at a computer, typing away. She handed me a brochure.

"It's in Boca Raton." Her smile was warm and proud. "One of the best. They've got someone driving up to get her. She'll be on her way by this evening."

It was a brochure for Willow Rehabilitation Center in Florida.

"She's going to Boca?" I asked.

"She didn't tell you?"

"She didn't." I looked down at the brochure. There was a picture of two ladies playing tennis and laughing on the front. She hated exercise.

"They surprise us sometimes, don't they, these people the universe shoves in our path and won't let us shake?"

Tears spilled down my face.

"Speaking of, Austin hasn't called out of work in years. You must've done something to him to get him to hand over that boat to my boy for the morning." She leaned closer. "It's about damn time."

26

AUSTIN

I'd be lying if I said the sting from our earlier conversation at the hospital had faded. I understood her relationship with her mom was complicated, but what lingered most was the fact that Sam was staying with me.

She'd be sleeping in a room. In my house.
Tonight.
Only a few feet away from mine, which was perfectly fine.
Totally fine.
I'd probably forget she was even there.

ME: How's your mom?

SAM: OK. I'll fill you in tonight.
I'm sorry.
For earlier.

ME: I don't know what you're talking about. ☺
Pugalicious there yet?

SAM: Ugh. On his way from airport.

ME: Be ready with your bags in 5. I'm coming to scoop you.

SAM: Knight in shining armor to the rescue again?

ME: We're going to watch the Mariners' showcase with Lexi.

SAM: As in, football?

ME: Yes ma'am.

SAM: Oh bummer.
I promised the paint I'd watch it dry tonight.
Rain check?

"I thought you were kidding." She answered the door of her bungalow wearing a sweatshirt with LET'S ASSUME I'M RIGHT plastered across the front that hung to her knees without any makeup on and her hair piled on top of her head. This girl was chipping away at my resolve every moment I saw her without even trying.

"I can't believe you still own that."

I looked down at my MARINERS CLASS OF '12 shirt. "Of course I do. What else would I wear to a football game? You, on the other hand, might want to change. Where's your luggage?"

"Right in here. Are you sure you're okay with this?"

"Yep." *Nope.*

Maybe I'd stay at Patrick's. I couldn't stop picturing my sheets wrapped around her legs. I had no idea how I was going to keep my mind functioning for two whole days.

"I figured you could just drop me off at your place on your way to the game. I'm going to leave the rental for Robby."

"We're meeting Lexi there." I hoisted her bags down the front step. What in the hell did she have in these things? Kettlebells?

"No, it's cool. Really. I'm not the sports type."

"You're not really the beach type either, or the fishing type, but they're on your list for work, right?"

She folded her arms across her chest and leaned against the doorframe. "I'm pretty sure Robby selfishly snuck the showcase on the due diligence list thinking he'd be the one to go. I'm not sure it's vital to the success of a new resort property to watch a bunch of teenagers run around tackling each other."

"Is your boss expecting you to check off everything that's on PugMasterFlex's list?"

She glared at me.

"How long do you need? Just curious. I left the car running." I pointed behind me. I loved getting a rise out of her.

"Can we go next week?" she whined.

"There's only one showcase. It's now or never." A fact that I was more than grateful for. I loved supporting the home team, but more often than not, whenever I was at the field, I'd get cornered into a conversation about when I was going to stop playing around with the ferry business, get my head back into the game, and take over this team like I was always meant to do.

She stood there and sighed.

"You're pouting."

"No. I'm slowly accepting my fate for the evening." She exhaled again even louder and turned around back into her bungalow. "I'll grab a paper bag," she shouted over her shoulder.

"For what?"

"To put over my face when I see everyone I went to high school with."

"Let's gooooooooo, Mariners!" Sam screamed at the top of her lungs. I looked over at Lexi. "Was she always so enthusiastic at our high school football games?"

"Definitely not," she whispered behind Sam's back.

"That call is bull, ump!" Sam shouted.

I leaned over but kept my voice down. "They're called referees." She glared at me. "I'm just saying, generally speaking, people refer to them as referees."

"Well, maybe I'd call them referees if they could DO THEIR JOB RIGHT!"

Lexi busted out laughing.

Sam sat back down all flustered and stuffed a huge piece of cotton candy in her mouth and sighed. Then she glared at me again. "This is awful."

"Looks to me like you're enjoying yourself."

"But it isn't as awful as I remember it being seven years ago."

"Maybe you just enjoy watching sweaty eighteen-year-olds tackle each other more when you don't have to sit next to them in chem class."

"Definitely not the case." She stuffed another enormous piece of spun sugar into her mouth. "And this may be the best cotton candy I've ever had."

After the showcase portion of the night, the players rolled right into a heated scrimmage. After the fourth quarter buzzer sounded, Rex's team rushed the field, clinching the win that counted for absolutely nothing. But regardless, in typical victory fashion, the quarterback and a few of the offensive linemen surprised Rex and dumped a large cooler of Cool Blue Gatorade over his head.

Once the chaos on the field calmed down, the team filed into the locker room and the stands emptied. Usually I didn't hang around after, dodging questions of when I was going to return and claim my birthright. But I told Lexi we'd meet them at Harpoon's in just a little. First, I wanted to show Sam something.

Once the stadium was clear, I hopped the fence and walked out across to the field.

"Wait, aren't we going to get arrested or something for being out here? We're not even players."

"For walking across a high school football field? I'd hope our boys in blue have better things to do than chase down riffraff that's scouring the football sign."

"We're going to scour the football sign?" The excitement in her voice plastered a goofy smile across my face I was thankful she couldn't see. As far as I knew, we were the only high school in the state where half the stadium backed up to a body of water. Made it rough for seating, but we had the best views by far.

"You sound excited."

"I've always wanted to do that!"

"Well, tonight is your lucky night. I want to show you something and the view's better up there."

She followed me across the freshly trampled grass. The main stadium lights flicked off just as we reached center field, leaving only the floodlights casting a glow across the grass.

"If we were in a movie, this is the part where the sprinklers would come on."

"Or, the killer would come out and murder us," I replied.

She hit my arm. "I thought you were into romances!"

"I mean, *or* thrillers."

Her eyes went wide. "Oh no, are you the hometown best friend's brother who kidnaps the girl who came back only to bury her body and they'll find me forty years later in an unsolved mystery case by some kid finding a shoelace sticking out of the ground and he'll pull it up and there I'll be?"

I blinked. "I don't think so. I don't like blood."

"Whew. Okay. Let's keep going."

I chuckled and kept walking. Where did she even come up with this stuff?

We slipped around the back of the old scoreboard, the salt of the ocean air wrapping around us, and started up the weathered wooden stairs. The creak of each step battled against the soft crash of the waves rolling onto shore just below us.

"What are we doing up here?"

"You'll see," I whispered back, a playful smiled tugging at my lips.

"Why are you whispering?"

"Why are *you* whispering?"

"Because I don't want the killer to know where we are."

"Makes total sense," I whispered again, trying not to laugh as we reached the top. I sat down, letting my legs dangle over the edge of the platform. She followed, her body close enough that I felt the warmth radiating from her skin. "Now that we're safe though, look that way."

Gently, I cupped her chin and turned her toward the mainland.

Her breath caught.

From where we sat, the view stretched out across the water like something from a dream. Against the ink-black sky, the shoreline glowed with twinkling lights from cozy bars and restaurants waiting to greet customers after the game. The water shimmered with the reflection of stars hanging above us. But just below the coastline of lights that skated across the horizon, the sea glowed with an ethereal blue light, swirling like a trail of stardust in the waves, the culprit of her stolen breath.

"It's called sea sparkle."

Her eyes widened with wonder. Her gaze traced the glowing blue and white ribbons that wove through the water, casting an otherworldly glow that hugged the entire coastline. "What is it?"

"It's actually called *Noctiluca scintillans*, but basically it's plankton that glows when it's pissed off."

She furrowed her brow, but her lips curved into a smile. "How do you piss off plankton?"

I chuckled. She was effortlessly funny and it made my heart swell. "It's pretty easy. You can just run your hand through the water and it lights up."

"Could you imagine if that happened to us?" she asked. "Every time we were really mad, we started glowing a different color."

"That would be pretty amazing actually."

"You'd glow a baby yellow. Super chill and sunny, but not too bright. You're one of those people who's calm, but then it's a total tsunami of bottled-up emotion once every ten years and you'd glow bright red."

"You'd glow pink."

"Pink?" she said with a laugh. "Why pink? I'd be steel blue or neon yellow for sure."

"Nope. Definitely pink. A light pink too. Like an, *aww-that's-cute-she's-getting-mad* kinda pink."

She narrowed her eyes on me. "You have no idea who you're dealing with, do you?"

We sat in an easy silence, watching the glowing water inch slowly down the coast. The moment felt suspended. The warm salty air curled around us, and the starlight traced her face in such a way that I would forever be able to recall exactly where her freckles ended.

"Thank you." She looked down at her hands fidgeting in her lap. "For today. The beach, the hospital, and being there even when I was kind of being a jerk. But mostly for the bacon." She leaned into me and put her head on my shoulder. "I really needed that. All of it. So, thank you."

I turned my head and rested my cheek on her. Her hair smelled like the moment just after it stops raining, when everything is clean and fresh. It felt like this was just how we always were. There had never been anything before this version of Sam and me.

A tiny sound pulled my attention to the edge of the field.

"Hey," I lowered my voice and nodded. "Look over there."

She followed my gaze to the edge of the field where a boy and girl leaned against the fence necking and giggling.

"She's wearing a cheerleading uniform," she whispered. "And that is *not* a football uniform."

I looked at the boy's tight black pants. "Aren't those what they call jeggings?"

"Head cheerleader makes out with class bad-boy nerd—black-rimmed glasses, brains, and jeggings to boot."

"Isn't that against some unspoken code or something?"

"Which is maybe why they're meeting incognito against a dark fence after ten p.m.," she whispered.

"They don't know we're up here."

"What hoochies."

"What if they're going steady? Doesn't that make them *not* hoochies?"

"Hmm. Good point," she agreed. "They're still clearly sneaking around though. It'll never last."

"Maybe it's a budding love story about the star cheerleader falling in love with the class nerd. Who wears jeggings."

"She'll get made fun of if it's public."

"But he'll take anything he can get."

"She ignores him in the hallways during school."

"Only to call him and talk for hours every night," I countered.

"All her friends are dating football players because that's the cool thing to do if you're a cheerleader…"

"But she wants real conversation. A man—"

"Boy—"

"A *boy*, who can talk about his feelings. Makes her feel seen," I continued.

"But she also wants a boy who can help her carry the groceries inside without getting winded."

"So, he'll join the gym," I countered.

"Then on the first day of senior year, he'll walk into school, all jacked up from pumping iron all summer."

"He'll have contacts and be wearing athletic shorts."

"And blond streaks in his hair that only lemon juice, salt water, and too much time in the sun can make."

I paused. "Something like that."

"And he'll walk into first period ready to claim his girl only to find out she's been dating some other guy all summer and it was all for nothing." She gave a big sigh. "Nothing lasts forever, everyone knows that."

"You are such a buzzkill." I leaned into her shoulder and laughed.

"Or a realist. Those stories never work out."

"They could though." I felt her eyes on my face, watching me track the waves splashing against the cement wall that boardered the field.

"How do you have such a positive outlook after all the crap you've been through with relationships?" she asked.

"I guess my parents still have the quintessential love story worth fighting for. Proof it could happen against the odds."

"Against the odds?" she laughed. "He was the star football player and she was the head cheerleader. How does that at all apply to what we're talking about?"

Yes, my dad was the star quarterback, but my mom was definitely not your typical head cheerleader. She was a total nerd. Head always in a book. Straight-A student who would rather do math than cheer at the games.

"Maybe being a cheerleader was a logical decision for her," she suggested. "She would technically have a better view of him when he played if she joined the team."

"*Logical* has no place in love. Perfect example in front of us."

She watched the two separate and link hands. "Do you think about it sometimes?" she asked. "What could have been?"

"You mean, what could have been if I took over?" She nodded. "No. There's not a single bone in my body that wants to be on the field, yelling at eighteen-year-olds to push harder than they already are. But it's still hard with my dad sometimes."

The two kids started walking to the parking lot across the field, hand in hand, smiles plastered on their faces. When they got halfway across the field, the sprinklers turned on, and they ran.

"Stop it!" She laughed, hitting my arm.

"See, movie magic can happen when you least expect it."

"Who did you pay to have that happen?"

"Well, if I was paying someone to make that happen they would have clearly missed their mark, wasting it on two lovestruck teenagers instead of us."

She tilted her head toward me and smiled. My eyes dropped to her mouth.

"It's not so bad, is it?" I asked, my voice hoarse.

"What?" she asked, barely a whisper.

I leaned into her shoulder and slowly tilted my head toward hers. My nose grazed the side of hers, giving her plenty of time to pull away if she wanted to. I didn't want to pressure her after the day she had. It had been complicated enough. Ever since our kiss at the bar, my insides have felt like lava around her. I just wanted to stop imagining the moment our lips touched over and over again and crash into her with everything I had.

She leaned in slowly and paused right before her lips touched mine. The heat of her breath seared my skin. I wouldn't move. It took every single ounce of self-control not to move a millimeter more toward her, but this had to be her choice. I wanted her to kiss me because she wanted to, not because someone was watching.

Then, she did.

It was soft. And so tentative at first.

Everything around us melted away and felt so warm. So perfect.

She pulled back and kissed me again. A tiny moan came out of her mouth and she barely pulled on my lip with her teeth, and the warmth turned into a raging fire. I gripped the back of her head and devoured her. I couldn't get enough. Her taste, her smell. The way her hand pulled at my chest to get me closer.

My other hand came around the back of her neck and cradled her head as she exhaled into me.

A *ding* came from her phone.

She paused, but just for a second. She leaned back in toward me and two more *dings* came through.

She pulled back again, and gently caught her lip between her teeth.

"Don't do that." I was shocked at how out of breath I was.

"Do what?"

"That thing where you pull your lip with your teeth. You're going to unravel me."

"Definitely wouldn't want to do that." She slowly grazed her bottom lip with her teeth again.

I leaned back in and took over, my tongue exploring every place of her with a primal need to consume every piece of her. I couldn't drink her in fast enough.

Another *ding* came through.

"Do you need to get that?" I whispered into her lips.

"No." It *ding*ed again. "Oh my God, okay, hold on." She reached into her back pocket. "It's Robby. He's here."

"Does that matter?" *Please say it doesn't matter.*

"He's at the hotel. We were supposed to meet tonight when he got in. I kinda forgot when you showed up and kidnapped me to watch boys in spandex wrestle each other to the ground."

"I can drive you back if you want." *Please say no.*

She closed her eyes and tilted her head back. "I have to go."

I fought against every bone in my body to stand up and held out my hand to her. I pulled her up so she stood less than an inch from my face. Her smile was perfect—part giddy, part mischievous. I wanted to kiss her again.

But instead I scooped her up and threw her over my shoulder.

"Wait! You can't carry me down stairs like this!" she cried out.

"Don't you worry, carrying in groceries is no problem for me." I smiled as she held on to my neck for dear life.

I carried her all the way to the truck kicking and laughing. "Harpoon's or no Harpoon's?" I asked as I set her down by the passenger door.

Her phone *ding*ed again. This guy was really starting to piss me off.

"He's waiting for me. Do you mind dropping me off? I'll take the rental back over once we're finished."

I handed her my extra house key.

"Are you going to go meet them?" she asked.

"Yeah, I'll head there for a little." *I'd rather take you home.*

I could see her wheels turning. She bit her lip, thinking. I looked down and thrust my hands into my pockets to keep from mauling her.

She bit her lip again. "I'll text you on my way back over, but it'll probably be pretty late."

How am I going to keep my hands off you for the next two days? "Yeah, that works."

"You sure?"

"Positive." *God, help me.*

～

The bar was packed after the showcase and I was dying inside. I couldn't get my mind off what she felt like. How she tasted. Something awoke in me at her touch I hadn't felt in a long time.

This was a very distracting situation to be in.

"Where's Sam?" Lexi asked.

"She had to meet that guy from work."

"This late?"

"Apparently."

Lexi was saying something about the quarterback as I was picturing Sam leaning over the dining room table with some other dude watching as her hair fell into her face.

"Did you hear me?"

"Huh?" I asked. "Sorry, wasn't paying attention." Also, didn't care.

"Clearly. I said, the QB still has two years left. Rex is grooming him to lead them to the state championships."

"Maybe even next year," Rex piped in. "He's got the raw talent. Just needs the situational experience. Kid's got a good head on his shoulders."

"Yeah, seems like it." This was torture. "I'm going to run up to the bar. Can I get you guys anything?"

"I'll come with." Lexi, no doubt, spotting a chance to grill me sans Rex.

We squeezed our way into a spot at the bar and waited on Becky. "Okay, out with it."

"Out with what?" I asked.

"You're smiling."

"That's a bad thing?"

"But you're grumpy smiling, which is an even more amazing talent. This isn't an *I've-had-a-not-crappy-day* smile. This is an *I've-got-a-grade-school-crush-and-am-losing-my-marbles* smile."

"I don't know what a grade-school crush is."

"Have you guys talked about it?" she asked.

"There's nothing to talk about." She made a little grunt noise. "Lexi, you're making way too big of a deal of this. We're just hanging out."

"'Hanging out'," she repeated.

I was terrified she was going to see right through me. "Yes. No strings. Nothing crazy. She's leaving in a week or two anyway." My heart dropped at the thought.

"Okay. That's cool. I guess it's a good thing because it's not like she'd move back. Ever." Her eyes stayed glued on me, watching every micro expression I made. "I mean, even if you guys did hit it off really well, there's more to it than that. She's got her job, that whole thing with her mom—"

"I know she's not moving back."

She tilted her head, and softened her voice. "I just don't want to see you hurt."

"Lexi, please. I'm good. We're just hanging." And we kissed. Twice. And now my entire life has been turned upside down.

"Okay, okay. If you're sure."

"I'm sure." Completely.

"Good, because she's coming to dinner tomorrow night."

Shit. "At Mom and Dad's? Why?"

"I invited her. Before I knew you were in love with her."

"You're so dramatic."

"You're going to get your heart broken."

There was something churning in my chest, but I wasn't exactly sure what it was. She'd met my parents a million times. Practically grew up at our house. But the thought of her setting foot in my parents' house again catapulted my stomach into my neck. I knew how perfectly she'd fit in at the dinner table. How she'd help my mom in the kitchen. Laugh at my dad's cheesy jokes.

But Lexi was right. She'd never be permanent. Her life was in New York and I couldn't offer her a single thing here. I was content with metal bleachers at high school football games and the simplicity of small-town life. The pace fueled me just fine while it left her wanting more. She needed the excitement of the city, the constant buzzing energy and electricity.

She'd never be happy here even if by some random chance she did stay. Which she wouldn't. And the sooner I accepted that fact, the better.

I had already been down this path with Vanessa. She never saw herself staying here, but she did anyway. For me. And I could see the same scenario play out in my mind with Sam.

She'd fall into the rhythm of the island again and the shiny things she saw in a new light would eventually dull. She'd say she was fine, but she wouldn't be and she'd slowly start to blame me without even realizing it. She'd come home one night and barely respond to me when I'd touch her. She'd think I wouldn't notice, but I would. She'd start flipping her phone over when we were home. Then she'd stop leaving it around altogether. Then one day I'd come home when I wasn't supposed to and find her there with someone else and it'd be my fault. Because I was stifling her. Because I trusted too much.

Because I needed so little, but it was everything.

I needed to get out of the bar. Too many people. Not enough air.

Becky dropped three cold beers in front of us and nodded toward our table. "No Country Barbie doll tonight?"

Lexi raised her eyebrows at me.

"Not a word." I turned back to the table, trying to shake off the familiar feeling of wanting to chase something that was already gone.

~~

Later that night, I stared up at the ceiling in my room for hours until the front door opened and closed. I eyed my doorknob. She hadn't texted. It was better that way anyway. I had shut the door when I climbed into bed earlier. I didn't need to fuel whatever this was. A cracked door was an open invitation, right? I didn't need to voluntarily step into a shredding machine for my heart. The second I felt her lips on mine again, I wouldn't be able to stop and it would only make things worse.

But, hell if I didn't stare at that doorknob with all my might, willing it to open on its own.

27

SAMANTHA

My eyes burned. Not only did I stay up way too late last night going over details for our staff call this morning with Robby, I also stared at Austin's bedroom door for over an hour when I got back to his place. Which was closed.

That was a sign, right? To stay away?

I could have knocked. Or texted him. But I was later than I thought I'd be and knew he had a full run in the morning on the ferry so I talked myself out of it. And Austin was already gone when I left this morning. No note. No text. And what good was it going to do anyway? I had a little over a week left here and there was no point in starting something that wouldn't go anywhere.

Even if he was an amazing kisser. A curling toes, stomach dropping, fingers raked through hair, goose bumps out of the blue—

"Earth to Samantha." Robby's voice cut through the constant replay of Austin's hand wrapping around the back of my neck.

"Sorry, what?"

"I'm sorry you had to drive all the way over here. I totally could have gotten another place. I didn't realize they were going to kick you out of this one."

"No, it's fine. I'm staying with a friend. It's no problem, really." Except the fact I wouldn't be getting a good night's sleep, staring at closed doors and imagining what could happen behind them.

"I bet you can't wait to get back to the city. I've only been here twelve hours and I don't think I've stopped sweating once."

There was a mixture of feelings buzzing around in my chest. This meeting was a pivot point. I had gone over the numbers last night with Robby and I had a good feeling about my recommendations to Glenn. Robby stayed pretty mute on his opinion, which was surprising. I knew Team Glenn wanted a massive skyscraper hotel and a monstrosity of a resort development, but based on what worked here and what was special to the island, I knew a neon slide and a time-share eyesore wouldn't be successful.

Ivy popped on the screen. "You guys ready?"

"Of course," I answered. My tone didn't even convince myself.

"Scoot together more, I can't see both of you."

Robby wiggled his chair closer and draped his arm over my shoulders. "Better?" He squeezed my shoulder and gave me his best boy band smile.

We watched Glenn and the rest of the team on my computer screen as they filed into the conference room back in New York. Glenn plopped down and rubbed his hands together, ready for battle.

"Samantha, great, you're already here. We've got some stuff to show you that we came up with. It's going to be perfect for the island, we just need to find the numbers to justify it all. Robby, you fill her in yet?"

"No, sir, not yet," he responded, shifting in his seat a little. "I figured I'd let you do the honors since it was your idea." His voice sounded a bit off.

"Did she at least see the racetrack thing yet?" Glenn asked.

"Racetrack? For cars?" I asked.

Robby leaned over and whispered. "It works in Daytona."

"I don't think Daytona is really the vibe we're after here." I glared at Robby as nicely as I could. He was sitting too close. "Actually if we've got time, I'd really like to start with my recommendations first. I've come up with a solid plan based on the due diligence I'm going to share."

"Sure, we can do that right after. Robby, you ready?" He swallowed next to me as my screen filled with the first visual of the presentation from Glenn's side. *Water Whizz Family Time-share Resort* splashed across my screen in neon green.

This had to be a joke.

"Robby, take it away!" Glenn shouted in what he probably thought was a great theme park host voice.

Robby avoided my very intense stare at the side of his head and started. "*Water Whizz Family Time-share Resort* is the very first family-style water park resort of its kind in the Southeast. With over thirty water adventures across the property, including twenty waterslides, a lazy river rapid, and a water bumper cars arena, it will be one of the most in-demand parks you can book. Home of the Green Giant"—the slide clicked over to the neon waterslide the duo had shown me from last meeting—"the park will be the talk of Florida."

Glenn clicked through as Robby narrated slide after slide of unnaturally colored plastic in their quest to convince the team of the sheer genius that lay before us all.

Through the clear view of the room on my computer, I watched Ivy slink farther and farther down in her chair.

Glenn's knee bounced up and down with excitement. "And look at this. There's plenty of room to build multiple hotel zones, each matching the color of the waterslide at its pool." He clicked through a few pictures of bright green and pink buildings, each thirty stories high jutting up in the air, screaming for attention right along with their matching waterslides. They were easily the ugliest buildings I had ever seen in my life.

Robby continued. "We'll build a racetrack that connects all of the different hotel zones. Ancillary businesses will be built along the track including a new ice cream shop, various restaurants, a movie theater. Even a big-box grocery store answering the need for a one-stop shop with everything anyone could want. Souvenirs and tchotchkes, rafts, bathing suits, sunscreen, even some packaged food items—you name it, it's there. It'll allow us to still charge tourist pricing, but manage it through one store, which is cheaper to run and stock. This will provide a reason for not only the tourists, but the locals to visit the property, negating the need for all these little specialty stores that are littered throughout the island right now."

"*Littered* throughout the island?" The hair stood on the back of my neck. He hadn't even seen the island yet. Did everyone but me forget he'd just landed *last night*? I lowered my voice to him. "These are businesses that have been here for decades, passed down from generation to generation. They don't litter the island. They *are* the island."

"You have to think bigger on these types of projects, Samantha." Glenn's slightly condescending voice made my jaw tick. "This revenue line captures business from the entire island now, not just the tourists and not just during peak season. We're making a destination for the entire island, not just the influx of new money during tourist season."

Heads in the conference room all nodded up and down, like those little plastic bobbleheads that people keep on their dashboards.

I turned to Robby, fuming. He knew this was where the pitch was going last night and he kept his mouth shut as I fed him idea after idea veering in a completely opposite direction. They were planning on building a flashy cartoon version of the island that would bring floods of people in that would boost the local economy, but would irrevocably alter the character of Rock Island, losing the authenticity of the place that's been created over a hundred years. And pushing all of the locals out of business while doing it.

I saw the creeping signs of destructive tourism leaving their mark already—brightly colored wrist bands, inflated prices for milk, gas streaks in the overcrowded water from too many motorboats plowing through. Resort staff roaming the beach in flashy colored polos asking beachgoers if they'd have time for dinner on the house later that evening if they'd just listen to a thirty-minute overview of the time-share opportunities.

"So, you're just replacing it all." My attempt to keep my voice even completely bombed.

"Enhancing," Glenn replied.

"By replacing. The idea of coming into an existing city is not to completely replace everything. It's to build on what's already there. Uncover unseen opportunities and elevate the entire town, not just build a bunch of new stuff to send everyone else out of business. Respectfully, you don't come at these the same way you'd come at a new development. I've got the numbers here to prove the town can sustain an injection of tourism that would preserve all they've built, but take them to a whole other level, focusing on strategies that make the town unique and buzzworthy. This could be a gem of a travel destination if we do it the right way."

"But you're missing the mark. This *is* a new development, Samantha. Which is why Robby's running point now, not you."

His statement hit me like a slap across my face. Both the realization and the hopelessness of it sank in. I had missed it. I was treating this like a redevelopment project because I was so close to it. But he was right. We hadn't been hired by Rock Island to revitalize their city. It was a new development, on new land.

My screen switched back to the full-room view and I saw Ivy's stormy face looking at me. She hadn't seen this coming. And there was no way to hide the shock from my own face.

"*This* will be a gem of a travel destination." Glenn pointed to the Water Whizz Family Time-share Resort logo behind him that filled the entire projector screen.

"It'll be something, that's for sure." Ivy had been silent up until then.

"And what exactly do you intend to do with the miles of forest and trees that are currently the future site of this Whizz Resort?" I asked.

"It'll be demoed." Glenn answered like it was obvious.

"Demoed?"

"Well, we can't build on trees, Samantha. I think she's had a little too much sunshine." Uncomfortable chuckles filled the air at Glenn's comment and Robby shifted in his seat again next to me.

I plowed through the insult. "There's preserved forestland there. And mangroves. And endangered species. And an entire dried-out birchwood tree forest on the beach that's protected."

My voice climbed an octave, but I couldn't hold my frustration in.

"A dried-out forest?" Glenn repeated slowly. "So, a dead forest?"

"I believe they refer to it as a *preserved forest*, sir," Robby chimed in.

"I'm sure we can find a way around it with the city council. Robby, you run point on that."

"Of course, sir."

My blood boiled. "The point of these projects isn't to *find a way around* the city that you're trying to help."

"Oh! And check this out," Glenn continued, switching the screen back to the presentation.

I stopped breathing.

"It's called the Dolphin Jet."

On the screen was a picture of the largest passenger boat I'd ever seen.

"It's an HSC." Glenn continued. "High-speed craft. They can go almost a hundred miles per hour and carry over five hundred people at one time. Multi-decked, top-of-the-line features. It can even shuttle cars across."

Robby leaned back with a grin. "I already looked into it. There's only one other ferry option right now that runs six days a week. Looks kinda dinky and small. We could probably fit their boat on ours if they wanted a lift to the island quicker." He cackled at his own joke.

Austin. He was talking about *Austin.*

Glenn beamed like a proud dad. "Our resort will have a top-of-the-line craft. Safe in, safe out, extend the whole resort experience from the moment they step on board."

I was panicking. "Why would we need to replace an already thriving business? Why not just use them?"

"Because we're building a resort with thousands of rooms, Samantha. You think a little dingy can shuttle people over fast enough? It'd take a whole day just to land enough people to fill up the bar at the main pool deck."

"But there'd be too much tourist pressure. Exceptionally high tourism traffic like this will endanger the identity and the cultural and social integrity of the island. What I've put together is more conducive to the natural habitat on the island—"

"Why don't you show Robby around and we'll reconvene in a few hours?" Glenn interrupted. "What's on your agenda for today?"

Robby answered for me. "We're taking an inshore fishing charter in about an hour. Best on the island. The captain's been around for over ten years. Knows the best spots, routes, drop-ins. Don't worry, we'll be taking notes."

"We've got a week to finalize the pitch to the investors. I'm sure you two will figure it out and come up with the numbers we need. I mean, who doesn't want to come to a resort filled with waterslides?"

"It's genius," Robby confirmed.

The video call disconnected and I couldn't tear my eyes from the blank screen.

I wanted to punch Robby in the nose. Hard.

"Soooo, the fishing charter should be fun." He looked down and tapped his pen on his empty notepad.

I gritted my teeth and kept my voice even and low. "You knew this was what he was planning and you didn't say a single thing last night or this morning."

His shoulders sagged. "I kind of liked your ma-and-pa on steroids idea once you started going. I wanted to see what you were thinking."

"Glenn's idea is awful. You'd kill off the entire town and turn it into a tourist trap. Have you even looked into insurance for something like that? What I showed you last night will work. And it will be more profitable in the long run. I have the numbers and the research to prove it."

"You do," he agreed. "But the reality is, Glenn's already made up his mind. Either you jump on board and show him you can hang with the big kids, or you swim upstream and eventually tire out anyway. Your choice, but they end up with the same result."

"Is that seriously how you operate? You just don't have any backbone whatsoever?"

"Oh, I've got a bone alright, I just choose when to let it go. You, my darling, are blowing your load on something that's not worth it."

"You're disgusting." I stood up and grabbed my laptop and bag.

"I thought you hated this town anyway? What's it matter to you?" he called after me as I stormed toward the door. "Okay, so I'll just meet you at the dock in a little, yeah?"

I let the screen door slam behind me. My heart sank. They'd put the entire town out of business.

Austin. They would put Austin out of business.

And there wasn't a single thing I could do about it.

28

AUSTIN

Sam bit her lip when she was thinking about work.

Sam hated cold coffee but it still took her four hours to drink a single cup.

Sam had six freckles on her left cheek that looked like the big dipper upside down.

I was not someone who noticed these kinds of things. But I noticed them with her.

Sam also walked like she was stomping cockroaches when she was pissed off, which is exactly how she came down the dock toward me. A guy in a white linen button-down rolled up to the elbows and navy-blue chinos was at her heels keeping pace, looking like he had just stepped out of a Tommy Hilfiger billboard ad.

Ah. So this must be Robby.

I hadn't spoken to her since last night in the parking lot after the game. I was up and out by dawn putzing around on the boat, trying to clear my head. Captain Harold texted me to see if I could bait fish for his early morning charter. He was taking out the little old ladies I met a few weeks ago from New Hampshire on a fishing expedition and his first mate was out sick. He also told me he had two last-minute tagalongs; *your friend Sam plus one.* I immediately gave Patrick the boat to run for the day and offered my help.

She walked down the dock with fire in her eyes. A flashback of her lips on mine crashed into my mind and stole a heartbeat, or two.

"You following me, roomie?" I asked when she was close enough. She stutter-stepped when she set eyes on me.

"Hi." She stopped and stared. "I jumped on an inshore at the last minute."

"*We*," the guy chimed in from behind. "Babe, you're going to face-plant in those heels."

Babe?

Sam turned around to face him. "Do not call me *babe* ever again or I will cut your balls off."

Robby peeked around her. "She's a feisty one." The way he spoke, like he knew her better than I did, made my blood boil.

"You must be Robby."

"This your rig?" he asked me, looking behind me to the *Sea King*, Captain Harold's monster of a fishing boat with at least twenty rigged poles poking out of the top.

"Nope," I responded. "Just helping out Captain for the day."

"You are?" Sam asked. I may have made it up, but I swore there was a tiny current of hope in her voice. "I thought you had to run the ferry today?"

"Patrick's on point today."

"Yeah, so you're like, the fish assistant?" Robby puffed out his chest and chewed his gum with his mouth open.

I blinked. Sam rolled her eyes. Was this guy trying to be funny?

"They usually call it first mate."

He gave a huff and looked around through his mirrored aviators. The small urge to punch him brewed somewhere underneath the surface.

"I get the delightful pleasure of showing Robby around the island today." Sam clenched her teeth. "We're starting with the fishing charter around the point of the island. Captain Harold said he could squeeze two more of us on short notice."

Robby's gum bubble popped obnoxiously loud. "Sam's going to show me all the make out spots on the island."

Yep. That urge was growing stronger pretty quickly.

"You're not even remotely funny," she snapped back. "You're lucky I even acknowledge your existence after the stunt you pulled this morning."

Stunt this morning?

Starting off the day with this guy would be rough, let alone spending the whole day with him. I didn't want her anywhere near him.

"Hey, why don't you come with me first?" I asked her, acting like the idea had just come to me. "I've got some water errands to do for Captain and we'll meet up in a couple hours."

"We're heading out on the charter *together*," Robby answered for her. He draped his arm over Sam's shoulder, which she immediately swept off her.

"We'll meet up with Harold's crew for the second half of the trip. I need to run out to catch Captain some live bait first."

His eyes narrowed in on me and a shit-eating grin crept across his face. "Nah, we're good, man." He draped his arm over Sam's shoulder, which she swept off. Again.

"Splitting up and covering more ground would be beneficial to your project. You probably want to map out the best places for bait fish. Right, Sam?"

"Yes. Yes, it totally would." She finally saw the out I was giving her. "I'll go check off the bait…places…with you, and Robby, you can head with Captain Harold and check off the first few fishing spots."

"Wait, what are you going to do?" he asked as she jumped on my skiff.

"You know, fish assistant stuff."

"Well, I'm coming with you," he argued. "Do you even know this guy?"

She looked right at me and answered, "It feels like we just met."

I swear the boat caught fire underneath my feet. I started up the engine once I remembered how to breathe again. "Boat's pretty small. And you need to get your sea legs first. That'll be easier on the bigger boat."

"I don't get seasick," he called out over the motor as we pulled out.

Captain Harold was walking the little old lady trio down the dock toward the *Sea King*.

"We'll meet you guys in a couple hours!" I yelled at him.

It was still early enough, so the water was calm and full of potential for the day, just waiting for a boat to come through and stir it to life. I felt the hum of the motor through my feet as we taxied out.

"I have a vanilla latte and a breakfast sandwich from the Mug in the hatch."

"You do not." Her eyes went wide and my heart swelled.

"I do."

"I love you." My breath stilled at the sound of that phrase.

What the hell, pull it together.

She reached past me to open the hatch and snatched the brown bag out. She stuck her whole head in, taking a huge breath.

"Wait, how did you know I'd be here?" Her head was still in the brown paper bag.

"Harold texted me this morning about the charter saying you'd jumped on last minute. He figured I'd be more willing to help since his first is out with the flu." We idled past the mangroves where the water started to open up. "Assuming your call this morning was less than ideal?"

"Ugh, don't remind me. Let's pretend it didn't happen." She took a huge bite, and with her mouth full, leaned back onto the cushion. "I love bacon."

"I know." I smiled down at my feet so she wouldn't see me blush.

She was quiet on the way out, sitting up front with a towel wrapped around her. I assumed she was still running through the call from this morning in her head. She wore the strain from work across her face but I figured it was more than that. She hadn't heard from her mom yet that I knew of. And being here without her must feel out of sorts. It couldn't be easy, just waiting around. I guess it was better than waiting around for calls at two in the morning.

But the effect of salt and sea air could be revitalizing. The water had a way of opening you up and spilling your guts out to it, whether you felt like it or not. I just needed to give it time. Let her bring it up if she wanted to talk about it.

We idled out past the markers and I sped up. She sat on the bow of the boat as the wind ripped through her hair. She looked back for a split second, the traces of worry and angst gone for a moment.

There was that feeling again where my stomach dropped and my heart tugged a bit. The urge to taste her lips was overwhelming. And distracting. But Lexi's warnings kept ringing in my ear.

I was starting to pay attention too much. I knew she'd be perkier after her latte, and if she didn't have one she'd get a headache soon. She preferred bacon over any other food in the world. Except cotton candy. I put an extra slip mat on the boat because I knew she'd be wearing heels, even if they were just heels disguised as *wedges*, whatever that meant. I also had a pair of boat shoes, size seven, under the seat for when she tripped one too many times and wanted to take her shoes off.

Sure, I needed to get bait fish for the charter, but my plan was to take her to a small, secluded spot where spotted trout were a dime a dozen. You could catch something with your bare hands if you stayed in the same spot for more than ten seconds. Fishing was an adrenaline rush the moment you hooked one, whether you liked to fish or not. I thought it would be a welcomed distraction for her and I wanted to help give her some relief, even if it was only for an afternoon.

After a ride through the open water, we hit a flat and I threw out my cast net to catch bait. Her eyes burned a hole in the back of my shirt as I worked to pull up the net. I've never been so intently focused on the surface of the water before.

"I thought we were fishing?"

"We will, just have to catch the bait first."

"I never got the whole cannibalism thing with fish before."

"The cannibalism thing?"

"You know, fish eating other fish to survive. It's kinda weird, right?"

"I guess I've never seriously thought about the survival of the underwater ecosystem before. Survival of the fittest?" I offered up.

She laughed and I stuck the sound in my back pocket for later.

"You know, I went out with your dad and Lexi a few times when we were little. Although I don't exactly remember fishing. I think it was more tubing and escaping from imaginary sharks."

I pulled up the cast net and sent the slivers of silver fish flopping along the deck.

"Catch 'em!" I yelled.

She turned to me, a mix of confusion and utter horror. "What? I'm not touching them!"

"We need to throw them in the live well before they die. Hurry!" I dropped to my knees, scooping up a small fish in my hands and throwing it into the live well.

She followed suit and trapped a fish with both hands, then

immediately screamed and pulled her arms back. "It's wiggling!" Her laughter cut the air like rays of sunshine.

"They're supposed to wiggle, they're alive." I watched her diving and hopping around the deck, catching the pinfish and throwing them into the well.

We got most of them transferred until there was one left, and she turned to me with it cradled in her hands.

"He's not moving." There were tiny water wells growing in her eyes, but I couldn't tell if she was serious or if her eyes were filled from laughing. "Should we give him a proper burial?"

I hesitated. "I'm not sure what that looks like."

"Aren't you supposed to kiss a fish before you throw them back?"

"I don't think that applies to dead fish."

"Are you sure? I feel like that would be the appropriate thing to do."

"You want me to kiss a dead fish?"

"I mean, this was your idea." She shrugged apologetically.

I leaned forward cringing as a smirk appeared on her lips.

"You're serious about this?" I was about to kiss a dead fish for this woman.

"It's the right thing to do." She pulled her lips into a fine line, laughter about to break through.

I leaned down and just as I puckered my lips, the fish bucked out of her hands and smacked me straight across the nose before flinging itself over the side back into the ocean.

"He's a fugitive!" She completely doubled over in laughter, holding on to her stomach with both arms. She couldn't catch her breath as I stood there, stunned, backhanded by a fish's tail. Tears were streaming down her face from laughing so hard.

I didn't want to look anywhere else.

I'd take ten fish slaps in the face every day to see her like this.

Ten speckled trout later, seven by her count alone, I pulled our boat next to *Sea King* and anchored.

We caught a glimpse of Robby leaning over the back of the boat.

"Oh no." Sam was trying not to smile.

Captain Harold walked along the railing and leaned over to us chuckling to himself. "Haven't had one puking this much since Dolores. Turned out she was ten weeks pregnant and didn't even know it. Wouldn't think the same excuse applies to your boy over there, though."

Robby heaved again. Some sea legs he had.

"Oh, look! It's Captain Handsome!" Shirley called out from the deck of the boat, waving her hands at me like an octopus.

"Look what she got!" Gail yelled overboard pointing to Ethel as she held up a decent-sized Spanish mackerel. "Reeled it in all by herself."

Ethel smiled proudly as Captain Harold came up behind her and gave a thumbs-up. My heart soared. All of her four-foot self was beaming. I had hoped they'd have some luck. Captain Harold had spent over fifty years on the water and tracked the fish like he was one of them.

"The bugger didn't have a fighting chance once this little lady got her eyes on it."

Gail had her camera out snapping away, catching every moment she could.

"I haven't caught anything yet," Shirley sang as she danced around the deck, "but Captain Harold dubbed me the official host of the boat. I've kept drinks filled, bellies full, and spirits up."

"We've caught more fish in an hour than my whole charter yesterday."

Shirley waltzed over the side of the boat and leaned over a bit to loud-whisper to me. "He says I'm the good luck charm."

"I might hire her full time just to have her prance around the boat all morning calling to these fish. I'm telling you, they come to her."

"They can't help but hear her voice decibel. You know, kinda like dogs." Gail rolled her eyes and got a close-up picture of Ethel and her mackerel. These ladies were a riot.

I helped Sam onto his boat and introduced her to everyone. Captain took a peek over at our boat and noticed the haul we got for the morning.

"Now, don't you be talking about your count in front of my guests. You'll make 'em jealous. No one can hold a candle to this guy and his captaining skills."

"She's got seven notches on her belt already this morning and it has nothing to do with me," I countered.

He lowered his voice to Sam but I could still hear. "Don't let him hoodwink you. He's the best fishing captain you'll meet in this channel, let alone this coast."

All three ladies were huddled up in a group staring at Sam and whispering, no doubt sizing up Sam's future wife score.

"The best? Coming from you that's saying a lot."

"I'll never leave the water for good, but the moment my nephew wants to chase his real dream, the fishing business is all his. Always has been."

Her eyes flicked to me filled with questions. I hadn't told her Captain Harold was my uncle, but if I drew her a family tree of the island, it'd take a while.

The sound of shuffling feet snagged my attention as Robby's green face poked around from the back of the boat. He saw me and straightened his back a bit.

"Looking a little green in the gills there, sailor."

"Aaron, good to see you didn't sink your dinghy." Robby swayed just a bit, fighting to steady himself.

"It's Austin."

"Yeah, for sure." He walked toward Sam on wobbly legs. "Ready to catch some big fish, Leigh?"

"Are you sure you're okay? You look a little queasy."

"I'm great. Just need a little sunshine." He held in a burp and grabbed the side rail. "Much better now that you're here."

I gritted my teeth as Shirley and the ladies started whispering.

Ethel's voice rang out over the others. "Well, I for one love a good pissing contest."

29

SAMANTHA

I loved watching Austin. The way he interacted with his little fan club made me feel all warm and fuzzy inside. It came to him so effortlessly, like he was born to show people the magic of the water. But the more I watched it, the less I loved it. Because then I remembered that his business would eventually tank because of my company. He seemed like such a natural helping them out. Maybe if I could convince him to follow his dream of starting a fishing charter, it could work out? Maybe it'd be a blessing in disguise, forcing him to follow his childhood ambition. He was clearly gifted at it. And he had Harold's business ripe and ready to be handed to him from the sound of it.

Austin and Robby had been at it all day, locked in an unspoken battle of who could outfish the other, as if the size of their catches could somehow dictate the winner of life. And the peanut gallery was making for quite the entertaining trio, cheering every time they hooked a fish like it was the final Hail Mary of the Super Bowl.

Austin held the record at forty inches—a beast of a snook he reeled in earlier with steady precision and a smirk that made me roll my eyes but my stomach swan dive. But Robby had a monster on the line, and the tension on the boat was so thick it could've been cut with a fishing knife.

"Aaron, you got the tape measure out yet?" Robby grunted through clenched teeth, the back of his breezy buttoned-up white linen shirt soaked through as he wrestled with the rod.

Austin's jaw flexed but played it cool, even though I could see him throwing Robby overboard in his mind as it played across his face. "Sure thing, Robert," he said evenly, not glancing at Robby as he coiled the line of his own rod. "And don't let go of that reel, or you'll lose him."

Shirley had her phone out, narrating the story as it happened. "And this, ladies," she sang for the video as she crept in for a close-up of Robby's arm, "is what it looks like when someone who works out reels in a fish." She zoomed in on his biceps while Robby flexed, making Gail laugh and Ethel cover her mouth and giggle.

The rod in Robby's hands bent almost in half as the fish fought back.

Austin's eyes flicked to me for a moment, his mouth twitching with the faintest trace of a smirk. "You might want to loosen the drag," he offered casually. "Unless you're planning to snap the line."

"Thanks for the tip," Robby shot back, "but this one doesn't stand a chance." The line creaked under the strain, and Harold hovered nearby, watching like a referee waiting for the perfect moment to blow the whistle.

The fish surfaced for a split second, its massive tail slapping the water as sea spray flew up and completely soaked the front of Robby's shirt.

Ethel smirked. "I was just thinking all we needed to get this party started was a wet T-shirt contest."

Robby let out a triumphant yell. "Did you see that? It's huge!"

"Yeah, it's a good one," Austin's voice maddeningly calm. "Let's see if you can land it."

Robby's face twisted with determination. The fish darted under the boat, and Harold barked a warning. "Keep the line steady or he'll wrap you up in the prop!"

"I know!" Beads of sweat formed on Robby's brow. He shifted his weight, trying to maneuver the rod as the fish took another dive. Austin stepped forward, ready to intervene, but stopped short when Robby shot him a glare.

The line whined again, dangerously taut. "You're going to lose it if you don't—" Austin started.

The fish broke the surface again, thrashing wildly as Robby reeled it closer. It was massive—easily the biggest of the day. Austin grabbed the net and positioned himself at the edge of the boat, his movements precise and controlled. "Bring him in slow. Let him tire himself out."

Robby ignored him, pulling harder, his breaths coming in short, frustrated bursts. The fish gave one last violent thrash, and Austin lunged forward, scooping it into the net with practiced ease.

Robby puffed out his chest, grinning as if he'd just won a gold medal. "Told you I had it under control."

Austin, to his credit, kept his expression neutral as he measured the fish. "Nice catch," he said, his voice even. "Forty-two inches. That's a monster." He genuinely congratulated him, a pillar of professionalism, but I didn't miss the way his grip tightened on the tape measure or the flicker of frustration in his eyes.

"Oooohhh, looks like we have a new winner!" Gail exclaimed, phone still recording. Robby turned to the camera, his aviators lost somewhere in the battle, and winked.

"That's a boat record," Harold called out, his tone impressed. "Looks like you finally got your sea legs, rookie."

As Robby basked in his victory, Austin glanced at me, and for a split second, I saw something there—something raw and unspoken. He wasn't just competing with Robby for the biggest fish.

He was competing for me.

The sky was a swirl of bubblegum pink and orange as we pulled back into the marina.

Robby stepped off Harold's boat and beelined it straight for me. He held out his hand to help me off but I jumped out on my own and gave him a tight smile, the memory of our call earlier snapping me back to reality.

"Austin wants to show me one more spot to check off the list for today." I kept my tone light but firm. "I'll text you later."

Robby gave me his best lost-puppy look, his shoulders slumping just enough to tug at the corners of my sympathy.

"But hey," I added, softening just a fraction. "Nice fish. For real. That was seriously impressive." I was being genuine, but I wasn't about to let him off the hook, pun intended, from this morning. Not yet. His wolf-in-sheep's-clothing act still felt too raw.

"You good to press down an actual button on a camera, Maverick?" Shirley asked Robby, recruiting him as their new sunset photographer.

The hum of the motor filled the silence around Austin and me on the smaller boat, and I didn't mind the break in the noise. The water was pure glass going back, reflecting the pink sky and fluffy clouds that looked like puffs of spun sugar. There were so many things bouncing in my head I couldn't think straight. The call from this morning, Robby lying, the monstrous ferry that would put Austin out of business, my mom whom I still hadn't heard from, the best kiss of my life... Why had his door been shut? What did that mean? He seemed fine today.

I gazed out over the water and leaped from subject to subject, wondering what it all meant.

Austin started to slow the boat. "You've been quiet since we left."

"Thinking about how to defend myself against the three little ladies who will most assuredly be kidnapping me in my sleep tonight."

"I've got one more place to show you for a picture, then we'll head in. It's just around the corner here. Sound good?"

"Sounds great."

He pulled around the bend and slowed the motor. It looked like any other inlet until I saw the gnarled tree branch sticking out of the water. It had the same twisted look about it that the branches did from Birchwood Beach.

"Do you recognize it?" he asked.

I looked at him, then back at the branch. "It can't be."

"It is. We're just at high tide."

I was dumbstruck. "So, the whole beach, it's under water now? All of it?"

"Almost. About half an hour ago it all was. Tide's going back out now so we'll start to see the tallest branches poking out here and there."

The evidence was small, only a few of the tallest branches reached out from under the water.

"I figured you'd have more of an appreciation for it if you actually saw it in person," he replied.

The water rocked the boat as we slowly made our way closer and around some of the branches. There was an entire world below us that absolutely no one would know about unless they saw it at a different time of day. It was amazing.

"I feel like there's a very important lesson about things not being as they appear on the surface here."

He steered the boat up close to one of the branches.

"I still can't decide if it's beautiful or sad," I traced the warped branches crawling out of the water.

"I think it can be both."

I took my camera out and started taking pictures, trying to document some of the scenery we were passing. I had a pretty good collection of photographs already from the island but no one would believe this unless they saw it.

"You going to include this in your research?" he asked.

I had originally planned to, but now I wasn't so sure. After finding out Glenn's plan this morning, which had zero care or concern about what the actual island needed, I was waffling. What would happen to this place? Would Glenn somehow pay off whoever he needed to on the city council, and they'd come in here with bulldozers and excavators and tear up whatever remained? There was something so special about this place. It felt like sending it to a certain death if I told anyone else about it.

"I haven't decided yet. I don't want to ruin it."

"Amazing how people's first impressions can be so off, huh?"

"Speaking of first impressions, Captain Harold is your uncle?"

"Married to Josie who owns the Starfish."

"Why didn't you tell me he was your uncle?" I asked.

"Never crossed my mind to give you the rundown of the family tree. They weren't around when you grew up here."

"The family connections never cease to amaze me on this island."

"They moved here about five years ago from the Keys. Josie is my dad's sister. She took over the Starfish and he transferred his charter business. Both started booming after about a year. They're good people. Both a little quirky."

"They're perfect for each other."

"They absolutely are. Soulmates." He winked and my stomach swooped.

"Why won't you take over his business?" I could tell he wanted to joke around but I wanted to know about this whole fishing thing. It would be the perfect out. I couldn't shake the morning call with Glenn, and to my knowledge there were no plans whatsoever for any fishing charters in Glenn's vision. If Austin really wanted to go that route, he wouldn't be a target.

"I'm not sure if you noticed, but I've got my own business to run."

"But isn't fishing what you really want to do?" I asked as he navigated the boat around the largest branch that stuck out from the water. It reached over our heads by about a foot.

"I'm happy where I am."

"But if you had to pick, what do you like to do more? Running fishing charters or running a tourist ferry?"

He narrowed his eyes on me. "Why are you needling me?"

"I'm not needling you, I'm just asking the question in different ways until you actually answer. I don't understand what's so scary about taking over the fishing charter business."

He exhaled. He took a second to respond. "The shuttle business is a need that I fill. It's where I fit right now."

"You can't do both?" I asked.

"How would I do both?"

I'd already thought through all the different options he could take if plans were approved on a fast track, the best one hiring a captain to run Scuttle's Ferry back and forth for the next eighteen months while the resort was being built. Austin could focus on building his fishing charter and by the time the resort opened, the charter business could be huge. He'd have no need to run the ferry anymore.

"Captain Harold's got the fishing thing covered."

"Sounds to me like he's teed you up to take over easily."

"Nothing's that easy, trust me." He huffed and turned away, like he was ready for the conversation to switch.

"He literally said, *the moment my nephew wants the business, it's his*. Explain to me how that's not easy?"

"Family's not ever that easy. You know that. It's not a guaranteed thing."

Well, nothing was guaranteed. Out of all people I'd assumed he'd know that, but it sounded as perfectly set up as it could possibly be. And if he took over, he wouldn't be forced out and left without a job. Or a company. "So you'd give up your dream of owning a fishing business because you don't want to fail at taking over an already wildly successful business?"

"That's not what I said, Sam."

"Not in those words, but what could be the real reason? That just sounds like an excuse not to follow a dream."

He leaned against the side of the boat and crossed his arms, the playful smile wiped from his face. "Wow. Okay. What about you? I'm sure your dream job isn't sitting in a high-rise working a ninety-hour-a-week job for the rest of your life with a human resources time bomb and what sounds like a dead-end promotion wise?"

I flinched. The look on his face immediately fell.

"I'm sorry, I didn't mean for that to come out so harsh."

"No, no. I mean you're totally right. I thought for a long time that's exactly what my dream job looked like. Climbing to the top floor of some cushy building where my corner office and secretary sat waiting. Turns out I'm not qualified for that after all."

"I don't think qualifications are the deciding factor in your position," he countered.

I looked out onto the horizon again. It was starting to turn dark and the water looked like black oil pooling around the orphan tree limbs.

"What would you want to do, if you could do anything? No restrictions," he asked. He was giving me an olive branch, trying to erase the last twenty minutes. But an image of the huge passenger craft on the water bulldozing his ferry popped in my mind.

"I have absolutely no idea anymore."

The last rays of sunlight drained from the sky and the temperature immediately dropped. We were quiet as he turned back toward the marina. The moon reflected off the water on the way back in the most peaceful way—while everything inside me churned like a squall at sea.

I bolted the minute we got to the dock, leaving Austin to his normal cleanup duties. I physically felt the weight of the last few days on my shoulders. I was tired of feeling so many different emotions in such a short timeframe with my mom. So tired of fighting with Glenn for my ideas to be heard. Heavy from the new guilt that had been put on my plate from this morning and the call.

Guilt for what that call meant, not only for Austin, but the entire town.

30

AUSTIN

I walked into the house holding my breath. There was a chance she decided to go back to her house since her mom wasn't there, but I know she felt uncomfortable there alone.

There was a note on the kitchen counter.

I'm sorry for being a jerk.
You are the best ferry captain in the whole wide world.
Do you forgive me?
Circle YES or NO

A relieved breath left my chest.

"Can I take that as a *yes?*"

I didn't see her bundled up on the sofa when I walked in.

She was there. On my couch, snuggled up in my blanket and not anywhere else. The smart thing to do was not lean into whatever this was. I shouldn't care. But the moment I saw her here, safe in my house, I wanted her to stay.

Even though I shouldn't.

I loved the way she stood up to me and bantered with me, calling me out on my bullshit. I loved her quiet vulnerability and her trust in me to allow me to see her for who she really was. But she was strong. Stronger than anyone else I'd ever met. To go through what she did in high school, losing her dad, the accident with her mom, and still be full of life and light was more than I could imagine.

She wasn't scared to push me. She wasn't scared to ask questions.

I loved the way she laughed. The way her face lit up when she caught me looking at her. The sound of her voice and the way she usually piled her hair on top of her head like a bird's nest and her skin and her smile. She drove me crazy, like a drug I couldn't get enough of.

I had this overwhelming urge to crawl up beside her and pull her in my lap, tell her everything would work out—her mom would be fine, she'd get the promotion, but if not, it was better that way anyway. That we could figure it out. She'd never have to take a call about her mom alone again. That I'd protect her and take care of her if she would just let me.

But I stood there, my feet glued to the floor, scared of what that all meant. I sat on the barstool facing her instead to keep myself from falling.

I grabbed the pen and circled yes.

She stood up and walked toward me cradling a mug of coffee in her hand, the steam curling lazily into the air. Strands of damp hair clung to her shoulder leaving a dark circle on her oversized sweatshirt—*my* oversized sweatshirt. She looked exhausted, and absolutely beautiful.

She leaned over my shoulder to glance at the paper and my heart tumbled at the smell of my shampoo on her. I didn't just smell it, I *felt* it—her nearness, the intimacy of it—everything she was wrapped around me in an instant.

I was falling for her.

"You're drinking coffee?" I asked, my voice a bit hoarse.

"I'm just holding it. It makes me feel warm inside." She nestled herself in between my legs. My skin buzzed everywhere we touched.

"I know the feeling."

She leaned into my lap and reached behind me to put her coffee cup down on the counter. "I think you make a perfect ferryboat captain," she whispered as she kissed my cheek. "And you'd make a perfect fishing boat captain, too." She pressed a kiss to my other cheek. "And you'd make a great captain of, like, anything else that needed a captain." Her soft giggle tickled my neck. My skin was on fire and my fingers were tingling to touch her. I grabbed her waist and pulled her closer.

"I hate to break the moment and all," she whispered into my ear, "but you smell like fish." She laughed out loud and threw a hand over her mouth.

"Hazard of the job." I closed my eyes and tried to calm the raging sea in my chest. "Give me five." I stood to pull the shirt over my head.

Her eyes darkened. "For the record, you should never wear a shirt ever again."

I smiled. This would be the fastest, hottest shower I'd ever had in my life.

As the scorching water rolled down my back, I thought about Sam leaving. It would rip my heart out. But did it have to? Could we somehow make this work? Could she be happy back here?

What about the city? I'd never been, but maybe there would be a chance I could make it work?

After Vanessa left, I was a wreck. For a while. I hadn't opened up my heart in a long time. But there was something about Sam that made my insides smile. I wanted to be near her, whatever it took.

I wanted her on my couch, snuggled up in my clothes. I wanted to wake up next to her and take care of her and protect her from everyone else in the world that would ever try and do her harm. I wanted her to fall into me at night and feel safe, feel taken care of, and know I wouldn't go anywhere.

I planned everything out with Vanessa—where we'd live, how many kids we'd have, the color of our living room walls. Maybe I didn't have to plan everything out. Maybe the city, or the house didn't matter. Maybe Sam and I could take it one step at a time and see where we ended up. The thought scared me. It terrified me.

I turned the shower off and threw on a pair of sleep pants. Maybe we could just see where it goes?

Her door was open a crack. If I stepped through that door, there was no turning back. I wasn't the kind of man who could have fun for a few nights and walk away unscathed. If I walked through that door, I'd be willingly handing over my heart, knowing it could go directly into a shredder. I didn't just want a day or two with her. I wanted the thousand little moments of her brushing her teeth by my side, her pouring coffee into her cup, putting groceries in my pantry. I wanted my bathroom to smell like her in the mornings after she got ready. I wanted her jeans left haphazardly on the floor by my bed because there wasn't time to do anything else when we got home but kick them off.

If I took this leap, there'd be a very real chance I could wake up one day alone and shattered into a million little pieces.

I stared at her cracked door and felt the ground shift beneath me.

I wasn't in jeopardy of falling.

I'd already jumped.

I was in free fall.

I pushed the door open slowly while my heart swelled with every step. I crossed the room to the side of the bed. She lay curled on top of the blanket, her shoulder gracefully rising and falling in a steady rhythm. Her head rested on the pillow, hair sprawled out around her, beautifully fast asleep.

My heart liquefied into a puddle at my feet.

I reached down and brushed a stray piece of hair from across her face, careful not to wake her. Her lips were barely parted, breath whispering through the room in little waves. For a moment, I just stood there, watching her. She looked so peaceful, as if the weight she carried all day finally had lifted for just a few hours.

Then, guilt hit me, hard and fast. Tonight would've only complicated things. I refused to be yet another thing she'd have to carry. I wanted to take every burden I could from her shoulders and put them on mine, not become one myself.

I tore myself from the guest room, every step heavier than the last, and slowly pulled the door shut behind me.

31

SAMANTHA

Mary Kay curled back in her patio chair with a crisp white wine that had frosted the sides of the glass. "So, tell me about living in the city. Is it everything they say it is?"

We sat around the table in the backyard with empty plates and full bellies.

My anxiety almost made me cancel. I woke up to Austin gone already. No note. No text. The last thing I remembered was the sound of the shower running. Could I seriously have fallen asleep? It was a long day—the sun, the stuff with Robby, and the call with Glenn. I hadn't heard from Mom. But I left my door cracked. I know I did. I've never stared at a door with so much anticipation in my life. But when I woke up this morning it was closed.

There was no way I had the wrong impression, right? Did I step out of line? Was he not interested? Did I read the whole thing wrong?

I knew I had been a little short with him on the boat, but I thought we were on a whole other path after he got home, then, nothing. I was nervous seeing Lexi's family again after so long and adding Austin on top of it just complicated the night. I was anxious about rewinding seven years and seeing people I barely knew anymore. My stomach was in knots, but the moment Mary Kay opened the door as I walked up the driveway and ran to wrap her arms around me, I knew I made the right decision in coming.

My eyes pricked with small pools of water. I was swept back in time the moment she hugged me, and the familiar scent of lemon cleaner surrounded me.

"To answer your question, yes. And so much more. There are five-star restaurants around every corner. I sat next to Robert De Niro at a random coffee shop just last month. You can order takeout at any hour, on any day. There are always people moving about and there's always something to do. Theater, ballet, musicals, parks, art museums, concerts. You name it, you can find it somewhere."

Bill leaned forward at the head of the table. "The entertainment capital of the world, right?"

"I think that's Vegas, Dad," Lexi said.

"Same idea."

"Seems like a lot of distractions to me." Austin hadn't spoken directly to me all night. He'd barely made eye contact since he walked in late. The worst-case scenario of me completely misreading our entire existence together morphed ten times over already in my mind. Were we acting like we didn't see each other? Like I wasn't staying with him? Maybe he could read my mind and he realized I'm an awful person keeping a huge secret from him and he hated me now.

Ugh, I had no idea.

"It can be if you're not intentional about creating downtime." I bumped my knee against his under the table but he wouldn't look at me. He'd been withdrawn throughout dinner.

Mary Kay beamed at me. "Well, I always knew you were made for something bigger. Every time you and Alexandra would play store, by the time you two were done you'd have opened a pretend ice cream shop, bakery, and coffee shop and had a full pitch ready to go to the city council on a new playground proposal."

Lexi lit up. "We definitely still hold the record for lemonade stands in a single summer on the island."

"You always had such an imaginative brain. They're lucky to have you up there." Her words melted my insides. I hadn't realized how much I missed affirmation from someone who actually knew me. Not just the business workaholic side of me, but the me who had always loved to dream and build and play for fun.

"Pretty sure you two funded our entire VHS tape collection with the proceeds from those lemonade stands," Bill said.

"I have Sam to thank for my obsession with Debbie Gibson." Lexi turned to me. "Do you remember 'Lost in Your Eyes'?"

"You mean, do I remember the best song of all time?" I dipped my head. "Maybe."

She pushed her chair back and grabbed her wineglass as a microphone. "I get lost..." she sang.

"In your eyes..." I replied as I snatched mine and stood. Then we both sang at the top of our lungs. "And I feeeeeeeel my spirits rise and soar like the wind. Is it love that I am in?"

Then we looked at each other and paused. "I can't remember the next line," I whispered across the table.

"Neither can I." We both fell back into our chairs laughing.

"Thank the Lord," Bill added.

Austin leaned back in his chair, a smile desperately trying to burst across his face.

I narrowed my eyes at him. "Don't act like you don't remember the concerts we used to put on. They were too epic to be forgotten."

"Pretty sure I was in my room playing Nintendo, although if that was a taste, it looks like I got the better end of the bargain."

"Oh, don't you play coy," Mary Kay said. "I'm pretty sure I have some pictures stashed away of your musical debut somewhere too, Austin."

"Now those I would pay money to see." Lexi pranced over and topped off my wineglass again.

"Lexi, that's enough," Rex piped in laughing. "She hasn't even finished *that* glass. We don't need to turn Samantha into an alcoholic."

The awkward silence that blanketed the table was excruciating. "What?" Rex continued. "Alexandra gets a little carried away with her hosting responsibilities is all I'm saying."

Austin turned his eyes to me right away, roaming my face.

Mary Kay reached over and laid a hand on my arm. "I'm so sorry, he doesn't—"

Lexi interrupted. "I didn't give him the whole story, I didn't think—"

"No, no, please, it's okay," I looked at Rex's confused face. "My mom is actually an alcoholic." His face turned beet red. "And, also partakes in other fun extracurricular substances sometimes too."

"Oh my gosh, I'm so sorry. I had no idea." His eyes desperately searched Lexi's face for a lifeline.

"Seriously, it's not a big deal, Rex. Please don't feel bad. You wouldn't have known."

"How is your mom doing?" Bill asked. "Austin told me about Willow Rehabilitation. Best place she can be."

"She's doing good as far as I know from the staff updates. She hasn't been able to make contact yet. I guess that helps acclimate their patients to the program without any distractions, but her counselor says she's doing great."

"I'm sure the moment she can reach out to you she will." Mary Kay squeezed my hand. Just her touch took some of the sting away, but I could feel the massive tidal wave of emotion creeping up my chest. The gentleness in her words cracked something open in me—something that had been quiet for a long time. "Now, you kids go relax. Let Dad and I clean up for once. Enjoy the time you've got left with Samantha here." She winked at me as she stood.

Rex stood, gathered a handful of plates and headed inside through the patio door as Lexi followed. "I'm going to run in and check on him. I'm really sorry, I should have given him a heads-up."

"It's nothing. Please, tell him it's seriously not a big deal."

"I will. I'll meet you two out there." She motioned to the Adirondack chairs down by the water.

Austin stood up without a word and started toward the water's edge. I followed him out and plopped down in one of the chairs next to him. The ocean slowly lapped up onto the shore, tumbling the rocks and stones smooth.

"Well, glad that wasn't awkward." My attempt to make him laugh failed. He stayed silent as we watched the waves roll in for a few minutes. I was starting to seriously doubt my interpretation of anything ever being between us. Did I imagine everything? Was he mad that I fell asleep? Did he consider himself lucky I fell asleep? My mind spiraled out of control.

"You worried about your mom?" he finally asked.

"No. Surprisingly." I was thankful he was finally talking to me, even if it was about my mom. "I'm just glad she's finally doing what I've asked her to do for years. It's a huge step. But I'm not going to get my hopes up about it just yet."

"Are you going to hang around until she gets back?"

"That could be over a month away. I'm not sure that's in the cards for me." The sun was just about to set over the horizon. "You guys really do have the best view of the entire island."

"They don't have this in the city, huh?" he asked.

"Not like this, they don't."

"Are you going to miss it here?" he asked. There was an edge in his voice and he hadn't looked me in the eyes since we sat down.

"I'm not leaving yet."

"You're not here for that much longer." There was a sharpness to his words. Could he still be mad at me pressing about the fishing charter stuff? Maybe that was still bothering him.

"Listen, I'm sorry I pushed so hard yesterday on the boat, about the whole job thing. It's really none of my business."

"It's no big deal."

"No, it is. I shouldn't have been so pushy. It's your business. Obviously, you know what's best, not some random person barging in with yet another opinion on how to run your life."

"You don't owe me anything, we were just making conversation." His words felt cold. He stood abruptly. "I'm going to grab some water, you want anything?"

"Lexi said she was bringing some out."

"Okay." He stayed standing, gazing out over the water like he was waiting on some long-lost boat to peek over the horizon.

"What's going on with you?" I asked. "Did I do something to upset you?"

"No, nothing. Just trying to enjoy the slow pace of life down here." He finally looked at me, and quickly walked by my chair back to the house just as Lexi came out. He didn't even look at her as he stomped by.

"Do I want to know what just happened?" she asked as she walked up.

"I have no idea, don't ask me. How's Rex?"

"Kicking himself. He'll probably still show up at your place tomorrow with flowers even though I told him it wasn't necessary."

"He seems like a good guy."

"He is." She plopped down into the chair next to me. She had the puppy-dog-in-love look glazed across her face.

I squeezed her hand. "I'm really glad you found him. You always did look good in love."

"I got lucky."

"I keep having to remind any cute guy I meet in the city that posting on your Instagram in hopes of becoming an influencer is not actually a job." She eyed me. "It's a story."

"It always is."

I loved the familiar lull. Being back here with her family, I was afraid I'd no longer fit in. Like this new person wouldn't have anything in common with me, and there'd be too many awkward pauses and weird looks. But I slid back in, just like I used to. And that scared me too.

There was something beautiful about being known.

"Speaking of cute guys, any chance I can ask you something without you completely freaking out on me?"

"Ah, I've been wondering when this would come up." She looked at me and gave me that kind smile she saved for *talks*.

"I'm just curious what's gotten him all hot and bothered tonight."

"You really don't know?"

"Please, enlighten me. I can't seem to figure out what I did wrong. One minute we're good and wonderful and the next he won't even look at me."

She took a deep breath and a healthy swig of wine. "How much has he told you about Vanessa?"

"Nothing really, beyond she left him for his best friend."

"You knew Austin and her were engaged, right?" I nodded. "Austin is such a planner, and he had it all figured out. They even had their future kids' names picked out."

I pulled my knees up and wrapped my arms around my legs. The thought of him and her with children sent me a little off-kilter.

"He was so blindsided by the whole thing. He's had a hard time trusting anyone since."

"So he hasn't dated anyone since that happened?"

"Oh no, he's dated people. Or, he's gone on dates *with* people, I should say. But nothing serious. I think he thought there was absolutely no chance he'd ever need to be back in the dating pool again, so when that all happened, it threw him for a while."

"But that was three years ago."

"While I'm sure seeing Vanessa and Tom walk into the bar didn't help, I also don't think they're the reason he's having a hard time right now."

"I hounded him yesterday about the whole fishing charter thing and following his dreams. I kind of read him the riot act."

"Oh, he's definitely not mad at you for that," she responded with a little snort. "We've all been doing that for years. Sam, you're the first person he's been even remotely into. And by *remotely into*, I mean falling headfirst at about a hundred miles an hour."

My heart took a tiny leap.

"I think it took him by surprise," she continued. "He knows you're leaving soon without any plans on returning at all. And I don't think he knows how to deal with it." She looked over at me and her eyes softened. "Listen, you don't have to pour your heart out to me, but he's a really good guy. And he's guarded his heart for a really long time. While I'd love to have you as a sister-in-law someday, I've warned him the odds are about one in a trillion that you'd ever stay here. If he's lucky. This small-town life isn't for you. And leaving it isn't in the cards for him. That doesn't leave much room for there to be anything but heartbreak. I think he's just trying to distance himself a little bit to avoid the inevitable."

My heart was skipping for joy and gasping for air at the same time. I looked back out onto the water and exhaled, the flutter in my stomach instantly turning sour. Because I could see it. She verbalized exactly what I knew but didn't want to put words to.

"All my life I've spent trying to run from this place."

"He knows that."

"There's no way I'd survive if I came back."

"He knows that too." Her eyeline shot above me as I heard footsteps approaching from behind.

"You ladies up for a round of good old-fashioned family Pictionary?" he asked. "Mom says it's mandatory."

"I call Samantha!" Lexi shouted as Mary Kay and Bill walked out onto the yard, huge easel in hand, with Rex trailing behind them.

"I think a round of boys versus girls is perfect for tonight." Mary Kay had a mischievous look on her face and a new bottle of wine.

I saw a glimmer of a real smile on Austin's face for the first time all night.

☼

"That is a hundred percent a *Tyrannosaurus rex*." Austin looked at his drawing on the easel.

Bill and Rex just stared at him, mouths open.

"Or, a raccoon," I was laughing so hard my lungs were on fire.

"Where do you see a raccoon!?" Austin shouted. "Look at its feet! Raccoons don't have talons on their feet!"

"Yeah, but their hands look eerily similar to your *dinosaur's* hands." Rex covered his mouth to stop the laugh from bursting out.

Austin scrunched down and put his nose on the easel, squinting at his drawing.

I could barely speak between breathes. "For the record, I don't think a *T. rex* has ears."

"At least not ones shaped like a raccoon's," Bill murmured under his breath as everyone cracked up again. Austin threw the marker at him.

After eight rounds, the score was tied. Turns out Rex was a pretty good Sharpie artist, and Bill was used to Austin's eccentric drawings, which gave them a leg up. But Lexi and I still made a pretty good team, and with her mother's drawings looking like professional sketchbook pieces, we were stiff competition.

"Last one, winner takes the title." Bill tossed Mary Kay the marker. She plucked out a card from the fishbowl, looked over to us and grinned.

He counted down with flare. "And three, two, one, go!"

Tiny grains of sand fell through the small hourglass as Mary Kay drew a stand with a pitcher, and two stick figures smiling with money in their hands. Lexi and I looked at each other and screamed, "A LEMONADE STAND!"

Mary Kay threw the marker up into the air and bowed. She came in for a tipsy winners' hug with the two of us as we fell back on the couch together in a fit of laughter, chanting "winner winner, chicken dinner."

"I mean, of all the cards," Austin mumbled under his breath.

"We'll get 'em next time, boys," Rex said, cheering them on in his best high school football coach voice.

Lexi crawled over to give him a kiss. "Always the encourager."

I leaned back all warm and fuzzy from laughing. I hadn't felt like a part of a family in a really long time. Hadn't had bellyaching laughs and inside jokes and a mother figure who looked at me like she knew what I was thinking but wouldn't out me.

I felt beautifully sad.

"On that note," Austin stood and faced me with his hand out, "let me take you home. I could stand to walk off some of this humiliation." My stomach flipped.

"Thank you for coming tonight." Mary Kay pulled me in for a tight hug. "This was the most fun I've had in a long time." She pulled back and kept me at arm's length with her hands holding my shoulders. "I hope it's not seven years before we get to see you again. We've missed you."

My chest sank a bit and it was a little harder to draw in a breath. I was having such a good time, I forgot I was leaving soon. With the weight of the looming promotion that had all but been officially decided lifted off my shoulders, I realized I let myself relax a little. Something I rarely did anymore.

Austin and I walked in a comfortable silence for a block or so, until I busted out laughing.

"What?" he asked, looking over at me smiling.

"I was just thinking of your dinosaur raccoon."

"It was totally a dinosaur."

"With ears."

"A dinosaur with ears," he laughed. "Exactly."

"They're amazing. I forgot how that felt." My voice caught.

"How what felt?"

"Having a family." I took a deep breath. "People who know you.

Like, really know you." My head was swimming from too much food and wine. I still felt the throbbing of my sore stomach muscles from laughter as we walked.

"I'm sorry."

When people found out I barely had a family, they usually tried to make me feel better by telling me how awful their family was. Stories about their annoying older brother teasing them, their sister stealing their clothes, their awkward uncle hitting on their friends at Christmas dinner. God, what I would give for a *burned-turkey-on-Thanksgiving* story of my own.

We continued to walk along quiet back roads until we hit his street. We heard crickets chirping, palm fronds swaying, and the sound of the water in the distance, but we didn't see a single car drive by. I had a warm buzz radiating through me. For once I wasn't obsessing about a call, or a report, or wondering what the next step was. I wasn't upset about the lack of people running into me or the background noise of honking and shouting that was all but absent.

I was happy.

"Your family is amazing. And hilarious."

"And they adore you."

"That's your typical Sunday night, then?"

"It's not typically *that* animated. It's usually more of a two-bottle-night adventure, not a six-bottle one."

We walked up to his house and he stopped a few paces behind me.

"I'm sorry."

I turned at the sound of his voice.

"About tonight and how I was acting. You haven't done a single thing to warrant me acting like an emo lovestruck teenager toward you."

"Lovestruck?" I questioned, raising my brows.

He blushed and shook his head, dismissing the comment. "You go on in and head to bed. I'm going to sit out here for a bit and clear my head." He nodded toward his front patio swing. "I'll see you tomorrow, Sam."

I could have said good night and walked into his house and shut the door behind me.

I could have thought about the fact I was leaving in just under a week and had no intention of coming back. Ever.

I could have thought the right thing to do would be to let him eventually meet someone here, and not make things more complicated.

I could have.

But I didn't.

I took a deep breath and stepped closer to him, within an inch of his face. His breath smelled of red wine and chocolate. He didn't budge as I crept closer, his hands quarantined to his pockets. His eyes darkened and searched mine, like he was desperately trying to uncover and catalog every shade of brown in them.

And he waited.

He waited while my insides went on a hundred-foot rollercoaster vertical drop and every word I've learned since age two left my brain. His eyes wandered down to my mouth and my lips barely parted, a wordless command my traitorous body was happy to follow.

I took a deep breath.

"For once, I'm not trying to figure out everything ahead of time. I'm not asking questions, not dissecting every possible scenario to guarantee it all will work out in the end and I won't get hurt."

"Okay." Flecks of gold swam around in his heavy eyes and his breath quickened.

"Coming home is really awful for me. And no one ever made this place less scary but you do. You make me think I may actually be able to survive my real life here."

I inched closer. He tilted his head down, his nose brushing the side of mine.

The heat of his breath filled my mouth, warming my chest, and time seemed to check out for a moment. He was close enough that the worn cotton of his T-shirt teased my hands, and I wanted nothing more than to tug the fabric over his head, and sink my fingers into his skin.

"I'm not a one night kinda guy, Sam."

I tilted my mouth up to almost reach his, closing the small distance that stood between us. His eyes didn't leave mine.

"Take your hands out of your pockets."

His eyes dropped to my mouth. "If I do, I won't be able to keep them off you."

My breathing was shallow, and his stopped, waiting for permission.

I leaned my hips into him and whispered into his lips. "That's kinda what I was hoping for."

In a split second, his hands gripped me and my back was up against the front door. The warmth of his fingers found their way to my waist, to the tiny sliver of skin that sat in between my shirt and the top of my jeans.

We stared at each other, every *almost* moment replaying in my head. Then his lips crashed into mine, hot and desperate, as his teeth grazed across my bottom lip. His tongue coaxed my mouth open as he tilted my head gently, his fingers laced through my hair, deepening his reach.

My stomach plummeted, a soft groan coming from the pit of my need into his mouth. His hum matched mine, the sound winding its way into my bloodstream.

"Samantha." The desperation in his voice sent a line of fire straight down my back to my toes. I sighed into his mouth as he kissed me over and over again, each lick and bite deeper, slower.

I grabbed his waist, pulling him closer, wanting to crawl into his shirt and bury myself into his skin.

This. *This* was what I wanted. What I needed.

He leaned into me, bracing one hand on the doorjamb as I reached behind me for the knob and flung it open.

"Your door's unlocked?" I asked through shortened breaths as we fell into his house.

"It's Rock Island. No one locks their doors." He bent down and swiped my legs out from under me, wrapping me around him as he carried me to the couch.

I ached for him as I straddled him, wanting to feel his skin on mine in every place that swarmed with him. His smell, his touch, the way his hands claimed my thighs as they gripped him on the couch.

His mouth slid down my neck, heated and ravenous, pulling at my skin with his teeth. Every inch of my body molded to his, like it was perfectly made to fit into every crevice his body had. A puzzle piece finally finding its fit. A spark finally finding the trail of lighter fluid it'd been searching for.

I didn't want slow and steady. I wanted everything.

All of him.

All of *this*.

He cupped my face and gently paused. "Samantha."

"That's the second time you've called me that."

He pinned my gaze, and took a breath, slowing us down. "I want you to be sure."

I inhaled deeply, searching his face and seeing my primal want and need reflected back right in front of me. "I promise you, I'm sure." I kissed his top lip. *"Austin Marcs."*

A sly smile bloomed across his face as he whispered his words into my mouth. "Say it again."

"Aust—" and he claimed me before I could finish.

32

AUSTIN

"Best condiment ever?" I asked. Our heads faced each other on the pillow. She lay naked, tangled up in my sheets with one leg draped over my waist. Her hair was in a messy pile behind her and she didn't have a speck of makeup on. This was my favorite look yet.

"Ketchup."

"Mayonnaise," I countered.

"Ew, gross! That stuff makes me gag."

"It's sent directly from heaven."

She giggled. That sound was catnip for me. "It's *gross*. Favorite color?"

"Navy blue."

It took her a second. "Red. Ruby red."

"I thought it was green?"

"I think I changed it." She beamed at me. "I think I just changed my favorite color." Her eyes were filled with disbelief, like a kid caught with a hand in the cookie jar and her mom just said, *Oh, go on, honey.*

"If you were an animal, which one would you be?"

"Ooh, that's a good one." She pulled at her lip with her teeth and a flash of her biting my shoulder last night crashed into my mind.

"How about a baby kangaroo so you'd have to carry me around all day?"

"You're too heavy to carry around all day." She laughed and palmed my face. I rolled on top of her and pinned her to the bed as she laughed. I kissed a line down her cheek, following each of the freckles on her face. I wanted to bury myself in her for the rest of the day.

"We're going to be here all day if you're kissing every one of them."

"That's—my—plan," I said, in between pecks.

Patrick and his cousin had been manning the majority of the ferry runs this week while I spent every waking moment I could with Sam. I wanted to soak in all I could with her. Some part of me hated to admit it, but they were doing an amazing job. Not only did it not sink or run aground, they weren't even late—not a single time. I even had a few emails in my box praising them.

So, I stayed with Sam.

I'd count the freckles on her face until she woke up in the morning. Then I'd make her breakfast, knowing she thought runny scrambled eggs were gross and a bite of toast not covered in butter was an atrocity. She told me how she never had bacon in high school. She was scared of the grease popping from the stove, and she never had anyone else to cook it for her.

So I did.

Every morning.

I paused after I kissed the faint white line through the middle of her brow.

"It's from the accident," she answered without me asking. "Doctors said I was lucky. They had no idea how I flew through a windshield and walked away with only a scar on my eyebrow. Well, and twenty-three screws in my arm." She turned her arm around and a faint line trailed down the underside of it all the way down to her wrist. "Oh, and a medically induced coma for three days but there's no scar from that anywhere."

"She came to pick you up that night?" I lay back down beside her and hooked my leg around hers.

"The night of the pep rally. I knew she had been drinking, she always did. I just didn't realize she was that far gone. She masked it really well."

I couldn't imagine living in a house with someone who would put her daughter in danger by choice.

"She'd wake up and have vodka in her coffee and I had no idea for months." As she talked she ran her fingers along my arm. "It was small in the beginning. I'd find her keys in the fridge or in the silverware drawer. She'd forget conversations we'd just had the night before. At first I thought she was just having trouble processing everything with Dad, but then I started to find empty containers in hidden places, like in our garage or in the trunk of the car. This one time I came home from school and there was a take-out soda on the counter. I took a sip and it felt like gasoline coating my throat. I coughed so hard I almost threw up."

"Did you ask her about it?"

"I didn't at first. I wanted to see what she'd do. When she got home, she picked it up, took a long sip and didn't miss a beat. When I asked her what she was drinking she said, *Just a Coke*. When I told her I had a sip and it didn't taste like Coke to me, she got snippy and said, *Well, it's the off brand, it's not going to taste like Coca-Cola.*"

I leaned in to kiss her scar again. I held my lips to her, breathing in her scent, wondering how many things she'd seen over her lifetime. How many times she'd been disappointed, let down, forgotten about.

I wanted to take care of her.

I wanted to be the one who showed her she wasn't someone who could be forgotten.

Her phone *ding*ed from the bedside table. She leaned over to check it and a sour sneer passed over her face.

"PuggyWuggy?" I asked.

"Ooh, that's a good one." The sound of her laugh belonged here, in this bed, with me.

She looked at me with sad eyes. "I have to work today."

When she sat up I pulled her arms back down and nuzzled her into the sheets.

"Not all day, just a few hours. Promise. Just enough to stave them off until Saturday when I get home."

The silence felt like a rupture in my stomach.

Saturday.

One day left.

"I'll make a few runs with Patrick and we'll meet up for dinner. Sound good?"

The last thing she needed was to feel guilty about me on top of everything else she was dealing with. I wanted to ask her to stay on the island. To ask if it were possible to work from here for a while. Or come back down. But I needed time to figure out how.

～

Patrick busied himself tying the boat to the dock. "Alright, spill it. You haven't let me run a day of shuttles across solo in, well, ever, actually. You've let me captain this whole week, and now you're walking around all smiley today like Shirley Temple."

"I am not *smiley*."

"What'd you do, get laid or something?"

I turned away from him so he couldn't see my cheeks flush.

"Oh, my good Lord up above, I was kidding! Look at you!"

"I don't know what you're talking about." I pulled at my work collar that all of a sudden seemed a bit too tight.

"You're sweating."

"It's ninety degrees outside."

"You're pulling at your collar and your face is flushed. And you're *smiling*." His million-dollar smile took over his face.

"I smile," I argued. "Aren't you supposed to be tying down something? Or cleaning something?"

He beamed at me. Then I saw the pieces click as his face lost a little bit of its sunshine.

"Wait a minute, you and Sam?" He paused. "Is that a good idea?"

"We're just hanging out. Now get to work."

He stared me down. It was the look he gave me after Vanessa cheated on me and I told him I was fine.

"She's leaving soon, man."

"And I'm not quite sure why everyone thinks it's their business to tell—"

"I'm just saying," he interrupted as his hands flew up, defending himself. "What are you going to do, give me the business and move up to the city? I can't exactly see you at an art gallery with tight pants and a glass of champagne talking about the rise of impressionism or pop art."

"What the hell is pop art?"

"Art based on modern popular culture. You have to know these kinds of things when you live in the city, dude."

"I'm not moving to the *city*." But even as the words left my mouth, I wondered if that was an option. What would it look like to wake up next to her every day? What did her apartment look like? Did she lay her clothes over the chair in the corner of her room like she did at my place?

"Just be careful, man, that's all I'm saying. She's a good girl, but not one who's going to stay. Your life's here, not there. You'd suffocate in the city."

"And I'm going to suffocate you if you don't turn your ass around and mop that deck."

He narrowed his eyes and turned to the bucket. "Okay, okay. For the record I'm happy you didn't forget how to use your wiener."

He ducked just in time to miss the ball of rope I threw at his head.

〰

I texted her on our last run back in. Her face was a constant in my vision all day. Her eyelashes. The stray hairs around her forehead that weren't long enough to reach her eyes. The little red marks she had on her lower lip from biting them. The dip in her cheek when she smiled.

I kept looking at the water and thinking about what she said. I had built this business from the ground up. We were successful, busting at the seams and looking to expand, but was it really what I wanted to do for the rest of my life?

I felt alive on the water. I couldn't imagine a day without being on it in some form. But I started to think about what I really wanted. What would life look like if I could do anything I wanted?

Patrick's comment about suffocating kept playing through my mind. Could you even go fishing in New York City? Was that a thing?

Maybe if her mom got better she'd consider coming back home. She didn't seem happy at her job, and based on what she told me over the last few weeks, the promotion she was gunning for was going to the pug guy anyway. I knew she and her mom didn't have a great relationship, but things could change. They had to if she got better.

The more time I spent away from her, the more I wondered what it would look like if she stayed. Or if I left. I tried to keep my mind focused on the present, knowing her plans to go back to the city were concrete, but my masochistic heart wouldn't leave it alone. The pendulum swinging gave me whiplash.

What if?

She texted me she'd be another hour. Patrick and I had locked up for the day. He was heading home and I had an hour to kill. If I went home I'd stare at the door and drive myself insane waiting for her, so I headed to Harpoon's instead. Most of the local captains took a night cap there and while I normally avoided a tipsy tale, a quick fish story would serve as a welcome distraction.

"What's up, Skipper?" A strong hand squeezed my shoulder and I turned my head to find Robby sliding into the stool next to me at the bar, a fierce sunburn surrounding where his aviators blocked the rays.

"Not much, Sea Legs. You feeling a little less green?"

"It's Director Sea Legs to you. Got word just a few minutes ago." He signaled for a beer to the bartender.

My stomach turned over. I didn't have to ask, but I did anyway. "What do you mean?"

"The job. It's official. I'm officially celebrating."

Shit. The promotion. I wondered if Sam knew. She was going to be a wreck now that the promotion was his. I checked my phone but it was a blank screen.

"Funny seeing you here," he continued, "although it's the only place I've found open for a decent beer on the island so far." He looked around, eyeing the weathered nautical rope hanging from the ceiling and the battered wooden beams that lined the patio water view. "The water views are nice from some of these places, but I still don't get why people love it here so much."

"Depends on your priorities, I guess." He stared at me, waiting for my answer. "So, the views, yes. The sunsets are pretty spectacular. But there's something about the way of life down here. It's easier. It's like places you read about in books, or see in movies, but it's all the time. Not just this special place you get to visit. It still has this charm about it, like an undiscovered cove that not many people know about."

"*Yet*. Not that many people know about it *yet*. Once we finish this resort and our marketing team gets moving it'll be a different story. It'll top all the travel lists coming up in the next couple years."

Sam seemed conflicted about the resort lately, like maybe she didn't want to bring throngs of people here. Or maybe it was the promotion. But every time I brought it up, she would change the subject.

"And you get to single-handedly deliver every one of those tourists flocking in. Aren't you a lucky bastard." He grinned, nodding to the bartender for a drink. "What are you going to name her?"

"Name who?"

"The new boat. I was thinking *Ferry Godfather*. That'd be pretty funny, huh?"

I shook my head, trying to latch on to what he was hinting at.

"You get too much sun, Skipper? Isn't the captain supposed to name their boat? I thought that was a thing." He chuckled and took a long swig from the bottle. "I told Samantha it's not every day you get a multimillion-dollar boat handed to you. I told her I thought you lucked out."

Lucked out? Multimillion-dollar boat?

I looked over at him. His typical arrogant smirk was dialed down. Like he wasn't aiming to poke me, just laying it out flat.

"Right, yeah, it's definitely a thing. Tell me more about this boat

I lucked out on." I kept my voice steady, hoping he wouldn't catch on that I had no idea what he was talking about. "How big is it again?"

"I don't speak boat, but it carries five hundred at a time, I think."

Five hundred.

He shrugged, like that was nothing. "It'll be a lot different than what you're used to, but I guess a boat's a boat, yeah? They've all got a steering wheel, and they float. Although I think this one drives itself. Hell, you could just sit in your cockpit and drink a martini, if you wanted."

"It's called a wheelhouse." The motion in the room slowed down around me, the hum of the bar muffled in the background.

"Whatever. I'm just glad you agreed to it. Would've been an awkward conversation if you wanted to keep your own ferry in business, know what I mean?" He laughed into the neck of his beer again as he took a sip.

My hand gripped my beer bottle hard enough to send it shattering. "Absolutely."

"Makes sense that it's you though, I guess. You still get to be out on the water, just don't have to deal with all the runaround of owning your own business anymore. Glenn will probably pay you way more than what you make with your boat anyway. I mean, no offense or anything. It's a win-win."

He clapped my back and all I saw was red.

"Yeah, sounds like it."

"Nature calls." He pushed his barstool back and disappeared down the hall toward the bathroom.

I stayed frozen, gripping my beer bottle, watching a single drop of water slowly slide down the side of the glass. Was this why Sam wouldn't talk about work?

Was it possible she knew the resort planned to incorporate a *five-hundred-passenger* ferry into its design?

Five hundred guests at a time.

Every hour. Every day.

The numbers swirled in my head as the drop of water fell to the bar top and vanished underneath the bottle.

Once that thing started running, I'd be out of business in less than a month.

33

SAMANTHA

When I was assigned to a new project at Goodrich, the first thing I did was walk around the city to see where my feet would take me. I'd watch where people would go, what stores or parks they gravitated toward. I'd let my mind wander. I'd start seeing things in my head played out like a movie. Community gatherings, parades, parks with signs announcing festivals, balloons floating in the air and ice cream dripping down kids hands, blankets spread out across the ground with dogs catching Frisbees, weaving in and out of people. The details would bombard my brain.

That hadn't happened here. Yet.

But I finally started to see it in my mind. It was still fuzzy, but it wasn't dictated by pool bar sales and occupancy rates. I saw families on fishing charters, and generations taking a family reunion picture on the beach. I saw small stores with hand-painted signs at local business fairs. Sunday morning markets with fresh flowers and smoothies. Kids riding resort bikes with seashell-filled baskets all over the property mid scavenger hunt. Things were starting to click into place. I just needed a bit more time to pull it all together.

I was on the couch and had just turned my phone back on when Austin walked in the door.

My phone began dinging back to back with notifications pouring in.

"Busy day?" he asked as my phone chimed again and again.

When I looked down at my phone, the room hollowed out.

> **IVY:** where r u
> **IVY:** answer ur phone
> **IVY:** pick up ive called you 10 times
> I didn't want 2 send over txt but ur not answering
> i dont want u to hear it from him first
> Robby got the promotion its official
> pls call me when u get this

"You okay?" he asked.

The room tilted.

"Yeah, it's just stuff for tomorrow," I lied as I got up from the couch and made my way to the front door. "I just need a sec."

I held my breath as I dialed her number. I knew this was coming, but to actually hear it severed the thin string of hope I still had with a blowtorch.

"God, where have you been?" she yelled at me. "I've been trying to get ahold of you. I was trying to get you to come back today."

I was in a fog, my insides still like Jell-O from her text.

"It's a mess. Glenn fast-tracked his decision, got the board's approval, and announced it at the staff meeting earlier, that you, for some reason, weren't signed on for."

I'd turned off my phone to brainstorm uninterrupted this morning, completely forgetting about the staff call. Once ideas started to finally come, I wanted to unplug and sink into them.

"Are you okay?" she asked.

"Describe for me what *okay* looks like." The image of me walking into Robby's corner office ran through my mind. It was decorated with lighted beer signs and a neon slide in the corner.

"You need to come back and we can fight this."

"Fight this?" I asked. "I'm not walking in with my tail between my legs for a promotion that he didn't give me. That's ridiculous."

"Everyone here knows you should have gotten it. They're all talking about it."

"Good to know I'm the subject of the watercooler gossip."

"Robby hasn't even done anything but lie in a hospital bed lately. It doesn't even make sense. Two analysts have already said they're quitting if they get transferred to him."

I looked out toward the water. I couldn't actually see it from Austin's front yard but I could feel it. I could hear the palm fronds rustling in the wind and the air smelled of salt.

The promotion was gone. The entire reason I agreed to come to Florida was to show I deserved this promotion. That I was the right choice for it. But being in Florida was now officially pointless. I was stuck here, gunning for ideas that were already dead in the water.

I couldn't seem to get enough air in my chest. What came next? What happened when I hung up this phone? Since everything I was doing was pointless anyway, did I hop on a plane and go back home? Did I go inside and pretend like there was still a chance I wasn't irrelevant?

Maybe I should still write down the ideas I had. They could serve as inspiration when I'd inevitably be job searching when I got back to the city. They were good but not clear yet. I just needed more time.

And I didn't have it.

There were too many emotions running through my body after we got off the call. I looked down at my feet and noticed the gravel in his driveway. It was made up of tiny white shells, small ones about the size of my fingernail.

The screen opened behind me and Austin stepped out.

"It's official. Robby got it." I couldn't even say the word *promotion*. It just felt dirty. And wrong. And so, so unfair.

"I'm so sorry." He walked toward me and wrapped his arms around me from behind. "I know you really wanted it." I settled into the warmth of his chest, his shirt sporting a faded football team logo. It was cotton, washed over a thousand times and smelled like detergent. "But look at the bright side," his words tickled my neck through my hair, "maybe now you can stay here instead."

I quickly drew my head forward and turned around. I had no idea what I was looking for as my eyes searched his face, but confusion and anger bubbled up, mixed in with the other emotions fighting for attention in my chest.

"Staying here isn't an option." I knew we had avoided the subject of me leaving but staying on Rock Island was never on the table. Ever.

"But I thought you just said Robby got the promotion? I thought you said if he did, you weren't going to stay there?"

"I don't know what I'm going to do. But we have a huge presentation to give and I'm pitching one of the biggest projects I've ever had. I'm not just going to bail out of that."

"Of course not." He stepped toward me and held on to my arms. "That's not what I meant. It's just, I assumed Robby's idea would be the one you would help pitch. I thought your idea wasn't in the cards anymore."

"I don't know what's in the cards!" My voice raised as I stepped back again. I had no idea if I'd be helping Robby and Glenn pitch their idea to the board. Or if I'd even have a job when I got back to the city. Or if I even *wanted* this job.

"Hey, hey." He put his hands up and lowered his voice. "I'm sorry, I just figured it wasn't that big of a deal now."

"Of course it's a big deal." Frustration brewed like a tropical storm in my head.

"I just thought..."

"You thought what? That things would change because we slept together a few times? I won't ever move back here, Austin. The island is a last resort for me. Actually, it's beyond a last resort. It's not even a possibility."

The only sign from him that he was upset was the deep breath he took.

"You really thought I'd stay here and give up my entire life in the city?"

"From what it sounds like, it's not much of a life you actually enjoy." His steady voice buried underneath my skin.

"You don't get to do that." I turned from him and headed back into the house, royally pissed off. I needed to grab my stuff and get some space. It was all too much. Too much feeling. Too much expectation. Not enough air.

"Do what?"

"Judge my life. You're the one sitting here running a business you don't even want because you're too scared to go after what you *do* want." I let the screen door slam shut between us.

"Kind of irrelevant since it's a company that's apparently being forced out of business within a few months anyway." The bottom fell out and I turned around.

He knew.

I was expecting his anger, ready to fight the wrath I deserved for holding this secret for so long, but he stood there with his arms at his side and a melancholy look on his face. He lowered his voice. "Thanks for the heads-up on that one, by the way."

I didn't know what to say. I didn't know how much he knew or where he heard it from.

"I heard I get to captain quite the ship," he continued. All I could do was look at the floor as he opened the screen door. "The thing I can't figure out is why you didn't tell me first."

"Did Robby tell you?" I asked.

"That's not the question you should be asking." His voice sounded so *disappointed*. I wish he would have been mad. I wish he would've yelled something so I could've yelled something back. I was mad at myself. I was mad at Robby. I knew I couldn't trust him. I should have seen this coming and somehow told Austin myself.

"And for the record," he continued, "I'm not too scared to go after what I want. The timing isn't right."

"That's always everyone's excuse." I was so tired of hearing that. Timing is never right. For anything.

"What's your excuse? Why are you so scared to be happy?"

"That doesn't even make sense." I turned back down the hallway to his bedroom. My clothes were scattered around, piled up on his chair and at the foot of the bed. I shoved dirty socks and shirts into my bag until it was overflowing.

"So you're just going to leave?" he asked.

"I have a plane to catch."

"It's not until tomorrow."

He grabbed my hand and stilled me. "Why?"

"Why, what?" I spat, wrenching my wrist free.

"Why are you so scared to fall in love with me?"

I looked at him to see if he was serious. "That's a ridiculous question."

"You're terrified of it. Why?"

"I'm not scared. Or terrified. I'm just not *interested*." Pajama pants. Hairbrush. I couldn't tell if I threw his clothes or mine in my bag.

"So, these last couple weeks, you've felt nothing? You're just, fine?" He followed me around his house, room after room, collecting the things I had scattered the last few days.

"Yeah, I'm *fine*."

"You've turned into a pretty good liar lately."

That stung.

"I need to go back to the city. You know, where I *work*. And *live*. That was the plan, remember?" I walked to his couch and threw around the cushions looking for my keys that had mysteriously vanished.

"Plans can change."

"My plans don't change." *TV stand, bar counter, by the fridge...*

"You can't say you don't feel anything for me."

"That doesn't matter." *Kitchen table, coffee table, kitchen counter...*

"*Everything* matters." He stepped in front of me and blocked my path. "Tell me you feel the exact same way about me that you did a month ago."

The truth was I felt *safe* a month ago.

I knew what was expected of me. I knew my job, my responsibilities. I knew where I fit and didn't. I knew nothing was guaranteed but if I worked really hard, there was a smaller chance I would be surprised by something and it would hurt. I could deal with an overconfident, selfish boss and a cocky coworker who made inappropriate sex jokes. What I couldn't deal with was someone laying out their heart for me and expecting me to do the same.

For God's sake, where were my keys?

I looked past him toward the door and there they were, in the key dish.

"Stay." The intensity in his eyes was blazing. They were pleading, aching, begging me to say something. He crossed the distance between us and cupped my face in his hands. His fingers laced into my hair and his mouth desperately consumed mine. My knees betrayed me as they melted underneath his touch. The familiar smell of the ocean cradled me as the room stilled.

Alarms fired in my head for every reason this was wrong. I felt the emotion pulling me down. If I didn't stop, it would drown me. There wouldn't be any coming back from this. It would mean everything would change. This life I had built brick by brick would come crashing down. No, not crashing down—bulldozed and set on fire with semi-grade gasoline and lit with a blowtorch.

I saw it play out in my head. I'd move back home and run into my old elementary school teacher at the grocery store newly pregnant, with a one-year-old screaming in my cart. I'd work in the concession stand on Friday nights at the football field handing over greasy aluminum-wrapped hot dogs to pimple-faced teenagers. I'd have a high school class reunion every Saturday night at Harpoon's where I'd strike up small talk with people I used to lock myself in my room over, their words spearing through my fourteen-year-old self-worth like a hot iron through ice cream.

I'd give up everything I've worked so hard to build the last seven years, and all for what? For the hope that this little flutter would grow into something more and actually be worth it? Trust that it would never leave me on the floor of my bedroom covered in tears and drowning in snot because he decided I was a little more broken than he thought I was? Or maybe I didn't want three kids and a dog but I wanted a corner office with a view and that just wouldn't work here?

Could I really roll the dice and hope he'd never get sick with a brain tumor, or trust that he wouldn't crack and break if something too hard came our way?

I pulled away from him. I couldn't do it. I couldn't say yes and give up everything.

His lips followed after mine.

"Don't." I put my hand on his chest and took a step back.

"Don't leave."

I grabbed my keys off the dish and walked out the screen door. I refused to look back. This wasn't going to be one of those endings where the girl changes her mind at the last minute, turns back, and runs into her lover's arms. My life didn't work like that. Pain didn't just go away. Ghosts didn't just decide to lie down and take a nap.

"What about your mom?" he called out.

"What about her?"

"What about when she comes back? You don't want to be here for that?"

"I'll pass on taking a front-row seat to the inevitable destruction that'll follow that one."

"How can you say that?"

"You haven't been here for every other time she's been *doing great*. It's great until it's not, then it sucks your soul dry."

"What about Lexi's wedding? She's getting married next weekend."

"Lexi doesn't need me there." I answered him without even turning my head as he followed me down the shell driveway.

"She wants you there."

"Don't use her to try and guilt me into staying. I don't have a choice, Austin."

"You always have a choice."

I kept walking. Just a few more feet and I could tie this up and shelve it right next to all the other boxes from this place. "You really don't think you deserve to be happy." It wasn't a question.

"My definition of happiness is very different from yours."

"You just want distractions to keep you from wanting more."

"You have no idea what I want." I opened the driver's side door.

"But I know what I want. I want you." He pushed the door shut behind me and pinned me to the car.

I blinked back the tears welling in my eyes. "It's not that simple."

"It is." He lifted my chin. "Sam, look at me. Everyone writes a story in their head that eventually becomes their life. If you don't write it for yourself then everyone else is going to write it for you."

Other people's circumstances dictated my entire life. It's how it had always been. It was time for me to choose what I wanted.

"You want me today. Maybe tomorrow. Maybe even in a few years. But there will come a moment when I won't fit anymore."

"Why can't you just trust me?"

"I do trust you. That's not it."

"Then tell me what it is," he pleaded.

"It's nothing, it's just not worth—"

"Not worth being happy?"

"It's not worth the pain when you eventually leave." The words burned like acid pouring out of my mouth. "Everyone always does."

There it was. The reason why I worked so hard. The reason I

buried myself in distractions. In this awful thing called *real life*, I could do everything—bend myself until I broke, give up every dream I've ever had, put everyone else above and before me, and it still wouldn't be enough for someone to stay. There was still a chance they could leave, whether they choose to themselves or not.

I belonged in the black-and-white of the world I'd built that respected time, energy, and effort. There were calculated risks for things I was willing to bargain with, and outcomes based on data. There weren't bad scans one day showing something under the surface that shouldn't be. Business proposals rarely got up and walked out the door because they didn't measure up to what was originally promised. At least, not on my watch. I didn't have to be *enough* to keep my work around, but with people I did. There was an overwhelming sense of the possibility that if I did something wrong or didn't do enough, they'd leave. God forbid I miss an expectation they had and I come up short.

"That's not fair."

"People leave. That's what they do."

"Not if they love each other."

"Love is never enough. I've learned that twice over."

His chest sank as he stepped forward and rested his hands on my neck. "I'm not your father. Or your mother. And I don't deserve that."

"You deserve a hell of a lot better than what I can give you."

"Good things don't always get taken away, Sam. That's not how it works."

"Oh, my bad. I guess I forgot the universe was *fair*." I hated how the crack in my voice betrayed how deep the anger ran.

"That's not what I'm saying." His thumbs traced my collarbone gently, leaving a trail of ache behind them.

"I'm due for *something* to work out, right? I mean, what are the chances? Enough bad has happened, I'm bound to have something good turn out. But that's not the way this world works. People leave. Sometimes they choose to. But sometimes they don't have a choice."

He was pleading with his eyes. I had to get away soon or I'd be done for. I wanted to change my mind. I wanted to sink into his arms and let him carry me inside and cook bacon for me every single morning for the rest of my life. I wanted to stay and pretend like the world could be kind, and life could be fair and predictable, but it couldn't.

It wouldn't.

I gently pushed him back and looked into his eyes. They had turned more brown than green.

I got into my car and pressed the start button.

I didn't have to look in the rearview mirror to know he stood there, willing me to turn around.

This was the right decision. I fit in a world of perfectly squared off city streets buzzing with life and electricity. Busy corners and traffic lights and merchants shouting at you. Magazine stands and tiny outdoor spaces a foot wide people convince themselves are big enough to be called patios, coffee shops on every block and an entire district of Korean takeout. Pencil skirts and work calls, conference tables and happy hour at O'Keefe's. That's where I belonged.

Not here. Not in this place that had only ever taken things from me. Not in this place where my heart swelled and hurt and leaped and felt everything I didn't want it to.

In the early morning hours, I sat on the old vintage couch in Mom's living room, the one that reminded me of grandparents I never had.

I paid an arm and a leg to arrange for a private boat to pick me up and head to the airport and needed to leave soon. The clock on the wall ticked down second by second as I blinked through the pictures of me smiling on the mantel.

Me on the beach holding a crab by its claw.

Tick.

I remember the way the water pooled at my feet and made little swirls in the sand under the waves.

Tick.

Me smiling with a Lisa Frank Caboodle on Christmas morning under a tree of ripped wrapping paper with sleep still in my eyes.

Tick.

I remember walking into the living room with my hands over my eyes as Dad guided me out, Mom holding a video camera on her shoulder that looked like it weighed a hundred pounds trying to catch my reaction to Santa visiting in the night.

Tick.

Me and my mom smiling at graduation, my arm wrapped in a bandage and sitting in a wheelchair.

Tick.

I remember the way the rubber on the wheels whirred as I rolled across the stage for my diploma. Mrs. Peabody built a ramp so I could cross just like everyone else. Except I was no longer just like everyone else.

Tick.

I had slept, but barely. My eyes stung. Even Taylor Hanson winking at me from the back of my door couldn't put a smile on my face.

Lexi's name flashed across the screen as my phone rang beside me.

"I told you this was going to happen." Her voice was kind but tired, like she had already talked about this at length with Austin.

"I can't just pretend I don't have a job and play house the rest of my life." I tried to exhale the weight of the coming day. "I was never going to stay. He knew that."

"Then you should have stayed away from him."

I closed my eyes and took a breath. The house smelled stale. "Lexi, I can't do this right now."

"Oh, okay, cool, just hit me up in seven years and we'll pick up right where we left off like nothing happened."

A tingle crept toward the front of my face and the burn of tears stung my eyes. "That's not fair."

"Neither is you coming back, uprooting his life, and giving him hope for something you knew wasn't going to be anything other than a fling."

"I didn't plan on it happening, Lexi. And by the way, it's not like this whole situation is only my fault." The tone of my voice surprised me. I was so angry. I was angry at Lexi for calling me out and for me realizing that's exactly what I did. At Robby for being an asshole and still coming out on top. At Glenn for caring more about bourbon and golf than work ethic and intelligence. At Mom for collapsing when I needed her most. At having to make my own breakfast, and lunch and dinner because she couldn't get off the couch. At being scared to cook bacon, for God's sake.

At my dad for dying.

And at Austin for worming his way into my heart when I tried so desperately to keep him out.

"It doesn't have to be that hard, Sam."

I knew she was trying to make me feel better, but it made me feel worse.

"Love isn't exactly a fairy tale for everyone else," I spat back. "We all don't get to bat our eyelashes from behind a bar where we're slinging beers for tourists and have some college coach swoop in and rescue us from our shitty bartending job that we didn't even need because our parents would float us the rest of their lives anyway." My face felt hot and my hands were shaking. I was pacing in front of the fireplace. "You get to play house with your cute little Cinderella story and pretend you did something to deserve it all. It's not like that for everyone else."

The line fell silent. My breath was short and fast and tears stung my eyes. Her voice came a few moments later as a whisper. "You want to know why I stayed here, Sam? Because of my family. They were worth staying for." Then her voice came through, angry and full of steam. "And then Rex. He was worth staying for. And my friends. And the life I've built here. That was all worth more to me than chasing some dream somewhere else."

"Yeah, well, we're not the same person."

"No, we're not. I decided to stay because of the people I care about. You decided to run to get away from the one person who didn't care about you."

It was a slap I never saw coming. If anyone understood what I carried, what I went through, it was her. For her to throw it back in my face wasn't just cruel—it hollowed me out, leaving me with nothing to fight it off.

"What I wanted to be didn't exist here."

"Don't pretend you left to chase a dream. You left to escape her at the cost of everything."

"You have no idea what it's like to have something ripped from you. To live in fear that every single thing you care about eventually gets snatched away or leaves."

"I'm sorry, Sam. I'm sorry for what you went through but it doesn't mean it's always going to end up like that."

I needed to be at the boat dock five minutes ago. "I have to get to the airport. I need to go." And I hung up.

I looked at the graduation picture again. Anger welled in my eyes as I walked over to it and slammed it face down. I didn't even bother to wipe the tears away this time. I just let them fall to the floor, along with all the expectations and hopes I had that maybe, just maybe, home could mean something different this one time.

34

SAMANTHA

My tiny city apartment refrigerator was stocked with fancy waters and prepackaged lunch and dinner containers. The fern in the corner of the kitchen looked livelier than when I left.

This was the right decision. I belonged in a world where honking and yelling drifted up from street corners below, where white and gray dominated color palettes with clean lines and angles. Where things were as they seem. And where there wasn't a godforsaken starfish in a ten-mile radius.

I didn't need homemade breakfast. I had a five-star chef just down the street who did that for me whenever I wanted. He cooked bacon too. Painted white wicker and sea creature sculptures didn't belong here. Neither did splashing waves or palm fronds rustling in the wind. No drunk dials in the middle of the night from some guy asking me to come get my inebriated mother.

And people wore *shirts*.

I took a breath. This is what I had worked my whole life for. To get *here*. Not to be stuck *there*.

ME: I've got an idea

IVY: does it involve burying a body

ME: Close.
You mentioned before
you've got a board connection

IVY: i said that?

ME: I need a 10 min slot with the entire board
at the meeting next week
to discuss the resort proposal.
Has to be before Glenn and the team
pitch their whizz calamity.

IVY: BEFORE glenn???

ME: Yes

IVY: i luv where this is going

ME: If I'm going down,
I'm going down in flames.

IVY: 🔥 🔥 🔥

There was a fierce kick at my door ten minutes later. I looked through the peephole and saw Ivy's eyeball peeking through a fern branch at me.

"You're a sight for sore eyes." I pulled the door open to let her and her entourage of bags and drinks come in.

She piled her stuff on my kitchen counter. "I brought you a venti vanilla latte with oat milk, Celsius for later, and a turkey-cheese wrap from Delco's."

"What's the fern for?" I asked, pointing to the one she held in her hand.

"That's a fake." She nodded to the perky one on my kitchen counter. "The other died of natural causes." She walked over and put the new live fern on the counter and threw the fake one in the garbage can. "There. Now it's alive."

"Oh. Okay."

"We have the presentation slot scheduled for four p.m. on Monday. The entire board has RSVP'd yes."

"Wow. That was fast. The entire board?" I asked.

"All twelve of them. You have ten minutes. And you're scheduled before Glenn, but heads-up, he'll be in the room. I've already requested an extra trash can for when he shits his pants when you start talking."

"How'd you pull that off?"

"I'd tell you but I'd have to kill you. So, we've got one day to blow their minds with your ideas. Office or apartment all-nighter? Your choice."

I just stared at her and blinked. Was I really going to do this?

"Let's reacclimate." She stepped in front of me, grabbed my shoulders, and slowed her voice. "You are no longer in Florida. You are in New York City, at your apartment. You are Samantha Leigh, kick-ass resort developer with a score to settle. Do you know who the president of the United States of America is?"

"Yes, but does that actually matter?"

"Aaaand she's back. Here, drink this, it'll help." She handed over a mixed green smoothie out of her Mary Poppins bag that tasted like grass with a tiny bit of metal stirred in.

She stared me down until I drank the entire thing. "Okay, now out with it."

"I'm fine. I just need to get back into the swing of things, that's all." Jet lag was a real thing. Most of the time.

"I'm going to ask you one more time, and if you don't want to talk about the guy yet, I get it. I will switch the conversation back over to work and how we nail Pugly Duckling and his harebrained ideas to the wall and prove you are master of all things beach town development. Now, are you okay?"

"Yes. I am fine. I promise. It's just going to take me a moment to shake the sand from my brain. Pun intended."

"Noted."

"An office all-nighter. This place is too sterile." I looked around and wondered why the monochromatic tone of the room never bothered me before.

"I'll buy you another plant. And a colorful vase."

"Good plan. And maybe a key dish."

"What in the hell is a key dish?"

I paused. "A dish for keys."

"That's completely impractical."

I nodded. "Right, yeah, exactly."

Ivy went ahead as I packed up to head into the office for the next twenty-four hours. I walked out the front door of my apartment building into the flow of people. Heads were down, paces were quick. I caught a lady's eye and smiled. She grunted and stepped to the side. She was probably just late to get somewhere important.

Thunder cracked above and a tiny droplet of rain landed on my arm. But it was fine because I loved the city when it was wet and shiny. It's like it washed away the moments of yesterday and made a way for something new and bright. This was *not* the predictable movie moment where the heroine walks through a rainstorm without an umbrella, the downpour indicative of her waterfall of sad emotions.

It started to really come down, so I scooted into an alcove of an apartment building and my foot squished into something.

Please don't be poop. Please don't be poop.

I looked down and my shoe was cradled by an old hoagie sandwich, puffy and slimy from the rain. I leaned against the concrete wall and looked out. People scurried under umbrellas and jackets. The sky was gray and bleak. Black clouds moved around ominously looking for a target to dump on.

Austin's face was everywhere I looked, burned into my mind like when I looked at the sun too long as a kid. But I didn't have time for that right now. He was just a distraction. A tan, salt water–scented distraction that wrapped around me like well-worn cotton.

For a second, I tried to picture it. I looked out into the flow of people and imagined him walking by, with his worn-in jeans, flip-flops, faded high school T-shirt, and backward baseball cap. Everyone knows you can't wear flip-flops in the city. I tried to picture him in Central Park drinking a green smoothie. He'd make fun of me for it and said it tasted like grass, which it did. I'd take him to the Hudson and look out over the water. He'd ask about fishing and I'd tell him people were allowed, but there were rules. It was catch-and-release only.

I couldn't see him in a cubicle at some nine-to-five job, wearing closed-toed shoes and a button-down that itched his neck. I could see him pulling at its collar already.

He'd miss the sand. The salt water.

He'd miss sitting outside his parents' house in homemade Adirondack chairs.

He'd miss Florida sunsets and Sunday night dinners.

He'd have to give up everything.

It couldn't work. There was no way I'd go back and he didn't fit here.

35
AUSTIN

Black clouds were never a good sign.

We had a full day of ferry runs across the water and the fact the sky looked how my insides felt seemed a little too on the nose for me.

"I'll grab the top deck panels." Patrick hopped up the stairs and started rolling down the plastic sheets that would hopefully keep some of the rain from accosting our guests. He must have picked up on my vibes from the moment I stepped onto the dock this morning because he had yet to drill me with questions about how I was doing.

Even though I hadn't slept a wink the last couple days, I was grateful for a full day of work ahead of me. Anything to try and distract me from the vision of Sam's face was a welcomed diversion.

The wind started howling the moment we latched the last panel down. As we escorted guests from the building on the mainland onto the boat, the rain picked up.

"Welcome aboard, everyone!" Patrick laid on his Jamaican accent. "You know what they say when it rains on your wedding day? Same thing applies to vacation. You're guaranteed a beautiful trip from here on out. But for now, please keep your butts in your seats and hang on. It's going to be a bit of a bumpy ride today."

My phone *ding*ed on the way out of the mainland marina. My palm was slick with rain as I took it out of my pocket, trying to quell the hope of it being Sam's name on the screen. It was a text from an unknown number.

> **UNKNOWN:** We've got a deal.
> My guy's going to captain it down
> for you this week.

It was the owner of the north Florida charter who was looking to dump his passenger ferry. After finding out the new resort development's plans for their monster ferry to the island, I wasn't in the position of offering what the boat was actually worth. I had maybe two years max making money with Scuttle's Ferry before I was forced out of business. I lowballed thinking there was no way he'd take my measly offer, but he did. I'd give her a once-over for maintenance, do a few cosmetic repairs, and have her shuttling people by the end of next week. I'd already done all the numbers and scheduled out the new routes. While we'd run six days a week still, we could cut down on trips across and almost double our capacity and revenue.

But we still wouldn't be anywhere near five hundred passengers a run.

All of Sam's star-chasing comments about fishing rattled around in my brain. Yes, that was the ideal situation but timing was important. My current business was important. My crew depended on me to put food on their table. It wasn't in the cards to give that all up and go follow a shooting star. At least, not today.

Lightning lit up the sky. A few of the guests looked around, unease painted on their faces. Storms like these were typical in Florida, but lightning and thunder hit differently when you're over water. You're more exposed.

I wondered if it was raining in the city. My Google search of *what is New York City like* came up with three things consistently.

There was a lot of brick and concrete. There were no palm trees. And it was the most populous city in the United States, with over eight million people jammed into three hundred miles. I couldn't fathom that. Where did everyone sleep?

But it was surrounded by water so it couldn't be that bad.

Who was I kidding? I'd look like a fool in the city. I was beer and sandals at a dive bar. She was espresso and high heels at a museum.

I had convinced myself there was a chance she wasn't one of those who left the island for good and never came back.

I had convinced myself the island could be a place of peace for her just because I was here, ignoring everything she had lost on it.

And I had done a damn good job of convincing myself I hadn't fallen for her.

But I had.

~

The storm cleared halfway through the day and the rest of the runs across went smoothly.

"Drinks after work at my place?" It was one of the few things Patrick had said to me all day. My hunch was that Lexi had given him a heads-up for what to expect.

"Nah. Not today."

"How 'bout you come on over and have dinner. Mom's making lasagna."

I eyed him. "Is that an official invitation?"

"She's expecting ya, if that's what you're asking."

"That's a low blow." And he knew it. You didn't pass up Mabel's cooking. It wasn't an option. It was the best thing on the island and when you got an invite, you went or she'd come after you for turning down her food. Took it as a personal insult. *Ain't nobody have so little time they can't eat*, she would say.

～

I walked through their front door and spotted Mabel over the stove decked out in a colorful doughnut-printed muumuu. She turned and wiped her hands on her apron and stomped right over and gave me a hug. A real one. The kind that pricks your eyes because you know how much love someone's trying to give you through it.

"Now, I heard you had a little run-in with love. We're gonna talk about it after your belly's full." She never beat around the bush. She set expectations up front and carried on. She shoved a plate of lasagna at me and told me to go sit down.

But the moment the plates were cleared she dove in.

"Patrick, you go on and clean up the kitchen. This boy and I got some life to do."

She led me out to the back patio and patted the small cushion on one of the iron chairs.

"Now," she started as she leaned back, the chair squeaking under her weight. "I heard that girl up and left, just like she said she would."

"Yes, ma'am."

"So, what are you gonna do with that?" She stared out into the garden in her backyard. It was overflowing with all kinds of fruits and vegetables, vines crawling up over each other and hugging the worn wooden fence. It was impressive on its own, on top of the fact that gardening in Florida heat was no small feat.

Words weren't coming to me easily that day. I didn't know how to say it felt like my heart was bleeding out without saying exactly that, which felt a little dramatic.

We sat in silence for a few minutes.

"You see all that?" she asked, pointing to her garden. "It takes time and attention. Lots of it. Those things don't just decide to pop up overnight. Stubborn little suckers sometimes. But I sit with 'em long enough, water 'em when I need to, prune 'em when they need it, they come back year after year for me."

"You're the only one I know with the luck to grow things in this heat."

"It's not so much about luck. But giving 'em what they need when they need it. Just hard to know what that is sometimes."

"Are you telling me Sam needs a tall drink of water?" I asked with a forced laugh. Mabel gave me her *look*, like now wasn't the time to be covering up emotions. "She's not coming back, if that's what you're getting it." My tongue felt heavy saying it, like my mouth had wet glue inside it. "I could give her all the space in the world. That's not what she's looking for."

"And what's it that she's looking for?"

I thought about how everything she talked about wanting revolved around work or the city up until a few days ago. "A corner office and a promotion, I think."

"What exactly do you think that's going to give her?"

I thought for a second. I was sure it was a trick question. "More money?"

"Please, that girl doesn't care about money. Keep guessing."

"A better view of New York?"

"You always were a bit of a sass." She narrowed her eyes on me. "That poor girl grew up too soon. Losing a daddy who loved her, and a mama who did too, just didn't know how to show it. Too caught up in her own grief to know the difference between up and down. Loss does that to people. It messes 'em up a bit, some for a good bit of time. She lost too much too soon."

"Her mom's in rehab now."

"Heard through the grapevine she's doing pretty well, too."

So many of Sam's words flew through my mind. "She said I should start my own fishing charter."

"You told me that exact same thing when you were eight years old." She closed her eyes and tilted her head up to the sky. "Do you want to?"

"I don't know what I want. I bought the ferryboat from that north Florida charter that sold. Patrick doesn't even know yet. They're delivering this week." She looked at me, and even though I was busying my eyes tracing a tomato vine, I could feel her gaze roaming over my face to see how I felt about it all. "Do you think the fishing thing is a good idea?"

"Do you?" she asked.

"Why do you always answer a question with a question?"

"Just trying to get my boy to think is all." She reached over and patted my hand. Her hands were warm and callused. "If people asked more questions these days, they'd be a lot better off."

"The ferry thing makes sense. Buy the bigger boat. Grow the business."

She sat there silent, watching her vegetables sit still.

"I remember the first time my dad and I ever took Patrick out. I can still see the look on his face when he reeled in the first fish he'd ever caught. He had this big old goofy smile plastered across his face that he couldn't wipe off for hours. I loved seeing that. Being a part of that."

She sat in silence nodding her head and smiling to herself.

"I don't know," I continued. "Maybe there's room for that too."

"When we share something we love with others it's hard not to spread that joy around. That goofy smile you're talking about? You have that too when you're on that fishing boat."

"But the business is doing really well. Although fast-forward two years and it may not be around anymore."

"Patrick told me about the resort and their boat. Don't count on other's intentions as concrete. Plans change. And you can't control what other people do. There's more to life than just work, you know that."

"It was easier when there wasn't," I replied under my breath.

"Aw, now where's the fun in that? Life would be boring if all you did was work and then die."

"Not with your job, it wouldn't."

She chuckled. "Well, now you've got me there. All the crazies keep me on my toes."

We sat for a few seconds as my fingers mindlessly drummed the metal chair. I took a breath, knowing I wanted to get something off my chest, but not sure my heart could take any more cuts. "She said she's worked since high school to get away from this place."

"This place looks different to her than it does you and me. We all have ghosts, they're just hiding in closets for us. Hers get to walk around the streets out here."

"I don't know what to do." It was the first time I had said it out loud and it felt good to just admit it. "I thought about going up there. To the city."

"And what thoughts did you come up with?"

"Patrick said I'd have to go to museums and wear tight pants."

"Oh, good Lord, could you imagine?" Her laugh was hearty and warm, like homemade bread right out of the oven. "Your father would have a heart attack."

I had imagined myself a million different ways in the city, but no matter what it looked like, it never fit.

"You know, I had an old man on our floor last night. Drunk as a skunk. Mean ol' thing. You know what he told me he needed? A liter of vodka and to get the hell outta there. That man didn't need no vodka. He needed a few hours of withdrawal and a swift kick in his rear."

I could see Mabel on the floor in her nurse's uniform, giving hell to some poor guy as he cowered underneath her shaking finger.

"Sometimes we have no idea what we actually need. But oh, we think we do. That's the fun part. We just need to put one foot in front of the other, and one morning we'll wake up and the answer will be waiting for us like it was there the whole time. Sometimes we see the same thing we've been looking at every day, but all of a sudden it looks different."

I hoped she was right. Because every way I looked at it, my heart was broken.

36
SAMANTHA

Robby's eyes narrowed in on me through my phone screen as I made my way to the subway. "What's this I hear, you're making an *alternative recommendation* to the board? Spill it, Leigh. What's going on?"

"I just have a different view for this place that doesn't include neon slides and racetracks." Bodies slammed into me as people ran past me down the stairs to catch their train.

"Glenn's going to be pissed. He's at his annual Hackers Cup, which he always comes back in a bad mood from anyway. You didn't run this through him. Or me, for that matter."

"Well, first off, I don't need to run things by you. This has been my project for the last month. And second, let's call it a surprise."

"Glenn doesn't like surprises." *Yeah, no kidding.* "Is this because I got the promotion? Listen, I tried to call you and give you a heads-up multiple times. This doesn't mean things have to change. I know how valuable you are to Glenn and the company. To me."

"Did that Florida sun soften up your heart, Robby?" The train pulled up and the doors opened.

"I'm serious, Samantha. Can we meet up? You're heading to the office, right? Do you need help? I don't want you to dive into the shallow end and break your neck."

"I don't think your definition of *help* is what I'm looking for."

"Listen. I get that I've been a bit—"

"Obnoxious? Shady? Inappropriate?"

"I was going to say, *hard to handle*. Look, Leigh, I know going home was hard for you. But you also know I understand the home thing better than most because of the issues with my dad. Bottom line, you know what you're doing. You're good at your job. Let me help, please. As a peace offering."

"I'll think about it." I was tempted. He seemed genuine, but I had to put everything I had on the line for this last swing for the fences moment.

"I just don't want—" I hung up as I stepped through the subway doors. His text came through ten seconds later as the train lurched forward.

> **ROBBY:** I'll meet you at the office.
> Or I'll put all the mice I bought
> in your house instead;)

The conference room was littered with papers, coffee cups, and take-out containers. We had been heads down sifting through numbers the entire day and night. My chest still felt like it was torn in two, but the distraction of work was at least keeping a complete meltdown at bay.

We had a basic outline of recommendations and the beginning structure of the box development plan, but it was still missing something I couldn't put my finger on. My eyes burned.

"It's as good as it's going to get." I face-planted on the desk.

"It's better than anything *they've* got." Ivy nodded at Robby.

"I can vouch for that." Robby leaned back in his leather swivel chair and rubbed his eyes.

"What do you think Glenn's going to do when he finds out you've joined the dark side?"

"Hey, I'm not wearing your team jersey or anything. I'm just going to sit back and watch, knowing I did everything I could to help you not drown."

"Wow, what a pep talk," Ivy scoffed. "Really, I'm surprised they don't give you more people to manage."

Robby got up and made his way to the door. "Glenn should be landing soon. See you two in the morning." As he passed by, he squeezed my shoulder. "For real, Leigh, this is good."

It was good, but it still didn't feel like a done deal. I had been ready to go toe-to-toe with Robby on the monstrosity of a development they had their mind set on. I'd go down fighting it, but not without a whole lotta flames. But turns out Robby was never a fan of the *Water Whizz Family* disaster anyway. He wasn't bold enough to jump ship and publicly declare his allegiance, but it was nice knowing he thought my ideas were good. And that they made sense financially and for the good of the development.

Once Robby left, Ivy fixed her gaze on me from across the table. "Spill it."

"Spill what?"

She straightened the last few piles of paper on the conference table and flicked a crumpled wrapper across the room, sinking it neatly into the trash. "We've done everything we can. There's no work left to distract you. So, let's have it."

I'd spent the entire day trying not to think about Austin, but he showed up in everything we did. Every picture we sketched, every idea I pitched to the two of them. She wasn't wrong—there was no avoiding it anymore.

"There's nothing to be done." I exhaled, the weight of it all finally pressing down on my chest. "He lives there. I live here. It's not going to work. End of story."

Ivy arched an eyebrow. "I feel like you're leaving out a few details."

"He also happens to be my childhood crush. And my ex–best friend's older brother."

"The Austin fellow?" She leaned in, curious. I gave a small nod. "Is it serious enough to want to continue it?"

I'd imagined us a thousand different ways, but nothing made sense. "Yes. No. I don't know. *Fish out of water* would take on a whole new meaning with him in the city."

"And you going back to the island is out of the question, right?"

"I've spent my whole life running from that place. To voluntarily go back would be a special kind of hell."

"Tell me what's so bad about your hometown." Her eyes were earnest, genuinely curious as to why I couldn't ever see myself there again.

I hesitated, then admitted, "My mother, for one."

"Who's in rehab."

"Yeah, but I've been down this path before."

"I thought the whole rehab thing was new for her."

"Technically, it is. But it's always been the same pattern. She promises to get better, stays clean for a few days—weeks if I'm lucky—then falls right back into it. Drinking, pills, or something else. It always seems to be a different kind of worse to deal with."

"And you think it's all on you to take care of her if you go back."

"It *is* all on me. If I go back, I won't have anywhere to hide. For the last few years I've been able to stay just far enough away to keep the guilt at arm's length."

Hope was dangerous. There was a chance Mom might change, but the odds said otherwise. I'd been let down too many times, thinking things were different only to get a call that she needed to be picked up somewhere. It's the same vicious cycle over and over again. When I was in the city, I heard about it after the fact. If I were on the island, I'd live her addiction in real time.

No guy was worth facing my demons over and over again every single day.

Ivy folded her arms. "Is there anything else holding you back from wanting to be there?"

My eyes drifted to the empty coffee cups, the crumpled Post-its, the scattered storyboards and sketches of ice cream parlors and miniature golf courses. I was running on too little sleep and too many suppressed emotions. And somehow, Austin managed to sneak into every corner of it.

"I can't move back for a guy, Ivy. It goes against every bone in my body."

Her lips curled into a knowing smile. "Even if every bone in your body is in love with him?"

"Ivy."

"What? It doesn't take a genius to see it written all over your face. What I can't figure out is why you're so scared."

I stared down at the table, knowing it was pointless to argue. "Okay, fine. You're right. I love everything about him. I love the way he looks at me like I'm someone he wants to take care of. I love how safe I feel when he's around, like I could face anything as long as he's by my side. I love how he makes me laugh so hard my stomach still aches an hour later. And the way his eyes sparkle when he looks at me...like I could mean the world to him if I just said yes."

Her voice softened. "I don't understand what the problem is."

"That's exactly why it won't work. People I love—*really* love—they always leave. One way or another. Sometimes it's by their own choice, but sometimes not. How I feel about him is irrelevant."

"That makes no sense." She shifted her chair closer, turning it to face me. "How you feel about him is the only thing that matters."

I closed my eyes as the weight of the insecurities bubbled back up to the surface again. I rubbed my palms against the fabric of my skirt, as if I could push the fear back where it belonged. "What if I move back and it doesn't work out?"

"If you don't give it a chance, I can tell you with certainty that it won't."

I gave a small nod, unsure of what to say.

"But, Samantha." She waited to speak until I looked up at her. "What if it does?"

But what if it does?

I swallowed the knot forming in my throat. "Let me get through tomorrow's board meeting first, okay? I promise, we can talk about this again." She tried to cut in, but I smiled and nodded. "I swear. I just need to use the little energy I have left for tomorrow, then I'm fair game for an intervention. Deal?"

Her eyes narrowed. "Fine. I'll let it go for tonight. But some things are worth doing scared, Samantha." I blinked away the tears pooling at the corners of my eyes. "Try and get some sleep. We've got an early start."

I felt good about what we'd accomplished. But beneath it all, my walls were crumbling fast.

A single strand of hair escaped Ivy's bun, the only sign of exhaustion from her after hours of brainstorming. Her eyeliner, still sharp and perfect, mocked my rumpled ponytail that flopped to one side.

"I'll finish up here," she said. "Go home. I'll see you in the morning."

"Are you ever *not* put together?" I asked, eyeing the high heels still on her feet. "When this is over, you need to spill how you got all twelve board members to attend."

Her smile was pure mischief. "Maybe."

The apartment was quiet. I looked around and realized I didn't have any pictures hung on the walls. I took out a piece of paper from my top kitchen drawer and wrote *Hang some pictures* at the top. I thought about who I wanted pictures of and Austin's face was the only one I could think of.

So I crossed it out.

I wrote *Keys* underneath. I always lost my keys. I could fix that. I opened my cabinet and grabbed a saucer. I put it right on the kitchen counter as you walked into my apartment and placed my keys on it.

"That's ridiculous." I put my keys back in my purse and threw it on the couch instead.

I stared at the empty dish.

"Okay, fine. Fine." My words aimed at no one in particular, I took the keys back out and put them back on the dish.

"It's official. I'm going crazy and talking out loud."

I jumped when my phone rang from my purse.

"Hello?"

"Hi, is this Samantha Leigh?"

"Who's calling?"

"This is Beverly from the Willow Rehabilitation Center. I'm looking for Samantha Leigh."

My mouth went dry.

"What happened? Is she okay? Yes, this is her." The words tumbled out like an avalanche.

"Yes, I'm sorry to alarm you, Ms. Leigh. She's doing great. We're really encouraged by her progress. As part of our program, we incorporate family therapy early in recovery, especially when a patient's addiction is tied to grief or the loss of a loved one. I'm calling to see if you'd be willing to come in?"

My knees gave out, and I sank into the nearest chair as the tension leaked from my body. I hadn't realized I'd been holding my breath until it escaped in a long exhale. She was okay.

A wave of goose bumps crawled over my skin. Was I ready to see her? What if she looked different? Sounded different? What if this new version of her was just a mirage, and seeing her would only confirm what I feared most?

Or worse, what if she looked the same? It hadn't worked. Nothing would ever work. And it would only be a matter of time before everything started to unravel again.

"Would you be available tomorrow or Wednesday?"

"I work this week," I answered. "Every week, actually. I'm not sure, I'm back in New York. Can I get back to you?"

What if when I saw her in person, it broke the illusion of the sobriety this woman on the other line said she had? I'd come and say, *See I told you, it wasn't going to work.*

"Yes, of course. But we think a session with you would be really beneficial—not because she's struggling, but because she's healing. I'll email you my contact information and just let me know what works for you."

"Right, okay, yeah, I'll get back to you for sure. Thanks." I hung up and stared at the floor. I took a deep breath and counted the light gray stripes on the white rug under my feet. They wanted me to visit mom. To come back to Florida. My mind was screaming at me—the promotion, Glenn, the board meeting, Florida, my mom, Lexi's wedding.

Austin.

I cradled my forehead with my hands and shut my eyes.

Walking the city at night alone wasn't exactly the safest option, but I felt like I was going to suffocate if I stayed in that apartment a second longer. I needed some fresh air.

The city looked different in the dark. Shadows grew longer and alcoves looked deeper. Noises from drains always made me uneasy in the daytime, but they sounded even more ominous in the dark. I walked by businesses closed up for the night. Neon lights flickered in the windows of bars still open, the sounds of chatting patrons floating out from inside.

I walked by Italian Marco's wooden flower stand, all shuttered up for the night. I opened my purse, took out a hundred and scribbled a note on an old receipt. *For last time*, I wrote and slid it through the wooden crack on the closed-up display.

"Hate to break it to you, but Italian Marco is married," a voice from behind me said. I turned around and Jack's blue eyes stared right at me, full of surprise.

"Samantha? Oh my gosh, I didn't realize it was you."

"Jack, hi." *Just pile it on, universe.*

"I thought some random person was leaving love notes for the local flower guy."

"Oh no, I was short on change a few weeks ago and he covered for me. Was just paying him back." I knew my ears had turned red. I was never good at lying.

"So, about the whole—" he started.

"Yeah, no, we're good," I interrupted.

"Yeah, but that wasn't cool. I shouldn't have just—"

"No, really, it's fine. All water under the bridge."

"Oh. Okay."

Normally I would rush to fill the awkward silence but I just didn't have it in me. So I just stared at him. I never noticed it before but his eyebrows were really well shaped. I wondered if he waxed them.

I was just exhausted. And tired. And ready to get back home, although the word *home* felt off.

"Well, since we're cool and all, I mean, would you want to go grab a drink or something right now?"

I was sure I hadn't heard him right. "With you?"

He stared at me with a very confused look. "Yes, with me."

A laugh burst from my mouth. Because *this* was what I needed—Jack coming to my emotional rescue and bailing me out of heartbreak. The man who calls servers over by snapping his fingers. The man who talks with his mouth full and upon further inspection, most definitely gets his eyebrows waxed. The man who takes dates to farmers markets while he's technically still in a relationship.

I couldn't stop laughing. Hysterically laughing. Check me into a mental institution laughing with tears rolling down my face. And I couldn't stop.

"Why are you laughing?" His beautiful brows pulled together like he was offended he wasn't in on the joke.

"I'm just sorry to hear things didn't work out with Sunflower, that's all."

"Sunflower?"

"Yeah, let's just call it a day on this one. For good."

"You sure? It's spring roll night at our pho place. I was on my way there anyway."

"You know, I don't like spring rolls. They actually upset my stomach."

"We ate there every Sunday night for six months." He chuckled and took a step toward me.

"I know." I stepped back.

He took a step forward again and tilted his head in such an endearing way. "You love pho."

I laughed, but this time it was small and came out as a huff. Why had I played it safe for so long? If I didn't like pho, it would mess up our weekly routine. And God forbid anything I do unsettle anyone else because then maybe I wouldn't fit here. Or with him. And it would be scary to not belong here. I was supposed to be here. "I'm going to go. Good luck with everything, Jack."

"You sure?" he asked again.

"Yeah, I think that's the right call here."

"Okay then. See you around, Samantha." He turned and walked away. I didn't get a bit of satisfaction when he looked back and slowed for just a second.

And then, my hospital-grade laughter turned to tears. Tears that refused to stop flowing. I went to lean against the wall but there was something that looked brown and gooey oozing down it. The city smelled like a dirty pipe and everything just looked wet. A man walked by me and saw me crying, then took a step in the other direction instead of asking me if I was okay. That's New York for you.

And I missed Austin.

I *missed* Austin. And it was a sharp feeling. Grief has a way of dulling out eventually. It's still there, and it hurts, but you start to build things around it. You start to color experiences near it and one day, Dad's still not there, but it doesn't stab like it used to.

But remembering the way Austin's skin felt against mine sliced through me so fast I didn't feel it at first, then I couldn't breathe. It seared me.

I missed his smell and his eyes and his laughter. I missed the way when I opened my eyes in the morning, he was already looking at me, smiling. His bacon was better than the five-star chefs down the street. I missed the way he buttered every single inch of my toast. I missed how my face flushed whenever he caught me looking at him. I missed that little muscle on his forearm that popped up whenever he did *anything*. I had no idea an arm could be so sexy.

I lay in bed that night, eyes wide open. The sound of rubber rolling down the wet street and rowdy patrons, their morning regrets still just great ideas, floated in through my window. How did I ever sleep with so much noise?

I sat up and looked out my window. A young man was kicking a can down the street and singing "chim chim cheroo." I looked around the city, *my* city, and for the first time in seven years, felt like I didn't belong.

Too many conflicting scenes played when I shut my eyes, so I opened my laptop instead. My Google search page was filled with pictures from Rock Island.

I clicked on one of the Birchwood Beach. The article explained how with the water levels being at an all-time low, it uncovered this beach only a few years ago. Water levels were continuing to recede, uncovering lots of treasures no one knew about underneath the water.

I clicked through a few photos. There was one of a few teenage boys hanging off a high branch. A few family photos, everyone in white and chambray, smiling for the camera. There was one shot far away of a man on one knee, and a woman with her hands clasped over her mouth. It was taken by a photographer hidden somewhere. The trees surrounded them at low tide, their branches reaching out around them like a timber cage protecting their sweet moment. In the far distance, a lighthouse poked through the bushes on the beach.

Wait. A lighthouse?

I clicked on the photo and tried to enlarge it, but it was too pixelated. I cleared the search bar and typed in *Rock Island Lighthouse*. The page popped up with only a few hits. The first was an old sepia toned picture of the lighthouse that looked to be from when it was first built. Its shutters were dark against the white wooden siding and a small porch wrapped around the building. Sand dunes surrounded the house, standing tall reaching up to the sky like brushstrokes.

The second was an article about the possible renovation of the lighthouse back in the early fifties. Ideas started snowballing in my head.

I reached for my phone.

ME: Have you ever been to the lighthouse at the Birchwood Beach?

LEXI: Is this your idea of an apology?

I picked up the phone immediately and called her. Just as I thought it would go to voicemail, it connected. I started before she even spoke a single word.

"I'm so sorry."

"Sam, I—"

"Wait. Before you say anything, let me get this out. I shouldn't have gotten so mad at you. I was trying to push you away because I was scared. I'm sorry I defaulted to the same thing I always do, leaving before someone can leave me, whether they want to or not. You were right. I ran before to get away from the one person who didn't care about me in the way I needed her to, and I left so many others who did. I left you. And I'm sorry."

She sniffled through the line.

The line went silent for five seconds. Then ten. "Okay, that was a pretty good apology." She laughed and sniffled again. "Apology accepted. But I'm still mad about Austin."

"About that." I took a deep breath and forged on. "I'm not sorry. I'm sorry about the way I acted and how I left it with him, but I'm not sorry about how I feel about him. But if you're open to it, I think I may have figured out a way to maybe fix it. All of it."

"I'm listening."

"The lighthouse. Is there one at the Birchwood Beach?"

"Yeah, didn't Austin take you to it? It's a pretty good trek through the bushes at this point since everything's sort of grown over. You can see it by boat better."

I pulled out the land survey for the Rock Island contract. At the northernmost tip, past Birchwood Beach, there was no sign of a lighthouse.

I looked back to the computer and the map on the screen clearly had it positioned at the tip. Thinking back to that day, we had eaten lunch, then I got the text about my mom so we left. We didn't walk down farther than halfway along the beach. And when he took me to see it on the boat, our time was cut short.

Something started to fall into place.

"Stay by your phone. I'm going to run something by you in a little. But Lex…"

"Yeah?"

"For the record, you're worth staying for."

I hung up and clicked through another couple articles on the computer and learned that the lighthouse had been used for almost twenty years steering ships around the island. A picture of an old keeper's log recorded the weather and a few ships that made it around the point. The entries were barely legible, dotted with watermarks and discolored from age.

The lighthouse was no longer operable. It had fallen into erosion and desperately needed repair. Provisions were made to automate the actual lighthouse itself back in 1949, but the building was closed to the public.

An idea started to spark. I could see it. It'd take a lot of research and a miracle, and I only had a single night to make a lot of changes, but I had nothing else to lose.

37

AUSTIN

My phone buzzed in my pocket.

CHARTER GUY: $30k all in for both.

I sat out back at my parents' and watched their vintage wooden speedboat rock against the dock. I caught my first fish on that boat as a kid. I also nursed my first broken heart on it. When I found out about Vanessa and Tom, I drove straight to my parents' and took it out. I sat there with my pole for hours and didn't catch a single fish. Then I took it out the next day, and the next, sitting out on the water, drifting aimlessly, slowly praying that if I sat out there long enough, I could somehow throw all the hurt and betrayal in my body into the sea and watch it sink to the bottom.

Mom showed up with plate after plate of brussels sprouts and chicken casserole, thinking a full stomach would cure a broken heart. Lexi became founding member of the I Hate Vanessa Fan Club. Patrick leaned in to try and fill the hole Tom had left behind.

Everyone rallied around me, loving me harder than I'd ever been loved.

But no matter how hard they tried, the looks of pity were still there. Silent *I'm so sorry*s stitched in their glances. Hushed tones when I entered a room. Quick glances flickered my way when people thought I wasn't looking.

But I slowly filled my time with other things that kept me busy. I threw myself into a job that kept me working from sunrise to sunset. I put what I wanted on the back burner to fill in for what was needed. It wasn't that I didn't want to start the ferry business, but it wasn't my dream job.

It was just easier to settle.

And at the time, I told myself I was okay with that.

I knew I wasn't going to chase her to New York City.

And I was tired of doing what everyone else thought I should do.

Did I want to be with her? Yes, more than anything. But not more than my own happiness. Not more than hers.

It wasn't that I would never move to New York. I'd do it in a heartbeat if I thought that's what would make her and me happy. But I know how that works, when one person gives up themselves completely. Vanessa chose to stay for me when in her heart, she knew she wouldn't be happy here. It only forced her to resent me.

I wouldn't set Sam and me up for that same fate.

Life was short. I was tired of playing things safe. Even though my heart still felt shattered into a million pieces, I wouldn't trade the last few weeks for anything.

I took Mabel's advice and started asking questions. Why couldn't I do what I wanted to do? Why couldn't I manage the ferry business, let Patrick run the actual boat with a dependable crew, and focus on what I've wanted to do since I was five years old? I didn't need Harold to hand me his business. I could build it from the ground up. I knew enough people, and I sure knew enough about the business.

The waves lapped against the dock. I ran my hands down my face and rubbed my eyes.

If I went down this new path, could it fail? Yes. Would it hurt? Absolutely. But it couldn't be worse than how I already felt.

There was one thing I could do that absolutely terrified me, but excited me more. Nothing cured a broken heart better than a little bit of salt water.

ME: Deal.

38

SAMANTHA

Twelve identical suits stared at me from around the conference room table. Funny how picturing people naked never helped me with anxiety, especially when they're men over the age of sixty.

I'd been able to make it through most of the presentation without looking directly at Glenn, who was still a bright shade of red, probably wondering how in the hell ten minutes of the board's valuable time had been allocated to me when he saw the agenda.

"This town isn't unlike many beach towns across the nation," I continued. "It values the small-town feel—the mom-and-pop stores that have been there for decades and handed down through generations. They have neighborhood general stores where you buy a pair of flip-flops for five dollars, a gallon of milk, and Children's Tylenol, all at the same time. It's the kind of place where the ice cream shop still makes their ice cream from scratch every single morning, and gives customers two scoops when they only ordered one.

"It isn't about money and margins and headcount. Although trust me, those are very important numbers to the success of this development, and I'm well aware of that. But it's an experience economy. People call you by your first name in these towns because they *know* you. You feel seen, loved, valued. These towns are built with the people as the foundation. The outpouring of that is loyalty and adoration, which translates into treasured memories and repeat guests.

"What you've seen presented here today are my ideas to not only create a development that's profitable and will draw attention from around the world, but one that's cherished by the people, both those who visit, and those who call it home."

My throat caught just a bit at that last word. *Home.* For so many years Rock Island was a place that held all of my pain. Every memory of my dad, every painful interaction with my mom, the looks and stares from all the people who pitied my situation.

But it had also been the place where I opened gifts on Christmas mornings as a toddler. Where I learned to ride my bike. Where I went door to door and said "trick or treat" and ate so much candy every Halloween night I'd throw up.

All these memories shaped who I was. They formed me, both good and bad. Both joyful moments and ones full of heart wrenching pain. The more I wanted to push it down, the more it stung the back of my throat.

The island *was* home. It had always been.

"Lodging. What does it look like?" A man at the other end of the table leaned back in his chair. He had a full head of silver hair and looked like a heavy Richard Gere. And there were little pink flamingos all over his navy tie.

"I was envisioning dotting the coastline with upscale cottages and a few bed-and-breakfast-type buildings," I responded. "In the current financials you see, I incorporated a few buildings that are more conducive to larger groups but think more along the lines of long porches with communal gathering, group nature walks, and golf cart rides, versus Disney and roller coasters."

A skinny guy piped in, crossing his arms across his chest. "Using cottages versus hotels? Our potential occupancy capacity rate would be shot."

Another picked up the thought. "We'd shrink our main revenue source. And what about all the other revenue lines—food and beverage, all the ancillaries that are built in?"

Glenn shifted in his seat. "Samantha's our little dreamer. Always has her head in the clouds." I knew they'd all pile on and he'd take this opportunity to come save the day and somehow find a way to slice my intelligence. "But we can't continue to build a multimillion-dollar company on cottages. We need something larger to sink our teeth into. You're not in the right headspace for this type of work."

"I agree." The skinny old guy tacked on. "This isn't even close to our portfolio of work."

"I realize it's a bit of a different approa—"

"Samantha," Glenn cut me off. "He's right. While I appreciate your creativity, we're in the business of making money. We'd be drastically cutting our revenue stream by decreasing the amount of people a development like this can accommodate. Speaking of, let's move on to an idea that will make us money. Robby, why don't you take it from here?"

Robby looked straight at me and a hint of a smile bloomed on his face.

"Actually, Samantha, wasn't there one other thing you wanted to go over before we move on? Something about making a ton of money and cutting a lot of the costs?" Robby asked me. And he winked.

Glenn's nostrils flared as his face turned from a blush to tomato red.

I straightened my back and took a breath in.

"This development plan, it not only works for Rock Island, but the concepts and ideas are transferable to other properties with similar geographic locations, as well as clientele with similar demographics. We've created the plan to be retrofitted into existing establishments, and have also included options for a new build, which will cut development costs and timelines in half."

"That's a pretty big statement." Glenn clenched through his teeth.

I saw both confusion and intrigue cross over the faces of the board members.

"It's called the Lighthouse Collection." I clicked through the presentation to a page with the logo, a thin elegant pencil and watercolor drawing of a lighthouse.

"Lighthouses exist to safely guide captains in and out of the harbor. They serve as coastal navigation, steering captains to their destinations. Our developments through the Lighthouse Collection will stand as a beacon, guiding travelers to the locations where they're built. Areas with similar geography can support these establishments. We'd make changes based on what's important to the specific clientele of the area, but essentially we'd use this plan as a foundation."

"A coastal city in a box." Richard Gere looked intrigued.

"That's one way to look at it. Every site won't have a gem naturally built in like Rock Island does with the Birchwood Beach, but every location will have something special and unique. We just have to find out what it is. It cuts the due diligence period by more than half, decreasing cost on the development side. Most of the time involved is focused on the core values of the ideal customers in these geographic areas, and finding out what makes that particular location unlike anything else. It enables us to tailor the plan in half the time, cutting costs without cutting important development considerations."

"And cutting the number of tourists we can take in by more than half," Glenn argued. A red blotch appeared on his neck.

"Let's reframe the people who are coming," I continued. Glenn's jaw ticked as the other board members leaned toward me, intrigued. "They're not just Disney World tourists looking for tchotchkes and cheap thrills. We're talking about valued guests, and our developments being a beacon of light for them. We're not aiming for a onetime customer. We're aiming for a lifetime customer. There isn't room for everyone all at once, and that's part of the allure. And there's also a large retail element for the Lighthouse Collection. Ivy?"

I nodded at Ivy, prompting her to jump in.

"There's a huge collectible soft lines opportunity." She confidently leaned forward in her chair. "And to help bolster the local businesses, there will be upscale home goods like custom-made driftwood furniture, locally poured candles, and art—all in limited, numbered batch runs. Once they're sold, they're gone."

"For excursions and on-site offerings," I continued, "instead of roller coasters and bumper cars, you have sunset dolphin cruises and inshore fishing charters. We'd be able to justify higher prices because it's a better quality experience. And yes, we'll still have pool bars and on-site restaurants, but the per head revenue is actually much higher coupled with these new higher-price-point offerings." A few of the board members were looking toward Richard Gere. "And, part of the proceeds will go to fund the wildlife preserves in each area along the coastline."

Ivy eagerly chimed in. "There are tons of endangered species and protected plots of land along these waters. We attract a different kind of traveler with this approach, one who appreciates nature and cares for the environment."

"And one who doesn't mind spending top dollar to make sure

they're not left out of visiting one of the most coveted gems in the South," I added. "These guests will want to visit all of the top Lighthouse Collection locations across the world. Here's a list of twenty potential locations I've already vetted from a desktop perspective."

The room was silent. I cleared my throat.

"We've worked the numbers, and although the property would accommodate fewer people, the additional revenue streams easily make up the difference."

Silence again.

Then, everyone started talking at once.

"Do you think the state would provide conservation funds—"

"The PR angle is interesting—"

"I love the idea of supporting local artists—"

"Top ten undiscovered—"

"Did you see the picture of the trees—"

"Ms. Leigh," Richard Gere's voice cut through the chatter and everyone went quiet. "I believe you've excited my board."

Glenn looked like he was about to puke. Robby was sitting there with his ever-present smirk on his face, and Ivy looked like she was about to have an orgasm.

"Thank you for your presentation. The board has quite a bit to chat about this afternoon."

I took that as my cue, nodded toward Ivy, and we both stood up and left.

"Holy crap, you just killed that." I could still hear the chatter from the boardroom outside in the hallway. She grabbed my arm and pulled me farther away.

My chest felt light and my fingers tingled. "I can't believe we just railroaded Glenn and presented directly to the board without his approval. I'm most definitely getting fired for this."

"If they hated your idea, I'd agree with you. But they *loved* it. Did you see their faces? They were completely bought in. There's no way they'd let Glenn get rid of you now, even if he wanted to."

"Your idea about the retail element. That was huge. I had no idea you had such a knack for that kind of thing."

"More of a hobby. Oh, and by the way, don't think I didn't notice how you lit up when you talked about the island. We are tabling that conversation for later."

My mind was still stuck on the fact that for the first time in a long time, I was thinking of Rock Island as home.

I had a clear view of the boardroom door as it swung open and a few people walked out.

"Hey, Richard Gere is coming straight for us," I whispered to Ivy.

"Who?"

"Flamingo Tie."

"Oh. Yeah, I'm sure he is," she mumbled under her breath. I watched as he beelined in our direction. He had his eyes locked on us.

"Samantha, I've heard a lot about you. It's good to finally meet you." He extended his hand toward me.

"You too, sir."

Finally?

"Call me Richard." I choked back a smile. "Richard Jones. That was a pretty compelling presentation. I'm thoroughly impressed by what your team pitched."

"Thank you, sir. They did a phenomenal job pulling it all together."

"Now I see why Ivy is hell-bent on staying by your side. You just reinvented our whole approach with one presentation. I don't think I've seen the board so frazzled and excited at the same time." He looked right at Ivy and beamed. "Well done. Ivy, did you help pull together those retail numbers?"

Ivy crossed her arms and just smirked at him without saying a word.

"She absolutely did," I answered after a few seconds of awkward silence. What in the hell was she doing? "Her ideas were pivotal to the plan."

"That's great to hear. Ivy, will you send me those numbers? I want to play around with a few things."

"Will do, boss." Then she *saluted* him.

"We'll be in touch, Samantha." He turned, giving Ivy a side-eye, and walked back toward the conference room door.

"Did you just *salute* Richard Gere?" I asked.

"Yeah, don't think too much of it. He gets a kick out of it," she brushed it off.

"How could you possibly know that?"

"He's my dad."

My mind came to a screeching halt. "I'm sorry, what?"

"He's my dad... And he's been super pissy about the fact I'm just your *assistant*, but I think he might kind of get it now."

I looked at her with my jaw on the floor. "How did I not know your dad was on the board of directors?"

"It's not something I put on my Insta profile." He had a large frame and a full head of shampoo-commercial hair. She could fit in a sardine can even with four-inch heels on and had pin-straight black hair. "I favor my mom's side. Obviously."

It all started to make so much more sense. "So that's how you got our time slot on such quick notice."

"Yeah, they typically do pretty much whatever he says. Based on stock ownership, technically he owns fifty-one percent of the company."

"All this time you've worked for me, how did I not know your dad was the majority owner of the company we work for?" I'm an intelligent person. There's no way I missed this unless she was deliberately showing me smoke and mirrors.

"My dad's always thought just because he's this big corporate guy that I'd want to follow in his footsteps. But I don't want to. He says he's worked his whole life so that I wouldn't have to work as hard. But that's not who I am. I'd be miserable running some big company, sitting in a squeaky leather chair and answering to a bunch of men who don't have enough hair and suck at golf."

"Does he know about your writing?" I knew she moonlighted as a writer under a pen name but we never talked about it. I tried to give her the privacy she's always granted me.

"He knows I dabbled in college. He'd kill me if he ever read any of the books though."

"Books? Wait, how many have you published, exactly?"

"Honestly, I didn't think I'd stay that long with you." She narrowed her eyes at me, avoiding my question. "But after the first few days of working for you, I knew you were kind of kick-ass. I've learned a lot from you. Things I wouldn't learn cushioned underneath some baby boomer who wanted to appease me because of who my dad is. So, I stayed."

I was speechless. I didn't know what to say. On one hand I was pissed she kept this from me. On the other hand, I wasn't surprised at all. It seemed like exactly the kind of thing she would keep secret from me and the world.

"I'm grateful you stayed. Even though it scares me how good of a liar you are."

"It's called storytelling, and don't get all emotional on me. New York is a right to quit state. I'm going to circle back and see what I can find out. We'll catch up later."

I spent the rest of the afternoon holed up in my office pretending I wasn't checking my phone every two minutes. Robby's head popped in the doorway.

"I can't stay long." He leaned against the doorframe. "Don't want Glenn to see me congratulating the enemy, but you nailed it, Leigh. For real." There was a genuine smile on his face.

"Well, we'll see if the board thought so too."

"Oh trust me, they were like kids on Pixy Stix after you left. You killed it."

"Thanks for doing that in there, letting me finish even though Glenn was trying to get you to railroad me."

"It was nothing. What you had to say was good. I wanted them to hear it."

"Plans after work?" I asked, hoping my olive branch would be seen as a completely platonic gesture. "We're either grabbing a glass of champagne to celebrate or a whiskey neat if I'm walked out at some point today. My treat, as a thank-you."

"Oh man, I'd actually love to but I've got this thing." For the first time ever, Robby blushed. He rocked back on his feet as he met my gaze.

"Okaaay," I drew out, happy to leave it at that.

"It's a girl, actually?" It came out as a question. "I met her down in Florida and it turns out she's going to school up here at NYU."

"Oh wow, okay. That's great."

"It's Charley's niece, Sherry? You probably didn't meet her. She's not a local."

"Doesn't ring a bell."

"She's pretty awesome. She's more brazen than me, if you can imagine that." His face turned a shade deeper. His eyes darted around my office like he was looking for buried treasure. "She has a good head on her shoulders. I think I like her. Like, a lot."

"Well, I didn't think I'd ever see the day you were twisted up about a girl. I'm happy for you. I hope it works out."

"And she's hot," he added as Ivy crashed into my office.

"Hey!"

"That's my cue." He turned around, beet red, and headed out. "See you, Leigh."

"What was that all about?" she asked as he beelined down the hall.

"Growth, Ivy. Growth."

She shook her head. "Dad's petitioning to steal you."

"I have absolutely no idea what that means."

"Nothing's final, *but* the idea is Robby would keep his promotion, obviously, but Dad's going to recommend you head up a whole new division for boutique hotels using your strategy for the Lighthouse Collection. Finding the properties, retrofitting them, everything we talked about in the meeting."

This was it. It wasn't what I expected—it was something better. I'd be able to find and negotiate multimillion-dollar deals and cherry-pick those I thought would make the best developments for the collection. I'd have a whole team at my disposal, and be able to find the unearthed gems of tourism.

And Rock Island wouldn't be turned into a neon dumping ground for high-density polyethylene. The quaintness of the island would be preserved. Locals would grow their businesses, not lose them. And new visitors would love and appreciate the island for what it was, not what millions of dollars of development could make it.

I should have been screaming at the top of my lungs, wanting to down a bottle of Dom and dance on top of a bar. It was officially a champagne kind of a night. I should have been over the moon.

But I wasn't.

This is what should have made me happy.

But it didn't.

Something was missing.

As I looked down at my desk, all I could think about was how proud Austin would be if I told him. He'd scoop me in his arms and tell me we were going to celebrate. He'd set me on the couch and tell me not to move. He'd make dinner from scratch for me and tell me how I deserved it, and how there wasn't a single other person in the world who deserved it as much as me. Then he'd kiss me once, then twice like he couldn't get enough. Then we'd forget about dinner as it got cold and spend the whole night wrapped up in each other.

She sighed. "You're thinking about him, aren't you?"

I shook my head to scatter the thoughts. I had finally let myself live a little instead of being scared that everything would fall apart if I made a wrong move. All my life I'd been running from that place and now, it was somehow finding a way to seep in through the cracks.

I had Austin to thank for that. For the first time, I let myself see something other than the hurt that's always been there. It's like I experienced a whole new place with him and now I couldn't shake it.

I didn't know if I wanted to.

"I don't see you just up and leaving everything to move back there. You're not exactly the damsel-in-distress archetype that gives up your entire life for some guy whose widowed mother owns a family Christmas tree farm."

"Oh, I'm definitely not, but I've got an idea. Can I ask you one more favor?"

Her eyes twinkled. "Always."

39

SAMANTHA

I scheduled Mom's rehab visit for the day of Lexi's rehearsal dinner. Might as well kill two birds with one trip.

The hallway smelled like bleach. Not strong enough to sting your nose, but strong enough you knew without a shadow of a doubt someone finished cleaning thirty seconds before you walked in.

The floor was white and shiny and my shoes squeaked as I walked down the hall to where my mom had spent the last couple weeks. I hated how it reminded me of the hospital.

"She's been really excited for this visit." Dr. Joseph introduced herself in the reception area as Mom's counselor. My deep dive desktop research told me there was a 47 percent chance she was an addict too. A former addict? Recovering addict? I didn't know the lingo or how you were supposed to address people.

I didn't want small talk. I was clinging to my mother by the last tiny bit of rope that was fraying anyway, and I wasn't in the mood for someone to act like they knew our entire dynamic. Like they knew what existed in the space between our conversations and our politeness.

It felt like walking down a hallway where a black hole was waiting at the end that I would disappear into forever. For so long we had done this dance of moving around each other and ignoring the massive rain cloud that hung above us. We were *fine*, with gallons of rain dumping on us, drowning us in our own heads.

I was ready to face it though. Whatever the outcome would be, at least we could stop pretending there was just Coke in the Styrofoam cup.

"She's been doing really well. Has checked off all the boxes and has held firm to all her commitments," she continued. "She's become someone people count on here. Other patients. Even some of the staff." She smiled and paused before we walked into her office.

"Your mom is working hard to change, and part of that is understanding how her choices affected the people she loves. This is an opportunity for both of you—not just for her—to process things in a safe place. You don't have to say anything you're not ready to, but your perspective is important."

"Sounds like fun." I felt uncomfortable in my own skin. While hell would be a welcomed reprieve at that moment, this was the right thing to do.

My fight with Austin pulled tight like a rubber band across my chest. Work was up in the air with unknowns and questions everywhere regarding what the board would actually approve. If I stayed under Glenn, which was still a very real possibility, he'd make my life hell for what I'd pulled on him.

It felt like my life was peeling back, layer by layer. Not necessarily in a bad way, but not the way I expected. If the island was ever going to be a place for me again, a place to call home, I needed to shine a light on every dark, painful shadow with my mom.

And it started here.

"Ms. Leigh, your mother's striving to be a different person with new habits and new perspectives. It's important that you don't fall into patterns you've always had. I encourage you to keep an open mind and ears during today's visit."

She pushed open the heavy door, and the moment I stepped inside, I barely recognized my mother. She jumped up from a couch that screamed *therapist office's* and made her way toward me before awkwardly stopping a few inches shy. Her eyes were already getting misty and immediately my shoulders straightened and I was on guard.

She smiled at me. It wasn't a fake vodka-soaked smile that told me the world was fun and exciting if I'd just wear a sombrero once in a while. It was a genuine smile that told me the world was full of pain and heartbreak, but that she was still here.

My eyes started to water and she pulled me in. I melted into her arms. I hadn't been hugged by my mom—my sober, loving, and fully present mom—since my dad died.

"I'm so sorry," she whispered through my hair as she held me tight.

All these years, she never apologized for any of it. I swallowed to get my throat to stop closing up. She pulled me back and put her hands on my shoulders.

"There's nothing I can do about my actions after the accident. But I need you to know how sorry I am. For a lot of things. I'm sorry I wasn't there for you after your father died. I was dealing with grief in an unhealthy way and I couldn't see past what I was feeling. I let it consume me. Eat at me from the inside out. And I neglected you." She cupped my face in her hands and smiled. "My strong and resilient daughter who needed her mother, and I wasn't there."

I blinked through my silent cascade of tears.

"I can never express to you how sorry I am for not being there when you needed me most."

I imagined this moment a hundred times in my life. But I never actually thought it would happen. I never truly thought I would feel remorse from her, but I did.

She hugged me again, and I didn't trust my voice to speak.

"Let's have a seat, shall we?" Dr. Joseph nodded to the couch. Mom sat in the chair next to me and the doctor propped herself on her desk.

Mom smiled at me. And it reached her eyes.

"I'm sorry for the accident," she continued. "I should have never gotten behind the wheel. You are and will always be the most important thing in my life. My actions haven't shown that to you, but I'm going to try and change that. I know my promises don't mean much to you right now, and I understand why. But now I'm going to do everything in my power to be better for you. You deserve that. And I deserve that too."

I wasn't sure what I was supposed to say. I didn't know how this worked. Was I supposed to roll into tomorrow like everything's changed? Sure, this felt different. She looked different—healthy— and she had apologized for the first time in her life, and I wanted to believe her. I really did. But when you've had your hopes stomped on a hundred times over, you just expect the boot to come crashing back down.

"I'm not asking you to forgive everything that's happened," she continued. "There's a lot we need to talk about and work through. I'm just asking that you give me a chance to show you that today can look different. That's all." She looked to Dr. Joseph, and off her nod, my mom asked, "Do you think you could do that?"

She wasn't asking a lot. She was asking about today. Could I trust her enough to give her today? "Yes."

It was such a small step. But so much weight lifted off my chest.

"Does this mean you're coming home?" I asked.

"The center has actually invited me to stay. I have the option of continuing my program since Dr. Joseph has offered me a job." My mom looked over at the doctor and smiled. "It's just temporary, but I'm not ready to jump back into life on the island just yet. My routine is still too ingrained in me there. It's not long term, staying here, but something that would be good for me right now as a next step."

"Is that what you want?" I asked. She sounded like an adult.

A proud smile spread across Dr. Joseph's face. "She's been working a lot with our younger patients. She's organized a couple events that the residents have enjoyed, and a few have really taken to her."

Mom leaned forward and lowered her voice. "You should see what these young girls in here wear. I mean, when did belly button rings come back into style? I always thought that was such a trashy thing."

Dr. Joseph gave her a narrowed stare. "I do think a little more time here would be beneficial for your mother. An addiction such as hers doesn't just disappear after a certain number of days. It's a lifelong battle she'll fight, so the better we can remove the temptations and consistencies she had back home, the better."

"I'm doing good here, but there's still a lot to work through."

She hesitated and looked to Dr. Joseph who gave a subtle nod again.

"Your dad," she started and paused. The bottom of my stomach fell. She took a deep breath and began again. "Your dad was everything that held me together. When he died, I was so angry. I didn't know how to wake up in a world where he didn't exist anymore."

It dawned on me that I had never heard my mom acknowledge the fact that he died. It was always *when he left*, or *after he was gone*.

"I spent almost four years watching you blame him for dying."

"It was easier to be angry than to be sad. And I was a coward. Remembering him hurt too much. I thought maybe if I forgot he was there in the first place, I wouldn't have to exist in a world where he no longer was."

I knew this. I knew how she felt, but her actually admitting it felt like it meant something completely different now.

"Is there anything else you'd like to say, Bonnie?"

"A lot more, yes, but I think that's a good start."

The doctor looked at me. "Would you like to say anything, Samantha?"

There were so many conversations we had over the years and I never felt like she heard what I was saying. She was looking at me, expecting me to say something. Now was as good a time as ever.

I told her how once Dad died, home became somewhere that had a lot of pain and it was all I saw when I thought of it. I wanted to leave so badly, thinking maybe if I got away from the island, away from her, it would get better. On the surface it did for a while. I had a great job. Lived in a busy city. Filled my time with to-do lists and spreadsheets and took on more things than I could handle just so I wouldn't have to slow down. If I did, it would all come crashing forward over me like a wave.

I had been running away from it for so long, it just felt normal to turn the other way. I didn't want that anymore.

"I don't want home to be somewhere I keep running away from."

Dr. Joseph gave a small nod. "Thank you for sharing that. Sometimes we're able to redefine a physical space into something different if we're willing to look at why it's not a safe space for us to begin with. By acknowledging and accepting what originally caused that feeling for you, sometimes that in and of itself can redefine it."

"I won't pressure you to come visit anymore. But know I'd always love to see you. And you don't have to stay with me. You could stay with Lexi. Or at the Starfish. Wherever you want. No pressure."

"If it's alright with you, I'm actually going to stay at the house the next couple days. It's Lexi's wedding weekend and the rehearsal dinner is tonight at the Marcs' house out on the water."

"Gosh, I feel like I've been out of the loop for so long. Josie sent me an email updating me on all the wedding weekend festivities. That poor Lexi and all her brother's drama right before her wedding. She'll be happy you're going."

My heart froze.

Austin.

"What drama?" Had she somehow heard about us?

"Bonnie." Dr. Joseph gave her a narrowed eye and Mom sat up straighter.

"It was only through email, and just this morning. No cheating, I promise. I haven't spoken to anyone." She looked at me and saw I was still worried. "Oh, honey, Lexi's fine. It's just that woman he was seeing forever ago. The nerve, coming all the way back here after so many years. You'd think he would have smartened up by now."

The room started to fuzz at the edges. "Vanessa?"

"Yes! That's her. Knowing that girl's family, it doesn't surprise me. She swings back and forth between men like it's an Olympic sport."

"Let's focus on what's in front of us, Bonnie. On what we can do today."

"Right, good advice. Speaking of..." My mother stood up, brushed off her jeans and tucked her hair behind her ears, completely clueless she had just shoved a lance through my soul. "I have a hitting lesson at two on the tennis courts. I'm completely awful at it but the outfits are cute, so there's that."

The only extracurricular activity I knew my mom to do was

barhopping. And now I could add shattering my world and tennis to that list.

"Thank you for giving me today, Samantha." She pulled me into a hug. "And don't worry about Lexi. She has you to lean on again and I know that means the world to her."

She walked out and I stood in a daze. That couldn't be right. There's no way Vanessa would come back. But even if hell froze over and she did, there's no way he'd take her back. You don't just run off with your fiancé's best friend, marry him, then change your mind years later and get welcomed back with open arms, right?

As I walked out of the facility, the pit in my stomach grew heavier. They had spent years together. We had spent weeks together. At one point, he had built his entire world around her and envisioned having kids. A house. A *life*. All with her.

But I knew how gossip was on the island. And I knew how my mom could blow things out of proportion. With her, it was like the telephone game with a firework finale; everything explodes by the end.

I was tired of letting elephants in the room squeeze me into the wall until I couldn't breathe. It was time to stop fleeing.

The moment I turned onto Austin's street I saw it. The bright red sports car was parked in his driveway like a flashing neon sign against all the little cottages. Leave it up to Vanessa to have an obnoxiously loud and irritating car that you just wanted to throw a rock at.

But maybe it wasn't hers. Maybe he had a new friend over. Maybe Rex bought Lexi a new car. Or maybe he had a toilet leak and the plumber happened to be a car fanatic.

I slowed the car down just before his house. The big picture window in the front of his house had the curtains pulled, but there was a little sliver of light popping through on one side. I couldn't see anything from the car. I'd have to get out to get a closer look.

If he saw me, it'd just look like I'm walking to the front door. I just needed a tiny peek to see if it was her or the plumber. Easy fix.

I pulled my car a house down just in case, and my feet carried me up the shell driveway until I could see the kitchen counter through the window. There was one barstool nestled underneath, and a pair of fair ivory legs, wrapped around the metal legs of the other.

My eyes wandered up. She looked more like a porcelain doll, one that would break if you shook her hand too hard. Her lips were a deep red, and against her ivory skin and long black hair, she looked like a version of Snow White if she didn't have all those dwarfs to take care of and got a boob job instead.

She was glowing.

And she was smiling.

And he was laughing. I heard it. I couldn't see him, but I knew that laugh. That was the laugh he gave when he was embarrassed. The one that started small like a chuckle then rumbled deeper in his chest. It was the laugh he gave me when I sat up on my knees in bed and lifted my arms above my head, waiting for him to make the first move.

She cackled and threw her head back. He leaned onto the counter and I caught a glimpse of his face. His head cocked to the side with a small smile creeping across it. It felt like watching a movie. A movie where you yelled at the screen, because the hero was about to kiss the girl who killed his mother, or kicked his dog, or cheated on him with his best friend and he didn't know.

A scene where two people who knew each other so intimately barely looked at each other and all their clothes just fell to the ground.

I stepped back. I was going to throw up. It couldn't be happening, but it was. She finally came to her senses and of course he would give her another chance. There was a time his entire life revolved around her existence. She had been his fiancée at one point, for heaven's sake. They had spent almost a decade together. It didn't matter that she had cheated on him. Or run off.

He had planned his entire life with her, and she had finally come home.

"Who are we creeping on?" I jumped at the voice from behind me.

"Mr. Crenshaw!" I whispered, swiftly backing up. "I was just leaving."

"Anything good going on?" he asked, trying to peek around me through the curtain.

"Umm, I don't know. I was just dropping something off. I'm done now." I turned and beelined it for my car.

"I've got something I want to show you," he whispered after me, hot on my tail.

"No! Definitely not." I ran down the driveway and to my car.

I looked in my rearview mirror at Mr. Crenshaw, and a bright red sports car responsible for the knife through my heart.

I had missed my chance.

40

SAMANTHA

My cursor hovered over the SUBMIT CHANGES button for a solid sixty seconds. If I clicked it, I could make the last flight out.

I paced around my childhood room as I drafted five different texts to Lexi, each explaining in various ways how I'd miss the rehearsal dinner and wedding. They ranged from *Hey! So I've got this flesh-eating bacteria thing happening so I can't make it* to *Hey! I'm in love with your brother but he's moved on with his skank ex and my heart is in a trillion pieces all over the floor and I can't find enough superglue, soooo sorry!*

I could hop on the plane and go back to my apartment in the city. Ivy would buy me a new fern. Again. I could put a picture or two up in my apartment. Buy a pillow that was an actual color. Maybe I'd even let her put me on a dating app, as long as she filtered out guys named Robby. And Austin. I could pretend Austin was just a fling. Like he wasn't the most amazing person I'd ever met. I'm sure the feeling of drowning all the time would lighten up. Eventually.

I didn't need to face Austin and have him hand my tattered heart back to me on a platter with the *V* word watching from the front row.

But fleeing was exhausting. Hiding was getting old. I was tired enough from the visit with Mom and running away took so much effort. I didn't need Austin's ghost haunting me for the next seven years.

I let my mind wander.

What would happen if I just chose to stay? Not forever, but just for the night.

What if I did the hard thing? What if I showed up at my friend's rehearsal dinner like I said I would and didn't run away? What if I choose to be a good friend, and smiled and cheered for her as she married her best friend? What if I didn't run from the pain like I did seven years ago and just stood still and faced it head-on?

What if I stayed?

It was a terrifying thought.

But Austin and I were grown-ups. I could apologize for being an ass and walking away like I did. I could wish him well on his journey and hope he wouldn't get cheated on. Again. Who was I to get in the way of true love?

Who was I kidding? That's total bullshit. I wanted to go egg her car at the rehearsal. But I could swallow it instead and be the bigger person. I didn't want the next seven years to pass and this still be something I wish I would have done differently.

I looked around my old room. The last time I was here I tucked that little picture of my dad and me into the corner of the desk mirror. The heartache of losing him had changed. It went from constantly gasping for air but never actually drowning, to tides of grief that would sneak up without warning.

But one day I remembered his smile without it sucking the air from my lungs.

My mom was just a dull ache that sat there, taking up every inch of me. But after seeing her at the rehab clinic, I started to see where maybe, just maybe, there could be room for something other than guilt and anger. Maybe we could make room for something else to grow.

This time, I wouldn't let it take seven years for me to face what I needed to.

I would do this the right way. And that meant telling Austin how I really felt, regardless if he was doe-eyed for his ex-fiancée or not.

Screw it.

I closed out the tab and put on my heels. I'd do this for Lexi. I'd do this for me, even if my heart would be ripped out in the process.

41

AUSTIN

The lawn was full of people chatting away. But instead of mingling, Mom was in the kitchen handing me a bushel of carrots to cut.

"Mom. You do realize we hired caterers for this, right? If you want to ask me questions, just ask."

"Okay, fine. Have you heard from her?"

"No."

"Have you called her?"

"No."

"Well, why the hell not?"

I don't think I'd ever heard my mom curse before. "How many glasses of champagne have you had?" I asked.

"She's a good one. You're supposed to fight for the good ones."

"Then what? I move to a city where I'd be miserable? Or she moves here, then she's miserable? I can't expect her to give up the life she loves to move back home. And she wouldn't expect that of me either."

"Sometimes love changes people."

But I didn't want it to change her. I loved her exactly the way she was. She was stubborn and particular, and when things didn't go her way, she got flustered. If she left her job, what would she even do here? Work for Josie at the inn? Become a barista? Sam loved what she did, and she was good at it. She'd grow to resent me for being the reason she stayed.

"What are you going to say when she shows up tonight?" Mom asked.

"Who shows up tonight?" Dad walked through the open sliding glass door.

"No one."

"Samantha," Mom corrected.

I don't even know why I bothered keeping anything private anymore. "I don't even know if she's coming. But if she does, I'm not riding in on some fairy-tale white horse. I'm sorry to let you two down, but my story's not the same as yours and dad's."

"Your dad and I got lucky, but we both gave up things. I'd be living in Martha's Vineyard owning a bakery or a bed-and-breakfast if it were solely my choice. And your dad, well, he'd probably move to Texas and start herding cattle. Who the hell knows," she said with a laugh.

"There's a lot of money in cattle these days." Dad opened and shut a few drawers around the kitchen. "Where'd you put my grilling supplies?"

"I hid it all. You'll never find them. Now, get back out to your daughter's party where there is *catering*." She hushed him as he began to object and steered him back into the yard.

She turned her attention back on me. "We compromised, honey. Sometimes love changes people, but mostly it changes what you *want*. I wanted a life with that man more than I wanted Martha's Vineyard. And we both fought for it. Still do. All those little moments can add up to something great if you let it."

I looked through the patio out into the crowd of people mingling. Patrick and his cousin had just walked around from the front, which meant the last of the out-of-towners were here from the ferry.

We made our way out of the kitchen just as Lexi walked over to where Mom and I stood.

"Do you see them?" Lexi pointed to the loudest group on the lawn. Rex, his four sisters and a few husbands piled around each other laughing. "They're telling stories of Rex when he was little. Apparently, he refused to take off his *Teenage Mutant Ninja Turtles* undies for weeks when he was eight because he thought they gave him superpowers to protect his younger sisters. His mom saved them and hid them somewhere in our wedding present pile because now he needs to protect me." She looked at Rex with stars in her eyes. "How did I get so lucky?"

Mom eyed me. "*He's* one of the good ones too. The ones you fight for."

Lexi looked at me. "What's she talking about?"

"Drop it," I said to Mom. "We were just talking about how happy you look, that's all."

Mom leaned over to Lexi. "We were talking about Samantha."

"There's no need to talk about Sam," I said. "I'm fine."

Lexi looked over my shoulder at the lawn. "Oh no, I think the ice table is out of stone crab."

"Oh no! I'll be right back." Mom hurried off.

"Wow. That was impressive."

Lexi chuckled.

"She's predictable. God forbid people be out of food at a party of hers." We watched Mom circle the table like a hawk trying to find the mystery hole of food.

My gaze ran across the lawn, weaving in and out of crowds of people.

"She's not here yet, but she's coming," she answered, even though I hadn't asked the question. "Are you okay?"

"Don't you worry about me," I answered as I put my arm around her.

"Have you guys talked since everything happened?"

"*I'm* the big brother. I take care of *you*. And I'm fine. You need to focus on enjoying yourself tonight."

"I am enjoying myself." Her eyes flicked across the lawn again. She's always worrying about other people, even at her own rehearsal dinner.

I wouldn't be a proper brother if I didn't rile her up just a bit though. "I saw Vanessa again today."

"Again? Austin, I swear if you're—"

"She's pregnant."

Her breath sucked in quickly. "Wait, what?"

"They're pregnant. Like, with a baby."

"The spawn of Satan?"

"You really didn't like her, huh?" I asked, laughing.

"Maybe if she hadn't nicknamed me *Sloth Baby* from the moment she met me..."

"You did hang around us a lot." I smiled at her. "I wouldn't have wanted it any other way."

"And she felt the need to tell you this in person, why?"

"Tom came too. They apologized, believe it or not. Together."

"Oh. Okay. I guess, better late than never?"

I didn't feel anything other than shock when I opened the door and they were both standing there. She apologized. He apologized. It was the first time they ever said they were sorry for what happened, and I actually believed them. It's a weird feeling, spending so much of your life with someone and then they're just gone one day.

I won't be grabbing drinks with them anytime soon, but it felt nice to have better closure.

"Tom wanted to tell me before I heard it from somewhere else. He and Vanessa are really happy. She was literally glowing. They'll be here more often now with the baby on the way and they didn't want it to be weird every time they came back. Grandparents and all."

"Well that was nniiiiii—not satanic of them."

"You can't do it, can you?"

"Nope." She smiled out at her guests, taking a moment to scan the crowd again.

My stomach somersaulted as Lexi drew in a quick breath. She and I saw Sam at the exact same time heading into the backyard from the side pathway. Sam was in a navy-blue dress that hugged her waist. Her head was down concentrating on the stone path, trying to navigate heels and patches of grass. We hadn't spoken since the night she stormed off. I sent her a single text letting her know I was here to talk whenever she was ready, but I hadn't heard anything back.

Lexi turned to me. "Do you love her?"

"Yes."

"Do you want to be with her?"

"Yes, but I'd never allow her to give up her whole life and move back here."

"Just make sure she knows how you feel. No question about it. No room for any other interpretation than you're crazy about her. Let her decide what to do about it."

"Look at you, being all wise now that you're almost an old married woman."

"I don't want you all heartbroken, driven to becoming a recluse who never washes his clothes and eventually wastes away and dies with all his cats and no one would know for years. Or something similar."

"I could see that happening."

Lexi side-hugged me again. "Plan of attack: you go take a shot. I'll intercept for a few. You come out when your balls aren't in your throat. Sound like a plan?"

"Don't think I could come up with anything better."

42

SAMANTHA

The street Mary Kay and Bill lived on was already parked up with cars and white golf carts were shuttling guests to the house, pearl-colored balloons whipping behind the back wheels. I sat in my car and checked my phone, trying to stall just a few seconds longer. Ivy had offered to come down and be my wingman for when I crumpled to the ground after confronting Austin, and I didn't hesitate to take her up on the offer. I was sure I'd need an emotional support buddy after the carnage that was about to go down, but she texted and was stuck at the airport after landing and would be late.

I was on my own.

Facing an entire bridal party and all the extended family was much easier thinking Ivy would be by my side. But I would do this the right way. No more running away, regardless of how much it hurt. And that meant telling Austin how I really felt.

IVY: how do u feel

ME: Like I'm about to throw up.

IVY: not ideal but workable

ME: ☹

IVY: still on tarmac
god help me get off this thing
fun fact…
did u know alligators usually mate in the water
i'll b there soon

I did not, in fact, know that. But I put my phone down. It was time to man up. I'd walk into that party, find Lexi and apologize in person first, then find Austin and voluntarily throw my heart into a meat grinder.

I walked up the Marcs' white shell drive to the perfectly manicured hedges and blooming hydrangea bushes that lined the small sidewalk leading out back. The sounds of music and merry voices drifted around the house as I walked down the stone pathway carved into the lawn. It looked like someone spent all day out there with a pair of baby shears, meticulously trimming each blade of grass with a ruler.

The backyard twinkled. Edison lights seemed to be suspended in thin air. Couches and little sitting areas littered the expansive lawn, looking out over the water. There was a small stage set up on one side with a string quartet. In the middle of the yard, a large seafood display sat on top of a sculpted ice table the length of a car, covered with snow crab legs, stone crab, shrimp, and oysters with lemons and small pots of cocktail sauce nestled in between king crab legs.

I took a deep breath and scanned the crowd. I spotted Rex on the far side of the lawn with a bunch of women laughing. They all doubled over giggling in the exact same way, laughing with their mouths open and squinting their eyes shut. His sisters, no doubt.

"Sam!" I heard Lexi call out my name from back toward the house. "You're here!" She bounded up to me and tackled me in a full-blown hug.

"I wouldn't have missed it." I pulled her back just a bit. "But before you say anything I have two things. One, I'm a total and complete jerk and I'm sorry for yelling at you. I'm the worst and I know it. And although I thought about heading back up to New York City to avoid seeing your brother tonight, I didn't. One step at a time. You're important to me and I love you and that's all."

She smiled. "I'm glad you're here."

"Me too. And two, I already know about Austin and Vanessa." She blinked. "I don't want to talk about it. It's fine. I'm fine. I want him to be happy."

"What about—?"

"And tonight's about you. And that's what's important."

"Did you—?"

"I saw her car. And I saw them through the window. I wasn't snooping or anything, it just, whatever. I totally was but I didn't really see anything but, *ugh*, she's the worst isn't she?"

"She is, but she's not—"

"It's fine if she's here," I interrupted. "He has a right to bring whoever he wants to your wedding and you should be supportive of him and that's fine."

"Agreed but—"

"No, don't tell me. I don't need to know. She can look at me all she wants with her little glowy vibe thing happening but I came here to say some things to Austin and I'm going to say them."

She cocked her head. "Like what things?"

"I need to apologize. But there's something I need to tell him that you definitely aren't going to love." I had never come right out and told Lexi about my feelings toward her brother, and I wasn't sure how she was going to take it. But I was running out of time and while I already had my big girl panties on for the day, I figured I might as well spill.

"You're in love with my brother," she finished. My eyes went wide. "Yes, I'm fully aware. Do you seriously think I don't know you that well? You've always been awful at hiding your feelings."

I was so relieved she was smiling. "I told him he wasn't anything special. That what we've had these last couple weeks is no big deal, but it is to me and I need to tell him."

"I know it is to you, and honestly, I was just scared that it would blow up from the very beginning. You both are too important to me to let something tear one of you away again."

"I completely understand, but I don't know if it even matters at this point. I mean, if he wants to go the whole Snow White route then fine, so be it, but at least he'll know the truth about how I feel."

"Snow White?" she asked.

"The whole vibe she has going on. You should have seen her. I'm surprised there weren't little gophers dancing around her and a bluebird singing on her shoulder. I don't remember her being that *glowy*." She looked at me like I had two heads. "I don't want to judge, but I might throw in that he really shouldn't trust her, like, at all. We aren't the only two options in the world but cheating on your husband with your ex-fiancé is kind of dirt. Right?"

"Right." She nodded slowly.

"I'm going to go find him but I think I might need to puke in the bathroom first."

"For real?"

"I just need a minute to send my stomach back down out of my throat."

"Right. Okay, inside you go. I'll keep my eye out for him. And Sam? Thank you for showing up."

"I meant it. You're worth staying for."

On my way to the bathroom, I heard a few voices coming from Austin's old room. I slowed down to listen.

"She's pregnant?" a deep voice asked in a whisper. I was pretty sure it was Patrick. "Man, when did she tell you?"

"This morning." All the oxygen left the room.

That was Austin's voice.

"Wow. She couldn't have waited until after tonight? Kind of big news to drop right before your sister's wedding."

"She always did like to upstage."

"Is she excited?" Patrick asked.

It felt like the air melted around my head. This morning someone told Austin they were pregnant.

Vanessa.

Vanessa was there.

Vanessa's pregnant? That explained the ethereal vibe she had going on. That was a thing, right? *But why would she tell Austin?*

Dread pooled in my stomach.

Austin couldn't be the father. There's no way that could happen. *Right?* But why would she have been at his house?

The dread was boiling now. Tom and her were together at the bar. But Austin wanted to get out of the bar fast when he saw them. He wouldn't do that to Tom. Seeing us at the bar must have sparked something for her again. Or maybe it was going on before that? He didn't tell me. Should he have told me?

I felt a bit faint. It'd only been a few weeks. Could you even know that early?

I ran outside and took a big gulp of the night air. My eyes searched frantically for Lexi. I didn't need to stay. Not tonight. I needed to leave.

I spotted her across the lawn and ran to her side.

"She's pregnant, Lexi." I couldn't believe the words pouring out of my mouth.

"Vanessa?"

"Yes, Vanessa. She's pregnant. How could you not tell me?"

"It's just the spawn of Satan. It's not that big of a deal."

Was she nuts? That was her future niece or nephew she was talking about. She looked over my shoulder and her eyes grew wide.

"Sam?" Austin's voice came from behind me and was like warm molasses dripping down my lower back.

Shit.

I closed my eyes. I could at least apologize. That's what I came here to do, without any sort of promise for anything more. Because clearly that possibility had been set aflame with a bottle of lighter fluid tonight.

I turned around.

"Hey, hi." I didn't expect the wave of nausea to hit me so squarely in the forehead.

"Hi." His smell circled us. The last time we were this close I was turning away from him.

I awkwardly looked around trying to find something to latch on to. "I guess congratulations are in order?"

"Yeah, I guess they are." He looked at Lexi.

"So, you're happy then?" I asked, acting like my entire life didn't feel like it was on the line with this one single question.

"Of course, I'm happy. How could I not be?" The blow felt a little more consuming than I was ready for, but I forced a smile. I had my chance, and I said no. I would be happy for him.

"Hey, Austin," Lexi started, "tell her what exactly you're happy ab—"

There was a tapping on the mic and all eyes went toward the small stage area. Rex caught Lexi's eye and waved her and Austin over to the head table.

"Don't go anywhere," Lexi ordered more forcefully than I thought necessary. "We'll chat after this." Austin gave me a small smile as he walked away. My body swayed to follow him, like it didn't understand I was meant to stay here.

Rex's dad took center stage, warning the guests there was no way Rex's four older sisters would miss a chance to share war stories of their brother as a toddler. So, with a grin, he handed over the mic. Stories of braces and awkward first dates topped memories of Tic Tacs up his nose and the one time he got stuck in the toilet as sister after sister outdid the one before her. After thirty minutes, every guest's face was streaked with tears.

Then it was Austin's turn. He was charming, and looked so handsome onstage. The corner of his eyes shined as he talked about Lexi as the little sister who would crawl into his bed when it stormed outside. He talked about how her giggle never ceased to put a smile on his face, regardless of how bad his day was. He talked about her obsession with *The Little Mermaid*, Debbie Gibson, and her tiny Polaroid camera she carried everywhere.

He mostly avoided eye contact in my general direction, but as he was winding down, he looked straight at me. "Sometimes people find a way back to each other against the odds. We all know Rex came back to the bar again. And again. And again." A murmur of chuckles filled the room.

"I'm excited as our family continues to grow." I swallowed the lump as he looked back at Rex. This was his family now—Mary Kay and Bill, Lexi and Rex, and Rex's massive tribe of hilarious sisters who looked so fun. And a new baby on the way. This was his little bubble that I would never be a part of. "I couldn't imagine a better guy to call my brother. Welcome to our family, Rex."

Everyone applauded and lifted their glasses. He was funny, eloquent, and genuine. Everything he should have been.

After the speeches, a small brass band started to play and people were mingling with fresh drinks. I scanned the crowd for Lexi and made a beeline toward her. There was only so much my heart could take before it bled out in the backyard.

"The speeches were beautiful and I can't wait for tomorrow, but I'm going to head out for tonight." I held back the tsunami of emotion that was threatening to overtake my body.

"Wait, did you talk to Austin?" she asked.

"No, but I'm going to find him, tell him, and literally run the other direction so I wanted to say bye now."

She grabbed my arm and started pulling me through the yard but I stopped her in front of the swan ice sculpture. "Lexi, I will find him. You go back to being the blushing bride, deal? I'm perfectly capable of shredding my heart in front of him on my own. I will find him and tell him I'm moving back."

"You're moving back?" she asked.

"You're moving back?" At the sound of Austin's voice, I turned around right into his chest.

"Just temporarily." I turned back to Lexi. "That idea I was texting you about, with Ivy? It worked. Sort of. But yes, in short, I'm moving back."

"Okay," Austin drew out.

"Right. Okay so, first I want to apologize." My throat felt a little tighter as I faced him. God, he was handsome. I didn't remember talking being such a difficult thing to do. "When Glenn first told me about the huge ferryboat he was planning to buy for the resort, that would basically force you out of business, I should have told you. Glenn changes his mind so many times though and, honestly, it's such a horrible idea, and I was really hoping to convince him out of it, but still, I should have said something. You've been nothing but honest with me about everything and I should have given you that same trust back. And I'm sorry."

"Okay."

He was uncomfortable, clocking the number of people pretending not to listen.

"And second, and I know this doesn't matter anymore, but I'm trying to face the music now instead of just running away so, I'm sorry about how I left before. The whole driveway thing. And for everything I didn't say that I should have after that. I kind of have this thing with running away when things get hard. That was immature of me to leave like that and I owe you a pretty big apology. I'm sorry."

He put his hands in his pockets and he continued to look at me like I was a puzzle to figure out. "Okay," he repeated. Was that the only word he remembered at the moment? A handful of guests quietly loitered around the seafood bar making no effort to hide their attention on us. And I felt my heartbeat in my neck. I didn't even know that was a thing. I wondered if everyone else could see the weird bobbing pulsing beneath my skin.

"Right, so one more thing." Into the shredder we go. "I understand this doesn't mean anything now, but I'm not walking away tonight without you knowing. You were right, about what you said before, about being scared to fall in love with you. Everyone in my life that I've loved has somehow let me down, whether it's their choice to or not. It's easier to just put a guard up than to constantly wonder when the dreaded moment will come. Or *how* it will come, which is even worse. So, I ran in the other direction instead of leaning into what we had, or could have had." His eyes were so intense, searching my face with a trace of sadness in them. The temperature outside skyrocketed.

"But the truth is, as much as I tried not to care and to not get attached, I did. You said I was scared to fall in love with you. But the truth is, I was scared because I was *already* in love with you."

His chest stilled.

"When I was back in the city, your face was literally on a constant loop in my brain. You were everywhere. You've never even been to my apartment but you would lie there with me every single night and the bed was empty in the morning and it was just so *sad*. It was torture. I am hopelessly in love with you and I'm an idiot for not saying anything sooner." His eyes widened just a fraction of an inch then he turned his head down, looked at the ground and took a deep breath. Maybe if this had come earlier there would have been a different reaction, but I needed to wrap it up and make a beeline for my car. I said what I needed to and now I was just unnecessarily embarrassing myself.

"But I know, I know, it's totally irrelevant now because you've moved on. If you want to be with Snow White, then fine. I get it—the history, the doe-eyed thing, whatever."

"Who's Snow White?" I heard Patrick ask someone.

"The *V* word," Lexi whispered back.

I forgot they were standing there. I glanced over and Mary Kay and Bill were standing behind Lexi and Patrick, with about ten other people who were pretending not to listen to our conversation. They quickly looked away when I spotted them. Apparently, there was something very interesting in Mary Kay's champagne glass.

"The *V* word?" Patrick whispered back. "What's the *V* word?"

"Vanessa, for God's sake," I answered, plowing forward. "And the *baby*. That's a whole other thing obviously. A whole other *living* thing but I didn't want you to not know and just settle for her. In case that's what you're doing. I mean, trying to work it out with your baby momma is not *settling* necessarily but—"

"Vanessa?" he asked.

It's not like I had anything else left to hide at that point so I let it all out. "I drove by your house earlier. To apologize. But I saw her car there. And her doing the leaning thing on your kitchen counter."

"Wait, you came to my house?"

"Yeah, and she was doing the whole, *I'm here, look at me leaning on your counter all glowy like Snow White with a better rack* or whatever."

"And did you see anyone else there?" he asked, eyes still locked on mine.

"I'm not mad. It's not like we were exclusive or anything. But I just assumed since she broke your heart before, you wouldn't give her another chance. And you doing the same thing to Tom that he did to you just seems so outside your whole *vibe* but—"

"Well, and the baby." He smirked.

"I overheard you in your room. I know she's pregnant. You would think two adults who understand how that works could prevent that, but again, whatever. I understand both parents are a necessary equation when trying to raise a kid into a well-rounded contributing member of society. You need to do what's right for your baby."

"*My* baby?" Austin asked.

Patrick gasped.

"Austin Francis Marcs," Mary Kay said sternly.

"Mom, shush," Lexi whispered.

"Umm, yes. Your baby." I looked around and noticed how many people were standing near us, watching my demise. I lowered my voice. "I mean, I get it, she was originally *your fiancée*, but admittedly it's a little shocking, I mean, geez, Austin, she's *married*..."

Austin was smiling. "So you think Vanessa and I hooked up and now she's pregnant? With my baby."

I looked at Lexi. She was biting back her smile.

"She's pregnant," Austin paused. "With *Tom's* baby. They came to tell me before I heard it through the grapevine. Thought they owed me that much."

Wait, what?

I looked at Lexi. "Sorry!" she whispered. "I kind of thought you had it wrong but then the speeches and, well, I didn't want to mess with the whole grandstand movie moment for you two when you realized you were wrong."

I looked back at Austin. "So, there's no baby?" I asked him.

"Oh there's a baby," he chuckled. "It's just not mine."

"There's no Vanessa?" I asked.

"There's no Vanessa." His eyes turned soft and my entire body melted.

And that was it. That was the moment I realized starting right then, nothing would ever be the same. The moment that would send my life in one very specific and beautiful direction if I didn't run. It felt like tiny flowers blooming in my bloodstream. His eyes were shining.

"Is this the grandstand movie moment?" I whispered.

"Well, we are at a rehearsal dinner." He glanced past me. "And there's an ice swan behind you, so...."

"Okay, then here it goes. To be honest, if I think about babies and grocery stores and elementary school teachers and Friday night football games, I feel like I'm going to puke."

His brow creased a bit in the middle. "I don't think that's how it's supposed to start."

"But here's what I know so far." I took a deep breath as every eye zeroed in on me. "I want to wake up next to you every morning and quiz each other on completely irrelevant, useless facts about ourselves. I want to stand over a stove and watch you make spaghetti sauce from scratch and tease you that you could just buy it in a jar instead and it would be faster. I want to take sunset rides on your boat, throw the anchor overboard and just sit watching the water, talking about the worlds that exist underneath us that so many people would see if they just opened their eyes."

Moisture gathered in his eyes, but he stayed perfectly still with his hands buried in his pockets.

"And I'm terrified." My voice faltered for a moment, but I forced myself to continue. "I'm scared to death that at some point you'll look at me and realize that maybe I'm not all that you need. That I won't check every box. My lucky streak with fishing will run out and maybe I'll end up hating it, and you'll want to trade me in. Or, worse, maybe you'll leave—and it won't even be your choice."

I exhaled, my heart thudding against my ribs. "I'm just saying, don't have too high of expectations for me. I can barely live up to my own expectations, let along anyone else's."

"Okay," he said softly.

"But the only thing that really matters at this point, is that I love you, Austin Marcs. And I'd really like to try and see if this could work. That is, if you'd have me...again."

"This is where they kiss!" Lexi whispered, swiping tear after tear off her cheek.

"Wait, you knew she thought it was Austin's?" whispered Patrick.

"I'm so confused." Mary Kay grabbed another glass of champagne off a waiter's tray.

"I'll explain later," Lexi whispered back.

He looked down at the ground, and the silence stretched between us until time seemed to stand still. "Samantha Leigh, are you sure?"

"I've never been more sure of anything in my entire life."

My heart swelled at the smile that lit up his entire face.

"Take your hands out of your pockets."

His brow lifted over those gorgeous green eyes that danced under the moonlight. "We both know what happens if I do that."

"That's exactly what I'm counting on."

He slid his hands free and took a step toward me, his fingers threading through my hair in one smooth, quick motion so fast he threw me off balance. His mouth crashed into mine and suddenly I was off my feet and into his arms. He tasted like salty tears and the ocean—and home. I clung to him, tightening my grip, unable to imagine a world where I'd ever want my feet back on solid ground.

Hoots and whistles around us grew as everyone started talking about Vanessa and Tom, and how wonderful it was that Austin wasn't tied to her for the rest of his life.

"Looks like I missed the big moment." Ivy sauntered up to the group looking like a million bucks. "I'm Ivy, Samantha's assistant. Apologies for my tardiness. Apparently two alligators saw fit to procreate on the runway today and caused a bit of a delay in my arrival." She turned toward Mary Kay. "Your house is absolutely extraordinary, Mrs. Marcs. Exquisite taste."

"Oh, why thank you." Mary Kay beamed.

She turned to Lexi. "And congratulations to the bride-to-be. You look striking."

"Ivy's my *former* assistant," I corrected.

A proud smile bloomed across her face. "I head up marketing for Sam's new division now."

"New division?" Austin turned to me. "Is it really true? You're coming back here?"

Ivy answered for me. "Short story is, yes. Samantha presented an alternate plan called the Lighthouse Project to the board at Goodrich."

Lexi's eyes lit up. "The special project you've been working on?" Lexi asked.

"It finally came together for me while I was in New York." I leaned into Austin as his hand wrapped around my waist, his mouth so close I could smell the champagne on his breath.

"Samantha's pitch centered around keeping the integrity of the island," Ivy continued. "The charm and traditions of the island were center stage. After hearing the pitch about the island and her vision, the board was totally in."

Ivy continued, "Rock Island is the first location of the boutique resort collection and Sam will be here every step of the way, making sure it gets done right."

"I'll be here most of the time, but I'll be searching for locations for future developments too, so I'll still travel a ton."

Austin squeezed my side. "Glenn doesn't seem like the type to let go of control that easily."

"He doesn't have a choice. Board already voted. Samantha's in. Complete autonomy. She doesn't report to him anymore."

Austin's jaw dropped. The corners of Ivy's mouth curved up.

Finally, I had the freedom to run the project from the ground up without Glenn looking over my shoulder, dictating what's best and making decisions based solely on financial gain. I turned to face Austin. "I'd like to take another shot at calling this place home."

He looked at me with that steady expression, his eyes sparkling. But then a small shadow of worry flickered across. "What about your mom?"

My heart swooned at his concern. "I'll tell you the long version later, but let's just say I'm hopeful for new beginnings."

He cupped my face and pulled me near, the warmth of his palms spreading down my neck to the tips of my toes. "So, it's not gonna be easy. It's gonna be really hard, and we're gonna have to work at this every day."

I laughed at his *Notebook* reference as tiny puddles of water pooled in my eyes. "You really are a closet romance addict, aren't you?"

"Shhh, I'm not done," he whispered into my lips, "But I wanna do that because I want you. I want all of you, forever. You and me. Every day." His smile stretched so wide it felt like the whole world brightened.

And as I kissed him again in response with my heart pounding, I realized I wasn't just choosing him.

I was choosing home.

43

AUSTIN

My face was warm and fuzzy from champagne. Of all the ways I pictured tonight going, this was by far more than I could have hoped for. After the rehearsal dinner, Lexi, Sam, and I sat on the seawall looking out over the ink-black water, the silver path from the moon shining across the top. The waves lapped against the shore in a steady rhythm.

Most of the guests had left, excited to rekindle the party for the wedding the next night. The ice swans stood tall in the center of the lawn, droplets falling to the ground from the tips of their melting wings. The band had gone home. The only sounds were the waves against the sand and the clinking of abandoned wineglasses and plates as the caterers cleaned up around the last mingling guests.

Rex and his sisters were laughing at the only table not folded up for the night. They were talking about the time Rex hid frogs in his oldest sister's bed because he didn't want his mom to set them free.

"They seem like a lot of fun." Sam looked over at the table where they were all trying to catch their breath. "Tomorrow's going to be beautiful."

She leaned into my chest and closed her eyes.

"You're beautiful," I whispered into her ear as I laced my fingers through hers.

"Cool it, you two," Lexi interrupted. "This is my weekend."

"I don't know what you did, Scuttle, but you finally got this boy to loosen his reins." Patrick came up behind us and clapped me on the back. He plopped down right next to Lexi. "Did you hear that you can call me *Capt'n* Bolt from now on?"

"Captain?" Sam asked.

"He hasn't told her yet." Lexi smiled at Patrick.

"You haven't told her yet?" Patrick asked me. "Dude! What are you waiting for?"

"It's not that big of a deal, really," I said, feeling my cheeks heat a little.

"The hell it isn't." Patrick nodded his head toward my parents' dock. "Take a peek at his new legs."

Her eyes went wide as she looked to the dock. It was hard to see in the dark, but alongside my parents' wooden speedboat was a vintage white and navy fishing boat bobbing in the water. The moonlight reflected off the center console and long poles pointed to the sky off the back.

"Turns out this kid just needed his heart broken again to finally follow his dreams," Patrick teased.

"It's yours?" Sam asked me.

I swatted Patrick in the chest then looked at Sam. "It's small. Just something to test the waters out. Turns out the owner from the charter business up north was also trying to dump this. Needs a lot of work."

"But it's a start." She was beaming.

Her eyes lingered on the name painted on the back as the boat rocked gently in the water, swaying in time with the waves—*As A Last Resort*.

She kissed me, soft and certain, and everything in me settled.

"It's perfect," she whispered.

I brushed my thumb along her jaw, the future suddenly something I could reach for.

Epilogue
SAMANTHA

Eighteen months later

The wind changed on the island once the tourist season officially ended. It became cooler, either from the lack of bodies crowding the local restaurants or the shift in weather—I wasn't sure.

It felt good to call the island home again. New memories started to take away the sting of the old ones and there were fewer landmines the longer I stayed. It didn't feel like a gut punch every time I drove by the light pole downtown. I still made Austin in charge of the weekly grocery store runs to avoid kindergarten teachers and late-night regrets of my mother. I was making progress, but no need to overachieve.

It was a strange and disorienting thing sometimes, walking around the town and living a new life where an old one used to be.

Mom ended up staying at the rehabilitation clinic and took a job as the activities director. She was the unofficial cheerleader of sobriety. Whether it was because she liked it so much, or didn't trust herself outside of its four walls, she never said. But I was thankful she was there, taking it one day at a time, sober. Her daily calls dripped with gossip from clinic patients instead of high school acquaintances, but her sobriety was more than I could have hoped for.

Ivy was on the island way more than she intended. I was beginning to think she liked it more than she let on. She was a beast at getting the media to pay attention. After a whirlwind deal and fast-track construction schedule, a small section of the resort opened early for travel partners, agents, and influencers, and the reception had been incredible. We'd been written up in the top travel magazines, touting "an unparalleled boutique resort experience that will change the landscape of tourism."

The few weeks we'd been operating under the radar couldn't have gone any better. The soft opening was scheduled in the offseason to get staff acquainted with the ins and outs of the resort as the rest of the compound was built. It wasn't even technically season yet and the weather was perfect.

I moved in with Austin temporarily. But that turned into a more permanent situation when he wouldn't let me leave. I still went back to the city every month for meetings, but I was happy when I got home, not missing the familiar noise outside my city window that used to lull me to sleep.

Austin's ferryboat business expanded. Patrick and his cousin—whose name tag read WILL SMITH—ran the ferries across, including the new five-hundred-person passenger boat the resort footed the bill for. We negotiated a partnership where Scuttle's Ferry was the exclusive party responsible for the Lighthouse guests sea transportations, which allowed Austin to focus his efforts on the fishing business. His uncle Harold still offered fishing charters but only deep sea, which apparently was *his* dream, which left inshore for Austin. His little old lady fan group made another trip down from New Hampshire and booked one of the first fishing charters he had. Ethel hooked a humongous tarpon and he had to help her reel it in. Her grandson had just downloaded TikTok on her phone before the trip and no one knew how to use it. Turns out Shirley was livestreaming the whole thing and had no idea.

And of course, it went viral. His schedule was booked up overnight. He now had a fleet of three fishing boats that ran weekly in addition to managing the ferries.

Austin and I took *As a Last Resort* back over to the Birchwood Beach. It had become a special place for us, being the inspiration for the Lighthouse Collection idea as well as one of the first places he took me.

I loved how Austin and I fit. He made me feel safe and loved. He made me think I could take on life without getting road rash. I thought about how much my dad would have loved him.

After we anchored the boat, he led me under and around the downed branches and laced his fingers in mine. "Ivy told me she's heading to South Carolina this week. You think it's the next one?"

We found a new plot of land for sale in a coastal South Carolina beach town. On paper, it was perfect. The spot mirrored Rock Island. Miles of beach stretched across flat land with a small community already established and thriving. But it flew under the radar from tourists and publications. Ivy was set to scout out the location, then was planning on being back on the island for the month after the grand opening.

"I think it's got potential to be our first retrofit for this place."

He sat on one of the trunks and pulled me down next to him. "I thought it'd be nice to catch a glimpse of the revamped lighthouse before the official grand opening. Kind of a good luck thing."

Some of the money from the resort development had been allocated to restore the original lighthouse, and not only did it become operational, it was a mini museum of the island with ship logs dating back fifty years and the full story of the Birchwood Beach.

Looking north, you could barely see the cupola from where we were sitting.

"You're not one for superstition."

"Figured it couldn't hurt." He scooped me from his lap and helped me balance standing up onto the trunk. I walked along it taking in the scene around me. I felt a sense of pride that this beach, a one of a kind as far as I knew, would be preserved because of what I had done. I still couldn't decide whether the beach was breathtakingly beautiful or heartbreaking.

I guess things could be both at the same time.

We got to the top and looked out below us. "It's still hard to believe this entire world exists underneath the water most of the day." I wouldn't have believed it myself if he hadn't taken me during high tide to see it with my own eyes.

He nodded signaling me to go even farther, so I started climbing. "If you climb to the top of that tallest branch, you'll see the rest of the lighthouse from here."

"You want me to climb all the way up there?"

"Well, Scuttle, at this point if you don't, it'll be bad luck."

I turned to face him and put my hand on my hip. "Don't you think it's time we retired that? I feel like I've done a pretty good job of growing out of that weird uncle nickname the last ten years, don't you?"

"Weird uncle nickname?"

"Yeah, you know—Scuttle is the weird uncle character of *The Little Mermaid*. He's always awkward, goofy, and rocking that *just-rolled-out-of-bed-after-an-all-night-bender* vibe."

"You think I nicknamed you Scuttle because you were the awkward one?"

I looked away embarrassed. "Well, obviously. I was thirteen and very off-kilter when you started calling me that."

He bit back a smile, then turned serious. "Scuttle is my favorite character in that movie. He makes everything in the room brighter just by being in it. You did that. You still do that."

The reality of what he said slowly seeped in. "Austin. I don't even—"

He squinted his eyes just past me.

"What?" I asked. I turned around and on a small part of the branch, something glittered. "What is that?"

"I don't know. Must be something that got caught during the tide change."

I scooted over and plucked a small shiny piece of metal off the branch.

And although I had never seen this tiny little circle before, I knew what it was, and I knew I'd hold on to it for the rest of my life. I turned it over in my hand—a silver ring with a solitary emerald-cut diamond. It was perfect.

He pursed his lips together, losing a battle with a smile. "I couldn't find any swans. Or ducks. But I have been growing this forest since before you were born and I think that's pretty romantic."

The sting of tears came swiftly. "It would smell funny if there were a bunch of ducks."

"And it would be loud," he added, tears pooling in his own eyes. "I love you, Samantha Leigh. There's no one else I'd rather talk about imaginary worlds that live just underneath the surface with. I promise to shield you from your elementary school teachers in the grocery store, forever and always, if you'll let me."

I laughed through the monsoon of water streaming down my face. "I'm in."

Sometimes, the last resort is where you end up, but it's exactly where you were meant to be all along.

Acknowledgments

We made it! And turns out, publishing a book isn't just a marathon—it's a full-blown relay race with, like, a *million* people passing the baton. I have so many people to thank.

Stacey Graham—Rockstar Agent Extraordinaire. It takes a special kind of crazy to procreate five times, and I'm so glad we share that in common. You're my kind of fearless. I'm still pinching myself that you're my agent. Thank you for believing in me!

Sabrina Flemming—Your insight into this book made it better than I ever could have imagined. For my first experience diving into the editing world, you made it so enjoyable. Thanks for pushing me to embrace the grit, so that the tender moments could shine brighter. You saw what I was trying to do with this, and you took a chance on me. I am eternally grateful for you.

To my early readers—Megan Bingham, thank you for always asking how my book was doing. It meant more to me than I can ever express. Sarah Lewis, you are a gem of a human being. You are a bright light in this world, and I'm so thankful to call you, friend. Natalie Putnam, you are my number one hype girl. My friend turned family. I am so grateful you are by my side, cheering me on.

To so many friends and family—

Katie Sims and Erika Picard, there's no one else I'd rather turtle with on a girls' trip when I'm ninety than you two.

Ashton/Colleen (*iykyk*) Keefe for being my sounding board for all the random questions at all hours of the night. Someday, I hope I get to return the favor.

Matt Putnam, for answering all my boat and real estate questions—but more importantly, for telling me Justin was in love with me in college. Thank God for you, or I'd probably still be single.

Dad, for lending your name to Captain Harold. My love for the water came from you.

To Kristin Mangas—my real-life Lexi—and Karen—my real-life Mary Kay. Family like you is once in a lifetime.

To Erzsebet Kurti (aka Ms. Lisa)—Thank you for sharing your travels and experiences with me. The birchwood beach was exactly what I needed to anchor Rock Island.

I believe there are people in life God hands to you on a silver platter, and Sarah Penner, you are one of those for me. I'm endlessly grateful for your encouragement, your belief in me, your wisdom, but most of all, your friendship.

Annabelle Monaghan—You lift up so many authors. The fact I asked you to blurb a book proposal is crazy. The fact you actually agreed means you're an angel. THANK YOU, a thousand times over.

To the Palm Harbor Library, and especially the Oliveri family, thank you for your lasting gift of the Madeline Oliveri Writers Workshop. Madeline's legacy lives on in every word I write. Your support shaped my journey, and I'm forever grateful. And to the people I met and have worked with through that workshop, specifically my Wolfpack: Whitney Harrison, Casey Brant, and Natalie. Thank you for asking the hard questions and pushing back on my ideas. Your candid feedback made me a better writer. I'm eternally grateful for your support and stellar brewery debriefs.

ACKNOWLEDGMENTS

To Erma Bombeck—If you're a comedy writer...go to the Erma Bombeck Writers Workshop. It's a nonnegotiable. End of story.

To my mom, who's always been a beacon of hard work, love, and determination. You're amazing, and through your example, you taught me I was capable of anything. I'm really lucky to be your daughter.

To my husband, Justin, who really is every good part of every character I write. This book wouldn't have been finished without you sacrificing so much. I'm delusional enough to want to do everything, but with you encouraging me, I actually think I can. And to all my babies: Lincoln, Everleigh, Montgomery, Remington, and Winslow... Thanks for giving me such a full and rich life to pull from. The fact that I brought five humans into this world still blows people's minds and honestly, it's my favorite flex.

I truly hope you, as a reader, find yourself weaved throughout this story. Life is messy, unexpected, and rarely tied up with a perfect bow. But man, I love a good redemption arc. Generally speaking, things in life often don't happen as fast as, or how, we want them to. So, thank you God for your faithfulness, delivering for me what far surpassed my expectations. Your path is always better than mine, even if I think I know better.

About the Author

Kristin Wollett's main goal in life is to make people laugh. While she's been an actor for over a decade in her "real job," she also writes romantic comedies, then dreams about who she can bribe to make them into movies. A University of Florida grad, she now lives on Florida's Gulf Coast with her husband and five young children and navigates life with an ample supply of dry shampoo, copious amounts of espresso, and the occasional glass (okay, *fine*, bottle) of wine.

As a Last Resort is her first novel (if you don't count the one collecting dust under her bed).

RAISING READERS
Books Build Bright Futures

Thank you for reading this book and for being a reader of books in general. As an author, I am so grateful to share being part of a community of readers with you, and I hope you will join me in passing our love of books on to the next generation of readers.

Did you know that reading for enjoyment is the single biggest predictor of a child's future happiness and success?

More than family circumstances, parents' educational background, or income, reading impacts a child's future academic performance, emotional well-being, communication skills, economic security, ambition, and happiness.

Studies show that kids reading for enjoyment in the US is in rapid decline:

- In 2012, 53% of 9-year-olds read almost every day. Just 10 years later, in 2022, the number had fallen to 39%.
- In 2012, 27% of 13-year-olds read for fun daily. By 2023, that number was just 14%.

Together, we can commit to **Raising Readers** and change this trend. How?

- Read to children in your life daily.
- Model reading as a fun activity.
- Reduce screen time.
- Start a family, school, or community book club.
- Visit bookstores and libraries regularly.
- Listen to audiobooks.
- Read the book before you see the movie.
- Encourage your child to read aloud to a pet or stuffed animal.
- Give books as gifts.
- Donate books to families and communities in need.

Books build bright futures, and **Raising Readers** is our shared responsibility.

For more information, visit JoinRaisingReaders.com

Sources: National Endowment for the Arts, National Assessment of Educational Progress, WorldBookDay.org, Nielsen BookData's 2023 "Understanding the Children's Book Consumer"